Praise for *for eve*

'Wilkins on form, as he often is in this book, is the best around.'
Iain Sharp, *Sunday Star Times*

Praise for *The Fainter*

'Outside the pages of Maurice Gee's fiction, there is no picture of contemporary New Zealand society as convincing as this one, and its creation of individual characters is unsurpassed.'
Nelson Wattie, *Dominion Post*

Praise for *Chemistry*

'A terrifically good book, so cleverly constructed and managed. It's a work of real tenderness . . . powerful and convincing.' Jim Crace

'Wilkins is brilliant at character . . . the writing is full of verve. Wilkins has an eye for telling detail, a great ear for dialogue and a dark sense of humour. It is easy to understand the acclaim he has already won in his native New Zealand.' *Guardian*

Praise for *Nineteen Widows Under Ash*

'Wilkins reminds me of some of the great American writers—Faulkner, Lowry, Richard Ford—where the simple story you are apparently reading deepens and broadens and throws out layers and shadows, and you are conscious of an underwater life and a sky overhead, but all the time you are immersed in what seems a limpid, even transparent medium.'
Evening Post

Praise for *Little Masters*

'*Little Masters* is an engrossing, fiercely readable book. It deals with classic themes of parents and children, love and exile, and the sadness of separation and dislocation. Damien Wilkins writes brilliantly about streetwise, smart children and adults searching for love and stability far away from home.' Colm Tóibín

Praise for *The Miserables*

'Wilkins has constructed a powerful portrait of family life . . . He handles the temporal shifts of the narrative with delicacy, precision, remarkable grace and apparent lack of effort . . . the prose is controlled, elegant, almost deadpan . . . A moving and subtle piece of work.'
Times Literary Supplement

Somebody Loves Us All

Damien Wilkins

Victoria University Press

TE WHARE WĀNANGA O TE ŪPOKO O TE IKA A MĀUI

VICTORIA
UNIVERSITY OF WELLINGTON

VICTORIA UNIVERSITY PRESS
Victoria University of Wellington
PO Box 600 Wellington
vuw.ac.nz/vup

National Library of New Zealand Cataloguing-in-Publication Data

Wilkins, Damien, 1963-
Somebody loves us all / Damien Wilkins.
ISBN 978-0-86473-616-1
I. Title.
NZ821.3—dc 22

Published with the assistance of a grant from

creative
nz
ARTS COUNCIL OF NEW ZEALAND *TOI AOTEAROA*

Printed by Printlink, Wellington

À Maree, Geraldine et Greta

Acknowledgements

This novel was written last year while I lived in Menton, France, as the recipient of the New Zealand Post Mansfield Prize. I would like to acknowledge the trustees and the sponsors of this award which allowed me time and space—an incomparable space—in which to write.

Many people in Menton helped us but I would like to make special mention of William Rubinstein and Luc Lanlo, whose friendship and support were crucial; also M. Loffredo, whose generosity at L'école de la Condamine helped make us feel a little like locals; and the staff at Collège André Maurois for their support; and our friends, John Dyer and Jo Short and their family, whose company (and language) we retreated to whenever in need of the English perspective. Paul Akins provided expert medical advice.

Finally, this novel owes thanks and love to my mother, intrepid cyclist, indomitable pedestrian.

Part One

1

That Saturday Tony Gorzo didn't call him. 'Speech Marks', Paddy's fortnightly column, had one dedicated fan or at least a reliably responsive reader: Gorzo. He rang Paddy every second Saturday to talk about the newest one. He never missed a column. Usually Gorzo rang in the afternoon, occasionally at night if he'd been out of town or busy during the day. There was a period when the phone would ring and Helena would call out, not bothering to answer it, 'It's Gorzo for you.' She said Paddy had a groupie and it was sweet. She'd never met him.

Paddy imagined Gorzo had an alarm on his phone or his watch, some method of alert, which told him to ring the man who'd saved his son from life as a retard. It was Tony's own terminology, and not true. Paddy had helped Jimmy speak again after a serious accident. He was a speech therapist. But Gorzo granted him powers, gifts. And to be honest, it was nice hearing from such a person.

There was no make-up call during the week either. And on Friday evening, Paddy went with his friend Lant to the bike shop and bought a bike.

Maybe Paddy got the bike as a replacement for Gorzo? It seemed unlikely. More momentous surely was the fact that his mother, following a persistent campaign led by Paddy and urged on by his two sisters, had moved into the next-door apartment, having finally sold the family home in Lower Hutt where they'd grown up. After all this time, he was back more or less living with his mother. Was this the opening of the period in which they'd end up mothering her? It looked a way off. Teresa was fit, active, mentally sharp, a young seventies. Yet one of those great wheels of life had begun a revolution, he thought—wheels, bikes? The last bike he'd owned, he remembered, his mother had given him. It had belonged to his poor father. Anyway, just then Gorzo's silence loomed larger than Teresa's presence.

He wheeled the new bike into the apartment and leaned it against the wall by his downstairs office. What was that poem's lovely ending, the boy staring at his bicycle, 'consoled by the standing of its beautiful silence'. One of Paddy's clients—the mother of a boy he was seeing—brought him poetry. Yet looking at his bike, he was not consoled. He thought he'd made a mistake, and he considered taking it straight back to Penny Farthing. He was no cyclist, not in thirty, nearly forty years. And to bike in this city? After each ride, it seemed, you were compelled to write a letter to the editor: To all the jerks behind the wheel, what am I, the invisible rider of the apocalypse? Do I not appear as a Christmas tree in front of you? Cyclists lived lives of great and impotent rage. They were righteous. Worse, they were right. They were the planet's future. He knew it and he doubted he was one of them.

Helena stood at the top of the stairs. 'Look at it,' Paddy said to her. 'Look at it go.'

He started explaining what the shiny machine was capable of, touching the gear levers, pointing at the disc brakes, trying to remember the sales pitch. In fact there hadn't been much of one. You were steered to the bike which best suited your needs and abilities. It was Paddy who'd tried to talk the bike shop guy into conceding something pricier might also work in his case. No, Mr Penny Farthing told him flatly, actually looking Paddy up and down—from his toes that slightly turned out, through his thick middle, the girlish bottom (the adjective affectionately supplied had been Helena's), and up to large and sloping shoulders, appraising the full package—I wouldn't bother if I were you.

10

Helena approached. She was about to do her charitable best. She smiled but she was dead tired, almost an exile in exhaustion. It seemed perverse of him to give her a new subject on top of all she was processing with her work. They'd not spoken much through the week. He'd sent her sympathetic looks. She'd apologised for being a drone, a worker bee. Actually, he said, a drone was different from a worker bee. The drone didn't gather nectar or pollen, or construct the hive, and on evidence she was doing all the above. He'd had a brief apiarist phase as a kid. Drones had bigger eyes than worker bees and didn't have a sting. They could help adjust the temperature of the hive by shivering or vibrating their wings. He went on a little longer in lecture mode until he saw Helena's nodding had become virtually a comic miming of rote attention. She was a queen bee anyway, he said. What, she said, clicking alert again, the single female among all those males? I'll pass. As a queen we feed you and dispose of your waste, he said. And what do I have to do in return? she asked. Basically, he told her, reproduce. At which point she'd emitted a grunt and left him.

In front of the bike, she was wary, blinking. Her first husband, Max, who was German, had done something with sports—Paddy couldn't recall the details—possibly a swimming instructor? He suspected physical activity in men was a shady area for her, with its whisper of discontent, odd regressive energies. What was Paddy playing at with the bike? What did it mean? In the three years she'd known him—he saw the calculation—he'd never even jogged, though they'd enjoyed walks together. They knew the hills. On Mount Victoria, they'd stood under a tree full of baby tui zipping around, playing a game of tag. The birds swooped among the branches, touching each other's beaks and then flying off. The craziness was surprising. They'd both thought tui would be solemn, importantly themselves, almost emblematic. Stately singers too. But here they were, thrilled and careless. Almost tuneless.

Finally Helena said of the bicycle, 'Is it the same one Jeremy's got?' She stood off a few feet as if it might start up on its own

11

accord. Helena didn't much like his friend, his oldest friend, which was why she always called him by his first name. To everyone else he was Lant. This was a pity, not that puzzling, but it had advantages. From time to time, Paddy had the pleasant, silly sense of being competed over, and an idea too that, with them both as intimates, he was tolerant, wide-ranging. Yet he knew he only had this pair, really. They were everything to him, without being equal of course.

Lant's involvement in the bike purchase was something he'd hoped to keep from her. Silently he conceded it was a strike against the project. *Two* men plotting physical activity was on a scale of untrustworthiness altogether different. He was influenced by Helena. He'd always been influenced more strongly by women than by men. Absolutely. He thought this was the way of the world and not just how countries such as, well, Italy worked. It was the world's not very great secret. And it was also one reason why he'd kept Jeremy Lanting as a friend. As a sort of balance, a statement about possibilities on the male side of things. He hoped men weren't hopeless. Resolutely he didn't want to join a men's group.

'Lant's is similar,' he said. He sounded to himself defensive, or defensive disguised as light, and not well. 'This is the one that best suits me. They tested me on it.'

'Tested you?'

'They filmed me on it, riding.'

'Where'd you go?'

'Nowhere. It was done with software on their computer. I sat on the bike, turned the pedals, and they filmed me.'

'How amazing.'

He asked if she wanted to sit on it, touching the sleek seat, which looked something like a sailor's hat, also rather cruel.

'No thanks.'

Under her gaze, the bike—an expensive one though certainly not top of the range, that was denied him—so thin and light, began to look flat, lacking a dimension, like a drawing of itself, the effect enhanced when he raised it an inch off the floor with

12

just two fingers. They were both wishing this insubstantial apparatus away. His cartoon bike.

She went upstairs again while Paddy went into his office, from where he could still see one of the bike's amazingly narrow wheels.

Above him he heard Helena clicking her tongue in frustration. She'd be at her laptop, the papers spread across the dining table. For the sound to travel was quite something. It was as if she was signalling him—not to come up but simply to understand the reasons why she'd been unable to respond properly downstairs. They'd never liked to leave anything hanging between them, at least until recently. The clicks were speech patently. He went to the door of his office and called up the stairs, 'All right on the upper deck?'

She called down, 'Grumble, grumble.'

When they both had work on, this was their evening pattern, to retreat and then reunite, sharing supper, though Helena had been working later than usual, coming to bed after him. Her language school was up for a review by the Ministry, who were reacting to rumblings from the new government. Everything was in order but she worried. The culture was punitive, the knives were out. A couple of rogue schools had put everyone under the same harsh weather. On the TV news they'd shown a man running to get into a black Mercedes, holding a newspaper over his face. Hers wasn't a rogue school but a model one, he told her. Yet the stress still played out and perhaps finally she wasn't wonderful at delegating. Helena held the whole enterprise in her head. It was her baby. That was a little chink in her armour. Her pride, or her voraciousness could it be called?

And in his head? His baby?

Two names he was thinking of: Tony Gorzo, naturally, and Sam Covenay, Friday's low-light, and his first appointment at Monday's clinic. Sam had been coming to Paddy for six weeks of speech therapy, with zero progress. From the time he'd had braces fitted on his teeth, Sam had more or less stopped speaking. He'd driven his parents insane until finally they said he could have the braces removed but the boy didn't want this either.

So was this the reason Paddy had bought the bike? To get things moving? That idea came to a crashing halt. In *Middlemarch*— probably his favourite novel alongside *The Magic Mountain*, which Helena had read in German—there was the salient warning. He knew the quotation almost by heart, having used it a number of times in presentations. That we all get our thoughts entangled in metaphors and act fatally on them. Everyone does this, 'grave or light'. That was his chink, he believed.

Forget the Covenays then.

At his desk he tried to come up with a topic for his next 'Speech Marks' column, and immediately felt everything had been said. This was entirely normal. This was writing. And yet after eight years in the newspaper, what was left? Was this the meaning of Tony Gorzo's silence? The reader had voted. Finito. Or, Greek, Omega. Columns of course had a natural life. His fellow columnists, though he'd never met them, demonstrated this truth. One year you're witty, geisty, on the button, and the next you're writing about how you hate jazz or the colour of the houses in your neighbourhood. Was he that bad? His column, a merciful follower might consider, dealt in facts, in ideas over personal opinion. Had the facts run out? This made no sense either. The world's data was infinite. One's ability to process, or just hang on, provided the limits. His thinking was somewhat manic, he knew. Over-available for capture.

The crook in the black Mercedes wasn't someone Helena knew, or even knew of. She was of a different class altogether, having read Thomas Mann auf Deutsch—a for instance he'd supplied when she looked in danger of using the term *industry colleague* as they watched the news and the man appeared a second or third time smelling the newspaper.

He looked up and saw the blank space on the wall where a picture had hung and here were the Covenays again. Alan Covenay, the father, had the picture. He ran a framing business, and was supposedly fixing it. The picture was a cartoon portrait of Paddy in fact, a gift from the newspaper. For years the cartoon had sat on the floor in the spare room of the house he rented after his divorce from Bridget. It wasn't until they'd moved into the apartment that he considered it again, or Helena did.

Helena's idea was that the cartoon created a natural talking point for Paddy with new patients. 'You could say to the kids, guess who that is?'

'They might not believe me when I say it's me,' said Paddy.

'So that's the talking point,' she said.

'How we fall apart as we age?'

'How we change, which is what you want them to do.'

He wasn't sure that was what he did want them to do. Did you say to the child with autism, I think you need to change?

'I think we can all change, learn, grow,' she said. 'I see it every day at the school.'

'Grow?' he said. 'I think we can grow paunches.'

She'd laughed, but unhappily, he thought, as if his flippancy had trampled briefly, harmlessly, on an important belief. He believed in it too, though not unproblematically. He didn't care for the coercion that often figured in the wish. It was the old psychiatrist and light bulb joke: the light bulb has to want to change. But where, for instance, did that leave civil rights, gay rights, women's rights, animal rights, environmental activism, any of the major progressive movements on which public opinion needed more than a prod? There was an argument for force. He'd had it with Lant over the years. Yes, yes, but there was also the collection of light bulbs that came each week to sit with Paddy in his office. Over a period, under a bunch of gently does it trial and error operations, suggestions, of games and fun, they turned on, these bulbs. They began to shine. He'd seen the light. I seen the little lamp.

Lant had a coercive solution for the Covenay kid. 'What you do is this,' he said. 'You walk over to him, you say, "I'm really fucking sick of this and so is everyone else", and then you reach down and pull his ear as hard as you can, lift him up by it. You'll never see recalcitrant vocalisation crumble so quickly.

Elective mutism? Elect this.' Jeremy Lanting was an educational psychologist. They'd worked together in the public system when he and Paddy were both starting out.

The other slightly manicky thing was that Paddy could hear voices, very faint, through the wall, and he strained to make out more in the murmur. His mother's radio left on? That was something she'd done for years, even before their father died— left the radio on to deter burglars. But perhaps this wasn't it at all. Paddy had been having trouble with his right ear recently. The sounds or interference came and went according to different stimuli. The noise was a hum, a pulse, and sometimes a soft sort of boom. Weirdly, he saw something: a person leaving a room, shutting the door after him. It occurred to him that this was his father. Occasionally he'd had things like this with his father crop up.

Apparently when he was a boy Paddy had been a frequent and vocal sleepwalker, arriving in the living room late at night, sitting beside his parents and taking up some obscure debate, trying to draw them in. 'Don't you see?' he asked them urgently. 'Don't you?' Evidently his father was terrified when this chatty zombie joined them. He couldn't do a thing, froze and stared, until Paddy's mother led the babbling sleeping boy out. He remembered none of it—did any sleepwalker? Plus he knew nothing about this when it was going on. It was never reported to him. He had to wait until he was an adult. He'd brought Bridget around to Lower Hutt for dinner. It was before they were married. Teresa told the story for no reason he could think of except this. Strangers i.e. non family members visiting the house could provoke her into saying things that were oddly disloyal and aggressive e.g. you're marrying into a line of possibly unreliable males. The sleepwalking wasn't especially funny in the narration though Teresa might have believed she was being entertaining. Visitors made her speed up. Anyway, listening to his mother Paddy felt his father mocked. The big idea about his father was extreme kindness, gentleness, forbearance. They loved his memory for that. The shadow was ineffectuality. That his son's sleepwalking could paralyse him was a direct hit. One interpretation was that Teresa was keeping the family clean of foreign taint, preserving the genetic stock, though presumably stock had to replicate itself to earn the name and how did she imagine things could go forward if she was blowing off potential mates? Not that it presented at all like this. Bridget didn't say a word afterwards. It was his sister Margie who'd always thought their mother sneaky and undermining. Certainly she had the shy person's combativeness when in situations that challenged her nature to lift a notch. She'd never been a good host. Too busy testing for the fittest.

Since Teresa had moved next door, he'd been far more prone than usual to such reconsiderations. Her very footsteps, though they went unheard—the building's soundproofing had holes but the flooring was highly absorbent—still sounded, still wandered in his direction. He listened. He found this out about himself. He was listening when he was in his office. Almost snooping. It was unexpected.

In his office he stood up and found on his shelves his yellow-stickied copy of *Middlemarch*. He read a few bits, flicking through pages, and several of the stickies fell out, having lost their adhesiveness. He'd always read with this system, fiction and professional journals and books. His flagged library amused Helena. The stickies had notes written on them. He'd thought it useful but as a system it was obviously flawed. Anyway, it was good enough to turn up the passage with the quote about metaphors. Casaubon, the dry religious scholar, about to marry Dorothea, defeating her other suitor, Sir James Chettham, and securing a match he'd hardly dreamed of—a lovely young brilliant woman whose only aspiration seems to be to learn at his knee and to help him with his big life's-work book—is surprised he doesn't feel greater excitement—'delight' is the word—when outwardly his situation appears so good. This, Eliot says, feeling 'more tenderly towards his experience of success than towards the disappointment of the amiable Sir James', is because he has fallen victim to metaphor. Casaubon, the antisocial bachelor, believed he had money in the bank, that he'd been saving up his pleasure for just this sort of day: 'a compound interest of enjoyment'. But nothing is saved. Casaubon feels blankness. The emotions, Eliot suggests, are only present in the present, made on the spot. It's an empty vault you open. You hoard air. This was how he'd deployed the moment in presentations and addresses. Children with speech problems weren't saving themselves for a later and miraculous fluency. It was best to unlock the vault now.

Then there was this from the same great book: 'Few things held the perceptions more thoroughly captive than anxiety about what we have got to say.' That could make said vault rather stiff to open.

Later the same evening—the evening of The Day the Bike Arrived—Paddy didn't believe it was coincidental—Helena told him that at his request she'd once covered first husband Max's body in a Vaseline-like substance and pushed him down a gentle slope of ice somewhere near Zurich. Paddy hadn't heard this before. At night she'd treated his burns. She'd been twenty-one, twenty-two, working as a maid in Max's father's hotel, overseas for the first time. Paddy, too, had worked in a hotel, though under very different circumstances, the details of which he'd never fully spelled out for Helena.

'All that from just a BA in German literature,' he said.

'BA Honours,' she said.

Her thesis was in a box somewhere in their lock-up, hardbound in black: 'Sorrows and Sensations in Nineteenth-Century Verse Drama.' He'd held it out to her once and she'd laughed, wouldn't take it from him, told him to put it back in the box. He saw her pride. Also she'd travelled quite far from all that. Not that there was any suggestion she'd sold out or anything daft. But she felt complex things about her past, he thought. This was part of the project of being together as late-in-life comrades, to gradually, over time, without hurry, find out such information. Or wait it out more likely. He wasn't going to push.

'Goethe would have been impressed,' he said. 'Especially with the Vaseline-like substance. What was it, an experiment?'

'I can't really remember.'

'At the hotel, did you have a maid's uniform?'

'Have we headed into some fantasy of yours?' She had a playful look in her eye, which he was glad to see. Lately he'd missed it. They hated crooks with their faces hidden by newspapers, but they also hated the Ministry of Education and poured curses on its procedures. Dodgy operators scamming in China and South Korea were evil, so was the word compliance. 'For the record, I wore a black skirt. White shirt, black skirt.'

'The classic look.'

'Well I had orange streaks in my hair.' She touched her hair in a remembering way. She wasn't wistful often and when it struck, you were affected.

She was greying now, from the front moving back. It was one of his jobs, to put on the slippery plastic gloves and rinse out the dye until the water ran clear—to be her hairdresser! It gave him a wonderful sense of loving to see the back of her neck, her ears. At forty, almost overnight, he'd lost most of his black and a good deal of the hair itself. Better that than the slow years of thinning. You mourned it and then you got on with things. If a miracle cure came through, you laughed at it and tried it. Noni juice, he recalled, from a fruit and vegetable shop in Newtown. 'Orange streaks? Was that popular at the time?'

'Among Bavarian chambermaids, you mean? I believe it made me stand out.'

'Chambermaids, what a word. It makes me think you were locked up in a cellar in a remote chalet, fed through the bars of a cage.'

'I'm pleased Max never thought of that.'

Later in bed, he was aware of Helena shifting onto her back, her position for talking. He'd already been there for forty sleepless minutes.

'Tony Gorzo still hasn't called,' she said.

'No,' he said.

'Why don't you call him?'

'Not how it works.' In the paper he'd checked the death notices.

He asked Helena about her work, the weekend, but her answers were quickly trailing off. She mumbled something about Dora, her daughter—usually a topic to be slightly wary of.

He listened to Helena's breathing. Was she asleep? She could switch off this suddenly, it was a great skill. Plus she'd been at the laptop throughout the week.

'What will you do, wear a helmet?' she said groggily.

After a moment he understood the change in topic. The bicycle.

She sat up and took a sip from her glass of water beside the bed—she needed constant brief sips, as if dehydrated by lifting an arm, moving a leg—and then lay down again. There was more to it. Helena had a chronic reflux problem. It sounded stupid even to him but when she first announced this problem, he felt his love increase. She chewed grey tablets the size of small biscuits and kept glasses of water in all the rooms. In the middle of the night she often woke suddenly, sitting bolt upright with a gasp, her hand pressed to her chest as though she'd been shot. She'd then take a couple of controlling breaths, a sip of water, and lie down again. When it happened the first few times Paddy was with her, he also sat up in alarm, thinking that someone was in the room. Who is it? he said. What's happening? Who's there? In a way, he supposed, he thought it was Dora doing this to her.

'Of course, I'll wear a helmet,' he said. He kissed her, told her goodnight, and she was sleeping by the time he turned his back.

2

Teresa stood in front of the meat counter at Moore Wilson's, asking for the sausages which Paddy, her son, had recommended as the best. Sausage heaven, he said. She'd never felt that excited by sausages or even food in general. It disappointed her whenever people started talking about great dishes they'd had. She barely remembered what she ate. Fishbones caught in her throat. Anyway, pork and fennel were apparently the ones to go for, made by the craftsmen butchers of Island Bay. The young man serving hadn't heard her order properly and she repeated it. 'Those,' she said, pointing in the display case. The sausages were in stainless steel trays, stacked in important mounds.

He grabbed a large handful and put them on the scales. 'You were saying "Island Bay", I get it now. Fennel.'

'Exactly,' said Teresa, or something like it.

He was putting more on, interpreting something else she'd said, hadn't said. 'Sorry.' He gave her a big smile. The sausages cost thirty dollars, which shocked her, and she'd got too many of them for just herself and Stephanie. She could give some to Paddy. In the refrigerated section behind her, she found a sealed pack of frankfurters and added these to her basket for the girls. They wouldn't be able to eat the fennel.

At the bread counter she said, 'Pain au chocolat, two please.' These could be cut up for dessert that night. But two, wasn't that a bit mingy for all of them? Amazing she still had to battle against this bending towards cheapness, still! Would there be fights at the ranch? She wanted things easy for Steph, aware too that Steph had a fear of bad dietary habits. She wouldn't have Coke in the house or anything except the plainest biscuits in the tins. That weekend Teresa was going to the Wairarapa with her daughter and her three granddaughters. Stephanie had planned it a month ago.

The woman hovered with her tongs. 'What was that again?'

Teresa pointed. 'There, pain au chocolat.'

'Okay. And how many? Just one?'

'Two.' She'd meant to increase the amount but she was flustered.

'Two?' The woman still seemed unclear.

Teresa held up the fingers. It was torture.

'There you go. Thank you.'

She couldn't find any goat's cheese in the refrigerated section. An employee was restocking close to her and she asked him if they had any.

'Coat?'

'Goat,' said Teresa.

'Gert?'

'No!' She laughed at him to see if that made a difference.

He kept a serious look on his face. 'It's a type or that's the company who makes it?'

'It's the animal that makes it!' she said.

'The animal is a gert, what do you call it?'

What did it take, an actual impersonation? Should she butt him? A creeping humiliation drained the comedy.

Vendredi, she thought. Novembre.

He looked over to a colleague who was behind the counter hanging salami on hooks. 'Hey Dorf, we got any cheese made from a grit?'

'A what?' said Dorf.

'A goat,' said Teresa, quietly now, beginning to doubt the animal herself. 'Goat's cheese.'

Dorf shook his head. Then he pointed at Teresa. 'You mean goat's cheese, right.'

Near the checkout counters she took a bottle of fresh orange juice from a stand and a packet of coloured pasta. It was possible to get through the payment part without speaking and this she accomplished.

Before Moore Wilson's, she'd been to Whitcoulls and purchased a pocket French dictionary. She didn't quite know why. This French business would fade, she thought. People woke up with afflictions of various kinds and they passed. While the girl was scanning it, Teresa saw a box of coloured pens and asked for this to be added to the purchase. They could come in handy in the Wairarapa. Stephanie had sent through photos of the place; there was a long window-seat in the conservatory and she saw the girls kneeling there, drawing pictures while Stephanie and Teresa read their books, drank their weak gins. At a certain point, once the girls were in bed, they'd talk about Paul Shawn, the children's father, and her daughter would cry silently, without too much passion. Then she'd sleep for twelve hours, waking to find Teresa had given the girls their breakfast and taken them to the park.

The girl looked up and said, 'How long have you been in New Zealand?'

'Me?' said Teresa.

She held up the dictionary. 'Your English is very good!'

'Thank you,' said Teresa. Absurdly, she felt pleased. The girl, she discovered, was grinning in encouragement, hoping to hear more. She turned and left, suddenly shy, a little hallucinatory under the fluorescent lighting.

I've been here seventy-eight years and counting.

That morning she'd woken as usual to the radio news. They were in the middle of a story from France, where truck drivers were going 'to make the snail', use their vehicles to block motorways. They were interviewing a truckie. His words were translated. Behind the English, you could still hear his voice. 'This is our message to the politicians and the oil companies. If you are stuck behind my truck in your limousines, you will smell my farts!'

She decided, in the abstract at least, she approved of French truck drivers.

Someone, a spokesperson, sober and measured and dull, was saying how pointless and harmful it was to the economy. Counter-productive. He was French but spoke in English. The behaviour, he said, was a 'relic', a *rayleek* she heard and the drivers were not snails but dinosaurs. Deenosaurs. She thought vaguely of Dean Martin, whom she didn't have a good handle on. He was different from Frank Sinatra, was he? She saw a thin drunk man in a dinner jacket with a cigarette, smiling at something risqué he'd just said, or was just about to say. *Risqué* was a French word. She couldn't think of anything for longer than a second before it headed towards this. Then she drifted back to sleep. When she woke again, it was vendredi. She had the word so far to the front of her mouth that she had to produce it, like the pointed stone of a plum. She said it aloud. She didn't have a shred of the language, yet here it was.

Teresa walked to the computer in the dining room, still in her pyjamas, and went online. This at least was normal. She always turned on the computer before doing anything else, going to the toilet, eating breakfast. She went to it as to an oracle. Of course the word meant Friday, and it was: today was vendredi. She said it aloud again, rather nicely. That was interesting again. Perhaps she had known the days of the week after all. Mercredi was familiar, like mercury, which as a girl she'd once had to spit from her mouth, having stupidly bitten a thermometer, a single melted bullet dropping and running through her fingers like something escaping her fever. Both her parents had stood there, unable for a second to comprehend what had happened; the act so far out of the range of her character that for a moment she thought: They don't know who I am. I could be anyone lying here.

Skype had opened and she read a chat message from Pip sent late the night before. How are you darling? Can't sleep. I keep having the same nightmare: I've come to live in Palmerston North.

Pip was her cousin, her great and long-distance friend. After a lifetime in Zimbabwe, she'd come to live in Palmerston North. Her husband had been killed, but that was long before Mugabe. Teresa had never met him, a Yorkshireman, only seen photos. David. He had a beard and was the manager on a tobacco farm before moving into the city after some problems. In a robbery, he was stabbed. David had been collecting the unsold bread from a supermarket to distribute to shelters as part of a church charity group. The crime belonged anywhere, Pip had said. It was mindless. She continued to love the people, the country, and she had stayed on. In the early Rhodesian days, there'd been the letters. Come, wrote her cousin, come, come, come. She described the streets, the things she'd seen in the markets, the local gardens, the giraffes 'mooching in the trees'. 'The dusty pink of the sunsets.' 'The blackness of the blacks.' She was swimming in a friend's concrete pool. The friend kept frogs to eat the pupae of the mosquitoes. Okay, then maybe I will. They'd both devoured *Sally in Rhodesia*. That book lit the fire.

How am I? Teresa wondered. Well, different, that was clear. When she looked in the mirror, she seemed the same. She spoke into her reflection and saw it. Her lips came forward and the muscles at the corners of her mouth were tight. She was acting. Her mouth felt sore. Her tongue was tired, which was a very strange sensation. The fatigue was astonishingly local.

It was Novembre, too, which she also pronounced perfectly, as far as she could tell, but how did she even know that much, that it was correct? The girl chasing the mercury around her wicker bedspread was monolingual, an ignoramus when it came to such things, though a student eventually of typewriters and foot-controlled dictaphones. You pressed down under the desk and a man's voice spoke in your ear. Dear Mr Peters.

She'd caught it from the *radio*? Maybe she was crazy and this was a sign, a symptom. She hadn't been waiting for it exactly, yet she knew she was now only five years younger than her mother had been when that mind, without pity on its owner, crumbled, admitting the barefoot dietician with the silken beard and the stopwatch.

In her eighties, her mother had grown to believe Teresa's father was secretly in love with the young Samoan woman next door and these were his illegitimate children coming through the hedge. He gave them eggs from his hens.

One afternoon, a few months before her mother died, Teresa had stood beside her as they watched from the window her father, a retired teacher, carefully handing the eggs to a young boy and girl. Her parents lived in a state house in Naenae. The wind flew against the high hedge at the rear of the property, turning it silver for a moment before switching it back. The leaves were glossy on one side and thick. They tempted you to touch them, and then they disappointed you somehow. Beyond the hedge, and through a little opening in the branches, there was barren public land that sloped down to a concrete waterway patrolled by stray cats. Teresa had always felt this place to be particularly desolate and despairing, though when they visited, her children often played there, if it could be called playing. You followed the waterway in one direction and came to a sports field which, in winter, smelled of rotting vegetation due to poor drainage. If you headed north instead, wading in the motionless shin-deep water, eventually you reached a culvert sealed off with a metal grill. She imagined in a flash her children swallowed into the darkness of the tunnel. Weeds and rubbish caught against the bars. She'd accompanied the kids once, Paddy walking in gumboots in the water, the girls on the grass. Lift your head and above the culvert you saw the hillside cemetery, the sun striking its tilted plane, where both her parents would one day be buried. Near the edge of the concrete waterway she'd almost stepped on the body of a dead rat. The hair on the body was brushed the wrong way. She'd scooped up Stephanie in her arms before she got a good look and jogged up to the line of hedges, calling to the other two who were bent over it. At such times she felt excessively widowed—widowed again and again, moment by moment, that it was ongoing and not a single event in the past.

'I can't believe he's done this to me,' her mother said at the window, 'but at least he has the decency to treat them well.' Then she took Teresa's hand and held it tightly. The neighbour's children were entering the chicken coop, bending their heads. 'How dark they are and him so pale!' The fantasy was cruel, hard on everyone, but it was also clearly interesting to her mother, a spectacle she hadn't anticipated. She found life immensely surprising, until of course she didn't. In her cupboards, which had once been full of home baking, chutneys, bottles of preserved fruit, there was only white bread, salt, pre-washed potatoes, mayonnaise mix in a packet. They discovered she was only eating things that were white in colour because of the dangers of what she called pigmentated food. Someone was telling her about this, a man she described as having a silken beard, bare feet and a stopwatch around his neck. Naturally no such figure existed in Naenae. She didn't speak boastfully about this phantom, but shyly, with a strange girlish smile on her face.

Was this what Teresa had coming? But then again, she didn't have a voice in her head, she had a voice in her voice.

She typed back to Pip, who was not online: Dear African Night Owl, all is fine. Teresa sent it before she realised she'd not replied to the line about Palmerston North. Her cousin would want something witty back, that was their style. She looked at the screen. No wit was in her, only a pressure at her temple, like a thumb. She went back into the bedroom and dressed quickly, as if something depended on it. Why wasn't there time for a shower? She put on deodorant. She had an urgent sense that she needed to be ready.

Although she had no appetite, she poured yoghurt onto cereal, chopping half a banana on top. For the time it took to eat this, through an old trick, she prevented herself from thinking. You imagined a white wall being painted, white on white. An odourless paint. The painting was important—the even sweep of the roller—otherwise you began to see writing, which led back to thoughts. She held it. In this blank space she hoped to return her mind to its normal routines, shaking off the foreignness that was only some ephemeral condition, the smudge that sleep had made of reality. Was she even properly awake? Then she couldn't hold it any longer. And the banana tasted like a banana and the yoghurt she poured in was wet and cold. There was instantly something grassy on her palate.

Once in Lower Hutt on High Street she'd been approached by a woman in her sixties wearing a tee-shirt that said across the chest: AIRBAG inflation on impact. Incredibly, the woman, it turned out, was from France. She was nice, very polite, cultured, with perfect wavy white hair. Her handbag carried exquisite scrollwork on its strap, the body of the bag kept elegantly plain. Could Teresa tell her where the art gallery was? They'd walked to the Dowse together, stopping to name the trees, admiring the fountain. Fontaine, she said. She loved the montagnes. Willow, said Teresa, pointing. Weeping Willow. The woman tried it and then they both laughed.

She thought about languages. She had learned shorthand, if that counted as a language. The name alone gave it away, as though the writer's tool had become a claw. Men spoke and as fast as it came out of their mouths, you stitched it to the page. Pip, she remembered, had wanted to be taught a few words; she was training to be a dental nurse and hoped to write rude things about the dentists who bullied her, who rubbed against her as they looked inside mouths. 'See here,' they said. She wanted to write such things in their presence, smiling and looking meek in the Pip way.

Pip's return to New Zealand had made Teresa think a lot about things she'd hardly considered for decades. Moving house too. Moving moved things, she thought.

Of course some people thought shorthand was magic, like spells inscribed on ancient tombs, secret code, but not the other girls from the pool. Shorthand was blindingly tedious, though you could use it to communicate to each other about boyfriends, pass notes under their noses. Pip's instinct was right. It was the language of disenchantment, of hopes up in smoke, which was a phrase that came back to her.

Come, come, come. You'll love it here. Oh yes? The mooching pupae, Teresa wrote back, things biting you in the night.

And who, Pip replied, is biting you in the night?

They were both virgins.

Teresa brought her tea into the bedroom and sat on the edge of her bed to drink it. Somehow this was better than being in the kitchen. There was a sort of intimidation still in the newness of the surroundings, in the wonder of it. Me? I live here?

In the alleyway between their building and the one beside it there were occasionally young men and sometimes a young woman, perhaps a prostitute, involved in some transaction though it wasn't a furtive thing. If Teresa happened to walk past, they didn't move off or attempt to conceal anything; they turned and stared at her, but not with hostility. They said, you? Are you also involved?

She tried to concentrate on the weekend ahead. Stephanie would pick her up that evening and they'd drive over the terrible hill, the three girls in the back, strapped into their car seats. Three dolls in a row. They always had fun. At the top of the hill Teresa would take over the driving while Steph held out bags for the girls to be sick in, and even this had a kind of merriment to it. Isabelle would want to hold her own bag. I've done more in mine, Mummy. And coming down the other side, there were the plains, which always made her think of the first explorers, the sunny knobbed expanse beyond the dark tangle of foothills. You breathed out seeing that, and felt pioneering, while also grateful the hard work had been done, the vineyards and cafés in place.

She packed a few things for the weekend. It was probably strange to be going away so soon after moving in—Paddy had wondered about the wisdom—but Teresa couldn't disappoint Steph. Of course Paddy wondered about the wisdom of that too. Make sure you get some time for yourself, he told her. Yet she truly didn't mind, did not experience it as anything but natural, the maintaining or supporting or doing something with the buoyancy of her youngest daughter, who was excitable and radiant, and who therefore required some solid backing. Teresa was solid. Not to herself of course but she was aware of an effect and part of that was reliability. Yes she would be there when she said she would, and surprisingly some people never managed even this simple thing. And she didn't mind it at all, the running around, the ferrying, the caring, though not many believed her. But she was also her daughter's audience and found that sustaining, interesting on a daily basis, as she did all her children's lives, even Margie, who'd always struggled with her younger sister's position, actually with any arrangement concerning the family. It was why she lived in Canada.

Darling Pip, I'm thinking of coming, I am. You know I won't and can't and how could I but I'm thinking of it, thinking of you under the mosquito net, among the grasshoppers, among the pink giraffes. Pip had been served first in a shop, despite the queue in front of her. Blacks. The thing is, Pip wrote, you can't not be served first. The blacks don't like it if you try.

Sometimes Stephanie entered the house calling out that she was there, expecting nothing less than immediate attention, and it was as if she'd come home from school for lunch and her daughters were kids she'd befriended on the way. Look who I found. She seemed very distant from them. Stephanie was a great mother and sometimes she desired, understandably, to be free of that, even to be not very good, helpless, lost. Teresa would discover her at the open door of the fridge. 'I'm totally starving! We all are!' Her voice itself not just the echo but the actual voice of the girl she'd been.

That was the old house. Now you had to buzz people in. They stood in the street, looking up.

After washing her breakfast things, Teresa had left the apartment building by the stairs; she was still not quite used to the lift. The alley was deserted. The shops weren't open yet and she walked in a large pointless circle, around the waterfront and back to Courtenay Place, taking in almost nothing. There was a small man in a yellow woollen hat juggling tennis balls, grinning at her. Had he been left over from the night before? Yet he wasn't drunk because he was keeping four balls, or even five, in the air. She didn't want to pause and count. She turned away from him as she passed and became aware that he was following her. He was bouncing a ball in time with her steps. After a few paces he stopped. In her head ran the same few words. Vendredi. Novembre. Mercredi. The thermometer's mercury again, the sounds of each word seeming silvery, globular, liquid, as they slid backwards into each other in a sort of song that was tiring, catchy, impossible to get rid of.

Leaving Moore Wilson's with the supplies, she felt her teeth become strange, heavy, partly locked, her tongue caught behind them, its tip pressed hard against the roof of her mouth. Her jaw was suddenly tight. She didn't seem to be willing any of this. A kind of paralysis, she thought. Stroke. I'm having a stroke. Why hadn't she thought of that before?

That the idea failed to bring her to her knees gave her a strengthening boost of pride; even if she were dying, there was a decent streak of realism in her. My speech has been affected in the direction of the Romance languages. And still she was able to swing her arms, carry her shopping, walk along this Wellington street. She didn't have the nice bag with its elegant scrollwork, the surprising teeshirt, the fixed wavy hair—there were no fontaines or montagnes—but she had still become this, a slightly French woman on her way home.

She moved through the covered car park with her bags, a little fearful, but determined. A van had to stop for her though she was only aware of it after she'd crossed in front of it. That woke her up to the world. The dread of collapsing in public did it. She'd seen these women, lying on crowded footpaths, their sweaty heads propped up on someone's balled-up jacket, semi-conscious, apologising; the deathless instinct to cover one's knees. Let me go in my own place, she prayed. She was carrying the world's most expensive sausages, chocolate bread.

People passed her, going to work. Gusts of wind struck at her in contradictory ways, wrapping the plastic shopping bags against her legs, and then releasing her, giving her a shove. Off you go. Her step was steady and fierce. She realised she was going past Helena's work and she kept her head down. She didn't want to meet the kind Helena now. Helena was a busy lady too. Such a meeting might easily knock Teresa off her feet completely. The temptation would be to fall weeping and close-mouthed into those arms. Unfair unfair.

She glanced up at the sign: Capital Language School. The irony stabbed at her, pin-like in the tops of her arms, a joke injection. Languages. A Japanese girl waited on the steps, cuddling her backpack to her chest, her smile fixed in terror and uncertainty. Perhaps it was her first day and she'd just stepped off the plane. The girl's eyes widened as they met Teresa's. Don't ask me a question, Teresa thought, ducking off. Where is art gallery? Look at weeping willow. *Reaping rillow.*

She walked on for a moment, thinking of the people she hoped not to run into.

Then Teresa turned back to see whether the Japanese girl on the steps of the school needed her help but she was gone and under this blow Teresa bent lower in her limbs. How heavy these best sausages were. Pith and rind were swimming and sinking in the orange juice.

It felt to her as though she was wearing a headband that had slipped down across her forehead; this was sweat she realised, putting the back of one hand there. I'm so hot! She was coming true, she thought, putting it to herself as strangely as that. The way she spoke to herself in her head was just a little out, a little off. Coming true to that thing she'd thought of earlier—did she mean that? She was herself as a young girl, so foolishly affronted by the thermometer stuck into her mouth, she bit down on it. The shock she'd engendered in her poor parents. They were older than her friends' parents, almost the previous generation, which gave their relationship a tone of—what?—care rather than love? But that seemed unkind. They were attentive, peaceful, bemused mostly. Her father had chosen her mother when she had few prospects—she was thirty-four—and they'd eloped to avoid a wedding in which the couple would be congratulated by a lot of doubters and smirkers, as her mother had once told her. 'They thought I'd have one sort of life,' she said. 'No one thanks you for proving them wrong.' Teresa remembered holding her mouth open for her mother to pick the pieces of soft glass off her tongue. Bloodless. Then her father, quick to recover, was pulling back the blankets to chase the mercury around the bed. 'It's the devil to catch!' he said, grinning at her. 'Help me, won't you?'

Her mother had left the room. 'I won't help wilful children,' she said.

Wilful? This hurt. Because she was not wilful and that was why her mother had said it, she thought, to establish a line everyone considered was very far away. Somewhere in the remote distance such a person, strange creature, existed, but not here. Her father finally scooped the little pool of grey matter into his palm. 'Got you!' Its moving surface like a mirror but also like the backing of a mirror, flashing light and dulling it at once. No, she was not wilful. Yet could a single act, one event, cause everything to change?

'Toxic,' said her father sadly, leaving the room.

She was toxic, she thought for a moment, poisoning their simple eloping lives. They'd nursed her through the rheumatic fever. She was better.

At the solicitors' office, she saved the fare for the ship, which took almost a year. And then she was saving some more, for living expenses and emergencies, though Pip said she could walk into a job in Salisbury no problem, be earning well soon after she strolled down the gangplank, if that was what it was called. Pip would come to Cape Town; she'd be waiting on the dock, and then they'd travel up together. Yet Teresa discovered she liked saving, the act itself. And as she became aware of her cousin Pip growing more expert in her new country, more casual about its astonishments, not as detailed in her letters—fewer giraffes—Teresa felt less inclined to go. She'd be starting from so far behind. Thinking about how much she'd have to learn was a great disincentive to begin on that process, she discovered. Pip would have to be her teacher, which hardly mattered, she knew, it was just that she felt she'd done enough learning. She was impatient for life to begin, not for everything to begin again. And then towards the end of the second year of successful saving, she met Brendan.

Finally, at the apartment building, Teresa stood in front of the lift, her arms incredibly tired from carrying the bags of shopping even though the bags didn't contain much, or any more than she was used to. She must be sick, she thought. Just then she became aware of two people standing beside her, a woman and a boy. They too were waiting for the lift. The woman caught her eye and smiled. The boy was looking at his feet. Suddenly Teresa turned away, pushing through the doors to the stairs with her shoulder. She had five flights. The stairs were a light well and sunshine fell on her blazing head. She began the climb. It was still vendredi.

3

In the early and dark hours of Saturday morning, unable to sleep, Paddy went downstairs to his office. A topic for 'Speech Marks' had come to him in bed and he had to check whether or not he'd already covered it: the glottal stop. Would that woo Gorzo back? What was he, his lucky charm? He found nothing on his computer and straight away made some notes. Then he turned off the machine.

On a bookshelf by the door, he saw the little bottle of oil he'd been given when he bought the bike. Next he was spreading newspaper under the bike and squirting oil onto the chain, slowly turning the pedal—just as he'd been instructed to do. It was nicely therapeutic. The cleverly interlocking links of the chain absorbed the oil and what they couldn't use fell in neat drops onto the newspaper. Then he carefully screwed up the paper and took it downstairs to the wheelie bin at the back of the building. Before stepping out, he paused, listening for any sounds. Recently there'd been a flyer distributed to all the residents of the building warning them to take care, especially at night, and to be security conscious. Don't hold the door open for anyone you don't know. Druggies used the alleyway. It was silent. From outside he could look up and see the lights of their apartment and also his mother's apartment. Her kitchen light was on.

The day after she moved in, she'd knocked on their door and said, 'So what are the rules?' What rules, they said. 'It's embarrassing,' she said, 'so I'll make a start. Rule one, I will not treat you as my new best friends. There'll be no open door policy with me, for me. We should behave as though nothing has changed. I won't be popping in all the time just because I can. I love you both dearly and hope to see a lot of you, but let's not make regular appointments either. Rule two, I won't come to you every Sunday with a pudding in my arms.'

'Why not?' said Paddy. 'I love your puddings.'

'I'm over puddings,' said Teresa. 'If you two don't cook, then why should I?'

It was true; Paddy and Helena didn't. She'd cooked for her husband and her daughter and he'd cooked for himself for years. They'd had enough of all that. There was a plastic box in the freezer labelled in Medbh's hand, 'Carbonara: eat for comfort!' This went in the microwave. Medbh was 'our girl', that was what they called her. Has our girl been in today? they said. What has our girl left us?

'Pretend I'm not there,' said his mother. 'Of course I'm here and it's marvellous. But don't listen out for me. Have you any rules for me? Please tell me one or make one up so it's not just me being officious and strange.'

And Helena had embraced her, surprising her. 'Teresa to consent to physical shows of affection from admiring, loving daughter-in-law.'

His mother was smiling. It moved Paddy to see this.

'Rule two,' said Paddy, 'Medbh, "our girl", will come to clean and cook for you once a week and we will pay for that.' They'd been over this before.

'I don't need a girl,' said his mother.

Helena said, 'Teresa, I wanted you to have her twice a week, like us, so I've already compromised. Can you meet us here?'

'But what will she do except twiddle her thumbs?'

'No, Ma, that's your job now,' said Paddy.

For Paddy's two sisters, Teresa's move was perfect. Whatever guilty worries they had about their mother—her possible loneliness, the need for help in emergencies—seemed neatly stored in the vicinity of their brother, her only son. Stephanie, the baby, with her small girls, no husband most of the time, and the right to kidnap Teresa whenever she needed to; Margaret, with the vague historical wound of antipathy towards them all, had a family and a life safely in Vancouver. What did Patrick have, the sisters wondered, except finally a settled and straightforward existence with a sane and grown-up person, in a nice apartment building? It had turned out that no one had really got on with Bridget.

For Helena and Paddy too, the move made sense. Helena loved Teresa as he did, for the qualities of her spirit: patience, selflessness, and a quietly efficient satirical streak. Helena also took reassurance from strains in Teresa's personality that for a son were perhaps more ambiguous: her independence and her vast privacy. She wouldn't pop in. Perhaps the women's hug had carried something of this too: as opposed to being the start of increased intimacy—his mother was not a great hugger—it was a special occasion, contract-sealing moment? Thank you for these rules. We will leave each other alone as much as possible.

He looked into the theatrical night sky above his mother's kitchen window. It was another windy night and in the foreground low dark clouds slid quickly over their building in the direction of the South Island, while behind them pale clouds were fixed in a stack, as if there were two skies. A rope might have been pulling the low clouds across a painted scene. The whole thing was backlit by a full moon. It was beautiful and intriguing, the setting for something, probably another round of ugly belting northerlies.

When they worried about emergencies with their mother they meant nothing much. A couple of months ago she'd fallen. In the middle of the night she felt ill and she'd gone to the bathroom where she vomited. It was something she'd eaten. She'd woken up on the bathroom floor, cold, and realised she'd passed out from the vomiting. She guessed an hour or so had gone by. She put her hand to her head and felt blood. In falling she'd struck her head on the side of the shower box. The wound needed stitches. It was not the reason she'd moved next door but it was part of the background to the decision, and part of Paddy's and Helena's insistence that Medbh be involved too. Another set of eyes.

Paddy had talked to Stephanie about this, who agreed. And maybe Steph would tread gently for a while, he said. How else do I tread? she said. His sister was hurt at once. Go easy perhaps, he told her. 'Easy? I'm easy! I'm the easiest one.' She was reddening in her face, already beginning to get teary. He only meant that with the girls she should be aware of not putting too much onto their mother. 'But she loves the girls! They bring her joy!' Yes, they were lovely and also young and tiring sometimes. He wasn't suggesting a ban or anything, merely a space. Stephanie had turned away from him and he saw her neck was a massive blotch. 'Are you taking her from me?' she said.

'Don't be silly,' he said.

'Then why is she moving into your building?'

'Because you live in a two-bedroom house full of bunks.'

She turned back to him, eyes glistening, her anger instantly gone. She looked suddenly grateful, as though he'd solved a problem she'd been hounded by for a while. 'Yes!' she said. 'Yes, where would we put her? In a cupboard?'

He slid back into bed as carefully as he could but Helena sat up at once and hit her pillow a few times. Then she took a sip of water from her glass.

'What's that smell?' she said.

He got out of bed and washed his hands again. Now he was a cyclist, he would need to buy special jelly for getting oil and grease out of his skin. He wondered what Lant used. By the time Paddy came back, Helena was asleep again.

*

Lant had taken Paddy to the bike shop and made him buy the right bike. Pretty much it was his friend's idea, though one Paddy had become curious about. Someone offers an idea about you, it's interesting. 'I feel you need to be fitter to face what you're going to face,' Lant told him.

Lant had been biking for about a year, following his marriage break-up. Since then he'd had a series of girlfriends—short-lived, immensely gratifying, he said—and he credited this success to a regular regime of punishing road work around the Wellington hills. He was fit. Lant was also trying other new things, having joined a band. This vaguely annoyed Paddy. Anyway, Lant had converted his hopelessly square childhood under a piano-teacher mother into a surprising guest gig as a violinist with a part-time countryish bar band, which put him in pubs late at night. Paddy saw his friend now had a collection of plaid shirts, a pair of boots, and even a denim jacket. He'd yet to see the costume in toto because he hadn't seen the band. Lant was coy about dates and times. Every so often, one part of the identity would get an outing—he'd be wearing a string tie, say. It was as if Lant was preparing Paddy, or even himself, for the transformation.

'What am I going to face?' said Paddy. Life with Helena had been marked by a deep and certain aliveness. They'd lived together for almost eighteen months. The apartment purchase was the clincher. He'd been no Casaubon. The post-Bridget years had not been about hoarding, frequently the opposite. Now he was happy, the real thing.

'Patrick, we're fifty now,' said Lant. It was a number with a certain weight and he added more by touching Paddy's arm as he said it. 'Fifty years,' he said.

For his birthday in July, Helena and Paddy had gone to Rarotonga and been happy there, delighted, warmed, rained upon. 'All right,' he said.

'How old were we when we first met?' said Lant.

'Twenty-four, five.'

'Two men of fifty. Standing on the earth. Pinch me, I'm dreaming.'

Paddy pinched him on the back of his hand. He flinched and pulled it away. 'Good news, Jeremy,' said Paddy, 'you might be ancient and of the earth but you still have feelings in the extremities.'

He rubbed his hand. 'That may be more than you've got.'

'Sorry,' said Paddy, 'but for me this last decade has seen major improvements. I feel in pretty good shape to face whatever's around the corner. Barring a massive coronary or prostate cancer.'

Lant looked at his friend with renewed interest. 'What are your symptoms?'

'None,' he said. 'I feel fine.'

'Good,' said Lant, disappointed.

Fifty carried a certain threat but it was the truth that at forty Paddy had felt worse by far with everything in pieces and nothing settled. Married to the wrong person. In the wrong job, or in the wrong setting for that job. He'd walked out of the hospital. Jimmy Gorzo, Tony's son, had been one of his last cases, a triumph. It was how he'd first met Tony. Paddy, together with the audiologist he'd worked with, had presented a paper on Jimmy at a conference in San Diego. That was Paddy's big final act. He'd looked into the lights of the convention centre, seen the outline of three hundred heads listening to him—pretty nice, he thought. The hotel pool, he remembered, was in the shape of an ear.

Then what? He'd come home and for the next six months worked first on the concierge desk of a city hotel before demoting himself to kitchen-hand in the hotel's restaurant. Such a massive retooling could probably never be accounted for by tracing incremental motions. It was all or nothing.

To Bridget he'd gone for nothing. She was a commercial property manager who'd watched her builder father die of asbestosis when she was sixteen. Of course they'd compared fathers. Anyway, she told Paddy he'd 'menialised' himself. Her sound conviction was that to fall below a certain salary band was to invite a health disaster.

There was a uniform Paddy wore: grey jacket with the hotel insignia on its pocket, black trousers, white shirt. Lant thought it wasn't quite the complete dissociative act. Hospitals, hotels, there was a connection of sorts. Institutions. The friends had suddenly grown interested again in each other after a period of not much contact. Lant now had a daughter too.

Lant wasn't to blame but Paddy had developed a fairly refined, if fluid, rationale for the havoc he caused, a part of which was the self-serving notion that we had several lives to lead not the single one we'd settled for. There was also the deep response to whim, conventionally thought of as light. Yet whim could enter any life and turn it in a new direction. It was a whip, spurring us on to unlikely achievements. To her ultimate credit, when he'd said something about all this to Bridget, she gagged on the spot, actually retching in front of him. She had her hand to her mouth.

One might retrain to fight cancer or to fly a helicopter, drive an ambulance even, but what he'd done was all negative, she said. Turned himself off at the wall were her actual words.

At the hotel Paddy volunteered to do nights, the room service orders. Soups at midnight, muffins to lovers at 3am. Creepy salesmen. It gave him more time to drift around the hotel, to doze and take part in hi-jinks. Bridget was properly terrorised. All his thoughts about her at this time were basically satirical. Cracking up but not going foetal, abandoning his profession but working quite solidly and responsibly, he was a ball of confusion to behold and he felt little humanity. Better for everyone that he was at the hotel, which was basically the home of satire, pranks anyway. He knew he was being a prick and a lunatic. He had to be very polite and obsequious there in a massive sublimation of the aggression he felt. (Lant.)

Bridget: Shift workers are the worst placed of any among the employed. People working night shifts have more accidents, contract illnesses. Statistically et cetera.

Paddy: Your fury at me is also a risk factor. Your blood pressure. (She was on medication.) The angry use themselves up faster than anyone.

It's you causing me to be angry!

You were furious before this, when I was helping keep our economic unit safe. And you didn't care for what I did before. (True.) You live in a state of agitation. I think you get something from it, being furious. Then you collapse. It's a cycle. (Tendentious and cruel.)

So you think I'm doing it on purpose?

No. But nor am I.

Nor are you working as a kitchen-hand on purpose you mean? That makes no sense.

He no longer seemed devoted to sense, she was correct. However, it wasn't all nasty invention. Here he was referring to the fact that after they were married, every six months or so, she took to her bed, inexplicably, struck down. Nothing to do with her blood pressure, which was the first thing checked. Initially, he thought it was a pretend illness, no, he thought it was very serious, then he was suspicious. Diagnosis-wise, there was nothing, but the suffering was real and he saw he had to swing into action. For three days, four days, longer, he nursed her. Meals on trays. They had to put the phone on silent ring because it gave her a fright. She asked him to examine rashes on her arms and her back, as if he were a doctor. He only worked among them, was looked down on by them. Real doctors had examined her and she applied cream to no effect. She had flaky skin around her nose. She had a shake in her hands, burning sensations in her feet. Once she told him it was as though she were lying on an oven tray. Night was worst because the oven door closed and she was in the dark. She was very scared. He was frantic to find out a cause when it recurred. Then after the fourth or fifth time, they adjusted domestically. In temperature and appetite, despite the fieriness, she was always normal. She had MRI scans that showed nothing. She was not mad though, which was what she feared. He knew she was fairly mad but that

42

was different, to be mad in private. Mad at him, or along with him. Two psychiatrists had given her the all-clear. Some sort of chronic exhaustion perhaps? Rest. Yet rest made her over-tired.

During these bouts she spoke with a tiny, dried-up voice, and she lifted her head off the pillow and pursed her lips for Paddy to apply lip-balm. It was this aspect that shocked him most deeply, the lips, the voice. Here evidently his professional sensitivities showed. Normally she spoke in flat, booming tones. She dealt with businessmen, she walked through cavernous spaces, empty office blocks she was trying to fill. She honked. Often she answered the phone carrying a calculator and announced numbers. There was not a trace of sales pitch in her voice. Perhaps this was connected with her success, the ability to remove hope, its ingratiating music, from her speech. To hear this unvarnished voice was to be persuaded of neutrality and the prospect of a good deal.

As she lay in bed, she sounded frighteningly girlish, beseeching and fearful and lost.

Just as quickly, she was better again. Her skin cleared up, the rashes were gone. She began again to carry her calculator. Her old voice came back. Shame clung to her for a short while. Contrition. Paddy felt this period was even worse than the bed-bound one. Her boldness, her strictness, her sweeping and unselfconscious power, even her paranoia, had been attractive to him once. He remembered how men like him thought they had to ask permission for everything. This proved to be a mighty misunderstanding. It was in retrospect a brief epoch of male grovelling, mourned surely by neither side. The first time they'd gone to bed, he'd tried to have sex without getting a full erection. Why? Was the penis a suspect tool? Well, he had one and she did not. These were the actual and not quaint terms of said epoch. A side-effect of feminism, late 70s early 80s local variety, was that nervous basically nice males, such as him, persuaded themselves their fears and insecurities were progressive. Quickly she put him right on all that. His courtesy was frankly problematic. If he were being a gentleman, gentlemen didn't he understand were part of the problem. She wasn't about to be broken as if she were a vase. She said, What is this? She was weighing it in her hand. What are we supposed to do with *this*? He responded at once, on command almost. From that moment on, sexually, their relationship had been satisfactory with an arrow heading up, indeed the only area in which humour could play a part. In bed, they both became childish, which sounded like the wrong word. When he held her, she talked about his one-bar heater. Her period was known by them as 'Mr Full Stop'. Her favourite position was on top, from where in week two, she asked him whether he'd thought of names for her breasts. Two names. He hadn't. Instantly he said, Maude and Claude. He licked his thumb and touched them in turn, saying the names. Hello you two, she said. Outside the bedroom, perhaps wisely, perhaps not, they never attained anything like this sort of tone.

He sometimes thought Bridget was humourless, meaning she didn't like his jokes, or the jokes he liked. She preferred Mr Bean to Preston Sturges. Everyone just shouted, she said. This was after *Sullivan's Travels*. Periodically he brought things home— books, videos—which he wanted to put in her way. The Henry Higgins aspect she sniffed a mile off. Higgins of course was a professor of phonetics. They'd even watched the video of *My Fair Lady* together. The first film in which an actor sang live though a wireless mic. Rex Harrison's cravat concealed it. Rex didn't think he'd be able to lip-sync because every time he did the songs it was different. Bridget hated this sort of information from him. I feel like I'm at your work. She never understood his work. On this they were even. What she actually did away from the house remained a dull mystery to him.

They were incompatible on a major scale, and this incompatibility turned out to be a kind of glue. From the outside they both saw the extent of the mismatch but they also sensed each other's defiance of opinion. Here was their commonality: to prove others wrong. Yet that made it sound too small and sour. Attempting objectivity, he sometimes tried to see the tape afresh, and more positively. They'd had some decent and interesting and harmonious trips overseas. Sexual satisfaction or plain availability went a long long way. Maude and Claude. And busy working lives. Theirs was decidedly not that couple whose fighting escalated to such a frenzied point that the only action left was, depending on the genre, murder or love-making. They had a gift for each other and they knew enough not to give it too often.

They knew each other's secrets, or a number of them. He'd once cheated in a university exam. She'd been a rampant shoplifter for almost a year when she was sixteen, connected, they both agreed, to her father's death.

She project-managed everything, including him. He thought of himself as one of life's foot soldiers. This allowed him to take a back-seat role.

What else? He had a weakness for punning. Her planet had banned it.

Children were an issue, sort of.

Midwinter, he recalled, they stayed at a bach. He was still at the hospital then. She was thirty-four, a kind of accepted Significant Number. On the near-deserted beach they came across a boy using a broken-off car aerial to repeatedly hit a large piece of driftwood. He held up the driftwood and lashed it again and again. Paddy said, That's something you wouldn't see a girl do. Earlier they'd been passed by a team of riders, all girls, on horses, in their policeman-type hats, ponytails out the back, trotting along the sand. The horseshoe marks went along the tide-line. Hello, the girls said.

I would, said Bridget, looking at the boy. I'd do it.

The whole weekend they'd discussed having children, pros and cons. It was a working bee type of weekend to clear this up. They'd known couples who'd split up on the question, or who'd been saved by it. But for them the vexedness was quite mute, or characteristically bungled. If she fell pregnant, he said, he wouldn't mind. And how was this going to happen exactly, she asked. Did he mean, she said, if the contraception failed? Or something more active, along the lines of not using any?

They'd had a bottle of wine at lunch, very unusual, and they were both in a good mood, teasing, gentle. The bach had a television fixed to a shelf so high it gave you a sore neck. The bed wore sacking. The poorness of the accommodation had made them relaxed. They'd both agreed on that walking in. They were both against its meanness, united. Their companionship had always flourished unpredictably though it tended to require a third-party target.

He said that if it happened, pregnancy, he'd be very happy. If what happened, she said. He found he was maintaining 'pregnancy' as key signifier as opposed to 'our child'. Then, he said, what do you think? Shine the bulb in your eyes for a moment, what would you like to happen?

After a while she said, I'm thirty-four now. I'm not on the dark side yet.

And despite this being in direct contradiction to earlier conversations, he let it go.

Ah, moment deferred. Time for a walk. They both were deep in scarves and gloves. She had small blue gumboots for walking on sand. She held his arm. They'd been together for almost nine years, having met in a corporate indoor soccer team for which they'd both been ring-ins on a night the team recorded an apparently rare win. She was tall and strong and showed decidedly unatrophied skills in scoring several goals. He was far more anonymous. Afterwards the team had celebrated at a pub. As newbies they sat together. She had two-thirds of an MBA done. Among his group any sort of economic activity, even that phrase, was incomprehensible, Muldoon-associated. He spoke to her as to a visitor from outer space, a sporty businessy woman with a mean left foot; or he was the alien. When he spoke she stared at him as though he had something in his teeth. He went home. Three days later he received a gift in the mail: a tiny soccer ball. No note. He couldn't think who would have sent it except the organiser of the team who'd called him in, some sort of thank you for that, which seemed excessive. A couple of days later, another gift: a referee's whistle. He rang his contact in the team, who denied it. Then he told Paddy that someone had asked for his address, the girl who'd played for them, Bridget.

The idea that he was being pursued produced conflicting emotions. Partly it was the Groucho Marx line about not wanting to belong to any club that would have me as a member. More strongly, the aphrodisiacal effect of flattery. Or simply that of curiosity. He wondered about her body. She was almost his height. Previously he'd observed the four-inch rule or whatever it was.

The boy thrashing away on the beach didn't look their way even though they were the only people visible. The horses had evaporated. He worked that aerial.

There was a scene he thought of, from the pivotal hotel night duty period. It was the morning and Bridget was going to work just as he was coming home. They met in the kitchen where he was hesitating in front of the cereals. Paddy said that it was hard to know what to eat and this gave her an opportunity to renew the attack. But why say 'attack', these were reasonable questions. He was a parody of male inconstancy. Years later when his sister, Stephanie, was left by Paul Shawn, Paddy experienced a shudder of knowingness. He hated Paul and the situations weren't the same at all and Paul's behaviour was far worse than his own since it involved small children and boundless and ongoing deceptions, but he recognised himself somewhere in that mess. Paddy had a sense of the mechanism at work. Was he having a crisis? Bridget asked. Was he seeing someone else? Was he losing it? Was he taking Vitamin C? He looked pasty, she said. He looked dreadful. He smelled of hotel.

'What does it smell like?' he said. It seemed the only part of the conversation that he could enter safely.

'Air,' she said flatly, 'air conditioned air. Tell me when you'll quit. Give me a timeline for this crisis at least, so we can plan.'

The shift-work made Paddy even more sharply her opposite. States of mind that were interestingly dreamy then oddly particular had begun to affect him. Sometimes he felt on his head for a cap he wasn't wearing. He had to repeat the action a few minutes later. He believed he was wearing glasses and reached to take them off. He said to Bridget, 'Have you ever seen in movies from twenty, thirty years ago, how they walk along the corridor of a hotel at night and everyone's put their shoes out?'

'No,' she said.

He could see his reverie was almost physically painful for her but he went on. He was sure they'd watched these movies together. Part of his *Pygmalion* phase perhaps. He'd rented the videos and sat on the sofa, her feet in his hands. She always had sore feet, his Eliza. 'It was a common practice. Perhaps someone came and shined them in the night, it was a service offered. But there are those scenes in movies, showing neat pairs of shoes outside each door. Someone walks along, trying to figure out who's behind each door from their shoes.'

'What's the relevance to you wasting your life? You'd like to shine shoes now?'

'No but I find that a very powerful and moving image somehow. The empty shoes of those sleeping guests.' He had other things he wanted to say but she cut him off.

'I don't know if you're even awake right now.' She peered into his eyes. 'Why is your hair all grey? Where is your hair gone?' She was studying him up close. 'Patrick,' she said, with a sudden and sincere curiosity, 'why do you hate me so much?'

This was the cue for them both to burst into tears. Simultaneously they gave way to an unacknowledged grief, which was both surprising and obvious. Oh yes, this. This pain. Their marriage had become a question circling each of them in isolation. Paddy saw the question as a particularly vicious and persistent creature, bird-like but not a bird. It comes and sits on our heads, he thought. It investigates our skulls with its beak-like implement. First it's my turn, now it's her turn. You're never

48

unaware of the other person's torment but there are intervals of reprise in your own. You mistake this for contentment. For now you are okay. Don't you realise that soon she will be watching you, equally paralysed, equally fearful, the creature, like something Peter Jackson could toss off in his lunchbreak, sitting, where else, on your skull. Obviously the ideal marriage would be something else, with fewer horned ghouls.

They stood together in the kitchen, not touching, shaking with sobs. He smelled his work-shirt: nothing. He felt gratitude to Bridget for finally putting some clarity into their lives, gratitude and loathing. Paddy didn't go to work the next day. They sat down and Bridget produced a piece of paper on which she'd written an outline of arrangements for the separation. Paddy felt both excited and bored looking at this piece of paper, as if they were planning a holiday. Yes, he saw the need but he just wanted to be there. Of course they changed their minds the next day—they had to stay together and see this through. They had to. Why exactly? She suggested they both make lists of the reasons they had for continuing to be married.

His list was 1. All we've shared. 2. All we might share. He was stuck after that, unhappy. It read very sentimentally. He wanted to add further items such as, My penis fits you, which was drawn from her verbatim account one night. Compliments were nice. He had a number 3. It was, Love question mark. He'd written it out like that. At the last minute he decided against presenting such a hideous piece of equivocation. Also not entered: 4. My need not to disappoint my mother. A great heaving sense of dejection and failure went through his bones when he considered having to announce to Teresa the end. This was separate from and even counter to any actual evidence that his mother would regard the matter with a similarly heavy heart. Yet it was like walking home with a bad school report. You looked into the Hutt River and imagined being swept away. You saw and felt all this even though you were a grown man.

They went to compare lists, sitting across from each other at the kitchen table. Except Bridget had come to her senses again.

49

She'd not gone through with hers. His list was the sole list. The situation was horrific, perfect. She looked at his list and then he reached for it and screwed it up.

More than two years before they split up, when he told Lant about Bridget's episodes of illness and the lack of any discoverable cause, Lant said at once, 'I think it's you, Card.'

'Me?' said Paddy.

'You make her sick.'

Lant stood outside the little curtained cubicle in the bike shop while Paddy tried on bike shorts. He handed Paddy different sizes. When Paddy walked out, he said, 'How do they feel? Are you ready to take on the world in those shorts?'

'They're padded in the groin area,' said Paddy. 'And behind.' They were pleasant, like nappies, though that sort of contact made you also feel a sudden desire to urinate, or the fear that you just had.

Then Lant reached inside the waistband and tugged unhappily. 'Too big,' he said. 'Why do we all want to hide our bodies?' He waved at Paddy's large teeshirt.

'The obvious reasons,' said Paddy. Lant was lean, with the physique of someone sick or extremely fit. When he was drunk, he smoked. He was no paragon. His genes covered more of his faults than Paddy's did. Both his parents were tall and bony. Paddy's father had been heavy, his mother was medium. Paddy thought he just looked normally comfortable, normally fattish. A person on a professional salary sits in a chair for twenty-five years, what is the surprise.

Lant made him buy hugging bike shirts as well, and a thin, vented wind-jacket in racing blue that tapered longer at the back. When Paddy bent forward on the bike he wouldn't be exposed in the kidneys. Clever little jacket. There was also a pocket back there, a pouch.

Later the bike shop riding analyst showed Paddy video footage on his computer of a middle-aged man trying to ride a bicycle. It was a side-on view from a fixed camera, with a fixed bike. Oddly, it was in black and white, or grey—the man was grey, his skin was a lighter grey than his clothes. There was a flickering quality to the image. He looked as though he was biking in the 1920s. 'See his head position?' said the analyst. Paddy did. 'Wrong. He should relax his neck.'

'I see.'

'See his shoulders? Wrong. He should be looser there.'

'Yes,' said Paddy.

'Look at his elbows now.'

'Yes, I see.'

'He should tuck them in, is he a duck?'

'A duck?'

'Waddle waddle.'

'No,' said Paddy.

'What does he have wings for?'

'Tuck them in,' said Paddy. 'He should.' For a moment he forgot who the duck was. He was the fucking duck.

'What about his foot position?' said the analyst.

'Wrong,' said Paddy.

It was exciting to be inducted like this, in duck-ted, to feel a new world appear on the horizon and to be told of its harshness, its standards, its strange customs, the language they spoke there. The provisions carried their own allure. There was much to buy. They were going on a big journey. Who was worthy? The challenge was invigorating, draining. The bullying was called for, totally. Lant was beside Paddy, observing, shaking his head, making sounds of disapproval at the video, which the riding analyst had now paused.

'At the top of his pedal motion, he should be here.' The analyst clicked his mouse and a horizontal line appeared superimposed on the video. The biker's foot was hopelessly raised above this line. 'In this angle,' said the analyst, 'he's losing about twenty per cent of his power.'

'That much?' said Paddy.

'People are always surprised.' The analyst peered once

more at the frozen screen. 'So, the head, the shoulders, the elbows, the feet. Apart from that,' he said, 'the bike is perfect for you.'

'And what about the shorts?' said Lant, unable to resist. 'Are we happy with the shorts?'

4

When Teresa woke it was dark, early morning, and it wasn't Friday any more. In fact, it wasn't even Saturday, which she expected now Friday was gone. Her radio, set on the timer, hadn't come on because it was too early. Usually she woke to the time pips of the 7am news. But she was wearing her clothes, she realised. This was what had woken her, the feeling of her shirt's thick sleeves, the touch of cuffs at her wrist, the weight of her trousers on her legs. She was wearing the same clothes she'd been shopping in, when she'd bought the pocket French dictionary and then the sausages and the bread. It felt a bit like someone was lying on top of her. She lifted her head a little—it was all she could manage—and looked the length of her body, a strange view. Just beyond her feet, which were in socks, stood her empty shoes. They were in an upright position. It looked as if they were being worn but not by her.

She let her head fall back again. Her shoulders were flat against the mattress, pinned in place, and she was cold and stiff. She moved a leg and the shoes fell off the bed, striking the wooden floor with a thud. This made her think of Paddy and Helena, next door. Would they have heard? She hadn't yet gauged which sounds carried and which were mute.

In the toilet her urine was an oaky colour, an extreme concentrate of black tea, as if she'd poured it from a pot. She found herself looking into the bowl, divining. This was clearly a long way from the golden straw her mother used to describe as optimum. Of course Teresa had missed meals and drinks. She drank a glass of water, put on the jug and then she went to the computer. It was dimanche. She couldn't work it out, how many hours that was, more than thirty-six. She looked it up. Deux jours, almost. Dormir. The screen was too bright for her eyes so she shut it down and went to the drawer for her dictionary. The book was not much bigger than her palm, with a plasticised cover, as though ready to be taken on travels of some kind. She sat in an armchair beside her small lamp and flicked through the pages. Presque. Almost. Presque deux jours. She'd never slept for this long before. She was like a person in a fairytale. And someone had come while she was lying on the bed and put on her shoes and walked around in her place, buying sausages and bread, and of course the travel dictionary. And when Teresa woke up . . . nothing had changed. It wasn't over at all. This was the beginning. Because she knew what it was, what she had.

Before she'd fallen asleep she'd put the sausages in the fridge. She remembered this now. All the food had filled her with shame and the box of coloured pens was heartbreaking. She'd texted Steph. She said she'd been vomiting all night, some bug. Bad timing! Sorry to the girls. She was going to bed right now. Go without me. Don't fret. Go! Yr sick old ma.

Almost at once, the phone rang and Teresa waited until it went on to message. Afterwards she listened to Stephanie. She said that was too terrible and could they do anything? She was always getting sick these days, she had to take care of herself. Well, Paddy was right there so she figured things would be okay. But could she face the drive by herself over that hill? They'd paid the money already and the house was waiting. Could Teresa really not make it, even if she groaned and threw up the whole way, she could have the weekend in recovery mode? But no, if she was contagious, perhaps it was best to lie low. One thing: she wasn't to get up in the middle of the night and fall over and cut her head open, okay? Loving you, Mummy, she said. Poor old you. Call me when you can on my mobile.

While she was listening to this, Teresa heard her mobile receive a text. It was Stephanie saying she'd left a message. Usually all this connectivity thrilled her. Now it was an assault. Anyway, the text said they would go. The girls had spent all morning sitting in the car, practising to drive over the hill.

Teresa was suddenly tired too, and weepy. Having created the lying situation, her body now seemed ready to make her honest. She did feel rotten. She swallowed a mouthful of bile. All the people she was letting down. Oh girls.

A surge of leaden dullness made her almost fall into the nearest chair. It was as if her senses were closing down, as if some surgery were happening to her while she was still conscious. They were taking out parts of her, the parts responsible for everything and someone was looking at each bit, saying, 'No, this isn't it.' Fault, they were looking for the fault. Maybe it wasn't a stroke. She was plonked in front of the computer, which for a moment she thought was the television or perhaps the black window of the microwave. One of her neighbours in Lower Hutt had found her elderly husband trying to watch a DVD in their oven. But if this was her mother's gift, Alzheimer's, where was the build-up, the misremembered things, the wandering lost in car parks, the secret looks of relatives?

Yet things had perhaps entered some new phase. The bathroom fall she'd had a few months ago had seemed to disturb her children greatly. Even Margie had phoned from Canada. For a week or so afterwards, Stephanie had stayed away. 'I don't want you scaring the girls with that ghastly bandage on your head. You look like a pirate or a loony.' Normal service quickly resumed. Steph wanted her as often as ever now, needed her to get through each week, gave her jobs, gave her the girls.

And Paddy? He had come warily closer, she believed, with a kind of curiosity, a sense maybe that time wasn't infinite between them, not that he said anything to indicate this. He'd asked her to go over the same story several times. She'd got up in the middle of the night, feeling sick, and she must have passed out. And then what? She woke up, cold, on the bathroom floor.

How long had she been lying there? Not long, she thought. She cleaned up the blood. Cleaned up the blood! he said. What was it, a murder scene? Then what? I went back to bed, she told him. I'd put a dressing on the cut. Had she used disinfectant? Had she phoned her doctor at once in the morning? Was she feeling all right now? He wanted to know everything about it. But he seemed to be asking something else too, along the lines of, What phase are we in now?

Not long ago she'd answered the door of her old house to Paddy and Helena in her gaming headphones. She was also wearing a microphone hooked over her ear. At once she saw it was a mistake. One's children were too easily disturbed.

'What are you, a call centre now?' said Paddy.

'Sorry, I'm playing,' she said. She'd been in the middle of a session and had forgotten the time. That was easy to do. It meant nothing.

Helena asked about the headphones.

'You feel more engaged wearing them,' she said. 'You're trapped in their sound world. All the senses are heightened.'

'How often are you on this?' said Paddy, disapproving.

'Every day,' she said. What was the point in lying?

She played Cushion, an odd game that was half-billiards, half a strategy test involving nineteenth-century diplomacy. You did deals on behalf of your country—sometimes you were at war, sometimes peace—and then you played your opposition in real-time billiards. That was the odd part. Two games really, joined, and without total success, and yet it was addictive. Cigar smoke drifted across the screen as you were taking your shot. The sound effects suggested drinks being poured, a strange spurting, which she'd worked out belonged to the soda fountain. You were building an empire, or losing it. It was impossible to explain. Her avatar was Cleopatra, which was also outrageous.

'What is an avatar?' said Helena. 'It sounds amazing.'

Her guests pretended to be interested for a while and then thankfully the conversation moved on.

The scenarios in Cushion were loosely historical and Teresa

was very good at it. Recently, she'd beaten someone in Belgrade who then sent her a message written in, she guessed, Serbian. The inserted smiley was a face with a penis being pushed in and out of its mouth. She'd annexed his country. The message board was normally a clean, polite place. Obscenities were quickly removed. But this one hung around for days. Finally she posted: At first I thought it was only your mind that was small. The next day Belgrade was gone.

Could someone with dementia do all this?

There'd been more from Pip on Skype: Why do people MOW THEIR LAWNS? Pip was struck by things. The cousins had not seen each other since Pip's last visit more than ten years before. They were planning a reunion and Teresa had promised to come to her, to see Palmerston North in all its glory. Pip had written: What is wrong precisely with GRASS?

Teresa began to type an answer and then stopped, changing her status to Not Available. She couldn't risk it. Her jaw was still, more or less, wired shut.

She knew what she had now. Bang.

The French dictionary was in the Whitcoulls bag and she put the bag in a drawer in her bedroom and lay down on her bed. She couldn't remember taking off her shoes. She knew what she had.

The ceiling was a set of exposed wooden beams, like the powerful skeleton of an ancient ship. The building was a converted factory and it still carried some sense of machinery, conveyor belts, men and women looking at things for dreadful hours, pulling flawed items from the procession and tossing them in reject piles. Indeed it had been a shoe factory. Sometimes when the lift doors opened and air came up from the shaft, there was the scent of glue, new laces. She imagined it.

Waking on Sunday then, with Saturday lost, and having looked into the bowl, Teresa finished her tea and picked up her fallen shoes, pairing them in her wardrobe. So finally she knew what she had. It was a tumour pressing on her brain, and the tumour had a French accent. Bonjour tumeur! The set of circumstances that had resulted in her selling up and moving house to be near her son and the rest of the family could be understood in this light. She wanted to die in their arms, the opposite of animals. This was the human mechanism's command. She didn't feel in control.

5

'Know what?' said Paddy, pointing out the door of his office. 'I really like keeping my bike in the hallway.'

The boy made no reply and failed to look where Paddy was pointing.

How could those wheels have supported him? But he'd been on them already, around the block before breakfast, and he'd come home in one piece, quietly exhilarated he had to admit, keen for more. He thought about telling this boring story.

The bike's spokiness, its dream of escape—had the boy even noticed? Maybe these thin bits of metal, the chain, made Sam Covenay think of his braces? For a moment, Paddy was tempted to put the question. But he didn't. His tactic was indirection. This was his simplest rule. Don't ask questions and never address a statement to the patient's face, client's face, person's face, come on. Speak into the air above and around and beyond. This was to create a roomful of speech, to avoid making communication an urgent business between two people, with all the attendant stresses—that could happen later.

The boy had been to a psychologist, two sessions, and then refused to go back. But he kept turning up here, and Paddy kept filling the air.

'I mean it's not going to last, that arrangement,' he said. 'I'm in a grace period. Soon I'll have to put the bike in our lock-up. A sad day that will be, but necessary. Goodbye bike.'

Today, even more than in most sessions with Sam, Paddy was struggling. He felt flippant, and a mild bullying instinct

59

took hold. He was even facing the potential erosion of his own precious rules. It had been such hard and unrewarding work. 'My guess is you don't ride a bike,' he said. 'I see you being driven everywhere by your mother. She does that for you, it's not taking advantage when she offers. I see you in the back seat, is that right? Even when there's space up front, you're in the back, chauffeured, looking out, like a person of importance, like a prince.'

Sam made no response. There was not even the defensive stiffening in his muscles to betray him. Bit by bit he was training himself to be fully absent.

The boy was dressed in black jeans, black school shoes, and a heavy black sweatshirt—always. If the backs of his hands sometimes appeared, they were invariably decorated in elaborate homemade scrollwork. Paddy did not imagine the pen pressing with any force into his skin—the touch and detailing was too fine—and he'd said as much to the Covenays, who naturally were worried this was a precursor to self-harm. More likely self-display, Paddy thought, part of the hide-and-seek of his current condition. Now you see me, now you don't. You think I'm a dead person, then here are creations of that morbidity. Behold my marks. Yes, there was a small skull sometimes visible. The tongue of a snake. Heavy metal dreams.

'Communicating with his father?' asked Angela. She meant the picture-framing business, that the pictures were directed back somehow there. Yet Alan Covenay appeared sympathetic and tender towards his son. No evidence of detachment. There were photos of them together, bent over a painting. 'I was teaching him gold-leafing,' the father had explained. It was often the case that one looked in vain for cause. Sam was self-created, his own artwork. The parents, any parents, always nod when Paddy tells them such things but they are not in agreement. Having it as their fault gives them at least a starting point. They are almost always guilty and ashamed. He understands the mechanism. To accede to visiting someone like him is a defeat for them. Deep down they do not believe in me, he thought. That speech should have a therapy seems bogus. They've read the Internet forums denouncing my sort, my science. They come armed. Deep down, it sometimes seems, they do not believe in their child, and he hardly blamed them.

'Did you know,' Paddy said, aiming softer now with the boy, speaking to the far wall, 'we all get lock-ups in the building?' He told Sam how there wasn't much room in theirs and that when they moved into the apartment last year they were combining two households in effect—Helena's and his. And Helena had a daughter, older than Sam—in her early twenties—but still connected, still with her stuff that her mother lugged around. Paddy paused. Did the boy even know who Helena was? They'd never met. Would he even be bothered to guess? And Dora, here was another name that meant nothing to him. 'You collect a lot of junk in a life,' said Paddy. 'You keep things you have no use for. You give this stuff importance it doesn't really have.' He was speaking for the sake of it, to keep himself company. The boy could make you feel sudden bitter jolts of loneliness, unworthiness almost, as if his decision not to talk was a criticism of everyone else's failure at self-control. The mute were superior and judgemental figures, ungiving watchers of the charade. With Sam, Paddy missed all the people in his life, perhaps even Dora. He thought of the small argument he'd had with Helena when they'd moved in and then he found he was talking about it to Sam Covenay. The kid was right, he had lost self-control. 'Helena has her daughter's schoolbooks, her primary school artwork. She hangs on to it. Okay, I get that. But she keeps her toys too. Her dolls and games, everything. I'm not sure why. So she, the daughter, can hand them on to her daughter? Then maybe you make a selection, right? Keep the best items, not everything. Anyway, it all sits down there, behind a steel door. In the dark,' he said. 'Like visiting the morgue. That's where my bike will be. If I can face it.'

The argument with Helena had had almost no heat in it, coming at the end of their moving day when they'd gone past any snappiness. They were automatons, wandering around with boxes. He wasn't seriously pressing for a cull of Dora's old things, and she'd admitted it was probably excessive to travel from place to place so loaded up. But, she said. What? Well, he'd never had to decide anything in this context. Meaning he was childless. Not any more, he told her. It took her a moment to understand he meant Dora. That's true! She kissed him. You know what they say, he said. A problem shared. She turned away, as if looking for something she'd misplaced, and he understood the joke had flopped. Proceed with caution, oaf.

And of course the lock-up wasn't like a morgue. It wasn't dark. You turned on the lights and the place was ordinary, well maintained, an expanse of smooth concrete, dotted with spots of car oil. But morgues, they were for boys, weren't they? It was an exciting concept, the dead filed away in drawers, like papers or huge dolls. Skulls and snakes. Heavy metal dreams.

Sam Covenay saw through this easily, or heard none of it. Impressively, nothing came from him. No sound, no motion, no smell—the last perhaps, for the adolescent male, his greatest achievement. In Paddy's presence he'd managed to slow his metabolism down to such a rate his body presented with no outward sign of activity. He was inert. A person entering the room might look for his coat on that chair and be surprised to find something animal.

The boy sat with his mouth full of metal.

Well, get this, Paddy himself had had braces. They'd talked about it, or he'd talked. He'd been forced to wear horrible little rubber bands that he had to take out whenever he ate. His sister Margaret would scoop them up, fire them at Stephanie. Someone will lose an eye! said their mother. Probably it wasn't until he was in his twenties that Paddy started smiling again with his open mouth. There were dark grooves on a couple of his lower front teeth. Even now it took a conscious effort to part the lips. He'd shared this. The boy had heard it. Big fucking deal.

Most annoyingly, the braces hadn't done much good. All that pointless suffering! This he didn't say.

Paddy had stopped speaking. Together they listened to the

apartment. It was windy again outside and the building made its periodic, far-off droning sound, a sort of architectural sigh from its lower reaches as the northerly banged into the neighbouring block and into them again, moving down the alley five stories below where they sat. At ground level you'd be able to hear the recycling bins scraping along the footpath. November. They couldn't ever hear traffic though they were in the middle of town. It was one of their selling points to Teresa. And the drug dealers were very handy too.

The permanent bass note, a deep throb, tuned almost to some vibration in the chest, was provided by the amenities carried through silvery insulated pipes visible in the building's corridors. At night you could almost believe you were on a vessel moving steadily through the water. He said this aloud also. He tried poetry, because why not?

An image came to mind—a very clear picture of another boy, years before, lying in bed, very stiff, partially paralysed in fact, scarcely able to move his head even, but raising an arm and opening and closing the fingers of one hand. Of course it was Jimmy Gorzo. His hand was somehow his mouth, expressive in ways his mouth couldn't yet be. That had been the first week of treatment. The moaning, and then the fluttering of hands. Paddy didn't think Sam Covenay, moving zilch, had much to do with producing this image of Jimmy. Paddy had Tony Gorzo again in his brain. Where was his friend? What accounted for his failure to call?

He was listening hard. What for—the phone?

Very faintly through the wall today Paddy could just make out his mother's voice, or someone's voice in his mother's apartment. He wondered how the weekend had gone. Stephanie's three girls were little, very short, and though they were perfectly formed, always with pigtails, always sunnily in dresses, three girls made of jam—pink-cheeked, sweet-natured, always sticky, you could have bottled them—they yet had the capacity to ravage the emotions as completely as any such trio. The three dwarves, Lant called them. Take the gin, Paddy had told her.

He tried again to decode the sounds from next door. Perhaps Teresa was on the phone. Or perhaps they were listening through the wall to her radio again; it seemed too pure for the TV, which he didn't think she had much interest in anyway. 'Can you hear that?' Paddy asked Sam. It was, after all, the boy's fault. He amplified any signal. You strained and strained to hear—something. Paddy thought again about Jimmy Gorzo hating the silence of the hospital room and complaining that his brain was growing dull. He needed sounds. Paddy too was growing dull.

Thirteen years ago Jimmy Gorzo, Tony's only child, had fallen off a quad bike while at a beach party somewhere up in Northland. Fallen on sand, as Tony liked to repeat. The stuff, he said to Paddy, they have in a sandpit, where little kids play. Tony had never got used to this indignity. 'They tell me packed sand is as hard as concrete but this was a dune. His mother's still combing it out of his hair ten, twelve weeks after the accident.'

When Paddy got to work with him, Jimmy had already spent a few months in the Spinal Unit at Burwood. He'd broken his back, which fortunately for him would mend pretty well. He'd also suffered damage to his cochlea, though this wasn't clear at first. On the first day Paddy met them all, whenever Jimmy tried to speak, his father would start talking over the top of him to cover up the sounds he was making. The boy would moan and point with his hands and Tony Gorzo would say, 'Hard to believe he was top of his class.' He took Paddy aside. 'What we want to know is, is this it? But no one will tell us. Instead we listen to Jimmy making his monster noises.'

Jimmy's mother, Ellie, clasped the boy's hands together and told him everything was all right and to be quiet. His hands flapped, opening and closing, if they weren't held. Later, Paddy understood these weren't spasms.

He was seventeen.

'The first thing I need to do,' Paddy told them, 'is to hear Jimmy.'

'You'll get the idea very quick,' Tony said. 'Animal noises, or like he's been punched in the stomach. Roughly speaking, we think all his sounds refer to the hospital food.' He laughed and knocked Paddy on the arm. Tony Gorzo had an awful cheeriness about him that at first Paddy mistook for shock; it was actually his way with the world. He punched everyone—everyone except his wife. Perhaps this counted for something.

'We don't think that,' said Ellie.

Jimmy made another noise.

'My wife has developed a system of communication through applying pressure to his hands. It's not sophisticated. One squeeze for yes, two for no.'

'He responds. He knows. It's still him,' she said, growing teary-eyed.

'If he wants to go to university, I don't think the lecturer will squeeze his hand like that.'

There was another Jimmy cry, this one longer. He used up all his breath with it, finishing on a sustained high note. His parents looked at him.

'He's never said that before,' said Tony.

Paddy asked for some time alone with Jimmy. On their way out of the room, Tony held his elbow and said, 'Whatever you can do, we'd be grateful. Even if you could only get him to be quieter with the shouting and carry-on.'

'I think your son is deaf,' said Paddy.

Tony nodded. 'Better than blind, I used to think. Now I wonder. The blind go about their work very quietly, don't they. Especially with a dog, or just a cane tapping. They're in the dark, where you have to creep around. We would love to have him whisper these noises, if only that.'

'I'll see what I can do.'

Naturally it was the father Paddy wanted to turn down, or turn off. He learned later that Gorzo was keeping Jimmy's grandmother, who apparently doted on her grandson, from seeing Jimmy except when the boy could be relied on to be asleep. He didn't want to upset her.

Tony Gorzo was a shallow figure, Paddy thought. A man of limited emotions, dealt a blow and unable to rise in any way to meet his family's suffering. Paddy tried to avoid him as much as possible but it wasn't easy. Gorzo liked to hold Paddy's elbow and tell him boastful things about his business. He owned a bowling lane place in the Hutt and a number of rental properties. 'I rent to the beneficiaries,' he said. 'Sickness, dole, solos. People say to me, "Tony, what you doing down the bottom end?" Because they don't understand the bennies always pay on time because the money comes direct from the government and they're long-term because they got no place to go.'

Tony was five feet six, overweight, balding, and with a huge, sputum-producing cough. He smoked thin brown cigarillo-type things that gave off a smell exactly like dog shit. The large oval gold-rimmed glasses he wore provided his face not with an owlish wise look but with the belligerent, peering, reproachful gaze of someone wronged.

He asked Paddy questions about his job and what he was trying with Jimmy but didn't seem able to take in the answers. Sometimes he got Paddy confused with the Ear, Nose and Throat surgeon, or Jimmy's neurologist, and once with the hospital dietician. He said, 'You specialise in back injuries?' No, Paddy started explaining about the range of people he saw on a daily basis. Stroke patients, Alzheimer's, cancer patients, Parkinson's, multiple sclerosis, coronary bypasses. He could see Gorzo start to tune out, actually flinching. 'People with dysphagia,' said Paddy.

'What is *that*?' said Gorzo, momentarily catching the word, and finding offensive what he didn't know.

'Swallowing, difficulty with swallowing.'

'Oh Jesus, don't tell me about it. Can't swallow? Take me out and shoot me, please.'

'No, you get cancer of the neck—'

'Oh fuck.'

'—we can help you regain normal function.'

He was already moving away, waving a finger: don't, just don't.

Gorzo would speak to his son's doctors while answering calls on his large mobile phone. He was one of the first users of the phones. It was always gripped in one fist. He'd thrust it at anyone passing and say, 'Call someone. Help yourself.' The phone was always running out of battery power. Ellie carried around the adaptor for it in her handbag—this was her task—though one time she forgot and Tony sulked in the corner of the room, staring at the dead apparatus. He needed to feel constantly aggrieved; the phone was a useful tool in his torment. Routinely he got lost in the hospital and would question nurses about why they kept moving his son around. When he was told that his son had been in the same room for a month, he wouldn't believe it.

His wife, Paddy noticed, also tried to avoid Tony Gorzo. Ellie and Paddy often met coming and going from Jimmy's room, slipping away furtively.

'I won't tell if you won't,' said Paddy.

She smiled weakly at him, thanking him for all his help.

It was a mystery how she coped but he'd quickly seen that she had the sort of reserves of self-possession required in that family, loyalty too. She refused to condemn her husband. She told Paddy that Tony was trying very hard. 'Jimmy is everything to him,' she said. 'He would take his place in an instant.'

Paddy had heard the same thing from Gorzo, and more than once. 'But Ellie, he can't take his place. That's the one thing he can't do. It's very important that we all focus on the things we *can* do for Jimmy.'

She nodded and took her handkerchief out of her bag, touching it to her eyes. Weepy, certainly, but she was still the person Tony didn't try to whack.

Jimmy Gorzo, it turned out, was intelligent, willing and resourceful. A quick study. Paddy's job was also made easier once the boy's hearing began to improve, which happened rapidly. An audiologist had fitted hearing aids but after a couple of weeks

Jimmy began to complain of distortion so they removed them. He also said that he didn't like the silence of the hospital room; he thought he heard better when there was a certain amount of noise. There was something counter-intuitive in this—didn't the deaf get distracted by background noises?—but Paddy talked to the audiologist about it and there was recent research which gave support to Jimmy's feeling. When things happened in a hush, Jimmy said he felt a dullness creep through his brain. 'I find it easy to give up.' They put a cassette-radio beside his bed, which stayed on more or less permanently. The doctors and nurses were encouraged to talk to their patient over the noise of the machine. No one was supposed to shout. Paddy's work with Jimmy also happened in the context of this acoustically boosted environment. Here were the beginnings of their conference paper.

Unsurprisingly, it was only Tony Gorzo who objected to the cassette-radio; he'd turn it off when he was with Jimmy. He said he couldn't hear himself think.

One day Paddy came across Ellie in front of the hospital. She was helping an elderly white-haired woman down the front steps. The woman, dressed entirely in black, walked with a cane and was bent over. She moved her legs by swinging them outwards as though they were weights only vaguely connected with her. Each step was followed by a pause, a regrouping. She was seriously incapacitated but also immensely sturdy. Her wide hips revolved with power and her shoulders were rounded and strong. If she fell, it would be serious, though at the same time she didn't appear fragile. On her face was a look of utter disgust. He knew at once this was Tony Gorzo's mother.

He waited until they were on the footpath before approaching them. Ellie was smiling apologetically. When he said hello, she dipped her head and performed a little step that was almost in the nature of a curtsy. There was a reverence he couldn't shift and they shook hands at an odd distance; he had to reach to find hers as she reversed, catching her fingers only. 'This is Jimmy's grandmother,' she said softly. He recalled the ban, the secretive aspect of visiting the patient.

The old woman stood with her feet set wide, looking from Ellie to him.

'Paddy Thompson,' he said. 'Pleased to meet you.' Her right hand stayed on her walking stick but with her left she gave his hand a light squeeze, studying his face. Her expression was one of wariness. She knew him to be a medical person. 'Have you been to see him?' he said.

Ellie nodded quickly. She spoke to the old woman in what he understood to be Greek, explaining something about him. The woman uttered a word; she hadn't got it: who was he exactly? Ellie said more, pointing at Paddy. Suddenly the woman's face changed and she looked at him, beaming. Her mouth opened but nothing came out. He saw her lower set of false teeth rise slightly with the pressure from her tongue. She held her left hand in front of her, searching for his hand again, which he gave. He felt her grip, and she leaned forward, putting some weight on him. Actually there was little weight to take; that impression of girth and force may have been an illusion created by the full black skirt, the manner of walking. Standing close, Gorzo's mother was tiny, an ancient figure from another land, a real peasant, her face fantastically lined.

She was nodding and smiling, quite overcome it seemed. He saw through her fine hair to the scalp. Her eyes were red and moist.

'She's very happy,' said Ellie.

'Happy,' the old woman said, or something like it, moving their hands up and down. A tear rolled across her cheek.

'Me too,' said Paddy. He laughed and Mrs Gorzo laughed, Ellie too.

They were happy because of Jimmy's improving situation. Successive scans showed activity in his auditory cortex was returning to normal. The cochlea damage had been temporary, though it was also clear that Jimmy's problems weren't wholly to do with hearing. Although his comprehension appeared unhindered, after a few weeks he was still having difficulty articulating certain sounds and there were memory problems. The neurologist thought Jimmy might have sustained minor frontal lobe damage in his fall, though the grooves in Broca's looked ordinary enough.

Nevertheless his overall progress was exceptional. When the orderly came to clear his meal tray, he said, 'Can I have some more please, please.' In fact he wanted more peas, but this was a massive advance on Day One's bleak moans. His voice lacked the full inflective range but he could modulate volume and pitch fairly well now and there was a realistic hope that over time he would regain complete control. He was also not deploying his hands as much to indicate things, although this compensatory tool would continue to appear even long past its obvious usefulness.

Paddy wasn't sure how Tony Gorzo would take his son's achievements. It wasn't perfection after all, nowhere near. Jimmy's voice still had a pronounced tonelessness, especially when he was tired, and there were gaps in his vocabulary. Cunningly, Paddy thought, the boy had developed a strategy for masking these gaps by pausing in speech and inviting the other person to fill in the blanks as if he hadn't so much lost the word but was passing over it since he had more important things to say. 'Last night I think I had too many . . .' 'Blankets?' 'I had too many on so I threw them off. Sorry if they got dirty on the floor, the blankets.' Paddy had watched him do this with nurses and it was very convincing. But would Tony think it sufficient?

Paddy got his answer in the week of Jimmy's discharge, in the hospital car park. Paddy saw him first. Tony Gorzo was bent over, moving things around in the boot of his car. He recognised at once his beefy back, the weight-lifter slant of his shoulders. In a flash he imagined him pushing further into the boot, settling the load on himself and lifting the car above his head to shake it. Paddy's car was parked just beyond his and for a moment he considered walking away, returning to the spot when Tony had gone. At that point Gorzo looked around and saw Paddy, or saw someone. He was trying to work out whether they knew each other. Here was another opportunity for Paddy to turn quickly away and move off between the cars. Gorzo was peering. Paddy stepped forward a few feet. Then finally Gorzo lifted one hand in uncertain greeting. Something was attached to the hand, but in the dusk Paddy couldn't make it out. As he got nearer he saw that Gorzo carried a bowling ball.

Paddy forgot in that instant that Gorzo owned a bowling alley. He only thought that for a man of this sort of pugnacity and ill will, the bowling-ball fist in a darkening hospital car park was terrible and perfect. In one of the lighted windows in the building behind them, his poor son had lain strapped and broken for weeks talking gibberish. Paddy associated acts of sudden and strange violence with this obtuse figure. He would use anything in reach to show the world his dumb muscle, and to cover the great deficiencies of his dumb mind. How could he not know me, Paddy thought, even after weeks?

'What size is your hand?' Gorzo said to him.

'Sorry?' he said.

Gorzo pulled his fingers from the ball and cradled it on his arm. Then he held his hand up in the air between them. Paddy didn't understand what he was doing. He nodded at Paddy's hand. 'Hold it up.'

'Hold up my hand?'

'Put it there.'

Slowly Paddy raised his hand, keeping it a few inches from the other man's.

He pushed his hand against Paddy's and kept it there. There was an unexpected smoothness to Tony Gorzo's skin. Gorzo was looking at how their hands matched. They were close in size—was this a surprise to him? He was judging something. Was it the prologue to some horrible trick? He'd drop the ball on Paddy's foot. Punch him in the ribs pretending it was a joke. Then it came to him: he was measuring Paddy for a ball. He was going to give him his own bowling ball right there in the car park. Nothing was beyond him. He wanted to show his gratitude.

They stayed in this position for long seconds, several feet apart but joined at the hand, though now Paddy noticed Tony had stopped looking and judging. His head was slightly bowed. He recalled Gorzo's mother's hair and the way she'd held on to him by the hospital steps. Paddy was looking at the top of his skull.

Then Paddy felt Gorzo's fingers move down between his own, and his responding, as they must. That was an eerie sensation, as of being swallowed bodily though the only contact was through the fingers. They clasped hands tightly and Gorzo looked at him, shaking his head. There was a slight trembling in the other man's fingers, as if he were just managing to restrain himself from something.

'You have children?' he said.

'No,' said Paddy.

'Wife?'

'Yes.'

'What's her name?'

'Bridget.'

'I want to call her.'

'Call my wife?'

'I want to say does she know who she's married to? Is she aware?'

'Okay.'

'Is she aware of the gifts of this man?'

'Of me? My gifts?'

'I can't believe you don't have kids.'

'I have my patients.'

He dismissed this with a snort. 'If I don't have Jimmy, all I'd do I'd get drunk. At the lanes, I have a bar. I'd sit in my bar all night. What do you do at night?'

'Me?' Paddy glanced around at the car park, the windows of the hospital buildings. Was he suggesting they become drinking buddies? No, the question was more than that. He was briefly overwhelmed. But by what? Then he had an odd moment. The many-windowed structure seemed capable of crushing the two men, rolling over like a child's block and catching them underneath, as though they were toy people themselves. He felt their deep insignificance. Steam was rising from the nearby laundry building, rinsing the air in the smell and taste of hospital linen. They were like that steam, shots of vapour disappearing in the night sky. Paddy had once come across a hospital room almost entirely filled with old pillows. He saw the room again now in a painful moment.

He liked what he did. He made a difference in his patients' lives. Had this idiot made him reflective, doubtful? No, my work is not in question, surely, he thought. But soon I'll be home. Bridget won't be there for a while. I'll have the place to myself. With a sort of terror he recognised this as his favourite time, when he could do whatever he liked, even if it were only to drink a cup of tea and sit absently in a chair, his book beside him, some music on. Gorzo hadn't made him see it, only admit it, and he wasn't sure what he'd seen anyway. The hot feeling of calamity, uselessness, waste, left him with cleansing speed. This was the true vapour, to give in, that was the nothing to be avoided. Jimmy Gorzo hadn't given in, and nor had his father. 'What do I do at night?' said Paddy, revived, grateful himself now, 'Nothing much, you know. I bestow my gifts.'

Tony looked at him carefully and for the first time Paddy saw something other than aggression and grievance. He smiled but he seemed unconvinced, disappointed, as if he'd hoped for something more from the man who'd saved his son. They'd come all this way and he'd paid the tribute, and Paddy had done little more than deflect him. What was this realm in which a man couldn't take praise? Who was this medical jerk in front of him? So skilled, so hopeless.

'Thank you,' said Paddy, seeing all this and wanting to make amends. Because he did feel he owed Gorzo something—strangely it was true.

Gorzo shrugged. Thank me?

73

They were still locked together. Paddy's arm was sore. Tony gave his hand a final raised shake and released them.

He turned back to his car, put the bowling ball into the boot, which Paddy now saw was full of balls, and closed the lid. Maybe he'd forgotten about giving him the ball, or he'd never had that idea really. He'd simply needed a way of holding Paddy's hand.

'You think he can go to university in a year or two years?'

It took Paddy a moment to remember that the subject was Jimmy. 'Why not,' he said.

'Think he can be less stupid than his old man?'

'I think he can.'

He laughed and opened his car door. 'Hey, Patrick, I won't call your wife, don't worry.' Paddy believed it was the first time he'd used his name.

Paddy watched him get in and start the car. He put it in gear and the car rocked forward slightly. There was a sound from his boot, a clicking as all the heavy bowling balls met and dispersed and met again. Then he realised Paddy was still standing there. 'What? Need a lift?' he said. Paddy shook his head and pointed in the direction of his own car and Tony Gorzo drove off.

It would be another three years before Paddy heard his voice again though every Christmas they sent a card. Paddy believed it was Ellie, Gorzo's wife, who wrote these cards.

The week after Jimmy Gorzo had been released from hospital, Paddy and Bridget had been to a party, mainly of her work friends. He'd thought he might speak to someone there about Jimmy—he was bursting with it, very up—but when he was at the party, somehow the impulse lost its appeal. A type of satisfying selfishness made him cling to the story, not let it out. Suddenly it seemed very personal, as if it vibrated with significance for him only and spilling it now would wreck the meaning somehow. This made him depressed though too. He felt he was at the party under false pretences and that he had nothing at all to say to anyone. He went outside and kicked a tennis ball into the dark.

He heard sounds, and a dog, a golden retriever, came out of the shadows of the lawn and dropped the ball at his feet. He kicked the ball again.

After they'd come home, Bridget said to him, 'We're talking to people, having a conversation, and I turn around and you're perfectly still, paused, what are you doing?'

'Am I?' he said. He was drunk.

'Yes, what are you doing?'

'Listening?' he said.

'For what?'

'For what's being said.'

'I think you're listening to something else. You're listening to *how* it's being said.' She resented his occupation, felt it gave him a spurious excuse to sit back while she did all the work. This was how she conceived of the social world, as labour. He thought she had a point.

'What and how,' he said. 'They make up speech.'

'*How?* How is easy. Is she excited, is she mad, is she this or that? You can get that straight away. But you stand there, stunned.'

'I wasn't aware of it. I'll try to be quicker.'

'And maybe don't tell people what you do.' She was sober; she'd driven home, changing gears with an aggressiveness that should have prepared him for this.

'Really?'

'Speech therapist. Everyone starts speaking funny.'

'More correctly?'

'More something. You may as well say hygiene inspector.'

'Then what do people do?' He was fascinated by her, how closely she'd watched him, and this after long periods when they seemed barely to notice what the other was doing. Was this, in the end, what marriage became—harmless ignorance and then a shattering act of intense surveillance? *You? I share my life with you?* Had she seen him outside with the dog? Of course she was the person whom he'd hoped to tell about Jimmy Gorzo and found himself unable to; it was the same now.

75

'They think you're dirty, unclean. Say you work with kids.'

'They might think at a kindergarten.'

'Right,' she was nodding thoughtfully, 'that you abuse kids in your care.'

'They'd think that?'

'If a man says to me he works at a kindergarten.'

'He's automatically a paedophile?'

'What does he look like?'

'I don't know, normal?'

'Anyway, just talk more, less listening. No one likes a listener.' She stared at him. 'I feel you're doing it again right now.'

'What?' he said.

'Listening.'

How had it happened that he was married to a mad person? He must have been mad too. Finally it had been the dog that had tired of the game with the tennis ball, wandering off across the dark lawn to its kennel and letting out a grand sigh when it settled—an astonishingly human sound, he thought. He and Bridget deserved each other and he wouldn't find anyone else. Slipping, he searched for the image of himself that Tony Gorzo had proposed in the hospital car park. It appeared and then it was gone. He had gifts and then he didn't. He looked at his wife. 'No, no, I promise. I haven't heard a word you've said.'

Here was the issue. He'd discussed it with Lant. We don't memorise, we memoirise, exactly the sort of word play Bridget couldn't stomach.

At Sam Covenay's fourth session they'd tried music. Paddy had asked Sam to bring along whatever he liked. They plugged in Sam's iPod. For an hour they listened to a sort of thrash, high male voices, lots of guitar solos. Paddy offered the odd comment, leaving spaces for anything Sam might like to say. Paddy was honest. He said when something excited him and when it was awful. 'Basically,' he said, 'I hate falsetto, except maybe in a black soul singer. Al Green, do you know him?' The session was the same as the others, a zero return. Not a hair on the boy's head moved while his favourite stuff belted out and while this sad grasping talking moron said stupid provoking things.

Strictly he should have moved Sam Covenay on after the first month, sooner, towards other realms of assistance. But Sam wouldn't see anyone else, his mother Angela said. He liked coming to see Paddy. He's said that to you? he asked her. No, she said, but she could tell. And he was always ready to go. Sometimes he was waiting for her in the car.

Paddy had heard her husband call her 'angel'. 'Do you have the car keys, angel? I haven't got them.' Automatically it seemed she'd reached across and touched the pocket of his trousers. 'Okay,' he said, smiling. 'I found them.' Angela and Alan. Paddy had watched their drama with the keys, lasting about four seconds, the first time they came to the room and he thought it exceptionally moving. A sort of nothingness to it that gripped him and rather alarmed him at the same time. To what was he attaching his emotion? He had the thought that these two adults seemed more interesting suddenly than their poor familiar son. Why couldn't they stay and let the boy sit in the car?

Sam had braces, a chin full of acne. To add to the conspiracy against him, he was fair-skinned and his hair, in this light, had a reddish tinge. Angela herself was apologetically freckled—she wore long-sleeved sweatshirts, shoes even on the warmest days. There were women who wouldn't show their feet—was she one? Was there a connection here? The mother who won't display her feet, the son who won't speak? Paddy made a few aimless notes. He remembered seeing his ex-wife Bridget brushing her hair in the bedroom mirror. She was pulling it back with one hand. He said to her that she should wear it like that. What, she said, and then everyone sees my *ears*?

In a year or so the braces would come off. Sam would grow into his face, his life, as we all did. It was probable that the Covenays were in that small percentage for whom the only action was inaction. This was what Paddy felt when he first met the family—time is a wonderful thing, and patience. He said as much to them. The Covenays of course felt that time had stopped. They looked harrowed. And, against this judgement, Paddy had taken Sam on. Why? To give the parents hope? That seemed unlikely. He treated his job seriously and wasn't prepared to indulge anyone, not even that deserving pair. So he must have said yes because he considered himself a god—this was Lant's suggestion. Yet what if it wasn't success he wanted, and the operation of those gifts Tony Gorzo liked to grant him, but failure? What did it mean to want something in front of you with which you could do nothing?

Surely this was granting Sam's display of adolescence in extremis a therapeutic potency it hadn't and couldn't earn.

Paddy glanced over at Sam now. He couldn't see his face, just the hair. They had an unspoken—what else—agreement that Sam could assume whatever position he liked. He could sit on one of the chairs, he could lie on the sofa, he could curl up under the desk. He always went for the same chair, the one closest to the door, in front of the cupboard that contained the games and toys used with the younger kids. He'd tried those too, as a way of explaining his profession to Sam. Here is what I do.

Often Paddy stood and moved around the room, finding books off the shelves, shifting papers. It was tactical—to relieve the target of his surveillance—but it also allowed Paddy to get some work done, some other work, non-Sam work.

He took some more notes for his column on the glottal stop.

Of course Paddy hadn't let the perversity of taking on the Covenay case prevent him from attempting, rightly, to end it. He wasn't a complete idiot. After a month, Paddy tells Angela that it's not working and he has real doubts about it ever working. She's the one who usually delivers Sam and collects him and now he's already waiting by the lift, ready to go down. They stand at the doorway, talking softly. But she insists something useful is happening. 'I feel there's progress with this,' she says, her eyes locked onto his.

'Really?' Paddy says, experiencing a surge of relief that he doesn't quite know what to do with. He finds himself looking at her shoes, which are running shoes, or rather walking shoes on their way to becoming some sort of sports footwear. They are lime green, with darker green laces. They transmit a kind of health. Angela walks on her toes, he's noticed, rocking forward slightly. Has this given her feet a bunched look that she wishes to conceal? She likes to stand close when she talks to you. So you can't see her feet? She's told Paddy she works part-time at a dry-cleaners owned by her brother and he imagines there's a faint chemical whiff when she enters the apartment. She's wearing a pale blue zip-up Icebreaker top and black stretch pants. She could be on her way from or to the gym or Pilates. He can't inhale because suddenly he thinks this would tell her he was trying to smell her. There's a brightness to her that seems ready to turn into exhaustion.

'I think so.' She pats his arm, rests her fingers on his shirtsleeve. Her hand is hot. She blushes. Her blood is running all over the place.

They both understand she's merely expressing a hope. She's not the person in charge. What can she know? Yet he's genuinely grateful. 'Thank you,' he says, almost adding 'angel'—does he swallow it in time? Sam is holding the lift open for her, one arm reaching inside it as though—okay, as though he's about to enter a large metal mouth. Back in his office, Paddy adds this to his notes. A lot of what he writes seems fictional, not just in terms of the made-upness but also in terms of images.

Paddy couldn't hear the voice through the wall any more. Yet he was sure his mother hadn't left her apartment; the doors made a distinct rubbery sucking sound when they closed, a little like the door on a new fridge. It was one of the quirks of the building that this sound penetrated. There were five other apartments on their floor. With dedication, one could learn a good deal about everyone's comings and goings. They knew the architect couple, the Harleys, who lived two along, went for walks in the city at the same time every night: eight thirty. They'd met them once, leaving on such an excursion. The Harleys said they liked to examine buildings reacting to night-light, the moon, the stars, the streetlights. The light from humans, Rebecca Harley said. What light? said Helena. The Harleys looked at each other as if it was a very basic question indeed. Then Geoff Harley, by way of a demonstration, held up his wrist and pushed a button on his watch, illuminating the dial briefly. Okay, said Helena. Rebecca Harley meanwhile had her mobile phone out. She held this up to their faces. Watches and phones, said Paddy, they have an effect on city architecture? It's a micro interaction, Geoff Harley said.

At one session, in search of a subject, Paddy had told Sam about the Harleys.

This he didn't tell: On Thursdays Geoff went out alone, a bit later, towards nine. Helena and Paddy had played a game. Where does Geoff Harley go on Thursdays without his wife? To examine buildings some more? Humans? What micro interaction was transpiring? One rule was it couldn't be sexual, that was too obvious. The Harleys already seemed a little wife-swappy, with their slightly creepy routine, their matching dark clothes. Their plastic poster cylinders under their arms. Paddy and Helena had soon created such a stockpile of stories about Geoff and his secret life that it was hard to meet his eye when they bumped into him. His smallest gesture seemed to confirm some detail they'd invented. The way he touched his shirt cuffs when he spoke. His smirk. The bag he carried. They had to stop. But they could still hear him if they tried every Thursday.

Before he started seeing Sam, Paddy set up his usual family meeting, so that everyone knew what was involved. He told them that he was all for speech but that speech took many forms and that elocution was not his business. Amazing how frequently the fathers made a joke about *electrocution* at that point. One in three, Paddy thought. 'No putting his finger in the plug socket then?'

Alan Covenay was not among this number. He'd listened carefully to what Paddy had to say. Towards the end, he'd stood up and patted his pockets, asked his wife about the car keys. The slight mournfulness he carried may have had nothing to do with Sam. In tall men who were drawn to cultural things Paddy had often noticed this air of melancholy, a feeling perhaps that the realm naturally favoured compactness. They didn't quite fit in their seats. You saw these stooping, guilty figures at the theatre, in galleries, at the orchestra where puckish men skipped around them. Then on his way out Alan Covenay stood in front of the framed cartoon that hung in the office. 'It's dropped slightly in the top left corner,' he said. Paddy stood beside him, looking. He was two inches taller than Paddy. Paddy hadn't noticed it but he was right about the picture. Inside the frame, the print hung crookedly now. 'I can fix that for you if you like.'

'Sure,' said Paddy.

'I could take it now, if you like.'

Paddy agreed.

'No charge.' He reached towards the picture, lifted it from its hook with a deft upward motion, and put it under his arm. When he did this, Sam made a quick sighing sound, or a sound of irritation. Had he watched this before? Was it something his father was prone to—walking into strangers' houses and leaving with the pictures off their walls? Everyone watched Alan straighten the picture hook.

'No charge? But you'll give me an invoice.'

'He won't give you an invoice,' said Angela, more sharply than she'd intended since she at once attempted to recover her tone by mumbling something else about the smallness of the job. It would take Alan minutes. The flicker of annoyance here seemed directed at no one in particular or at everyone. Was she simply thinking of the bigger task they were handing Paddy and that it didn't seem a fair swap? The difference was Paddy was charging them ninety-five dollars an hour.

Again from their son came the short breath of displeasure, more like a pant this time. When Paddy looked at him, however, there was nothing on his face but perfect tight blankness.

And no one had commented on the content of the cartoon, the caricature of Paddy done some years before but recognisable. Perhaps not. They're leaving with me, he thought. It was not an existential moment. Strange to see his picture exit the apartment though. He seemed to have had no control over it happening. Alan Covenay would have got his picture no matter what Paddy said.

And then the picture didn't come back and so much time had gone by that Paddy had begun to think it was now appropriate for the repaired picture to arrive at the conclusion of the therapy. He would give them back their son and they'd return him to him, as it were.

He was that stuck. And he had the bike to prove it.

He'd told Helena about Sam one night in bed. 'If he puts his fist through a window at school or pushes his mother against a wall, I could refer him to Lant.'

'Do you think that's likely?' said Helena. She was reading *People* magazine. She had a stack of them in her bedside cupboard. Trash relaxed her and he wasn't to scoff. Nor was her pleasure ironic. Dora gave the magazines to her after she'd finished with them. It was a vital and ritualistic connection between mother and daughter. They bonded here. Whatever was fraught and difficult and shifting between them seemed insignificant, soluble almost when they regarded the star system, its eternal dilemmas, its alcoholism, its abandoned love children, its surgeries. The relentless sinking of hope. They were briefly lifted. It also meant Helena was free to talk with him while still reading. As she'd pointed out, were she ever to open the 700-page journal of Christa Wolf which Paddy had given her for her birthday in a burst of highbrow Germanic fervour shortly after they got together and which delighted her so much she kept it permanently beside the bed, then all conversation would have to stop.

Sometimes, to prove this, she opened the book at random and read a sentence in German aloud to him. It was like being in bed with someone else.

'I don't know,' he said. 'It's possible. I feel so useless with this kid. He sits there in a black heap of unresponsiveness and occasionally I make stupid statements which hang in the room.'

'But he likes coming and his parents support it.'

'They might just be clutching at straws.'

'You're the best straw there is,' said Helena. She'd turned the magazine towards the light better to examine someone's unwanted pregnancy. Paddy could read the headline from his side. Helena studied the photo, shaking her head. Did she believe the pregnancy or not? Often Paddy looked at the *People* pictures, lying beside Helena. Even though she'd assured him the candid photos were mostly set up by the stars' agents, the furtiveness of the famous carried a charge. As they 'rushed' from restaurants where they'd been 'spotted' or made 'flying visits' to 'anonymous' suburban shopping malls in big hats and glasses and wigs, their hauntedness seemed real rather than performed. After all, these were not, as a rule, great actors. They couldn't pretend all that well, could they. 'That's very kind of you,' he said. 'I could use that in my advertising. "Looking to clutch at a straw? Ring Patrick Thompson."'

'You don't advertise,' said Helena. 'Jeremy Lanting seems premature to me anyway.'

'Fine, you might be right.'

She flicked over another page. Paddy read the words 'Rehab Horror'. The thought didn't flow directly but it came nevertheless. To what extent could it be said that Sam was acting? He came to the sessions so that Paddy could be his audience. 'Can I ask you one other thing, unrelated,' he said. 'What part of your body do you prefer not to show?' He was thinking of Sam's mother mostly, of Sam too, Bridget and her ears, but also the general furtiveness of the human race. He was not excluded.

For some reason he was also thinking about the tree full of young tui they'd come across on their walk in Mount Victoria.

That was the opposite, wasn't it. Where you expected hiding, you got display. There was a performance angle, though the birds seemed unaware of being watched, if that were possible. Often a bird's life had figured as a mind-bendingly anxious business, alertness without rest, the flicking head, the almost ceaseless flight from predation. He was taking as his sample the birds around them, in the city and the hills. No doubt his theory was garbage when you considered—what? Some long-legged creature, wading on a beach at sunset. He didn't know names. Or an albatross. Anyway, birds had never seemed to him strongly connected with beauty. Careworn, he thought. Small engines of fright, who, when they stopped in trees to recharge, were still charged. They were always plugged in to a current of crisis. They darted around, thinking what next, what next? It was terrible they had to know the present was over, the future was dire. Except these tui.

Helena put down the magazine. For this, she needed all her attention. 'What part of my body do I prefer not to show? To whom? Give me a context.'

'No, it doesn't matter. Perhaps when you look in the mirror.'

'Easy, my neck.'

'Your neck? What's wrong with it?'

'Come on.' She touched it as if it were sunburned.

'No, really, I don't know what you're talking about. Your neck looks fine to me.'

'Hey, I'm its owner.'

'One careful lady owner,' he said.

'As is where is. Some wear and tear. Highly motivated vendor.'

'Can the buyer collect? Because I'm interested.' Paddy ran the backs of his fingers down from her ear to her shoulder. 'I love your neck.' She closed her eyes and smiled. 'See?' he said. 'Whatever's the problem here?'

'Stroke it and it says, "I like that." I mean, it works fine as nerve endings, as pleasure centre. As a stand-alone neck, it's a disaster. It leaves my shoulders from the wrong place.'

'From here?' He gently kneaded her left shoulder with his knuckles.

'You make a good case for it.'

'As pleasure centre.'

'Right.' She gave a loud moan of delight, only half-faked. 'So much tension. Stupid work. Helena hating the school.'

'No, it's temporary, the school, I mean.'

'Temporary for now, yes. But next time? Probably this is the future too.'

He thought about her success, none of it assured, in total admiration. Having returned in a hurry from Germany in the wake of a nasty split from Max, and needing anything to keep going, she'd become a part-time gardener for a landscaping firm while her daughter was in school. Her CV was the very imprint of will-power. She'd started organising the staff roster and had then discovered a talent for business management. From there she'd managed a café in a garden centre, then a horticultural wholesaler where she bought an interest in the company with money she got after her father died.

There was all that German literature, *The Magic Mountain* and the verse dramas, but she insisted it was by chance she'd moved from plants back to words.

She'd once had a contract to provide indoor plants to businesses—dentists, lawyers, banks, and a language school. She'd struck up a friendship with the director of the school, also a Germanist, who was about to retire. He offered her friendly terms to buy into the franchise. Now the language school was part of a national network in which she had a financial interest and she was on the board of the governing body. The vital connecting strand throughout these moves was an instinct for investment. Helena had always made sure of something more than salary.

She claimed to have had a lot of luck and to have known good people but she was the person good people wanted to know, that was itself a singular gift. Yes, the future probably did look like this: a bad back, the chewing of grey biscuits, rising at night as if being murdered in her sleep. Yet she loved her school and was proud of it and would never give it up.

Paddy had met her when he was invited to give a seminar for Helena's staff based on a series of his 'Speech Marks' columns. These had dealt with English as a second language from mainly a physiological perspective. The title of the seminar was 'I Can't Get My Tongue Around It'. Naturally, this was always mentioned in the story of their courtship.

He continued his one-hand massage. She turned towards him and they kissed, the *People* crackling between them. He moved his lips to her neck.

'You don't have to keep kissing it,' she said. 'There are other places, you know.'

One thing with Helena he always marvelled at was that sex was normal, without being attached to an idea which announced smugly, this is normal, get over it. He knew from her German days she was used to nakedness. Swimming naked in lakes et cetera. And she was ahead of him in this. But it hadn't become dogma. Clothes were good too. Once he referred to her magic mons, and she laughed but there was no question of this sticking, or becoming the starter in a private jokey vocabulary. She inspired him somehow with sex. She was extremely attentive and nothing was dutiful. This was modelling of a very high order. She let him see straightforwardly how sex enhanced her mood, her spirit. Its effects could belong in the realm of ordinary life, and not be confined to the near-dark, or comic release. Once you got over your shame at the woeful inadequacies of the CV you carried there, you felt waves of gratitude for learning this! A torrent of humble joy! He remembered telling her he still felt that it was a bit flattering from the male point of view to be involved in the female orgasm. She shouldn't take this the wrong way but there wasn't much to do. He was laughing as he spoke. Great to watch though, she said. Always, he said. And I could say the same thing about the male orgasm, she said. They talked about penetration, which seemed to him to change the rules, involving her in ways that were, um, inescapable. But clitoral stimulation, she said, didn't feel 'outside'. I'm in a pretty extraordinary space, almost like a house, when that happens. There's a, don't laugh, a staircase, a bunch of steps I go up. Thank god I don't recognise it as any place, not my family home or anything. Stairway to heaven, he said. Now that would be flattering yourself, she said. It was the sort of disquisition he'd never had before. Solo's not the same, he told her. Ditto, she said.

She said, why do we say he *performed* oral sex on her? You perform Gilbert and Sullivan. Does one expect applause having done it?

I feel like clapping, he said.

'We're done,' he told Sam, with a sharp snap of his hands on the desk.

The boy flinched at the noise. Paddy had never done this before and he regretted the cheap trick of it at once. Stupid to try and scare them out of hiding. He thought of Lant's advice of pulling the boy up by the ear. 'Same time next week.'

Then in one fluid movement Sam wheeled off the chair and was out the door of the office. When Paddy reached the front door, Sam was there waiting for him to open it, a bit like a dog looking to get outside. It was part of the regime that Paddy controlled entrance and egress. Sam was catching a bus home today because Angela was busy—she'd phoned before the session. They were standing near the bike.

Paddy couldn't finish like this.

They were both aware that this session had been marked by something new and not altogether pleasant on Paddy's part: aggression, a weird current of malice. Chill. 'I might go for a ride later,' said Paddy, his hand on the doorknob. It was untrue. He needed Lant with him. He was still self-conscious in his shorts and his shirt and his jacket on those trembling, thin rims. In his shiny blue helmet. Then there were shoes that clipped directly onto the pedals. These could prove a special humiliation.

Upright it was more difficult for the boy to hide himself. He had his father's height. His features were smudged though. The acne was so inflamed as to present almost a second mouth. They'd tried dermatologists, medication. His lips bulged slightly with the concealed architecture. He looked quickly in the direction of the bike, then back again at the door. The action was accompanied by a sound somewhere between a cough and a laugh. A flash of braces. It was easy to imagine his contempt for Paddy and his bike. 'See you then, Sam.' Paddy opened the door and he ducked through it, passing so close to Paddy in his hurry that their shoulders touched.

Paddy watched him scoot off down the corridor in the direction of the stairs. He wouldn't take the lift since that meant further confinement, the possibility of human interaction. Sam Covenay was a shifty dark person, moving erratically. Flight aged him, filled him in. Had one of their neighbours opened his or her door at that moment it would have been to guess that a middle-aged homeless man was loose in the building. He was someone to be reported.

Then it occurred to Paddy something might have just happened a few seconds before. Sam had engineered the physical contact at the door. There'd been room to get by him. Paddy had stepped back to allow him a safe exit, that is, one without collision, without touch. But the boy had carefully, accidentally, made sure of this connection. He'd not barged Paddy either. He'd brushed him, a delicate action.

At the end of the corridor Sam was gone. Paddy looked at the door to his mother's apartment for a few moments, thinking he should check. Just knock and say hello. That was allowed by the rules surely. Then there was a noise. The door was opening. Medbh stepped out. Our girl.

'Hello, Paddy,' she said, 'what are you doing lurking in the corridor?'

It was Medbh's first day at his mother's. Now she was coming to cook for them. It had been Medbh he'd been listening to; his mother had been talking to Medbh. He'd forgotten. 'I was just seeing off Sam, one of my people.'

'The boy who doesn't speak?'

'Well, okay,' he said.

'And by the look on your face, I'm not supposed to know that, am I? How do I know that?'

'How do you know that, Medbh?'

'Well, I don't know the kid's last name.'

'Thank God for confidentiality.'

She walked over to him. 'Moving right along, I'd like to cook eggplant parmigiana for you, Paddy. And also, time allowing, a beef and beer casserole. Is that too wintry? It doesn't feel much like spring anyway. Helena was going to leave out the recipe. Promise I won't ask whether there was any progress on the case which I know very little about involving a person who recently left the building.'

'Promise I won't express relief at being able to experience finally the give and take of normal conversation.'

He let her in the apartment.

'Nice bike,' she said.

6

Lundi. Teresa looked out the window. She'd woken at the proper time. The radio was on. No more about the truck drivers. They'd made their snail. Oil prices stayed up but were predicted to fall. The apartment building wasn't moving, the windows were soundless, though she could see down at street level an advertising sign billowing, the giant picture of a car inflating and deflating. She asked her tumour what the word for wind was: vent. The vent blew and blew. Le vent souffle aujourd'hui. She tossed the dictionary back in the drawer.

In the shower she spoke English aloud and it came back to her as something else, as if she was being translated on the radio—she heard two parts.

At the computer she felt a sharp loss. She was missing Cushion, her game. Cleopatra. But she'd lose. In her current distracted state, clever people, and even the not-so-clever, would take advantage of her. Her empire would be endangered by obscene inhabitants of Belgrade and she'd be wiped out.

Self-disgust almost made her rush out of the apartment at that moment. What was she hiding from? What was the point?

Standing near the front door, she heard Helena leaving for work and a little later someone arriving at the apartment. This would be Paddy's first patient. She waited a few minutes until she was sure he would have turned off his phone and then she sent him a text. She explained about missing the weekend with Steph. The bug had gone on and on. She was a lot better now but would lie low for a while longer. Love to H. Review this week? Good luck, knock 'em dead. It was two texts.

Her mobile bleeped. Steph again. Teresa had already replied to the first volley of messages. The Wairarapa had been good, not as good as it could have been with you know who, but good. Girls fine, tired. Sleeps today. Last night a late one.

She sent a quick one back. Kisses to my sweet puddings! Too soon to come. Will call later. Sleep angels. You too.

Desk. Cup. Keys. Coat-hanger. Goat hanger? Gert? She was back in Moore Wilson's. Carpet. Electric jug. She walked around the apartment touching each object as she named it aloud. Paper towels. Photograph. Ironing board. Ironing board. She was touching this last thing with her toe but she reached under the bed and pulled it out, set it up, and then tried. Ironing board, she said. It would not come. You, she said to the ironing board, I hate.

Pillow. Moisturiser. Sleep. She couldn't touch sleep of course but she sounded wonderful saying it. Sleep. As if summoning it, or being summoned by it, she lay down fully dressed on her bed and closed her eyes. Why was she so tired? Because her body was fighting it.

She opened and closed her mouth, moved her tongue around. She thought of the children Paddy dealt with in his work. They got delivered to his door. Was it a door she should knock on and ask for help with her speech? It struck her in a confused instant that somehow they'd brought this on, Paddy and Helena. They'd persuaded her to move into their building, to sell up and come into town, to enter her dwelling by means of a lift. Look at the life you'll have in the city. What's the point of staying on in that big house, of living on in Lower Hutt? Which weren't their words, she knew it.

This was accurate enough: they'd advised her to sell lots of things since where else would it go. The framed maps that had been Brendan's passionate hobby as a boy, then as an adult, his rather canny interest since it turned out there were collectors desperate for the stuff. Gone. Okay, you needed a good deal of wall space. Plus it was Paddy's line, that longitude described what it felt like to look at a map, and to be honest she'd not spent much time gazing on them over the years. Still they were there, or had been and they showed an aspect of her existence; they were maps of that much.

Wasn't it something that two of the maps remained in the family, sent to Margaret's boys in Vancouver since they happened to show parts of Canada? She'd received no acknowledgement of that consignment, and did not expect it. Oh Margie. If she watched her children as audience, let her have this right, to also dislike some parts of the show.

A man had come from an antiquarian bookshop in Wellington and given her an appraisal on the maps, also quoting on some books Paddy had selected for chucking. She'd trusted Paddy utterly in this, not even bothering to look in the boxes, though now she felt she should have, if only as a tribute to the person who'd thought them at one stage necessary to their life together.

Her children were older now than their father had ever been.

The man from the shop was attractively weary, dejected even, as he moved through the rooms. In his grave attention, he seemed to be giving the objects in her house the sadness they deserved, and she had to excuse herself once to get a glass of water. She'd explained the situation exactly, that it was a great excitement to leave, despite which he persisted in his little grieving manner, stooped and tentative. It was as if he didn't believe her and that leaving was always wrong. She noticed his shirt, one button undone, had come loose over his belt. Extremely crooked teeth that somehow suggested gentleness. He carried a catalogue and referred to it from time to time, making small notes with a pencil. At the end, he passed Teresa a piece of paper with a sum written on it. She didn't really know whether it was more or less than she was expecting though the amount was considerable. 'Good pieces,' he said in a murmur. Really he was condemning her actions.

'Thank you,' she said, again moved and feeling it was all a mistake, or feeling the temptation to renounce what was done. At some point though, ten, twenty years after Brendan, she'd begun to stop considering herself widowed. That was a surprise. And what was she? Something unnamed. No, this antiquarian man didn't know her at all.

Before this, Helena and Paddy had arrived for a big clean-up session. The result was her house had been chastened. They'd filled their car with boxes of stuff to take to the St Vincent de Paul. These were the things no one would want, he said.

'Except the poor and the desperate,' she said.

'No,' Paddy told her. 'Walk into those places now, it's the middle class you're fighting with over bargain furniture and vintage clothes. The poor and the desperate shop elsewhere for new.'

Paddy also arranged the sale of the printing press, which had sat idle for decades in the garage, and on which their father made them birthday cards they weren't allowed to touch with dirty fingers. Brendan had known he shouldn't have acted with such preciousness in this area but it was the only such area, which drove him mad all the more. In everything else he was carefree, indulgent, irresponsible even. She had to be the disciplinarian, at which she had little talent. Love, he wanted, love all the time, and the ceaseless generation of happiness. In this way, she thought she was more grown-up than he was—and he agreed. 'You're the wise one,' he told her. 'The sensible one.' Dying young, however, was a sort of vindication of his way.

Somewhere there was a box of these cards. She insisted to Paddy that each of the children be given a metal mould as keepsake. She was not breaking up any sets by doing this since these were novelty items collected more for fun than anything else. They were the symbols Brendan often used for the children, on gifts. Stephanie got a duck, Paddy a man in a hat, and she put aside a sun for Margie. She thought that when her oldest daughter got around to complaining about the heedless dispersal of precious family things, the lack of consultation, she would present her with this sun. The risk was that Margie would see it as satirical, a sly commentary on her nature, but this was always the risk and on balance it was better to be suspected of mild offence than to appear to have neglected her altogether.

Of course it was ridiculous to blame Paddy and Helena for her current state or to even think that the move had happened against her will. She'd wanted it and badly, it turned out. The great luck of the next-door apartment coming up for sale! She'd had to lie down briefly on her first afternoon there from happiness and shock. Where was everything? The maps. No one was to blame. This was the tumour telling her things that weren't true about the world. Like the old maps. They were wrong. Whole landmasses were in the wrong place.

Someone was ringing the bell. She sat up at once. If she were quiet, they'd go away. It wasn't time yet to share her tumour with anyone. That would happen, of course it would. She saw it all. She almost wept then in a gushing pity for herself and for the faces that came to her with utter distinctiveness, the faces of her children and their children, watching her. Her bearing under these gazes would count for everything and she had not yet found the mode for it, for telling another living person she was not going to be one of them for much longer. She did not feel at all solid. They wouldn't recognise her. She didn't believe in God. Why not? Because there was too much suffering. But now, as a sufferer, she felt aggrieved at being banished from God's sight, at doing the banishing.

The bell rang again, longer this time.

She stood up carefully and crept towards it. At this point someone put a key in the lock, the door opened and a girl stepped inside. Was this a drug person, finally come?

'Oh! God, I'm so sorry! You are here. Sorry! I was ringing

94

and I thought you were out. I'm Medbh.' She was holding out her hand, smiling. 'Hello Mrs Thompson.'

But she was too attractive, too nice. Teresa took the girl's hand. 'Is it cold outside?' she said.

'Sorry?'

'Cold?'

'Oh, it's not bad. I'm just set cold, that's all. It's my temperature.' She was taking off her coat. 'So you just point me in the right direction. If it's okay with you, Mrs Thompson, I'll cook first, clean after. It's very nice to meet you. Is it okay to come now? It's all right, yes?'

'Yes. I'm . . .' she found it, the thing she had to say, 'Thérèse.' It was the tumour's name.

The girl studied her for a moment. 'Hi!'

Then she was following the girl into the kitchen. 'Tell me some of your favourites. What do you like to eat?' The girl was opening the fridge and looking in, pulling out the vegetable drawers. She held up the bag of sausages and felt them through the plastic.

Teresa nodded. Yes, those need to be used.

'I can do that.'

The girl wouldn't let her go. There was a string of rapid-fire questions about where things were, which Teresa answered by opening drawers, by pointing. There. Finally she crept from the room. She went to the computer and sent Pip a Skype message: Grass is a great evil. I must visit your wonderful city and educate you in our ways. We must mow together. When can I come?

7

He was watching Medbh slice and mince garlic. She chopped an onion. Paddy had offered to help but she'd turned him down. In her hands their knives seemed sharper, more professional. He remembered his time as a hotel worker. One night he was in a party that superglued a spatula to Chef's hat.

He'd known a Medbh in high school, an exchange student from Dublin, and not one since. Paddy had sat next to her on a school outing and said, 'Tell me, Medbh, about Van Morrison.'

'Who?' she said. 'Well I hate his music.' He remembered she always wore lace-up boots that went halfway up her shins. She had a white pair and a red pair. In class she was constantly reaching down to lace them up or unlace them. It exasperated the teachers. The leather was so thin you could see the knobs of her ankles. Obviously she was lying to him. How could anyone not think *Astral Weeks* a masterpiece? But then again, obviously he was lying in pretending to be interested in her opinion, at least about music.

'Tell me about Thin Lizzy then,' he said.

'Who?' she said.

'Thin Lizzy. "The Boys are Back in Town", you know. They're Irish. Two of the original members actually played in Them, with Van.'

'There you go, you know it all, why'd you need me for.'

Why'd you need me for. For some reason the phrase had stuck in Paddy's mind and he'd made it his goodbye statement at clinic when his client—boy or girl—walked out of the last session feeling, if not completely better, then better by far. And they did. Mostly, mainly, they did feel better, in their mouths, in their minds. Sometimes Paddy got a high five, though he was careful never to initiate. It was speech therapy. But no one made a speech, that was forbidden.

'You're a surprisingly good cook for someone involved in the lower reaches of the splatter movie business,' he said to this current Medbh.

They'd come by Medbh through Dora. Dora and Medbh had been friends from university, were now partners, lovers, artists together. They'd made several short films in which young women, usually played by Medbh and Dora themselves, suffered gory ends while hitchhiking around New Zealand. Helena had given them a series of long-term, interest-free loans. One of the films had been shown at a queer film festival in Sydney, where Dora's father now lived. The film received a Commended in the Cultural Understanding section of the jury awards. He remembered the day Dora had brought the certificate around to the apartment, tossing it Frisbee-style at her mother. 'That,' said Dora, 'is what you get for a thousand hours of work.'

Helena held the certificate in her hands, her eyes growing moist. 'Look at this. Look at this.' Dora might have been seven years old fresh from her first ballet recital.

Dora sniffed. 'A piece of paper, a pat on the head.'

'But a pat on the head from important people,' said Helena.

'Self-important people.'

'Congratulations,' said Paddy.

'Right,' she said.

She always rumbled him, even when he was being sincere, which in this instance he wasn't. He kept it light: 'Does this mean investors can expect a return?'

Dora gave Paddy a look: who are you again?

Helena flourished the certificate again, waving it to bat away any negativity, and moved to her daughter and kissed her on the cheek.

Then Dora had told her mother not to bend the certificate

and had taken it from her. Oh it mattered. There followed bubbles, not inexpensive either. The seven-year-old took three glasses thank you very much.

In the kitchen, Medbh told Paddy, 'We don't call it splatter. Other people have labels. Horror. Gore. Sicko. We just make films.'

'Films in which the female leads are routinely eviscerated and left to die by the roadside. And in which the flagrant disregard for continuity is built into the aesthetic, as is the use of strings of sausages for the victims' intestines.'

'I see you're a fan, Paddy.'

'I liked your early work.'

'*Muff Must Die*?'

'Was that the one? Anyway, your recent turn to a more political cinema raises questions for me which seem problematic.'

'*Hitch-Dykes*?'

'I'm no good with titles. In this one the two women overcome their assailant and it's *his* sausages we see spilled. Quite a reversal, don't you think?'

Medbh was the fun one in the couple. This was Helena's own appraisal. She said she hated to admit it but her daughter had chosen to be the difficult one, the moody one, the hostile one. Dora needed Medbh. They all needed Medbh. She finished an onion and when she released her fingers it fell into a million pieces.

'You're over-reading us, Paddy. We were just sick of getting that stuff on our clothes, in our hair, everywhere,' she said. 'Plus we had a wedding to go to the next day. You shower and shower and it still smells. It was the bloke's idea. Kill me, he said, why not kill me?'

'My God it's a pragmatic art form, isn't it.'

'Filmmaking is ninety per cent weather. Scorsese said that.'

'He's had some pretty good weather throughout his career.'

She gave a short laugh. The slices of salted eggplant were laid out and sweating on a tray. She bent her head close to the tray, inspecting.

'What are you doing?' he said.

'The moisture that pops out, why can't we ever see it happen? I mean, they're not exactly small drops, are they.' She stood up again. 'The truth is, Patrick, Dora and I are a bit tired of our cinematic direction.'

'You've hitchhiked all over New Zealand. You've had your throats slit from Kaitaia to Bluff.'

'*Bluff Muff Must Die*,' Medbh said sadly. 'That would have been a good title.'

'All that disembowelling, all those sausages.'

She peered into the oven. 'We're interested in doing something without talking, no dialogue.'

'I liked your dialogue. "When will we get there?" "Soon, doll." "What's this dirt track? This isn't the way to Auckland." "It's a shortcut."'

'We're interested in silence.'

'Silent movies. Of course that's been done. But how would the women tell the men who pick them up where they're heading? Would they use sign language? Deaf women getting murdered?'

'No more hitch dykes.'

'Big change.'

'Actually it's how we got to know about Sam, the boy who doesn't talk. We were with Helena the other week and telling her about our idea.'

'The idea of silence.'

'Right. So it came up then. I guess we were brainstorming. Dora said, Most of our time in real life is spent *not* talking. We sit at a desk, we chop an onion, we walk home.'

'You're chopping an onion *and* talking.'

'Because you're here. By myself, I wouldn't. I won't be saying much on the way home either. I'll sit on the bus, not saying anything. I'll look at all the people on the bus and on the streets, not speaking.'

'Except on their mobile phones.'

'Would you please be quiet?'

'I'll be silent.'

'But go to a film and you hear all this talk. Why is that? So then Helena must have mentioned this person you're seeing. Dora thought it was really interesting. Sam became something of a hero, an example anyway.'

'You know you're in danger of stepping on my toes here. If we're talking about Sam, and we're not because that's patient confidentiality but a case such as Sam's, a theoretical boy called theoretically Sam, if he's the subject, I kind of *want* that Sam to talk and so do his parents and his teachers and the world. And so does he.'

'You know that for sure? That Sam, theoretical Sam, wants to?'

'I know he's not happy currently.'

'Talking will bring him happiness?'

'Talking is something he used to enjoy—I know that, I've seen that. The family gave me videos, photos. For some reason he doesn't do it any more. I think that's worth finding out about.'

'Silence is worth finding out about, yes!'

'But Sam's no monk with a vow. You don't look into his eyes and see pools of contentment, the unsayable mysteries of the universe. He won't let you look in his eyes. He's too frightened. A hero? I banged my hands on the desk this morning and he jumped out of his skin. And that was private information. Not to be repeated.'

'Of course.' Medbh gazed at him.

'It's not an approved treatment method, banging the desk,' he said. 'Probably I was a bit frustrated.' Already he'd said too much.

Medbh was also the beautiful one. Dark hair, alert eyes behind her fringe, a graceful poise in her limbs. He'd seen her die a few times. Dora—fair, somewhat bland and open in her face, solid-bodied, all attributes of her father—loved killing her. Medbh had an astonishingly even temperament. As such, she was lousy at being mutilated. She seemed to lie back and take it with complete equanimity. The man came at her with an axe or a spade or a weed eater—whatever he had in the back of his ute—and she looked as if she'd been promised a massage. She screamed a bit but her eyes were basically welcoming. That feels good, now lower, that's it. Her accession to the indecencies she suffered on-screen presented, Paddy supposed, exactly the difficult subtext required by a certain sector of viewers. He knew from Dora, however, that this was simply a result of a failure in the performance. Medbh was too good-natured for the role. In the outtakes—they'd had evenings of outtakes at the apartment—they could hear Dora, directing, asking for more horror, more fear, more pain. Sometimes Medbh laughed audibly when she was stabbed.

'God, you have a great job, Patrick,' she said. She appeared utterly sincere. 'Helena told us you were like one of the top speech people for kids.'

'Well, we don't get ranked. There's not a league table where we go head to head against one another.'

'No but you make a difference. You get them to talk, these difficult cases.'

'I'm not a child-whisperer,' he said. 'The kids I see don't hear me and just agree. Look at Sam. Plus I like silence too. Don't get me wrong. It has its place.'

'When do you like it?'

The question took him by surprise. This was a quality both Medbh and Dora had, a directness, a sheen of self-possession and confidence in the presence of people older than themselves. A conviction that they would and should be taken seriously. This was new, he thought. For his generation the idea was *not* to be taken seriously by anyone. 'When? I don't know. Watching a sunset. That for me is a silent moment. You don't need talk to complete it, right? You sit there with your mouth open.'

'What else?'

'Fishing.'

'Fishing?'

'Fishing on a still lake.' There were real memories tied up here though he hadn't been fishing for years. They'd had a holiday at Taupo. His father had taken him and Margie out one evening in

101

the little boat; Steph would have been a baby. 'That's silence like a held breath, isn't it.'

'Until you catch something, then all hell breaks loose. I fished with my uncles in the Sounds.'

'But I never make the mistake of catching anything.'

On Lake Taupo they'd fished for an hour or more, he and Margie, while their father trailed his hand in the water and baited their hooks. Between baitings, their father closed his eyes. It was intensely quiet and the hush and the sight of him with his eyes closed encouraged them reluctantly to give up speech, to listen to the water lapping against the side of the boat and the birds lifting out of trees by the shore. They got bites and when they pulled in their lines the bait was always gone. The nibbles kept them interested, and the exotic peacefulness of the lake almost persuaded them of the value of this moment. They had an inkling of adult melancholy that was not wholly repellent, he thought. Even Margie was prepared to tolerate it for a time.

But there was something wrong with their father's method of baiting the hooks, perhaps even a deliberate incompetence. Should they actually catch a fish, this atmosphere would be spoiled. There would be a life in the boat that needed to be ended and suddenly he couldn't imagine his father having a part in that.

Paddy grew desperate to do the hooks himself but he couldn't bring himself to ask. Margie too had begun to suffer. In the car driving to the lake, they'd already argued about the best place to stick the knife in a flapping fish, and where exactly was the brain? What right had their father to impose himself so languidly on their needs? They swapped looks: you say it! Yet they continued to bob up and down in the stillness.

At a certain point Paddy saw Margie quietly lift her line out; the hook was bare again. Instead of reeling in and moving the hook over to their father, rousing him with a few drops of water falling from the line on to his arm, she let the sinker drop soundlessly back into the lake.

His sister sat in dumb fury, turned away from Paddy, while their father continued in his trance. Suddenly she stood up and threw the whole rod into the lake, shrieking as she did so, and wobbling the boat. Their father gripped the sides; he was totally disorientated. 'What's happening? Margie! Your rod!'

'I got a huge bite!' she said.

'My God!'

'And it just snatched the thing clean out of my hands!'

'Were you holding it properly?'

'I was, I was!' She started to cry.

'Okay, okay, never mind. We can easily get the rod. Don't cry now. No big fuss.'

'But you said I wasn't doing it properly and I was.'

The boat was still rocking. Margie stamped her foot in the boat. It made a useless hollow sound and she tried again without much improvement. A boat on a lake was not a floor. She was utterly estranged from the normal apparatus of her temper. Paddy could have laughed but he was watchful in the boat. There was always the chance his sister's violence would have consequences more lasting than the sharp passing disturbance which was her speciality.

'Will you sit down, Margie dear. Please. Sit down dear, there's no problem. My, that must have been a big old fish who liked your hook, eh. Did you see it, Paddy? Did you see the bite on the line?'

Margie had sat down in the boat and buried her face in her knees. Now she half-turned to look at Paddy, to see what her younger brother would do. It was in her nature to desire carnage and upset within the family. She was especially incensed by their father's temperament, his good humour and gentleness, none of which she'd inherited. Yet she hated to be found out; it was the point on which her desire for trouble was finally half-hearted.

Real nastiness on both sides might have required her brother to tell on her; to offer them all up into further noise and unhappiness. Their father hated unhappiness more than anything. Paddy wanted Margie punished. She deserved something. But how could it be done? He saw how it would go. She'd woken their father up and distressed him with her distress. Soon she could expect a hug, which she'd accept ungraciously. He ached with the temptation to bring it all down around them, to sink them properly.

'Yes,' said Paddy. 'It was a big one. Margie's rod almost broke, I think.'

'How wonderful!' said their father. 'Good girl,' he told his daughter. With care, and a slight stagger as the boat shifted, he stepped across to her and put his arm around her. She burrowed into him at first, and then began to wriggle as if he wasn't quite doing it right, as if it was his comfort that needed to be accommodated and she was doing him a favour.

One time Margaret had come home for Christmas. She'd planned to stay for three weeks but changed her flight and left after two. Something was happening with the boys, she told Teresa, and she needed to get back. It was a miserable lie that her mother saw through at once and accepted with a nod. Paddy had driven her to the airport. While they waited for her flight he told her it was a shame she was going back into the cold of the other hemisphere. She looked at him closely and said, 'I find it very cold here, Paddy. In that house, with her. There's no warmth that I can get. It all goes in the usual direction.' She meant Stephanie and her kids.

'She loves it when you come back.'

'We have nothing to say to each other. After a day, she goes on the computer and I read my book. I can read my book in Vancouver. I tried last week to get a flight but there were no seats.'

'But what do you hope to say to each other?'

'I don't know, something to carry back. The truth is I don't know what mothers say to their daughters, that's the problem. Really we have no history.'

'Don't cry.' His sister was tough but she'd never eliminated that volatility, that self-surrender. She was victimised by what she felt, as if her feelings came from somewhere else. They surprised her. It was like watching someone get tasered.

'Why? People will think I'm sad about leaving.'

'Aren't you?'

'Sad, relieved, frustrated beyond belief. All of the above, I suppose.'

'Is it silly to ask you to come back now? We could say the flight was cancelled. Stay a few more days, Margie. Don't get on the plane like this.'

'And you think she's not right this minute breathing more easily now I'm gone? You're so innocent, Paddy. There's a lot you choose not to see.'

'Is that the same as innocence?'

'Maybe not, I don't know.'

'I know she thinks about you a lot.'

'Yes of course. It's part of the problem. When she sits at her computer and I'm downstairs with my book, she's thinking about me all the time. It accounts for the tension. With me too, I read a chapter and I forget what I've just read. Basically we don't seem good for each other. We remind each other of some problem.'

'What problem?'

'That's just it, what is the problem?'

A few months after they'd divorced, his mother, who'd never behaved in any way that was obviously anti-Bridget, said to Paddy, 'She had no imagination, Bridget.' They'd been sitting in the kitchen of the old house, in the last of the evening's sunlight, while the silverbeet boiled in a pot. He was staying for tea. She invited him out of consideration and kindness and concern. He was not especially well.

He baulked at the plainness of his mother's sudden judgement. It wasn't that she was wrong. What disturbed him was that she'd felt this and concealed it from him. Not for the first time he was irritated by the distance from which she delivered her verdicts, her skill at foreclosing someone's character while her own remained invulnerable, beyond discussion. Her humility was in the end not only a shield but also a powerful weapon, and under the cloak of her own negligibility, she could be brutal. Who was she, this person who desired so much to be nothing? He was suddenly drawn to argue with her, contradicting the truth of her statement about Bridget.

Well, let's face it, you were never supportive of her, he said. You gave her no chance. He walked to the pot on the stove and lifted its lid with a fork, dropping it when steam came up at him.

She had asked what he meant.

What did he mean? he wondered.

He said, You presented her with that curious and ugly smile that really means I can't stand you. Do you think she was too stupid to see that? You never took her seriously even though you were relentlessly kind and understanding.

He couldn't look at her and she remained sitting, one of her shoulders in sunlight, as if pinned to the wall by his terrible harangue. There was always that caution and carefulness and you never gave her anything, any moment of true emotion but always humoured her, as if she was a simpleton. He had to leave the room but he couldn't. Not a sound or movement came from her, which he found doubly infuriating. You always looked amused when she spoke. The truth is, that's the way you've always been. You can't bear that we've grown up. You act nicely and there's a deep hole in you. The caution is you stepping neatly around this hole. You give decency a bad name. You drive people away. You have no friends. An adult woman with no friends, who's ever heard of such a thing?

The lid on the silverbeet pot danced a little and spat at him. He felt it on the back of his hand.

They remained fixed in position for a while. Then she stood up and moved towards him. He stepped away, dizzy with the fright of what he'd just done.

'I need to turn this down,' she said at the stove, speaking to no one in particular.

After that, he'd not talked to his mother for weeks. He walked about in a state of unhappiness that was physically painful. He had an ache in his side and it hurt to twist in one direction. It was never spoken about again. Oh, it was not forgotten, he didn't imagine. What was?

Medbh swept the peelings from the garlic and the onions into the bin. Paddy thought: even disposing of the rubbish, she seems more skilful than us. She was rinsing the eggplant and drying it on paper towels. 'Funny, I don't associate you with boats.'

'What do you associate me with?' he said.

'A chair.' She shrugged apologetically.

'A *chair*?'

'Sorry. Just thinking about your office, your newspaper column. Work. What about me then?'

He was wounded. 'I associate you, Medbh, with a defiled corpse. But a strangely happy one.'

'That was the old Medbh.'

'Anyway,' he said, still feeling tender from her image and finding an outlet in a new stridency, 'there are precedents for this sort of thing. Go to Russian movies, or Swedish ones, they don't talk for hours. Someone washes a cup, it lasts days. They look out the window and see themselves as children running through a field, endlessly. I can't watch them. And I can't watch silent movies. Just can't. I've tried. The great classics of the silent era. The silent era, they call it. I've got to leave the room.'

Medbh was flipping the eggplant slices skilfully around to coat them in oil. 'It's probably why you became a speech therapist.' She looked at the ceiling, as if the idea had come from there.

He reached for his mobile phone, needing to show how lightly he'd been touched. 'Because I hate F.W. Murnau?' He turned it on and now read his mother's text. 'Oh no,' he said. Medbh asked him what was wrong and he told her about Teresa missing the weekend away. The change in subject helped him recover immediately. 'But she was okay when you saw her? She said she's feeling better.'

'She didn't mention it,' said Medbh. She was opening the oven door. 'But I didn't know your mother was . . . French?'

He sent a text back and then looked up. 'French?'

'Is it? Her accent?' Medbh arranged the eggplant on the oven rack, checked the grill setting, half-closed the door, and went to the fridge. She took out a plastic container of fresh mozzarella. At the bench, she began to slice the cheese. 'Isn't she a bit French or something?'

'Not that I'm aware of. French? Why do you say that?'

'Just the accent.'

'What accent?'

'So you're not French, either of you.'

'I did it to the fifth form. My mother, to my knowledge, has had no dealings with the French language at all.' He thought of her Internet game, the circles of European diplomacy, something there she'd picked up on while wearing her headphones? 'She's been sick too of course.'

'Yes.'

'Au revoir, she said at the end.'

'You still want the job, Medbh? My crazy French mother. Next week, she could be Russian. Dressed in scarves. Asking you to clean her samovar.'

The street-level door buzzer sounded on the intercom. Paddy checked his watch. It was his two o'clock. He pressed the button on the door keypad, 'Come on up,' he said. There was a snatch of street noise and a voice saying, 'Thanks.'

He turned to Medbh. 'It's Julie with her little boy Caleb.'

She held her hand up to stop him. 'Confidential,' she said.

'Le petit garçon.' He moved towards the door.

Medbh looked up from her slicing. 'Because did she think Medbh was French? The name.'

'No. How? We're all from Ireland originally, our lot. She has a granddaughter called Niamh.'

'Ha, that's what I was going to be called but they went for a totally different set of problematic consonants instead.'

8

Helena arrived home late that evening, which was becoming a habit as the review approached. They'd already submitted many documents to the Ministry: budgets, business plans, projections. Someone would come soon to spend the day at the school, observing a class, and there would be sessions with a randomly selected group of interview subjects drawn from students past and present. 'My mind keeps going back to Janet Frame,' she told him. 'As a young teacher, with the inspector at the back of the class, she runs from the room and never comes back. It's in the film. She runs into the trees, she's free.'

'And a little bit mad,' he said.

'She's not mad to run though, under that gaze.'

'I don't think you'd even think of running. You'd return the gaze with interest. It'll be the inspector who'll run into the trees.'

'But that doesn't sound very good either. Anyway, I hope it's a man.'

'Why?'

'Women are tougher,' she said.

There was no doubt this Ministry person, man or woman, would find that Helena ran a thoroughly professional organisation with a high degree of client satisfaction. But it was still worth telling Helena this every night. At Christmas she got sixty or seventy cards from happy graduates.

It was after ten and Paddy had eaten his half of the dinner

Medbh had prepared for them. A leek and bacon flan that had survived its reheat perfectly.

He was back in the office, working on his column. If anyone asked him how long it took to write the column, he always said it was only six hundred words, not long. In truth they took ages, days. The more astute questioners would wonder whether it was harder to write with that level of compression, and Paddy would agree with this. Again, the truth was different. Right then, four hundred words would have suited him, two hundred.

Helena kissed him on the forehead and he put his arms around her waist. Paddy's head was pushed against her stomach and she stroked his hair. A perfect evening arrangement. Her clothes carried the chill of the wind, and also some ricey fragrance she'd collected in the Thai takeaways just around the corner from the school. She hadn't phoned him to say she wouldn't need her half of Medbh's dinner, which was still waiting in the turned-off oven.

'Green curry chicken?' he said.

'Do I stink?' she said.

'I could eat you, or at least your coat. How perfect is the most perfect language school in all the land tonight?'

'Far from perfect.' She slumped down in one of the chairs. 'How goes the glottal stop?'

'It's stopped.'

'What exactly is the glottis?' She'd asked through a yawn.

Paddy stood up and moved over to her. 'Open that wide again and I'll explain.'

'I don't think I can open anything.'

He began to unbutton her coat. With her sitting, however, this was surprisingly difficult to do. She pushed his hands away abruptly and stood up. 'Let me,' she said. She pulled at the buttons. 'I'm sorry, all day I'm with people who can't do what I ask them to do and so I have to do everything myself. I don't mean you.'

'No but then you come home and your beloved can't even get the buttons undone on your coat. Where can a person find

111

decent help these days? We could ask Medbh to stay and she could put us both to bed.'

'Sorry, Patrick. How was your day? Or did I ask that already? Sorry. It was Medbh's first day with your mother. Dora reminded me at work, I'd totally forgotten. We should have reminded Teresa.'

He thought at once of the French business. It seemed too odd, too diverting for now. 'Dora came to your work?'

'They want to make a silent film.'

'I know.' She looked at him intently for a moment but not really because he was on her mind, he saw that. 'We must make sure they stay together.'

'It's the slit in your vocal cords, part of the larynx, close it completely and you've probably said something like *chillun*. All God's *Chillun* Need Love. Glottal stop. Why do you think they might split up, apart from the fact that Dora would be a very difficult person to live with, while also being rewarding of course?'

Helena was very still, eyes wide, alert for something. Paddy wasn't convinced she'd heard what he'd said.

'What is it?' he said.

She returned her attention to the room and looked straight at him. 'Yes, in Arabic, that makes a consonant. The glottal stop is a consonant.'

'You knew all along,' he said. 'Why'd you need me for?'

'I'd forgotten I knew it. Iyob works in the office. Duh!'

Iyob was from Syria. He'd moved from graduate at the school to administration. He'd come to the apartment for a work party one time. Had he worn a bow tie?

'Maybe you should be writing this column. But then again, I thought Arabic was more pharyngeal, putting it near the epiglottis. Front wall of the pharynx articulates with the back wall, no?'

'Iyob is actually one of my headaches at present. Tonight I'm generally not in favour of the glottis or the epiglottis or any other glottis. With apologies to Arabic culture around the globe.

112

In fact I'm not so keen on any of the languages of the world, not even my own. Now I need to be pointed towards bed. I'm in search of utter darkness.'

'And silence,' he said. He was thinking also of Sam. It was not the time to bring up Helena's indiscreet talk of his patients. They lived in a small town. 'Why do you think Dora and Medbh are in danger of splitting up?'

'No reason. But we must always be on guard.' She took the hand he offered her. 'Show me the way,' she said, her eyes closing.

He led her to the bedroom. 'Dora came to your work. She never comes to your work, does she?' There was a sort of agreement mother and daughter had reached.

Helena groaned. She was feeling under her pillow for her nightie. 'Oh, Paddy, I gave her a job. A few weeks ago. In a moment of weakness. With the pressure on from the thing.'

'The Ministry thing.'

'Data entry. Please don't say anything right now about it.'

'How's it going, the data entry with Dora?'

'You know, I like having her around.'

'Maybe this will be the making of her.'

She looked at him blearily. 'I'm way past knowing whether you're being sarcastic.'

He knew sadly no other way to be. The daughter was Helena's Achilles tendon, which was a Lant saying. He, Lant, had snapped his years back on a flight of icy steps. The tendon was now his Achilles heel, he said. Between them, they said tendon. It was juvenile and as persistent as most juvenilia. Dora made her mother hobble, he thought. Having left Max, having forged a new solo life, having been unavailable twenty-four seven for her young daughter, Helena now watched Dora's adult misery with a troubled conscience. What if what if. He understood it, he did. It was the contemporary dilemma: the haunted woman. Also he saw the daughter understood it too and refused to concede that she was a maker of her own life, that her lines were not being written daily by her kind and loving mother. Because that was what bugged him: Dora was loved and still acted as if crippling deficiencies in this realm were keeping her from her goal. She'd cripple someone back. Okay, he should have felt more sympathy for the girl given his own experience. They had Margie in their family, making his mother, come to think of it, also the contemporary woman.

He went into the bathroom and put toothpaste on Helena's toothbrush. She came in and took it from him.

'It's got the stuff on it already,' she said, looking at her brush, unimpressed. 'You did it for me.'

When he was married to Bridget he'd done this during the periods she'd been sick in bed but he'd never done it before with Helena and it seemed to have happened in some sort of flashback. Had he forgotten for a moment where he was?

'Ma got sick,' he said. 'Stomach bug, she had to cancel with Stephanie. She spent the whole weekend in bed.'

'That's dreadful, why didn't we know? She was just through there all the time.'

'This is part of her "I don't want to be your new best friend, I don't want to knock on your door" thing.'

'You should have checked on her.'

The accusation surprised him, annoyed him. 'But I thought she was away! If I'd known, of course I would have checked.'

She'd started to brush, though she spoke a few words mid-brush.

'I can't understand you,' he said.

Helena was too tired to read even a page of *People* that night. Her light was off when he looked in after a few minutes. She was already sleeping deeply, pushing air at a steady rate through her nostrils, her lips slightly parted and vibrating. How much oxygen did she need for this sleeping? Sometimes, as now, she looked half-drowned, pale and with one hand caught oddly behind her ear, as if she'd been flung on the sheets. It was unfair to catch her like this and also one of the great privileges, he considered, of cohabitation. What has she seen of me asleep, he thought, what ugliness?

He found himself looking carefully at her neck. Nothing had changed about her neck of course. Yet her self-criticism had somehow made a difference. It was, he saw, slightly malpositioned with regard to her body. Lying down, this appeared more obvious. His cruelty was disturbing to him. Not for the first time, he blamed it on his failure with Sam. What did it mean—that he had such a limited supply of sympathy the boy could exhaust it? Yet he'd felt cruel at times towards him also.

Paddy finished the column in his office and emailed it to the paper. He was early with his copy. Clearly this was some way of getting to Tony Gorzo.

In the Gorzo Christmas card they sent their love and they provided news of Jimmy, who went on to university and became an engineer and now lived in America. Paddy never replied—not for any special reason, just that he didn't send cards and didn't want to start. Each Christmas the Gorzo card came, along with a few others, and he was very glad to get them.

When his column started up, Tony rang him, very excited. Paddy hadn't heard his voice since the night in the hospital car park a few years before. Tony had read the column and he'd recognised Jimmy's story, which Paddy had drawn on for a piece about the relationship of hearing to speech. Of course Paddy hadn't named names. This seemed to disappoint Tony. He told Paddy that Jimmy was studying in Auckland, and that they were all proud to see themselves recognised in this way, no matter that it had to be anonymous. Hell, *they* knew.

He asked after Paddy's wife and Paddy told him they were divorced but that had made his life better. Gorzo sounded as though he didn't believe this. He said if he ever lost Ellie he'd die. Paddy believed this and he said so. Gorzo wanted to know if Paddy was still at the hospital and Paddy told him about leaving shortly after Jimmy was discharged, about setting up in private practice. You're the boss, Gorzo said. It's the only way. Except

GST, said Paddy. But Gorzo said he could tell him the name of a good accountant.

'Why does the phrase "good accountant" always sound like "cheat"?' said Paddy. Gorzo didn't respond to this. Generally he didn't like the frivolous.

Paddy heard himself asking about Gorzo's mother, the old woman on the hospital steps. She was ninety-two years old and refused to go into a home and refused to move in with them. What about his father? He'd died when Tony was fourteen. Paddy said this made them twins. 'Really?' he said. 'You too? Actually we have a lot in common besides Jimmy.' Paddy couldn't think of much they shared but found he liked it being said. The assertion was somehow a hopeful one. This was the Gorzo style: say it and it was so.

It was interesting to hear from him but Paddy thought that would be it. The impulse to make contact was satisfied and he'd slip out of Paddy's life again.

Two weeks later his second column appeared and Gorzo rang again. 'How many of these things are you doing?' he said.

'Every fortnight they'll publish one,' said Paddy.

'We read it and it's not about Jimmy but still it was interesting.'

'Thank you.'

'Now I got to read it every two weeks.'

'Sorry about that.'

'You think a lot about speech.'

'Too much.'

He didn't like this and spoke earnestly. 'Why'd you put yourself down? Someone else has that job already, I'm sure.'

Paddy thought back to Gorzo's squeamishness in the hospital. Certainly musings on language were more tolerable than the idea someone couldn't swallow, but perhaps Gorzo had also matured. Still he didn't quite know why he was calling.

Then Gorzo told Paddy what Jimmy had been up to. Paddy asked him about his mother. He seemed surprised Paddy knew

116

about her and Paddy reminded him they'd spoken about it last time. Still he wondered aloud why Paddy had remembered such a thing. No change there anyway on the mother front, he said. She was stubborn as a donkey, he said. Mule? said Paddy. He wondered if Greeks said 'donkey'. Whatever, said Gorzo. 'We talked about our Dads though,' he said.

'Yes we did.'

There was a pause on the phone.

'You never told me how your Dad died,' he said.

'He was swimming—' said Paddy.

'Shit, he drowned!'

'No.'

'Thank Christ for that.'

'He'd had a swim, at the Riddiford Baths, and he came home—'

'He was too tired from the swimming, he dropped dead at home.'

'Hey, Tony, can I tell you?'

'Sorry, I always want to know the end. Sorry, Pat.'

'It was an aneurysm.'

'Ouch.'

'Ouch? Well, I guess. It's over fast though.'

'My Dad was fast too. A concrete post came through his windscreen.'

'Ouch,' said Paddy.

'You bet.'

There was a silence. They didn't know where to go from there. They'd ground to a halt. Having given each other news of perhaps the most painful moments in their lives in such a wonderfully incompetent fashion, what next?

Incompetent, yes. But also accurate. Paddy hadn't talked about his father in a long time. Obviously he'd been waiting for Tony Gorzo to come into his life, to twin up. The night in the car park came to mind again when suddenly Paddy's future took on a different shape. He missed his father terribly. Someone I loved and needed, gone forever, he thought. The piercing simplicity and starkness of that fact. Astonishing to proceed in the face of it. How?

'So, like—no warning signs, nothing?' said Gorzo.

Before he died the worst thing his father had were varicose veins. Then kapow. Kapow? Paddy might have cried his eyes out then on the phone. Instead he began laughing. Not because of the varicose veins but because of the absurd way he and Tony Gorzo were finding their way through all this. His impression was that Tony Gorzo listened to his laughing with a completely straight face; perhaps he'd even be concerned. Some people didn't laugh and he thought Tony was one of them. But he listened. Paddy believed the other man thought Paddy was terribly lonely and unhappy and he was the only real human contact he had. It wasn't the truth but it gave their conversations a necessary freedom, a sort of wildness and spontaneity that soon came to be something like fondness. Anyway, he rang the next time.

'When are you going to stop writing in the paper?'

'Never,' said Paddy. 'You're going to have to read me for years. Tell me about Jimmy.'

'Why'd you ever give him the power of speech if all he ever does is ask for money?'

They talked for a bit, and then Gorzo said, 'What's the next subject of the column?' Paddy told him that was always a surprise. 'Create suspense,' he said.

'That's right,' said Paddy.

'But I hate suspense, will he, won't he. Just give me it straight, I say.'

The day he found the room full of pillows at the hospital, Paddy had been trying to avoid seeing one of his colleagues who had some kind of boring administrative task for him. He'd simply opened a door and walked in. The pillows weren't bagged or covered in plastic slips; they formed a mound which took up more than two-thirds of the floor and which was higher than the windows. The pillows were clearly used, perhaps on their way

118

out or being stored prior to reconditioning. There were always circulars about re-using things, avoiding waste. The pillows were grey, minus their pillowcases, and many of them carried stains. It was impossible not to see turning heads, suffering heads, the heads of all those people who can't properly sleep, who sit up suddenly in the middle of the night to say things of great urgency to people who aren't there.

His sister Margie had once told him she couldn't look at a bed without wanting to lie down and go to sleep in it. No matter if she was tired or not, she felt the urge. At dinner parties she had to avoid catching sight of beds.

Certainly for Paddy right then it was not a question of lying down among the many pillows. He moved quickly on, down another corridor, looking to get away. The hospital was a great place to hide.

At two forty in the morning, Helena sat bolt upright in bed and announced a word he didn't understand. Was it a word? A demonstration of the glottal stop? Perhaps it was Arabic, connected with their talk earlier, her problems at the school. She hadn't been able to tell him about giving her daughter the job. Hadn't been able to say the name Dora to him. Some therapists believed nocturnal speech was revelatory in this manner: asleep we spoke what we were unable to awake. It sounded a little like someone clearing her throat. Or the action we make after swallowing an insect. A raspy word of great importance to her since she declared it with complete conviction. She seemed content once it was out. Whatever it was, the moment had a different quality to her usual gastric outbursts, and she'd not held her chest. He asked whether she was all right and she looked at him without surprise, smiled dreamily, and lay down again to sleep. A few moments later he heard her sipping from her water glass.

In the morning she had no memory of it. She said she hadn't slept well and she didn't feel like eating. He made her a cup of tea. Perhaps she was getting a cold, Paddy suggested. The stress of the school inspection. Brusquely, she rejected this. 'I had a dream I was with my mother at some sort of market overseas.' Helena's mother had died before they'd met. 'I was trying to buy a belt. My jeans were too big for me and I needed a belt. I was the age I am now, about. So my mother was handing me these belts and pulling them around my waist, tightening them, seeing if they fitted. Except she was choosing smaller and smaller belts. And she was yanking them tighter and tighter. Almost cutting me in half.'

'I see,' he said. He didn't know what to say.

She sipped her tea, looked at her watch. Her work bag was already on the kitchen table. She opened it, took out her mobile phone, regarded it unhappily and put it back again. She looked annoyed it hadn't rung. 'The old parent tries to strangle the child routine, huh?'

'But the belt was around your waist. Can you strangle someone by doing up their belt?'

She shrugged and walked out, leaving her mug on the table, something she never did. She always rinsed it and put it in the dishwasher. She'd not put a coaster under it either. He heard her in the bathroom, brushing her teeth with the electric toothbrush. Paddy had stopped using his because it gave him the low-volume sound for an hour or more afterwards in his right ear. This was one of the stimuli he'd identified. Helena had told him to get the ear checked but he hadn't. There was no hearing impairment, no pain. Self-diagnosing, he queried mild otitis media.

When Helena walked back in, ready to leave, he said, 'What did Max do?'

'Who's Max?'

'Your husband, Max. What was his job when you were married?'

'Diving coach,' she said. She continued to appear irritated by something. 'Why?'

'I'd forgotten what he did. Diving, right.'

120

'That was a lifetime ago. What are you thinking of him for? Sometimes it seems like it never happened that whole episode.'

'You have a daughter by him.'

'And she's a constant surprise.'

'You gave her a job.'

'Temporary, very temporary.'

'Also you told me the other day about getting Max layered up in grease for his naked slide down the mountain.'

'Near naked, he was wearing pants.'

'Anyway, you'd placed him in my mental field.'

'That was connected to the diving, I think.' She left to do something else and came back again. 'But Paddy, what about Teresa? She's over this bug, right?' It was said in the manner of, don't bother correcting me, please, I require simplicity and obedience, and not because you are my inferior but because I'm stressed and you can help me.

'I think so. I'll check on her this morning.' He helped her by again not saying more.

They were moving towards the door now. 'How did that boy go yesterday?' she said.

He saw again that she was trying to be normal. He was touched for one second. Then this pained him somehow. He didn't want them to be trying to be things.

'Sam?' He thought of that odd moment at the door when he'd brushed past Paddy—he couldn't say 'reached out'. He couldn't start telling Helena now about that. It needed some different space, that story. He'd rush it. She wouldn't be able to take it in. Perhaps it was momentous. 'Oh, you should have heard us. We talked and talked,' said Paddy.

'Really? No. Okay. Well. Maybe try the belt trick.'

'I'll strangle him into speech.'

She smiled at this. He was pleased. Her straight even teeth showed. Yes, she'd had braces too, he remembered, and they'd worked. Then her bag began to ring and she pulled out her phone. In doing so, she knocked her knee lightly against his bike. 'Fuck,' she said. The bike began to slide down the wall and

Paddy caught it as she skipped out of its way. She bent to inspect her trousers, brushing at the spot. She pushed a button on the phone and they kissed hurriedly across the bike. He watched her walk the length of the corridor, talking to someone, still flicking at her knee.

A slight far-off booming had also entered his right ear. As a trial, and perhaps even in response to Margie in the boat when they were kids, he stamped his foot on the floor to see if it helped. Nope.

From the apartment he rang his mother but it went to message. He texted her. Did she want to go out for coffee that morning?

He rubbed at his ear and shook his head but the slight fuzzing remained, a watery sibilance accompanying his every step. Perhaps he'd been too close to Helena's electric toothbrush both the previous night and that morning. She usually had the bathroom door closed. Was it enough now to be within hearing range for the effect to take hold? He'd once had what he thought was a repetitive strain injury along his wrist until he traced it to a new razor he'd bought which used a battery to vibrate the blades. Small things, small things. The Harleys came to mind, with their micro-interactions.

Over the next hour, Paddy listened to his own ear. He read things. A box from Amazon had arrived. He'd totally forgotten ordering the book, which turned out to be a biography of Churchill. Why? Part of his wandering research into speech patterns of the famous? He had a folder on his computer. Lawmakers were an interesting subset. Thomas Jefferson's lisp. Robert Kennedy's spasmodic dysphonia. Moses. Moses, who hates public speaking, is speaking to God. How is anyone going to listen to me, who am of uncircumcised lips? Because he'd burnt his mouth as a child, causing him to lisp, was a theory. He'd heard a paper on it once. Norman Shelley was the name of the actor said to have impersonated Churchill for the BBC. He'd taken out his own false teeth to mimic Churchill's impediment. Paddy understood he was delaying.

In the phonebook he looked up the number for Tony Gorzo's

bowling lanes in the Hutt. Perhaps Paddy had offended him in some way? Yet when he replayed their last conversation, which had been about nasal resonance, he was sure there was nothing in it that had gone wrong. They'd finished the call on the same friendly terms. Gorzo had repeated the same thing he always used, 'Don't tell me the subject of the next column, will you, Pat. Let me stew here for a fortnight.'

'I'll let you sweat it,' said Paddy.

'I'm a nervous wreck,' he said and hung up.

Paddy rang the number. His call went straight to voicemail. He hung up. If Gorzo didn't want the contact any more, fine. He knew where Paddy was. Sometimes you have a lot to do with a person and then, for no reason, the connection is lost. He had people in his life like that, everyone did. Tony Gorzo had appeared from nowhere and he'd gone back into that place.

9

That afternoon he met Lant outside the apartment building for their ride together. Paddy, wheeling his bike, walked towards his friend on his cleated shoes, toes pointing upwards, in his shorts and shirt and jacket. He wore his fingerless gloves like someone from Charles Dickens, a pickpocket. His helmet. Paddy felt sleek, vaguely Italian. An Italian pickpocket. The bike went forward alongside him on no more than the lightest pressure from a single guiding hand. He was aware of the hairs on his legs. It wasn't a warm day. He'd been told not to wait for nice weather to bike in. They lived in Wellington. You just got out in it. What if it rained? he'd asked Lant. You put a tiny umbrella in your pouch, he said. Really? said Paddy. No, said Lant.

'Look,' said Lant, 'the duck who can ride a bicycle.'

'Shut up,' said Paddy. 'I'm in no mood for the sort of self-deprecatory humour I've formerly indulged in with you.'

Lant looked at him closely and got on his bike. His outfit was red, predominantly, whereas Paddy's was blue. Did red mean something, something better? Had Lant tricked him into buying bunny blue? 'Okay,' he said, 'so you ready to put some k's on that baby?'

'Is that the way we talk now?'

Lant rode forward slowly, adjusting something on his bike, looking at his legs. Did he shave his legs? 'Let's ride!'

Paddy stepped into his pedals, clicking the shoes into place. By the time he looked up Lant was far off down the road. 'Bastard,' he said, starting after him. 'Bastard!'

Some days you had the legs for it and some days you didn't. Lant had also told him this. It was the mystery of biking. 'Fuck, it's the mystery of life,' he said. Lant saying this, and Paddy remembering it, wasn't the reason Paddy felt as he now did. Something bitter was passing through him, like a mild flu. A vague impatience. A generalised wish for progress. Let's go.

Today Paddy had the legs for it. They were going around the bays, all the way to Seatoun and back. But there'd be hill work thrown in. Up to Hataitai, then down again. He overtook Lant going past the New World supermarket. Lant laughed. 'Two more hours to go, shitbrain!' he called out.

They met a headwind. It watered the eyes. Beside Paddy, the sea sucked against the rocks. There was the smell of seaweed. Cars passed in moments of sudden noise and disturbed air. A small truck rocked the bike, causing it to snake, then settle. Paddy almost hit the curb.

By the time they turned up towards Hataitai, Lant was back on his tail. Then Paddy missed the right gear, nearly lost his chain, and Lant went ahead. Paddy caught him about halfway up, at the steepest point. Paddy was out of his seat, pushing the bike from side to side. Lant's technique was probably smarter. Of course it was, Jesus. He stayed in the saddle. His bike scarcely deviated. His feet made nice arcs. Paddy's thigh muscles ached and he could feel the phlegm drying around his mouth. Was he grunting? Probably. Still he went away from Lant, pushing two corners ahead. His toes were jamming hard against the ends of the shoes, which he knew shouldn't be happening, and he was gripping the handlebars so tightly a cramp shot along one arm forcing him to release for a second. He lost power. Whatever rhythm he'd had now disappeared. He made the mistake of checking over his shoulder. Lant had popped up behind him, still a corner back but gaining. Lant had his head down. His bike was steady. Air entered Paddy's open mouth, stinging his throat. He tried closing his mouth but that felt too constricting. He needed everything open, everything pulling.

It wasn't a race. It had never been a race. Lant's stylish and persistent riding was hugely aggravating. He was provoking Paddy, who shook out his hand again on the cramping arm and pressed more heavily with his legs on the downward stroke of the pedals, trying to imagine the correct version of the man he'd seen on the bike shop computer, the perfect horizontal at the apex of each push, the elbows lined up, the shoulders relaxed, the weight going neatly forward. A bullet not a duck.

His side hurt.

He heard a car coming up the hill behind them. Their bikes were going not much faster than walking speed.

Twenty yards ahead someone was trying to parallel park. A woman carrying a baby and a baby-seat waited on the footpath for the person in the car to complete the manoeuvre. But the car wasn't in properly and it was coming out of its park, angling across the narrow road.

It was hard to hear with the helmet on and the wind rushing past. Paddy thought perhaps Lant had called out to him. The car coming up the hill must have almost passed Lant but Paddy didn't want to look back and lose power again. He had momentum once more. The top of the hill was a couple of bends away. What was so urgent that he had to call it out now? He was the sort of person who'd do anything to win, Lanting. He was a psychologist.

The woman with the baby was looking in Paddy's direction. He saw the baby lift its head. How old was it? Five, six weeks? Very small, with a ball-shaped uncovered head, startlingly round. It was turning, looking for something. The baby had no words but only a sense that this was the direction to turn in. Paddy came closer and saw its mouth open. Mouth, nipple. Communication didn't get any clearer than that. We'd all started there. Even Lant. The mother was watching Paddy.

The gap ahead in the road opened a little as the reversing car made another move into its park. Paddy swung his bike out over to the far right-hand side. He could sense the car behind him coming very close. But where was it going? Nowhere. It would have to wait for the other car. Paddy had the road. Paddy had the machine.

The driver of the reversing car saw Paddy now—an older man, in his seventies, the baby's grandfather perhaps—and he stopped, unsure what Paddy was doing or where the front of his car was in relation to the bike. He was letting Paddy past. Paddy tried to acknowledge this, smile, present some gesture of gratitude. He was only a couple of feet from the car window. The man had no idea about Lant in his racing red, urging on this whole show. Paddy's look was supposed to express some of this. How important it was to pass him now without stopping. A friendly, firm nod to indicate he was doing the right thing. Stay there Grandad.

Probably the driver saw only a grimace, a look of desperation, strain. Paddy was pleading, demented, dangerous. He was the biker he'd write to the paper about, the paper in which Paddy's column appeared. Paddy was a figure of increasing concern. He was thoughtless. He would be involved in a serious accident. Paddy could hurt himself, which was fine, what mattered were the innocent people caught up in such moments of idiocy. 'My granddaughter, six weeks old, was almost involved in this piece of thoroughly avoidable madness.'

Paddy did feel a bit mad.

Then a car appeared in front of them, coming down the road too fast. This had probably been Grandad's point. Paddy was moving around the halted car. The downhill driver had to pull up with a sudden jolt. Paddy saw his body rock forward and slam back in his seat. Jerk was travelling too fast. The driver sounded his horn, threw his arms up inside the car: what the hell! His voice was muffled and far-off in his car. This time Paddy kept his head down. They had nothing to say. He biked on. He could see the top.

At Seatoun, they sat on the beach watching the interisland ferry slide past in what appeared to be about six feet of water.

Lant had beaten him by three minutes.

Against the muted backdrop of grey cloud, dark speckled

sea, brown grasses, metallic-dull sand, Paddy thought they must have appeared, in their bright biking clothes, garish and showy. Visible from the ferry. Beaconish. The ferry itself was luminous, hugely white and gleaming. They seemed joined to it somehow in their vivid declarations.

'It's not a race,' Lant told him.

'I know,' said Paddy.

Lant flexed his leg in front of them. He'd taken one shoe off to pick at something. Sand clung to his long toes. 'The reason I went past you on the flat was because I wanted to stretch out a bit, see how the bike was handling,' he said.

'Right,' said Paddy. His toes ached but he didn't want to take off his shoes. He didn't want there to be a comparison made between Lant's toes and his own, even a silent one. Paddy knew his weren't long like Lant's but that wasn't the whole point. He felt the need to remain as separate in his actions from Lant as he could. Paddy was refusing to unzip his jacket since Lant had done that. He'd taken off his gloves when he saw Lant hadn't. Paddy said, 'The reason I went past you on the hill . . .'

'Yes?' said Lant.

'Was to bury your conceited and padded ass. Which I did.'

'You almost got knocked off too.'

'Did I? Was that how it looked from behind?'

Lant laughed sourly. 'There were children watching that.'

'It was a baby. They can't focus.'

'Now you're accurately assessing the age of that infant from where you were on your bike on the road?' Lant lay back on the sand, shaking his head. Then he reached into a pocket somewhere—Paddy had noticed Lant's outfit was subtly different from his own, superior in clever, unostentatious ways—and took out a pair of sunglasses that he put on to look at the overcast sky.

'Where did *they* come from?' said Paddy.

The sunglasses curved neatly across his face. Wraparounds usually made the wearer seem cheap, mean. These were shaped elegantly, sportily. They made clean lines of Lant's cheekbones.

'Did your eyes start stinging in the wind when we went around by the sea?' said Lant.

'Yes.'

'That was salt carried by the wind.'

'They really stung.'

'These help.'

'Why didn't you tell me about getting glasses before?'

He sat up again, took the glasses off, and offered them to Paddy. 'You could wear them on the way home.'

'I don't want to wear them.'

'Wear them, try them.' He held the glasses closer to Paddy.

'No, you keep them, they'll be covered in salt now.'

'They're made of a compound that repels all that, maintaining a clear surface. Self-cleaning.'

'You believed that? They're self-cleaning? Nothing's self-cleaning, not even self-cleaning ovens.' They did seem extremely clean.

Lant shrugged and lay back down again. 'These aren't the reason I beat you, you know. They aren't magic glasses. I beat you because I'm more experienced and smarter than you, Card.'

'I'm glad we sorted that out.'

The ferry slipped around the corner, heading into the ferocious Strait. The northerly had changed to southerly a few days before. Paddy pulled on his gloves.

'Do you remember Dave Marshall?' said Lant. 'Obstetrics? I used to ride with Dave. Trouble was the pattern of our commitment tended in opposing directions. He couldn't make it a lot of the time, and then I couldn't. We were always cancelling, trying to reschedule. It was really annoying. So I said to him, "Dave, what's up this time?" And he tells me he'd got to see, let's call her Alison, I've forgotten exactly. Got to see Alison. "So we'll make it earlier, yes?" But no, he had to see Alison. So I figured it out. I wanted to bike more when I was *in* a relationship. He was less keen when he was seeing someone. To have a girlfriend was for him an act of devotion, he was consumed by that and everything else fell away. Whereas for me it was an act of celebration to bike. It was an extension of—well, let's not muck around here, fucking. I was energised. But Dave only biked if he couldn't fuck. In a way we were both humping our bikes, weren't we?'

'They didn't talk about this at the bike shop,' said Paddy. 'If they had, I might not be here now.'

'Dave biked doggedly, a hunched man trying to get through the dark times. You know what his favourite ride was? Uphill. He liked to be in pain.'

'So I'm Dave Marshall? I beat you on one hill climb and you want it that I'm sexually frustrated and masochistic? It's a long bow, Dr Lanting.'

'No conclusions drawn. But something in that ride just now reminded me of Dave. You both have heavy thighs. But no, wait, you're different too. You have a girlish bottom.'

Why on earth had he confessed that to his friend? Paddy picked up a handful of gravel and threw it at Lant, who ducked.

'Hey, whatsa matter? You're a happy man, you told me. Woman of your dreams, nice place to live.'

'I am happy.'

'Good.'

'Listen,' said Paddy, 'the mistake people make is they think happy is one shade.'

'Okay.'

'But happy is a range, it's a—scale.'

'And right now, you're at the other end—of happy.' Lant sat up again, taking off his glasses and examining the lenses. 'Okay, fine, all I care about really is having a stable riding partner, someone who says yes more than no. So far so good, Card. Fortunately for you too, I'm rarely alone at night.'

Paddy drank from his water bottle. There still the plasticky taste of a new bottle.

'Lant, how good do you think I am?'

'At biking?'

'Not at biking, no.'

'In what way then? Morally?'

'Professionally. How good at my job am I? Do you think I'm one of the top speech therapists?'

'In Wellington, you mean?'

'Go as wide as you like.'

'In the country? How many speech therapists are there in the country?'

'Doesn't matter. Put me somewhere. You know I've given papers in Australia. One time in the States.'

'Australasia now? America? I think I need the numbers.'

'Why?'

'Establish the mean.'

'Forget the numbers. Am I in the top bracket?'

'Yes,' said Lant. 'Depending on the size of the bracket. Yes. Definitely.'

'The size of the bracket? What size?'

'I don't know, you won't give me the numbers.'

'I've written a fucking newspaper column for years.'

'Syndicate the column is my advice, Card. I've always said that.'

'So I'm not in the top?'

'There's a smaller bracket, I guess, a tiny number, above your bracket. These would be therapists of great prominence. The theorists of it all perhaps, rather than your practitioners. These would be the thinkers.'

'Who?'

'I don't know their names. It's not my field.'

'Right, so why are you pretending to know all this stuff?'

'These are general observations. I thought I'd been invited to make a few of those.'

'You weren't invited, Lant. I asked you a simple question. *Merde.*'

'Murder?'

'*Merde*! *Scheisse*! Shit! You know, shit.'

'What's up with you, Card? What's happening?'

131

'I don't know. Nothing. I sure don't want to fuck my bike though. This isn't sublimation.'

'Everything's sublimation.'

'Okay, Tony Gorzo didn't call.'

Lant looked at him. 'Gorzo didn't call about the column and it sends you spinning?'

'He never misses.'

'Maybe he's sick.'

'Gorzo doesn't get sick.'

'On holiday then.'

'And he leaves without telling me? Once he called me from Fiji to apologise.'

'Dead. He's been killed. His wife did it or his son, stabbed him in his sleep.'

'Gorzo can't die. Impossible. Those things he smokes will make him live forever. Anyway, I've been looking in the paper.'

'Looking in the paper? Why not just call him then, find out.'

'That's what Helena says.'

'It would be normal advice. Call him.'

'And show him my weakness? Anyway, I tried. Got his voicemail.'

'Okay then, voilà, progress.'

'Didn't leave a message.'

Paddy stood up and walked over to where their bikes were resting under a tree. He thought of them as resting, as if they were horses, tethered there. Good boy, he said to his. Lant called out to ask what he was doing. Paddy told him they had to go. Lant looked down at his bare foot. He didn't have his shoe on yet, he said. Paddy had strapped on his helmet and was wheeling his bike across the pebbly part of the sand towards the road. Lant was standing now, struggling with his shoe, losing his balance, swearing. Paddy heard him shouting but it hardly carried. The wind had begun to move across his ears. Paddy was away. He watched his front wheel begin to spit up a tiny continuous fizz as if he were carving something into the road.

At certain moments it was clear to Paddy why Helena didn't much like Jeremy Lanting though she'd never said so. She was bothered, it seemed at first, by his profession. He could be superior, Paddy knew that. Smug. Conceited. Oh yes. He dealt with a lot of violent teenagers, accomplished criminals. 'Because he listens to terrible things all day, kids with knives making their sisters become prostitutes, I wonder if he thinks he can't be shocked,' Helena said one day. 'Probably he looks at someone like me and thinks I live complacently. True enough. But how long would Jeremy last on the street? He has a season ticket for the orchestra.'

'He doesn't think you're complacent,' said Paddy. 'Your life is full of refugees and immigrants, people who've risked everything and given up their homes and travelled. And these are the people who you help. He admires you tremendously. As for the orchestra tickets, I'm grateful for that because we get to use them sometimes.'

Helena thought for a moment. She might have been considering how effortlessly he'd lied on his friend's behalf, and was deciding whether this was sweet or not. Or she might have believed him. Lant had never spoken about Helena's working life to him. Why couldn't he have the thoughts Paddy had given him though?

She said suddenly, 'Why do you think he chose seats up behind the orchestra rather than down in the main auditorium?'

There was more inquiry than attack in the question, and the promise of a fresh direction. It was a quality in her conversation Paddy enjoyed, the ability to move around rapidly. She was never stuck. 'It's a great view,' he said.

'Where you lose the soloists. They play with their backs to you.'

Soloing was their word for masturbating, which of course wasn't what she meant here. The appellation could have disastrous results, as in the time they both had to leave an orchestra concert—thank you, Lant—when a visiting Russian pianist plainly adjusted his crotch prior to the opening bars and Helena whispered to Paddy that they were watching a great soloist. He put this from his mind now. He said, 'But you see almost inside the orchestra. You stare into the great machine. You see how the parts are all working. The musicians, they can look totally unconnected, looking inside their instruments and fiddling around, pulling bits off, then preparing to blow for two bars or something. You see them getting ready. How they exchange little looks with each other. The timpanist swallowing a sneeze.'

She appeared grateful to have left behind the direct subject of his friend. 'I always miss those things. They seem a bit bored to me, the musicians. Or just prosaic. A woman plays an extraordinary piece on the trumpet and then she tips the spit out on the floor.'

'I love it when she does that!'

'Yes, maybe that's the difference between us. I don't need to see the spit. Oh, it's all interesting but I prefer to close my eyes.'

'And fall asleep.'

'And concentrate on the music.' She looked carefully at him. 'And fall asleep.' Helena laughed. Her face in repose was surprisingly serious, her chin pointed purposefully, the lips set more tightly than she meant perhaps, her brow showing concentration; yet there was the sense of parody too, as if she didn't quite believe in such earnestness but had learned to do it. With her glasses on, she looked like a university professor, though better dressed. When she laughed the reward was terrific, a huge, lighted expression, a wide and white and perfectly corrected set of teeth, the eyes brilliantly brown.

'You've fallen asleep to some of the greatest music in the canon,' said Paddy.

'I begin with good intentions. Anything with a flute in it, I drift off.'

'And very loud drums. Was it Tchaikovsky?'

'They soothe me, drums.'

'Mmm, something from the womb perhaps.'

'I was an emergency Caesarean, born with the cord badly tangled. It took them twenty seconds to get me breathing. It was touch-and-go.'

'I was born in the afternoon, then I let my mother sleep.' How simply they slipped into these riffs on all they'd done and seen.

'I had colic the first eight weeks.'

'She always had to wake me up to feed me.'

'What was wrong with you?' said Helena.

'I loved to sleep. I loved my blankets.'

'You remember your blankets?'

'I have a sense of them, yes,' said Paddy. 'The silky bit stitched on the top of the blanket which pressed against my cheek.'

'How extraordinary.'

'Oh, I think being a baby was sort of a highlight for me. Of my life.'

'You were the perfect baby.'

'I was,' he said. 'That was before my mother became Cleopatra.'

His sense was that Helena didn't much care for his friend because he pre-dated her so completely and because they tended to communicate in a manner she almost certainly found annoying. Lant. Paddy was Card. Patrick, Card-Trick, Card—somehow. She'd never worked in a hospital. It was like going back to high school: nicknames, sexual depravity, problems with the toilets. Her language school was very grown-up in comparison. It was a serious business, learning the language that would help you survive. Studious people with bottles of water in the side-pockets of their backpacks reading the notices on the noticeboard by pressing their fingers under each word.

When Lant visited, she usually left them alone after a few minutes.

*

Back at the apartment Paddy met Geoff Harley in the lift. The doors opened and his neighbour stood there, carrying a box. He said he was on his way to the basement. He moved aside and Paddy wheeled his bike into the lift.

Paddy was sweating and sore, still wearing his helmet. He'd come in a hundred metres ahead of Lant. However, in a move designed to rob the moment of any satisfaction, when he'd checked behind, Lant was coasting, not holding the handlebars at all but with his arms folded, looking about the streets as if he'd never been engaged with him. How long had he been like this? Did he do it when he knew he couldn't catch him? Or had he eased up to give Paddy his victory? At Seatoun Beach Paddy had certainly provided sufficient reason to think his self-esteem needed a boost. Then why grandstand it with the arms folded? In fact Lant had a great professional scepticism around the whole issue of self-esteem. He thought its promotion created unreal expectations. Quite a lot of us, he'd told Paddy, had good reason to think not very highly of ourselves. More than once he'd offered that the Covenay kid, far from being deficient in confidence, probably harboured a champion cast-iron ego.

When they parted outside Paddy's building, Lant shook his hand in a suspiciously warm congratulatory manner. 'Did you see the dolphins?' he said.

'Yes,' Paddy lied.

'Did you see them? Were they feeding or something?'

'I think so.'

'I've never seen them so close in before.'

'Yeah,' said Paddy. All he'd been doing was keeping his eyes on the road and on his wheel. They could have been biking through one long tunnel.

Lant lifted his special glasses off. 'So how do you feel now?'

'I could throw up,' said Paddy.

'There's a pocket for that.'

'A self-cleaning one I hope.'

Lant laughed and put his glasses back on. 'Tell me, what are they saying, the dolphins, when they talk to each other? What do the noises mean? Is it talking as such? Is it stuff about the tides, the presence of a school of mackerel they fancy? "This is a nice bay we're in, isn't it?" "Weren't we here last year?" They're social creatures, right? It's not a million miles from the chatter of chimps, I think. But what do we know, Card? What are they saying?' He was obviously making his speech as long as possible to demonstrate control of his heart rate, his oxygen.

'Who am I, Dr Dolittle?'

'No, but come on.'

'A lot of it is conjecture.'

'Conject away.'

'Lant, I have sweat running into my underpants.'

'You're wearing underpants?'

'Oh please. The guy at the bike shop never said anything about that either.'

'It's a personal choice area.'

'Dolphins test their environments with sonic squeaks.'

'Right, how deep the water is, where the rocks are.'

'As far as emotional affect, no one's sure. There's been work done on happiness—'

'Happiness again!'

'—the sound of happiness. Pitch, volume et cetera. Whether there's even a melody, a tune for certain states. Most of the studies are done in captivity. There was some evidence that loneliness had a distinct sonic pattern.'

'Sad dolphin.'

'That in an aquarium, a dolphin which had lost its long-time performing partner was saying or singing a different tune, if you like. Of course a lot of this stuff is anecdotal. Trainers hearing new sounds, reporting changes. But then you map it through computer analysis and the graphs show no change. Look, I'm no expert.'

'People want the dolphin to be grief-stricken so badly, they imagine they're hearing the sad notes. Fascinating.'

'Or the software for registering such things is just not subtle enough.'

Lant nodded, slipped his feet into both pedals of his bike and held it steady. 'You're in the top bracket, Card,' he said.

'Oh, please not now. Don't try to repair the damage.'

'What damage is this though?'

'It's nothing,' said Paddy. 'It's the periodic wave of profound self-doubt that washes over us every so often and gives us the sensation that all our beliefs and values exist untested and that we live in a state of extreme vulnerability.'

'I've heard of it,' said Lant. He reached out and squeezed Paddy's shoulder. 'Sad dolphin.' Paddy became aware that Lant was using him to stay upright and he pulled away. For a moment Lant wobbled and almost fell. Then he straightened. 'Nasty dolphin,' he said. He biked in a circle around Paddy.

'So next time we see you,' said Paddy, 'you'll be on stage.'

'What are you talking about?'

'Your great gig at the school.' Stephanie had told him about it weeks before. Lant's band was going to play as part of a fundraiser at the school her oldest girl attended. Lant's daughter went there too.

'You're not coming, are you?' Lant looked suddenly concerned.

'Thought I might.'

'Some little school thing, I don't even know if we're playing.'

'Anyway, I'll be there. I promised Steph.'

At the lift Paddy had had no intention of putting his bike in the lock-up, not yet. He was going up. Geoff Harley somehow had persuaded him, or Paddy had simply followed a lead, taken an opportunity. A surprising amount of life was like this. A door opens and we step inside. It was something Lant would offer. On the ride home Paddy had been thinking of Sam Covenay again. His feeling was he'd trapped himself in the pose of The Boy Who Won't Speak. Perhaps the solution was not to try to break that but to offer him a new role, a fresh pose, to replace the self-defeated performance not with a simple return to the happy twelve-year-old Sam—he wasn't twelve, he wasn't that person any more—but with something as interesting, as radical as his current title.

To have had these thoughts—no matter how misguided they might turn out to be—to have created the mental space while biking, was suddenly extraordinary to Paddy. He'd failed to see the dolphins not because he was hopeless, or not only that, but because he was thinking, working almost. At some point on the homeward leg, the pain must have been managed. It was a tunnel but not an empty or uninteresting one, and if Paddy had set out hoping to eradicate all thought with pure action, he was returning strangely full of ideas. The nausea too was passing. His ear didn't hurt though it was surprisingly cold. For the first time Paddy felt reconciled to the bike. Everything else he'd done—leaving the bike in the hallway, oiling the chain at night, encouraging Sam to think about it—had been preparatory. Here was the thing. It was coming. He'd moved from wishful to actual, it seemed.

'I didn't know you were a biker,' said Geoff.

'It's all new,' said Paddy, regretting it at once.

'It's a good bike.'

'Do you know something about them?'

'Alas,' he said.

'Alas what?'

'I can't.'

'Can't what? Bike?' Harley was a disagreeable conversationalist, clinically MEF, meaningless enigmatic flow. Paddy could feel his good mood weakening under the spell of the other man's knowingness. Geoff believed he'd already been Paddy. He'd had a bike. He'd done all that. Paddy regretted especially not having taken off his helmet but it was too late now.

'The word came down,' he said.

'From?'

'Exactly.'

Geoff flexed one of his legs, displaying perhaps some significant stiffness that Paddy should inquire after. Paddy ignored the leg. The basement seemed a long way off. They both looked at the bike in the tiny space of the lift. Suddenly it seemed stupid and ugly and desperate. The bike was totally inadequate to the task it had been given, which was to carry forth the hopes of men of their age. Was this Helena's silent point too? Paddy's biking shoes made a loud clacking noise on the metal floor of the lift as he straightened the bike with an odd sort of roughness. What did he hope to achieve by this—to suggest that he was past the tender stage, that the bike was really nothing much to him? He'd already told Geoff he was a newbie. Finally the doors opened and Paddy pushed quickly away from Geoff Harley.

He called after Paddy. 'I met your mother earlier, delightful.'

Paddy waved his hand over his head without turning around. Delightful? Why use that word? She was nice, his mother, she was agreeable, but no one had ever said she was delightful. She had little desire to charm. Perhaps in the Harleys' world it made sense to say such things. These were the people who went out at night to watch for the light from wristwatches and mobile phones. He felt the temptation sharply to ask about these Thursday nights, Harley's absences, but kept walking.

Paddy removed his shoes and took the stairs back up to their floor, thereby avoiding Geoff, who was still moving things around in his lock-up. He'd kept looking over to where Paddy was putting away the bike, hoping to get him on his way back to the lift. Paddy carried his shoes in his hand and opened the door to the stairs as soundlessly as he could. His socks left sweat marks on the polished wooden corridor. At his mother's door he paused and listened. Nothing. He rang the buzzer but got no answer. If she were in, she'd be playing her game anyway. She'd be in her headphones, in Vienna or Geneva or Berlin or Paris.

He found he was wrong. Teresa had pushed a note under their front door. She'd caught the bus to Palmerston North to see Pip and wouldn't be back for a few days. Well, she was her own person. And the Pip visit had been something she'd spoken about before. Paddy couldn't remember the precise details but there was a tragedy in Pip's life. Her African husband had died. She'd stayed on. But now with Mugabe that was impossible. As girls, his mother and Pip had been close, and for a time they'd written to each other. The Skype contact had been recent.

10

Paddy woke up on Monday morning without Helena beside him. The phrase *his heart sank* occurred to him. He'd never been one to think, Good, the bed to myself. Usually they were in accord here, their feet hit the floor at the same moment.

He found her working at the kitchen table, doing spreadsheets on her laptop. She'd been up since five. She'd worked every evening until late, and had gone back into the school on both Saturday and Sunday. The Ministry had put in a last-minute request for more information on the school's business plan. Helena said they were also behind on several budget items. Then two of her staff had gone down with a stomach bug following a catered lunch designed to boost morale ahead of the review.

He brought her coffee. He modulated his voice to the carer's tone. Kissed the top of her head. She turned to him briefly and smiled. Her face was waxy in colour. There was a slight tremor in her eyelids. She'd been rubbing her eyes often. How had he managed to underestimate this so badly? He should have felt remorse for his comparative idleness, and he did, and he also felt irritated—at what? Sad but true the idea that Helena, poor Helena, with her thoroughly admirable dedication, was the cause of his trashy response. She was a fraction deranged in throwing herself this completely at working towards an end that didn't seem in doubt, and ideally there might have been something surprising and winning at his verbal command, a spell to break the spell. Recall the tui! But the ground he stood on was shaky. He felt vulnerable. His own crisis was small c. Hers took in the livelihoods of others. His was vague, mid-lifey, not very interesting. His was existential-focused, hers was existence-focused. She won. He agreed she won. Hers also, however, had an endpoint. The review would take place. There'd be a result.

In the midst of her travails, he'd been biking every day, also deranged. He'd gone out to Island Bay, concentrating on keeping an even pace and trying to maintain a calm disposition in the traffic. Adelaide Road, Lant had warned him accurately, was busy, fairly narrow, and a funnel for crap drivers to enter and leave the central city. Twice Paddy yelled at cars. 'Don't let them spoil your ride,' Lant told him. Private cursing he believed was the worst. Look closely and you saw lots of them, the muttering cyclists, people with valid grievances, driven inside themselves, stuck on complaint. Better to vent, call it to the wind, let it be blown behind you in a burst of saliva or be sucked ahead, words that you could then bike past. But Lant also said that gestures and shouts were generally useless; motorists understood finally only one thing: damage to their vehicle. A bang on the roof with the fist, a kick in the side panel. Of course you had to choose carefully when to express yourself like this. Lant said he'd once been pursued by two big blokes in a Falcon, finally losing them in an alley off Hania Street in Mount Vic.

At Island Bay Paddy sat on the stone wall looking out to sea. It was very Rita Angusy—the blue water oddly still, fixed in permanent agitation. A single fishing boat, painted in blazing red, rocked forcefully on its mooring between the little island and the shore. The beach was empty except for a woman far along from him who was throwing a stick into the water for her dog. It was a ruminative scene, he thought. Meaning it might have drawn from him a series of reflections. Here was the space, on the edge of land, in easy reach of elemental forces—sea and wind—where a person, alone, might consider things. Yet he found himself considering only the ride back along Adelaide Road. Already he was preparing himself for the battle. Biking seemed to refer to itself all the time. It was about biking. Perhaps this would change over time and there'd be an automatic set of

143

motions, allowing the free flow of thoughts. He'd had a taste of it on the homeward leg of the Seatoun ride with Lant.

Behind him on the road, a car was pulling a small trailer full of branches and garden rubbish most likely towards the tip. A few branches were hanging over the side of the trailer. Leaves flew up behind as he went around the bend into the next bay. Unsecured load, Paddy thought. Hazard, he thought. He saw himself riding behind that fuckwit.

The phone had rung a few times over the weekend. It was Dora. Helena had taken these calls in the bedroom, closing the door behind her. It wasn't usual though she said afterwards that she hadn't wanted to disturb Paddy. Each time the phone went he thought of Tony Gorzo, who still hadn't called. Now with the daughter on the phone, Gorzo couldn't get through. He'd asked whether things were all right with Dora, and Helena had only said that by now he had a good sense of her daughter. Paddy didn't know if this was true. He had *a* sense. He had his army of prejudice. More significantly, the non-explanation rankled. It was unlike Helena. There was something chain-of-command about it.

His mother had texted to say she'd be back from Palmie on Monday.

That morning he saw Trudy (language delay), Kevin (pragmatic language) and Caleb. He'd bumped Sam Covenay into the afternoon, claiming an emergency. Friday's session had been more of the usual. Blank boy, thwarted man. Paddy felt he needed a few wins under his belt. A straightforward run of appointments would be good for everyone.

It was Caleb's last day so Paddy said, 'Why'd you need me for.' The boy looked very puzzled but smiled. Why wasn't Paddy getting out the paper and pencils, the Lego, the little cars they sometimes played with? Caleb was six years old and he was better—he knew it. When he'd started sessions a few months before, he used a more or less private language with his mother Julie and then she would translate for everyone else. The first couple of sessions he wanted her there with him in case Paddy didn't understand. He refused to have his hand held but he wanted her there. It was a mix of fricative problems and consonant clusters that Julie had instinctively understood. He said *geen* for green, which was easy. He said *single* for jingle. But there were other trickier things, and recognising that he was having trouble being understood, he'd developed articulation issues through classic over-emphasis. Kids like Caleb often started by shouting words in frustration, mangling them even more, and usually ended up mumbling, simply passing over the troubling sounds to make themselves understood with the minimum fuss. When he first came to clinic Caleb was somewhere in between. Success with his mother—her cleverness in deciphering the sounds—had meant his frustration levels were manageable. He was also smart enough to see he was going to have to broaden his language base beyond his clever mother if he were to go forward. Now with his consonants in order and improved articulation through exercises, he knew he wouldn't have to rely on the translation process.

When she arrived, Julie, a published poet, handed Paddy a sheet of paper. She was his poetry supplier, lending him slim vols. On her recommendation he'd ordered Elizabeth Bishop. He now had it beside his bed. His poetry reading had floundered somewhere in high school. He was still wired to read poetry, more or less, as fiction, or for sense, which he knew was fairly arrested. He had to admit he liked people in poetry, stories. Bishop's characters and narratives were appealing. Aunt Consuelo at the dentist, the fisherman with his fish that had skin like ancient wallpaper, the oil-stained family who run the petrol station, or 'Filling Station' as the poem is titled, with their dirty dog lying on a greasy wicker sofa. The person in the poem has pulled in to get petrol and amid the oil and dirt, she sees, sort of horrified, there's an embroidered doily on a table, Why oh why the doily, and a begonia, which she calls the extraneous plant. Then the visitor thinks, amazed, sort of humbled, someone embroidered the doily, someone waters the plant, or oils it, she quips. It was also very funny, Elizabeth Bishop's poem. The poem's last line he had by heart, could summon easily and did so from time to time in a jokey fashion: 'Somebody loves us all.' Meaning not God but simply a person close by. He approved. A somebody trying to make a difference, a mark. The somebody was also the poet herself, he saw, whose lines, at the very moment they appeared to judge and to discard, yet loved the things she described. A big hirsute begonia.

Julie said she'd written a poem with them in it—Caleb, Paddy, Julie herself—and she hoped he didn't mind. Paddy asked her to read it. The poem used her son's language to tell the story so it was punctuated with the seeming nonsense of his earlier speech as well as celebrating finally his success. It was also sad somehow. The poem suggested, very lightly, that in getting better, something had been lost. She'd baked Paddy some ginger gems that were in a shopping bag inside a plastic container. 'I don't need the container back,' she said. She had tears in her eyes and Caleb ran into the corridor. 'Be careful, Caleb darling,' she called after him. Then she looked at the wall. 'But you took the picture down,' she said. It had been in the poem. Paddy explained that it was getting remounted. 'I made up a few things about the picture, I hope that was all right,' she said. 'Do you mind me asking what the real story is behind it. I hope it was you!'

'It was me,' he said. 'And I liked your version better.' In the poem the cartoon had been the gift of one of his clients, someone a bit like her son. This had surprised and pleased him, he said. The technique, the freedom to invent even with this most real of events, her son's triumph. Paddy told her the cartoon had been done a number of years ago by a newspaper cartoonist, and that his partner, Helena, had thought it might be fun to hang it in the office.

They were standing in the doorway to the apartment to keep

watch on Caleb. He was putting an eye to the handrail that ran along one wall, trying to see into it.

Paddy remembered how Bill Goldson, or W.G. as he was known, had been commissioned by the editor to do the portrait cartoon after some anniversary, Paddy's first year or his second. The offer of the column had come in the same week that Paddy had officially been confirmed as divorced from Bridget and not long after he'd set up his private practice. One of his first clients had been the son of the deputy editor at the paper and the father had asked him whether he was interested in writing for them. There would be a trial period at first and there wasn't much money. Paddy agreed to it because he thought it might help his business. Surprisingly the thing took off. There were a lot of letters to the editor as well as a steady stream of inquiries to use Paddy's services. Having worked in hospitals, he'd had little more than a hunch about the market demand for more broad-based speech therapy. It happened that setting up his practice coincided with a growing anxiety among parents around their children's abilities to communicate effectively. The question of whether it coincided with a matching increase in such problems was itself part of Paddy's work. He did a lot of assessments that steered potential clients away from him into other more profitable areas for them, namely family guidance sessions, budgeting services, occasionally the family court. Still, soon he had a waiting list.

The letters to the editor waxed and waned though he was assured that in reader surveys the column continued to be very popular. Then he was asked if he wanted a portrait done. This honour usually went to retiring long-timers but there'd been a mini-exodus of star columnists and some shoring up was in order, even involving rather arcane contributors such as himself. They would also use the cartoon, in miniature form, alongside the column each time in a design revamp. There'd previously been nothing except the column name and a by-line. It was a little sweetener and Paddy was touched. In fact the true sweetening was for W.G., who was just then being wooed by their rivals. The commission for drawing the cartoons was foolishly generous, as W.G., breaking his own confidentiality clause, cheerfully informed Paddy during the little presentation ceremony at the pub. 'I'll buy you a drink or seven, Patrick,' he said.

In one corner of the cartoon he'd drawn an object Paddy couldn't identify.

'Cards,' said W.G. 'Playing cards.'

'But I don't play cards.'

He pretended not to hear this. 'They also represent your fate.'

'What is my fate?'

'It's in the cards, Patrick,' he said, moving off with his whisky. No one at the paper knew that Paddy's nickname was Card; the coincidence wasn't amazing and yet it was the one stupid aspect that he grew to like about the picture, this accident.

In those days of course he had a little more hair. Bill, W.G., had suggested through a few wavy lines, some abundance. The cartoon Paddy also had his mouth open, apparently making an 'O'—reference to his profession, which W.G. had not the faintest idea about. His sister Margie had said that it made Paddy look like a slightly uglier Lord Byron about to receive some dental work. Open wide! He'd been given a collar that was too big— this may have been the Byronic echo—a collar on some puffy shirt he would never have worn. Was this some lab coat? He'd asked W.G. about it. 'A cartoon exaggerates, Patrick,' he told him. 'Why choose my collar to exaggerate though?' said Paddy. The rest of him was more or less Paddy. W.G. had no answer to that.

Paddy stood holding the baking and the poem as Caleb's mother smiled. She still had teary eyes. Finally they chatted about Elizabeth Bishop. He should read the letters, Julie said. Caleb came back to them along the corridor. She reached down to pick something off her son's shoe. It was one of Paddy's yellow stickies.

*

148

When the apartment doorbell rang around noon, Paddy had to check his watch. Sam Covenay wasn't due for another hour. Then just as he was opening the door, he had a presentiment of some unwelcome news. Afterwards it felt too occult to be this, yet at the time he thought he heard it in his right ear, the tinnitus of trouble.

The person Paddy wondered about most sharply in that instant was Tony Gorzo. He was coming to tell him why he hadn't called. In all the years of their phone calls they'd only met face to face three or four times. Somehow it suited them. Voices down the line.

He stood in front of Paddy, holding out his hand. 'Good afternoon,' he said. 'I am Iyob.'

Paddy shook his hand. 'I know. I'm Patrick, Paddy.'

Why did Paddy not then say, 'Come in, Iyob'? For some reason, he found himself waiting for the other man, Helena's ex-student, now employee. He'd come from Syria with some business training apparently and Helena had been very pleased to have him on her team. Apart from his skills, the presence on staff of a graduate was itself a great advertisement for the place. Yes, he had worn a bow tie, though not today. He wore fawn-coloured trousers, a white shirt and a blue zip-up windbreaker. Running shoes. He was a neat and compact man, with a black moustache, cropped hair greying at the temples. He was any age from forty-five to fifty-five. Also, as Paddy remembered, he was the source of some recent problem.

Paddy stayed there in the doorway, waiting as if Iyob was trying to sell him something. Except Iyob also seemed to be waiting. As if Paddy were the one who'd dragged him out here, as if it were Iyob's door they stood at.

Finally Iyob spoke again. 'May I come in?'

'Helena's not here of course. She's at the school.'

'Yes, I know this.' He lifted a finger, pointing it at Paddy's chest. 'I am sorry to arrive but you are the one I would like to see.'

'You want to see me?' Paddy began to explain that he worked

149

from home and that he had a client coming soon. Maybe if Iyob rang later.

Iyob held up his hand, showing Paddy five fingers. 'Five minutes. If you are available.'

They sat in Paddy's office. Immediately Iyob was looking at the space where the cartoon used to hang, now marked by the dirty lines on the wall. Paddy felt drawn for a moment to explain, but he held out. Iyob didn't need to know.

'Where is this picture of you?' he said.

'I'm getting it repaired,' said Paddy. 'How did you know?'

'At the party, we leave our coats here. I see this picture.'

'Do you mind me asking how you got in the building, Iyob? Only we're supposed to have this security system.'

'A man in the other apartment.'

'He let you in?'

'The architect.'

'He was an architect? How did you know that?'

'On the buzzer I pushed. I say I make a mistake.'

Meaning he'd done this in a calculated way or that he really had made a mistake? 'You pressed the buzzer for Harley Architects and Geoff Harley let you in?' It seemed wrong to mention Geoff by name, as if Paddy were exposing him to some risk, but this was his fault after all.

'I don't see the name of Helena there. I looked for her name.'

For some reason only Paddy's name had been put on the buzzer panel at the time they'd bought the place and they'd never got around to fixing it. 'We have different names, surnames.'

'Because you are not Dora's father.'

'Dora? No. But how do you know Dora?'

'From the school. She works there.'

'Of course.'

'This is the reason I am here. A problem with Dora at the school.'

'Iyob, I really think this is something to take up with Helena,

150

your employer. I'm not anything to do with the school. Helena is the total boss. I'm not involved.'

'Sorry but you are involved with Helena, true?'

'That's true, with Helena, not the school though.'

'Not the school. I understand.'

'So you see I can't be of help here. If you have an issue which is employment related, you must take it up with Helena. She's a very fair person, you know.'

'I know. She is very fair. She has been so kind to me. But she is the mother to Dora. It's difficult.'

'I think you'll find her very fair even in matters which concern her daughter. Dora's temporary anyway.'

Iyob looked puzzled.

'Not forever,' said Paddy. 'She'll be at the school for only a short time.'

'You know this, you are involved with the school.'

'Not involved in any official way. Helena just mentioned to me, casually you know. We chat about her work sometimes.' This wasn't the line to go down.

'About me? Do you chat, do you know?'

'About you? No.'

'Already I tell Helena, her daughter is not the best for the school.'

'So you've discussed it. Good.'

'Not so good. Because she won't listen too much. Helena is too busy, she is too worried for all these things.'

'The review.'

'The review, yes. Very stress.'

'Stressful.'

'Stressful with everything. Not a good time for another problem, I know.'

'Perhaps after the review, you should bring this up again. Helena has a lot going on. Plus maybe by then Dora will not be there.'

Iyob sat back in his chair, studying the floor. 'You know she makes movies, films? Dora.'

'I know.' Surely she hadn't been having screenings in the lunchbreak.

'You seen?'

'Seen her movies? A little.'

'Good?'

'Silly. Funny.' Paddy shrugged, at a loss. He thought of the prize they'd won in Sydney.

'Comedy?'

'Sort of.'

'I can't believe this. Dora is not very comedy.'

Paddy laughed. Iyob was no fool, no slouch. 'This is true.'

Iyob clasped his hands together and drew a sudden short breath. Was he asthmatic? 'At work she points the camera on me.'

'At work?'

'She puts the camera on her desk and points it on me but I don't know. Is it on, is it off? She says off but I say show me the camera and she says no. She doesn't let me look to check.'

'You think Dora's been filming you secretly?'

'Secret, this is right. For this secret film, I go back to fucking Syria, you know?'

He looked up at Paddy in a sort of challenge, leaning forward as though about to leave his chair. Paddy saw that Iyob was wearing a gold chain around his neck and that it held a cross. Was he a Christian? What difference did that make, were the Christians persecuted in Syria? He'd have to Google it. Syria was next to Iraq. Suddenly Paddy's hideous ignorance about Iyob's life must have been deeply apparent to that life's owner.

'Right. But why would she do that?'

'This girl.' Iyob threw up his hands.

Paddy told him he'd done the right thing, he'd told her he didn't want it to happen, he'd talked to his employer about it. That was all good. He couldn't do any more than that.

'Maybe I break the camera,' said Iyob.

'Oh, sure, break the camera! Why not. But no, not a good idea.'

'I ask her this, please don't put the camera on the desk. First time I look over and start smiling, saying cheese. Good mood from me, you know. Stop, she says. She don't want that. I say, I don't want this film. Fine, she says. No sound on the camera, she says. Okay but don't film please. Sure, sure, she says. Next time she puts the camera in her bag with a hole.'

'Peephole?'

'Peeping! If she was not Helena's daughter, I should take this bag and throw it out the window on the street.'

'Probably you don't want to do that, Iyob. She'll have the message by now, I think.'

Iyob looked around the room. 'Mr Thompson, it's not *Eye*ob. Iyob.'

'Sorry, Iyob. Call me Paddy.'

'Piddy?'

'Paddy, with an a.'

Iyob slumped back in his chair. 'When will she leave the school?'

'Dora? I'm not sure.'

'She tells me, what do you want to hide? Why are you afraid? What is the reason you don't want this film? You work at this desk, what is wrong if I film this? It's life. I make a film of life.'

'You have your privacy.'

'A man from Syria comes to work in a new place. It's interesting she says. There's no smiling. She says I look sad when I work. Perfect like this. Sad man from Syria. Homesick and lonely and suffering. But hey, listen to this. Paddy, I'm not sad! I have my wife, my son. A place to live. I work hard, I like this. I'm very happy to work. New Zealand is a great country.'

'She's making assumptions.'

'She says, I film you, you look very lonely, lost. Lost? Me? You kidding me, I say. But she won't believe it. Incredible, this girl. I say, okay, I make a film too. Girl comes from Thorndon, not happy. She's very angry about something. I don't know, maybe she needs a boyfriend.'

'Okay.'

'She says, no, she don't think so. And I say, a boyfriend to make her happy. Get married. No, no, she tells me. Because she has a *girlfriend*, she tells me. This girlfriend makes her very happy. Then I say, well, this is not the same thing. Paddy, what I believe is it's not right for this to happen. Homosexuals. See, it's my beliefs. You have different beliefs maybe, or the same.'

'Different.'

'Sure. But you are not homosexual.'

'No. But I don't have your beliefs.'

'Okay. And you stand up for your beliefs. Like me. But Dora, she says, no, because I'm a—bigot, she says. A bigot. I know what it means. In my upbringing, I think she has a perversion, okay. I say this.'

'This is where it went wrong, I think.'

'I don't tell her what to do but I believe it. No, she gets mad, says I am harassing her. I can't work here if I have this belief. So on, so on. Shouting, whatever. Goes to her mother, tells her I'm a terrible man. You think I will lose my job now? I think so. But before Dora comes, everything is very nice at school, very good work, very happy people. Dora doesn't like happy people. If you are very unhappy, you try to spread this. What everyone is, they try to make this the same in everyone. I'm mad so my English goes fucked. But you try to make the same as you, this is what's happening everywhere. These terrorists, you know, it's like it. They love death, so it's easy for them to say, you can be dead like me. Boom! Now I lose my job. Fair or not fair? Ask me.'

He'd finished this speech standing up and pointing his finger, his face coloured with the effort. He took a handkerchief from his pocket and wiped his mouth.

'I don't think Dora is a terrorist,' said Paddy.

'Not what I mean,' said Iyob.

'I understand.'

Iyob gave a brief noise, like a laugh. Then he held up five fingers. Five minutes. 'What you can do?' He shrugged. Was he asking Paddy what he could do, or was he expressing the notion that there was nothing to be done. Having spoken so forcefully, he now seemed almost at once to be completely deflated. Perhaps he was simply exhausted. It had cost him an enormous amount of energy to come to the building, to find Paddy, and then to say all of this. He shook Paddy's hand and thanked him. Paddy muttered something about talking to Helena and how he hoped the situation could be resolved. Iyob barely took this in.

Paddy looked at the bag that was beside his desk and remembered the gift from Caleb's mother. He took the container out and opened the lid, passing them over to Iyob. 'Please,' he said.

Iyob moved his face close to the baking. 'Who made this?'

Paddy explained briefly about Julie and Caleb. He found himself showing Iyob the poem. Iyob took the sheet and spent several moments scanning it. It was if he were reading it for clues as to what he should do in his situation with Dora. Perhaps Paddy hadn't explained this very well. Iyob used his finger to move along each line and he made slight noises with his lips. Paddy ate a ginger gem and waited. Iyob then passed the poem back to him. 'I understand, then nothing,' he said. 'Is this English?'

'It's English being tripped over,' said Paddy. 'A person trying to say sounds.'

Iyob held a ginger gem, turning it around and investigating it. The shape, with its flat top and angled base, did look strange. Then he wrapped it in his handkerchief and put it in his jacket pocket. 'I bring you nothing.' He looked disconsolate. Paddy told him he didn't need to bring anything. Still Iyob seemed unconvinced.

After Iyob left, Paddy called Helena but she wasn't available. She was sourcing new whiteboards in Petone.

When Angela Covenay arrived with Sam, Paddy asked if he could speak to her in private for a few minutes. Sam immediately turned away and walked off a few paces down the corridor. Paddy had invited him to wait in the living room but to no effect. Angela told her son not to disappear anywhere. Paddy noticed that after she'd spoken, she waited a few seconds, looking at his back, as if sound took this long to travel to Sam Covenay. They left the door to the apartment open a little and went inside where they sat in his office. Paddy didn't like the boy in the corridor but there wasn't anything to be done. Sam was going out the way he'd come in, Paddy thought, in a pose of direct contravention, piggish and staunch and stupid.

'How do you think Sam is?' said Paddy. This was more or less the most dishonest opening possible in the circumstances and in the moment it took Angela to adjust herself to the question, he took up his own inquiry. 'Because I don't think it's working.' Bluntness sprang from him. He'd imagined something more shaded than this but also he didn't regret it. He'd tried this once before and he needed to be more forceful. Also the agitation of Iyob's visit was still with him. Angela was wide-eyed, as if she'd been slapped. 'He could keep on coming here and sitting in the corner but it would be a waste of everyone's time. Yours, mine, his. It would be unprofessional of me to continue to treat your son, Angela. I can't do anything for him. In fact, he's gone backwards since our first sessions. I'm very sorry about this. I'm suggesting we end the treatment. Obviously we won't meet today and I'd like to revisit the fees over the entire period. I feel I've done nothing for you but I know you're unlikely to accept any conditions that put you in a position of appearing to have gained an advantage. Angela, you have not gained an advantage. I've failed here. It happens. I should have spoken up sooner, that was negligent. Sam needs someone else, not me.'

She was staring at him, amazed and hurt. She seemed determined not to cry. Her face was flushing. 'You don't think something, something small even, is happening? Might happen?'

'No, I don't.' He thought at once of the moment that ended their clinic a week before, but he believed he managed not to let this tiny and confusing piece of information show. That had been pure hopefulness on Paddy's part. Sam had just wanted out of there as fast as possible and had accidentally bumped him on the way past. And the moment hadn't been repeated at their last clinic.

Angela was regrouping, looking at her feet, which were in black brogues, almost like a school shoe. Her entire outfit was more businessy than normal. As if answering his thoughts about her appearance, she said quietly, 'I have a job interview later on. Council job.'

He wished her luck and she flinched slightly.

She sat silently for a while and when she spoke again she sounded more solid. 'Your professional opinion is very valuable to us, Patrick. And you've worked very hard, despite what you say. We appreciate that. Let's not even mention fees and money. Let's not. This is Sam's future.'

The sunshine was coming into the room, polishing the wooden floors. The southerly had whacked the city for a while. Now they got the reward. Intense blue sky, sunshine, stillness, the smell of the trees. He wanted to be on his bike.

'I agree, which is why it's important not to linger here.' His mind went quickly in search of the idea he'd had on his ride with Lant, something to replace Sam's current pose rather than cure it. He was cutting the Covenays loose but with this notion: Sam was now The Boy Who Couldn't Be Cured. Maybe this was what he'd been looking for all along, to defeat Paddy. Then let him have it. Everyone could move on once he'd been granted the victory. It had only been Paddy's pride that had kept the relationship going so long.

'Linger?' said Angela. 'Malinger, you mean?'

'I didn't mean that. He's a boy of tremendous will-power.'

'Sometimes I think he's the devil.' It was a statement of precision, delivered as if the facts were practical in nature, almost obvious. *I think he has shingles.* She'd lifted her heels and let them fall as she spoke, giving emphasis. She glanced in the direction of the door as if Sam might be listening. 'I'm not religious at all. This would be a secular devil.'

'With saints for parents,' said Paddy.

'We're certainly not that, Patrick. He drives us insane. Half the time I want to hit him very hard.' She clenched her hand involuntarily into a fist and regarded it with surprise, releasing immediately. She was blushing all along her neck now and up her ears, which looked painfully red. 'Alan is better than I am. He has control, or he did have. The feeling of rage is there. It comes out in unusual places. Last month he resigned from his cricket club where he's played for twenty years. Turns out he punched a man, his teammate. This is Alan! My gentle giant. He can't remember the circumstances but it was over nothing. He wrote a letter of apology. He doesn't return customers' calls sometimes. I'm just as bad, worse. At the dry-cleaners a few weeks ago I had a horrible woman complaining. She left some things, special care items. I took them to the dump bin out the back and threw them in. When she came back I watched my brother looking everywhere for the clothes. I'll pay him back. Hence the job interview. This is why I think my son is the devil. But we're the devils, aren't we. He does nothing but sit back and watch.'

'I can give you the name of an educational psychologist for Sam.'

This failed to penetrate. It felt such a weightless offer. They'd already been down that route. She looked up at the space where the cartoon usually hung. 'I have one more confession to make. This week Alan finally got around to fixing your picture. He was very sorry about it and how long it took. Ridiculous.'

Paddy started to say that this wasn't important but she held up her hand to stop him.

'Anyway, it's all done. He brings it upstairs and leaves it by the front door so we'll remember to bring it today. It's wrapped in brown paper. That was two nights ago. When I saw it again the next morning, the wrapping paper was torn a bit though the picture was still there. I asked Alan whether he'd had to do something else to it but he said he hadn't touched it. Sam was in his bedroom of course, music on. We both had a bad feeling about it, so we took it into the kitchen and pulled out the picture on the table there. You may remember, well of course you will remember, the cartoon was free floating in its frame.'

'I remember.'

'Sam had remounted it on card, given it a border. He'd worked with Alan's stuff that he keeps in the garage. He'd done a nice job, very neat. He has an eye for it actually, which is what Alan always said. You probably think it strange that we looked at that first but I suppose for me I was imagining the whole thing torn up or something. But it was well presented. Alan said he'd thought of card-mounting it himself but didn't want to bother you with it and he was feeling silly about the length of time he'd had it.'

'No,' said Paddy, 'because the space where it used to hang has itself been a great talking point. I'm thinking of keeping it like that. Why not let everyone imagine their own story around that gap?'

Angela looked as though she didn't quite follow this. She was struggling with some other thought. 'The frame is the first thing. But it's not what matters. It's the picture that matters.' She splayed the fingers of her right hand and looked at them. 'You know the work he does on his hands, Sam's hands. He likes art. I think. What do I know? Patrick, he's redrawn your cartoon.'

'I see.'

'He's the devil.'

'What has he done to me?'

'Removed a lot of the hair.'

'Okay.'

'Changed the mouth.'

'Yes.'

'Adjusted some of the clothing, I think.'

'Are my collars gone? I had big collars.'

'You wear an ordinary shirt now.'

'The boy's a genius. Anything else?'

'You're older. It's photographic almost, the likeness. What does he do every session but get a chance to steal looks at you.

He's been looking closely, he must have been. The detail. Don't think I'm excusing it in any way. It's an outrage. A crossed line.'

'Can I see it?'

'It's in the car. I didn't want to have it with us straight away. I was going to give it to you and explain when I picked him up. There was some crazy idea I had that he would apologise to you.'

'That was crazy.'

'No, that actually perhaps this was some special crisis point in, in—the treatment. Something?'

'I doubt it.' Again the moment in the doorway came to him.

'Okay.' She dropped her head. 'It was Alan's idea first to simply get rid of it, throw it away and say he lost it, it was stolen, something. Give you money. Then we thought at least show it to him.'

'How amazing.'

'I'm deeply deeply sorry, Patrick. It's ruined. It's just vandalism. We're ashamed and horrified. Yet I brought him here today for help. From the very person he's abused. Tell me what we can do. But we can't do anything.'

At that moment they heard voices coming from the corridor and they both stood up. There was a knock on the half-open door and Geoff Harley stepped inside. 'Sorry to barge in,' he said, 'but I met your mother downstairs.'

'Yes?' said Paddy.

Geoff turned and ushered Teresa inside the doorway. She was dressed in her nightgown. She was wearing her headphones around her neck, the microphone attached and hanging against her chest. Her eyes were glassy and her mouth hung open slightly. She looked wrecked, sleepless.

'She seemed a bit disorientated. She was checking her mailbox and then she couldn't remember her apartment number. I'm afraid my French wasn't quite up to it. Her English is really quite good but she did seem confused.'

'Ma?' said Paddy.

She looked up at him. 'Oui? Yes?' She reached for his hand. 'Patrick!' she said. *Patreeck*. 'How stupid of me. I haven't been sleeping well. This building, I got a bit lost, that's all.' *Beelding. Loss.* She turned then to Angela and tried to smile.

'Bonjour,' said Angela. 'Je m'appelle Angela and voici mon fils, Sam.'

Teresa turned to Paddy. 'What did she say?' She faced Angela again. 'I am sorry for interrupting. Please excuse me.'

Then Sam Covenay stepped forward from the shadows and Paddy watched him bend down and kiss his mother on both cheeks.

Part Two

1

He called Lant, who called someone in neurology—Murray Blanchford, whom Paddy didn't know. Blanchford called back within minutes. They quickly went over his mother's immediate condition though Paddy didn't say anything about the French accent. Let him come upon that. He talked about confusion, disorientation, some speech issues. Blanchford knew who Paddy was since Lant had told him. He wanted to know whether Paddy had observed any behaviour that might suggest dementia. Paddy said there'd been nothing. Mentally, his mother had been very sharp. This was more in the nature of something sudden. Then Paddy drove his mother to the hospital, phoning Helena on the way and leaving her a message to the effect that they were getting things checked out and there was no actual emergency. 'She's walking around by herself,' he said. He also left the same message for Stephanie. Through it all, Teresa sat quietly, responding with nods to his questions about how she was feeling. She kept bringing her fingers to her lips and lightly pinching them together. She apologised repeatedly.

In the car they stopped at some lights and a school party crossed in front of them.

'Who are they?' she asked suddenly. *Oo are dey*?

'Schoolkids,' said Paddy.

'I know they're schoolkids, Patrick. I mean, from which school?' *Patreek*.

They were dressed in blue blazers, caps. Boys mainly but a few girls. He said he didn't know.

'I don't really know the Wellington schools,' she said.

He reached over and pressed his hand against hers. She made a small sound of surprise at this, as if he'd got the tone wrong and reassurance wasn't what she needed. She was deep in her stoic mode now. In profile, looking straight out through the windscreen, she was a statue of classical indifference. He'd never seen her cry actually. When his father died, and then his uncle, in that vortex of tragedy, she'd gone into her room and not a sound was heard. She'd emerged to cook dinner for them. He was full of anxiety now. But also he was excited, he had to admit, enlivened almost. What had happened to his mother? He wasn't unfeeling.

At the hospital they went straight into an examination room where Murray Blanchford soon joined them. He was small, serious, with a short grey beard over some rough scarred-looking skin. He rubbed a pen through the beard when he listened, which produced a slight rasping sound.

He asked Teresa whether she'd like to sit on the bed or on a chair. She pointed at a chair.

'Let's begin,' he said. 'How do you feel, Mrs Thompson?'

She shrugged. 'Foggy.'

'I'm sorry, could you repeat that please?'

She said the word again. *Fergy.*

'Foggy,' said Paddy.

'And when did you start feeling like this?'

'I don't know.'

Paddy explained about the morning, how she'd been disorientated in the building.

'You've felt okay leading up to this morning?'

'Yes.'

'Any moments in the past week or so where you've forgotten things, mislaid things, felt confused?'

'No.'

'Have you had any episodes, that you can recall, when you may have blacked out, maybe lost some time? Anything like that?'

She shook her head. Then he asked her if she was taking any medication. No. They'd get some blood tests done, he said. Liver, kidney function. Just normal stuff.

Blanchford worked his pen through the beard, noting nothing though he had a file open on the desk in front of him. 'I'd like to ask you to do some physical things, very simple, to see how everything's working, Mrs Thompson.'

Teresa nodded, felt her lips.

He asked her to hold out both arms, palms upwards, as if carrying a tray, and to close her eyes and count to ten. For a moment she didn't follow this and Blanchford mimed it. The Barre manoeuvre. Paddy watched her hands. They remained level. Good. Then Blanchford got her to lift one arm slowly above her head and then the other. He asked her to flex her fingers. He wanted her to turn her head from side to side and then to look up and down. Covering one eye with her hand, he asked her to hold out an arm, then to repeat the action on the other side. 'Now raise both arms together, keeping your eyes closed, please.'

Paddy watched his mother's arms come up at the same rate and to the same height. Good again.

While remaining seated, she had to extend first one leg, then the other in front of her. Standing, he got her to move her arms out to the side. 'Now could you just walk across the room and come back.'

Paddy had seen all of this before. But he'd never seen his mother do it. He was watching in a sort of trance. She accomplished each task carefully, solemnly, and when Blanchford told her to relax, she slumped in her chair, drained. He wrote something down. Naturally she'd been terrified of failing one of these tests. That they were finished meant little. For Paddy, there were no obvious signs of weakness but Blanchford might have seen something he didn't like. They weren't to know.

'Now I'm going to just feel very lightly around your head, if I may. Please tell me if you feel any discomfort, pain.' Blanchford walked behind her and rested his fingers on the back of her head. Then he began feeling around. He was looking away from her as he did this, as if to watch his own hands would interfere somehow with their deeper sensory knowledge, or as if he was some brilliant musician, turning away from his instrument when he played. It was a bit quacky, or he was deeply talented.

Teresa had closed her eyes.

Blanchford stopped at certain points, resting his fingers in her hair. Above her right ear, he lifted the hair and looked. 'When did this happen? You had a little cut or something here.'

Teresa opened her eyes. She appeared puzzled.

'It must be from where you fell last month,' said Paddy. 'In the bathroom, remember. She had a few stitches put in.'

'Any problems since then?' said Blanchford. 'Headaches? Dizziness?'

Teresa shook her head. 'Nothing.' *Nuteen*. She gripped the edge of her seat as if she was about to topple over.

A subdural haematoma? Paddy should have considered this possibility earlier.

Blanchford was writing in the file with sudden fluency. He was reassuringly old-fashioned in this regard, being unable to talk and write at the same time.

The room contained the sheeted bed, four chairs with metal legs, and a computer workstation where Blanchford was writing. There was a keyboard but no monitor. The cord for the monitor sat above the keyboard, as if someone needing a monitor had come and snapped it off. This was probably what had happened, Paddy thought. A set of shelves above the workstation carried a single box of tissues. By the bed was a tall metal cupboard, and in the corner by the door, a rubbish bin with a paper bag liner. There were no windows. Paddy had spent years in such rooms.

'Can we go home now?' said Teresa.

Murray Blanchford looked up. 'So I would like to talk about speech.'

Of course she'd said *ome* for home.

'Okay,' said Paddy, 'so this is not her voice.'

'This is not my voice,' said Teresa.

168

Blanchford had stopped writing. 'Okay.'

'I don't sound like this usually.'

'There's been a change,' said Paddy.

Blanchford sat back, considering. He looked at his pen. After a moment, he held it up. 'Can you tell me what this is, Mrs Thompson?' Blanchford held up his pen.

'A pin.'

'And this?' He indicated his chair.

'Cheer,' she said. 'Char, you know.' She gave Paddy a panicked look. 'Seat, okay. Where you seat. I know what it is! The main problem is I haven't slept. So you're seeing me at a low point, I'm afraid.'

They took the lift to radiography and then, while Teresa was being prepared, Blanchford led Paddy along the corridor, looking into offices. They found an empty one with a computer and Blanchford sat down behind the desk, tapping quickly at the keyboard. 'What are you doing?' said Paddy.

'It's a powerful diagnostic tool.'

Paddy walked around behind him. Blanchford was Googling accent acquisition.

He pointed at the screen. 'Here. Astrid L.'

Together they read about the Norwegian woman, knocked unconscious in a bombing raid in 1941, who'd come around with a strong German accent. Her neighbours then drove Astrid L. out of her home town on suspicion she'd been a spy.

'Where does your mother live?' said Blanchford.

'In town.'

'Probably safe then. From the intolerant neighbours, I mean.'

So they were by themselves, they could joke now? Paddy stayed grim.

Foreign Accent Syndrome. FAS. An urban legend sort of condition that Paddy had paid no attention to. A team from Oxford University was working on it.

Blanchford sat back in the chair. 'Sorry, of course this is not a diagnosis at all. We're surfing the Internet for God's sake. We need the scan and so on. Probably not meaningful to give your mother this information at the moment, but up to you.'

In most cases of FAS, the change was temporary. The accent disappeared after a few hours.

'You've not seen it yourself then in your work?' said Blanchford.

'No.'

'It's certainly more refined than the usual word salad. Dysphasics are ten-a-penny but French? My wife speaks French. She considers it horribly lazy and arrogant of me, which it is, but personally I'm waiting for all the world to catch up with us and speak English. It's happening, you know, even in France.'

Paddy turned from the screen to look at him. 'Sorry, I wasn't listening.'

Helena and Stephanie arrived together at the imaging room. They'd met each other in the hospital car park. Paddy was hugged fiercely. Stephanie held on to him. He marvelled again at his sister's physical power. Post-motherhood, she was a sturdy, ample person. Her cheeks were always red and full. The young Steph, his little sister, he remembered as narrow, wan even. Having babies had not robbed her of a certain nervous tension but it had given her an entire sphere in which she was not tense at all. Her daughters, remarkably, were not fussed over. She'd dumped them, she said, with a neighbour. 'What are they saying, Paddy, is it a stroke?'

'They're not saying anything, Steph.'

'Dementia? Alzheimer's? The kids are so young for this to happen.' She meant her kids. 'Who's told Margie?'

'All they're doing is some tests. We should ring Margaret afterwards.'

'She had the stomach bug and no one went round to see her!'

'Could be totally unrelated, Steph.'

'And then she skives off to Palmerston North! Alarm bells should have rung then. She was hiding, was she? Poor Mummy.'

'Probably didn't want to be a burden,' said Helena.

'But that's what people are to each other, burdens,' said Stephanie. 'Look at me!'

'We should call Pip too.'

They were sitting in a row of chairs along the back wall of a room mostly taken up with the controls for the scanner, which could be seen through a viewing window. A technician entered and sat in front of his board of lighted switches, making adjustments. They began to speak in whispers as before a show or a play.

'Where is Teresa now?' said Helena.

'Being sedated for the scan,' said Paddy. 'They're getting her ready.'

'Sedated?' said Stephanie. 'Is that normal?'

'She wanted it,' he said. 'She'd developed this shake she couldn't control.'

Stephanie made a whimpering sound. 'I want to see her before it happens,' she said. 'She's my mother.' Paddy remembered something Teresa had said to him once about his little sister, 'Everything comes out. Stephanie says all the things we think. It makes her seem stupid. But we're all stupid aren't we.'

Helena took her hand. He was grateful she was there.

A voice came through a small speaker above the glass panel. The technician pressed a button and said something in response. Then their mother walked into view.

Stephanie gasped. Paddy was aware too that Helena drew back. Teresa looked tiny within the frame of the window. A hologram almost, performing in a spray of fluorescence. Dressed in a hospital gown, she wandered towards the glass, looking directly at them it seemed, feeling with her hands for the way. She pressed a hand against the glass. The technician on their side was gesturing to her to move away and sit down. It was

171

fantastically theatrical, grotesque. Where was everyone? How could she be alone in there? On reflex, Stephanie stood up and said their mother's name and held out a hand before realising what she was doing. The technician glanced around at them. A nurse appeared beside Teresa and drew her back towards the scanner. Stephanie sat down again.

Paddy had never lived easily with the next image, the human body tied down and inserted into the narrow perfectly machined space. MRIs were worse but even the CT doughnut was hard to take. He'd attended a few of them in his time at the hospital. In the bad old days of Bridget's mystery illness he'd had to be here and Bridget's own calm in the face of the procedure was no help. Her submission threw into sharp relief his near panic. He got through it now by studying his watch. The gesture observed by anyone would have suggested great calm, even boredom perhaps. But, he thought, we are all stupid.

For the time their mother lay confined there, strapped in, her head fed into the gleaming cylinder then pulled out again to be reinserted, the process happening several times, he felt pressed upon by thin wet sheets of metal. His watch-strap was silver and it seemed to turn too in his eye.

They couldn't hear the scanner through the glass panel but he could easily imagine the noise, which was a whirring, and this entered his ear somehow, causing his familiar symptom. His cochlea could be examined with a CT scan, but it was something he hoped to avoid. He was a health professional and finally as squeamish as Tony Gorzo had been, shaking his finger, trying not to hear what could happen, what did happen, every day, to someone. Someone like this.

Helena whispered beside him, 'What are they looking for?'

He had to wait several moments before he could answer. 'They're just looking,' he said finally. The haematoma would be picked up easily. Lesions could be trickier. A tumour. CTs could miss those. They'd have to come back in a few days for the MRI anyway. The CT was precautionary more than anything else, to find out whether they needed to start emergency stroke medicine. Blanchford would be looking in Broca's especially. If something was pressing there, the vocal cords might be affected, the length of syllables. Odd to think of such units now, that a syllable had put them all in this place. A flush heated his neck and travelled up.

They were allowed to take Teresa to the hospital café as long as they returned her for final clearance once the sedative had worn off. She was back in her clothes and she seemed like a different person, different again. Still not her.

'What do you feel like eating, Ma?' said Stephanie, who'd walked her arm-in-arm along the corridors.

'Every-ting!' said Teresa. She squeezed her daughter's arm and giggled. She began loading muffins and sandwiches and cakes on her tray.

The change in her demeanour was striking and almost totally a side-effect of the drug in her body. Paddy wasn't sure she'd fully taken in what Murray Blanchford had just told them having looked at the scan images. No evidence of stroke, no evidence of tumour, and no evidence of haematoma.

'That's strange then, isn't it,' said Teresa.

Stephanie had begun to cry quietly at this point.

'But I'd still like to do an MRI for a better picture,' said Blanchford.

'Then you'll find the collpreet.'

Blanchford leaned forward, trying to hear the word.

'Culprit,' said Helena.

At the table Paddy said, 'What's happening, Ma? How do you feel?'

'Great. I feel fine.' She clapped her hands. Everyone had to laugh at that.

'You sound like a frog,' said Stephanie.

'Very bizarre, I know,' said Teresa.

'What will the kids say when they hear you?'

'They'll chase me around and say do dee do dee do!'

173

'When did it happen, Teresa?' said Helena.

'Thérèse,' she said, smiling, making her name fully French. 'Trees are green. Thérèse, never. Vendredi. It was last vendredi.'

'What are you, bilingual now?' said Stephanie.

'No. Just a couple of words. I bought a dictionary. She told me my English was very good!' She laughed and put more food in her mouth. She was ravenous.

'French pig!' said Stephanie.

Paddy exchanged looks with Helena. He hadn't yet had a chance to say anything to her about Iyob, whose visit seemed ancient, belonging to another zone.

'Mummy, are you kidding us?' said Stephanie. 'Are you having a joke?'

'Yes.'

'You are?'

'Yes, you are.'

'Well that doesn't make sense to say that. "Yes, you are." Don't go crazy as well, please.'

'I wondered whether you've been playing online against someone from France?' said Paddy.

Their mother stopped eating to consider this question but then failed to answer.

'Do you feel tired at all?' said Helena. 'Tiredness can make the brain do all sorts of things.'

'You had that bug,' said Stephanie.

'Then the bus ride to Palmerston North,' said Paddy.

'Where?'

'Palmerston North, to see Pip.'

'Pup?'

'Peep,' he said.

'Oh,' she said vaguely. 'Yes, now she told me to get it checked out. She's full of—sense, Pip. But we laughed all the time too. You know I don't know what I'm doing here. I feel completely normal, except for . . .' She was searching for the way to complete the sentence but finally gave up.

174

'You sound, when you speak English, utterly French, you know that?' he said.

'Patrick, I'm not mad! I can hear myself. I'm fully aware of this.' *Theese.*

'Have you taken any new medication?'

'Oh my gosh! Yes, I took these new French pills, do you think that's it?'

'What French pills?'

'Oh, please, I was joking!'

'Joking just for that or the whole thing?'

'For that, about the pills. I haven't done anything, taken anything. I woke up last Friday and I thought, "It's vendredi", that's all. So I looked it up and it meant Friday. And I knew how to say it, apparently. There'd been an item on the radio.' *Rardee-o.*

'What item?' said Stephanie.

She explained about the French truck drivers, the snail. 'Voilà!'

'Voilà?' said Paddy. It was something Murray Blanchford should know.

'Thinking about it, you know, maybe here's an opportunity, I thought to myself.'

'For what?' said Stephanie.

'For . . . enchantment.' She regarded her plate of food happily. 'Although I wonder how I'll feel when it wears off. I must talk a lot until then! I must embrace it. I must!'

They ate in silence for a while after that. Despite her excited announcement, his mother appeared to be running low. She rallied again however. 'I don't like the idea of having my brain scanned,' she said, seemingly unaware it had already happened. 'If I've had a stroke, then it's a done deal. I've had a stroke. Now get on with it. If I'm sick another way, if there's a tumour in there which is doing all this talking, I feel okay, let him or her have a brief say. We've never heard from a tumour before, or at least I haven't. A French tumour!'

'Let's not talk about things like that,' said Stephanie.

175

'Okay, darling.'

Helena's phone rang and she moved away from the table to answer it. There were only a few other people in the café. Every so often a café worker appeared to look over the food and to take away empty plates.

Now there seemed a strange sullenness to things. The druggy fun they'd all taken advantage of seemed cheap, unreal. Soon they'd have to drive home. The clean CT scan had delivered an odd sort of result: one that was both deeply promising and deeply puzzling.

It was dark outside. They'd lost sense of time. A woman in a stained white tunic flicked off the lights above the warm food counter. An orderly appeared at the door with a mop, looked around the café, and then reversed out in the same direction moon-walk fashion, grinning. Paddy recognised at once the little provoking amusements of hospital life.

Helena came back and apologised. When Paddy looked again at his mother she'd paused almost in mid-bite. She held a piece of cake, which after a few moments she returned to her plate. She sat glumly watching the cake. There was a sense of utter emptiness in her look, as if the sedation's exuberant tide had suddenly sucked everything from her. She raised her head. They were all looking at her. She was afraid of them. What did she feel like right then—a foreigner? 'Don't lock me up, will you?' she said.

They had to listen carefully now since the accent was very thick.

'What?' said Stephanie. There were tears in her eyes. 'What did she say?'

'Darling,' said Helena, taking his mother's hand.

He sat with Helena in his mother's kitchen. The only light came from a lamp in the hallway. Teresa was asleep in the bedroom. Stephanie had stayed for an hour or so and then she'd had to pick up her girls and get them to bed. There was the barbecue fundraiser the next evening at Isabelle's school, Stephanie reminded them. She was expected on one of the stands. 'Your friend's band is playing too,' she told Paddy. 'But we can't go, can we. We can't. What are the rules now? What do we do?' They agreed to decide on all that in the morning.

They'd found a note from Medbh pushed under the apartment door—everyone was pushing notes under their door!—saying she could come later in the week and she'd ring tomorrow to confirm. On their phone there was a message from Angela Covenay who was sending her best wishes. She hoped everything was all right. Stephanie would be phoning Margaret, which was most likely a mistake though Paddy was glad not to have the job.

Helena and Paddy had been over the possible causes, the possible outcomes. They were both deliriously tired. For Helena of course it was a compounded tiredness. How had she kept going? On her laptop they'd read again as many Foreign Accent Syndrome stories as they could handle. There were references in German she'd struggled through, though these cases were from the early 1900s.

More recently, these. An elderly Egyptian woman in Cairo wakes up speaking in a thick Scottish brogue. An Argentinean polo player falls off his horse and speaks what one observer identifies as Gaelic. A young professional Czech speedway rider, Matej Kus, crashes in a race in Glasgow and is heard to speak perfect English to the paramedics attending him. Kus has only ever been able to speak a few English phrases with a heavy Czech accent.

'A boy at my high school,' said Paddy, 'his mother became a witch, which is not the same thing, but this reminds me of that. They got a special oven in their backyard.'

'Coven?'

'Oven. Do witches bake something?'

Helena didn't know.

'Part of me thinks, just go with it,' he said. 'Take her lead. Take Teresa's lead, or Thérèse. But which one? The enchanted mother or the one scared out of her wits?'

'The key thing is that the whole business is temporary, that seems to be the pattern.'

'Already she's lasted longer than most.'

'I have a good feeling about the morning,' said Helena. 'I believe in the basic goodness of sleep. If only I could get some.' She closed the laptop. This gave him an unexpected and strong feeling of loss. Their options for finding out more and more seemed over now. It was the first time he'd ever felt this way about the Internet. Helena leaned across and kissed him kindly on the forehead. The kiss sent a little buzzing right down his left leg to the sole of his foot.

Often the apparent oddness of Foreign Accent Syndrome could be explained through some distant connection. The Egyptian woman with the brogue had had a Scottish nanny, something like that. In none of these cases did the sudden rearrangement last longer than a day or two and frequently the victim returned to normal in a matter of minutes. The Czech motorcyclist, Kus, was particularly disappointed. Speaking through an interpreter, once he'd recovered—that is, lost—his facility, he said, 'I was hoping I could go on speaking English like that. It's very important to travel and compete on the international circuit to have English but now I'll have to learn it like everyone else, which is a real pain. I think I'll try to have another smash.' He was a member of the Berwick Bandits and the team's English promoter said, 'I never really believed it was possible but this incredible thing was happening in front of us.'

There was an exception they found.

'Poor Linda Walker from Newcastle kept going for weeks,' said Paddy. 'What happened finally, we don't know. There was no follow-up piece that we found. Did we look every-where?'

Following a stroke, Linda Walker had developed an accent that was a mixture of Jamaican, Canadian and Slovak. She jumped around from day to day. 'I've lost my identity, because I never talked like this before. I'm a very different person and it's strange and I don't like it. I didn't realise what I sounded like, but then my speech therapist played a tape of me talking. I was just devastated.'

Away from the Oxford team, there was another theory about FAS. If the brain was unaffected, there was the possibility it was a fine motor skills problem, an adjustment of troublesome phonemes. The speaker, unable to make the old distinctions, begins substituting sounds and ends by mimicking the whole accent. That was potentially the best news they'd heard all day. Phonemes were his kind of thing. Pad, pat, bad and bat.

Helena placed her hand on the laptop, sealing it even more completely. 'Your mother hasn't had a stroke. On first look. That's a huge plus.'

'True.'

'A huge plus, I'd say.'

'On a first look, no stroke. I agree. And no evidence of a tumour, on a first look. CTs miss lots of tumours, we know that.'

'But nothing yet.'

'And there are no huge blood clots there, so that's good.'

'Very good.'

'The brain is a strange beast.'

'Sometimes there's a knock to the system. Then things settle down.'

'One scenario, there was a haematoma from her bathroom fall, it dissipated naturally, she'll return to her old self.'

'It's a definite possibility.'

They'd already been through all this. Yet it was good to hear it once more. Their terms of reference weren't at all high-flown or particularly informed but it was Murray Blanchford himself who'd given them nearly all their statements. These were his words they traded and somehow even an adjective as weak as 'strange' took on an almost medical depth. Once he'd given up on humour, Blanchford had proved a straightforward and decent person.

'We know that the brain,' said Helena, quoting Paddy from

several minutes earlier quoting Blanchford, 'has extraordinary powers of recovery.'

'Extraordinary powers full stop,' he said.

'Who knows what decisions are being made by it as we speak, as she sleeps, recovering. Who knows?'

'We can only guess.' Paddy took her wrist and held it. He felt the broad bones and against his thumb, the tendons. He felt the pulse. Perhaps it was his own pulse beating in the tips of his fingers as they touched each other in the circling grip. 'Or, you know, it's not brain-related at all.'

'Motor skills,' she said.

'Exactly. Before all this, she probably knew what French bread was, a baguette. She's been to England and Scotland and Ireland and to Canada but not to Quebec and she's been to Australia. I think that's it. The adventures of an Anglophone. Pourquoi Français? Because she listens to a thing on the news?'

'It's not really French though, is it. It's just what it sounds like. Still, we have the trigger, possible trigger. We don't know how that works but still. The radio. That's good, I think. That's a cause which is entirely harmless. It's motor skills and the radio thing.'

'I think we've solved it!' he said.

'Oh, Paddy.'

He brought her wrist close to himself and placed it against his chest. This, he thought, was calming, one of those gestures that seemed about to unlock forever the mysteries of our individual selves, the way we're trapped in private spheres and the way we long for some kind of curing connection. He saw again the young baby turning its head towards its mother as they stood on the hillside footpath watching the cretinous possessed man bike past in his stupid frenzy.

'You know, Paddy,' said Helena, 'that she might need speech therapy.'

'Crossed my mind,' he said.

'In some ways it's like the orthodontist whose child needs braces.'

The comparison made him think uselessly of Sam Covenay and his closed mouth. His own adolescence even. Orthodontists were psychic vandals, weren't they. 'You think a discount is in order?'

They checked once more on Teresa and left her to it, her astonishing recuperation. Yet even this seemingly peaceful view had its own unsettling dimension of newness and strangeness. She looked pensive and poised somehow, as if ready to snap awake and say something of extreme intelligence. Was this her normal look? When had he last seen his mother asleep? Dozing in a chair perhaps, nodding off in the back seat of a car, but lying in the dark in a bed, watched as a child is watched—never, he thought. He didn't like it. She seemed aware of them.

In the morning he told Helena about Iyob. She listened without saying much, asking for clarification on a couple of points, and then she thanked him. At the mention of the language school she'd switched into a different mode. Paddy felt briefly as though he were someone who'd come to her with a set of problems that she would need to rank in order of importance. As he spoke he felt she was already making calculations, sifting, preparing to gamble. Her eyes flickered with some private boss-like thoughts. She withheld judgement, on either Iyob or Dora. That Iyob had come to the apartment drew no comment, likewise that Dora had presumably lied to her. Would she have admitted filming her mother's staff?

Helena was surrounded by situations of this nature on a daily basis, this was the impression she wanted to give. Her task as leader was to drain emotion from such events and recast them as a set of soluble facts. She and Paddy both knew this was an act. And perhaps she was right to attempt it. She was just trying to make it past the Ministry review. Behind the calm managerial front he saw dead tiredness crossing into resentment. *You bring me this now?*

'What'll you do?' he said.

She stared at him—*you're asking me?*—and then she told him with a controlled sigh that it was very difficult. He'd delivered a message—fine—but he had no rights to know the message's implications. This was when she said thank you. When they stood up to go next door to check on his mother, he half expected them to shake hands. Instead she said, 'You don't need this right now.' And again she kissed him drily on the forehead. Dismissed.

Teresa didn't look wholly revived though she told them she'd had a wonderful sleep. She was dressed and had eaten breakfast. She said she didn't remember certain parts of the day before and hoped she hadn't disgraced herself. Her speech was shy and vaguely singsong. She was attempting to disguise the Frenchness. Each give-away noise was an ill-concealed humiliation for her. She attempted to ask about Helena's day, to commiserate with her on the wretched review process, but this was all done through such contorted and fragmentary phrasing that progress could be made mainly through guesses on their part. Paddy was reminded of Caleb, his most recent graduate, with his ploys at getting his message across. Jimmy Gorzo too, waiting for others to fill in his gaps. Paddy's mother wasn't nearly as practised. She didn't yet know which words were trouble for a French speaker of English. Her sentences were a series of self-ambushes. He had the terrible impression she was trying to listen to herself say each word before it came out, testing it with her brain, burying it back in her larynx, waiting for it to form correctly. Her mouth was terribly tight.

'What are you going to do today?' he said.

The question was awkward. What could she do? What was expected of her now? What was the future for her? He'd meant little more than to make a casual inquiry. 'Nothing special,' she said, horrified, smiling. *Nuteen.* Stephanie was coming over later.

He told her that Murray Blanchford from the hospital was

likely to call. He had her number but he also had Paddy's, he said. If he called her, she should ask him to wait and then Paddy could come and be there as well when he talked to her. There was a possibility that she'd have to go back to the hospital for further tests but that probably wouldn't happen today. Did she understand all that?

She nodded carefully and put the back of her hand against her nose.

Helena stepped closer to her and said, 'We'll be here for you, Teresa. Whatever you need, whatever happens.'

'Thank you so much,' she said quietly from behind her hand. 'I feel so silly.'

After Helena had gone to work, his mother rang him and said, 'I need some milk.'

'Okay.'

'And bread. I tried Steph but she's out already.'

'I can get them for you.'

'Maybe some biscuits for the kids when they come.'

'Sure. Anything else?'

'A little block of Edam cheese.'

He didn't understand her. 'What sort?'

She repeated the word, finding the English pronunciation. Was he going to the supermarket?

'I could go to the supermarket, no trouble.'

'Potatoes. Fruit, I have no fruit. Where did all my food go? I have a list, Paddy.' *Leest.*

'Look in the freezer though. Medbh came and cooked for you. Do you remember that?'

'Of course I remember that.'

The last thing Murray Blanchford told them was that it might be best to carry on as normal, do the same things. Be positive. Maybe all that had happened was Teresa's system had taken a knock, he said, and until they found out otherwise, life should be life.

'You think that will help?' said Stephanie.

Blanchford had shrugged. 'It can't hurt.'

'Be normal, yes,' she said. 'Like nothing's happened.'

Teresa had already stepped into the corridor.

'But keep an eye on her.'

'Of course!'

'I don't know, try not to think of her as sick.'

Stephanie was smiling through tears. 'I don't think of her as sick. She's always been incredibly healthy. Right, Paddy?'

'She vomits once and gets on with things. She cleans up the blood.'

'That's so true! That's her.' And she leaned across and kissed him on the cheek. 'Good old Paddy.'

With this 'return to normal' in mind, on the phone Paddy reminded his mother about the school barbecue. He could still take her if she wanted to go, if she was up to it. They could sit quietly in the corner and watch things for a while. They wouldn't stay long and she'd get to see the girls. The school was very close to the apartment.

'But I couldn't go to that,' she said.

'Okay. Probably you want to rest. I'm not sure if I'll go.'

She was silent on the other end of the phone. 'Don't change your plans because of me, Paddy.'

Then at the point of saying goodbye she said, 'I'm not a prisoner, am I? Then why don't I get the things, why don't I go to the supermarket?'

He thought again of Blanchford's advice about a normal routine. This was too fast. Physically Paddy didn't trust her yet. 'Because I'll go. Because you need to take it easy.'

'What's easy?' she said.

He didn't know whether she meant this philosophically or that simply she'd forgotten what the word 'easy' meant. There was a third and somehow even more distressing possibility, that she'd had trouble understanding him, picking *his* accent. Was this the future? No, the future was phonemes, fine motor skills.

'Can you do one thing for me, Ma?' he said. 'Can you say the word b-a-t?'

'What do you mean can I say it?'

184

'Can you pronounce it for me?'

'Another test?'

'Okay, you don't have to.'

'Bad,' she said and hung up.

When Margaret heard about their mother, she said, 'Don't be stupid, Steph. Let me talk to Paddy.' And then as Stephanie outlined the events, the trip to the hospital, her older sister said, 'Thank God Dad's gone and we're not children. It would have destroyed us all.'

Stephanie phoned Paddy the moment she finished talking to her sister. The call had upset Stephanie, which wasn't unusual with Margie. But this time Paddy figured Margie would have been especially tough. Wrong-footed, she came out fighting. She'd be annoyed Stephanie had known before she had, and then angry that he'd got Stephanie to make the call. Steph, she'd once told him, was lightweight. The only thing holding her up in life was Teresa. Her younger sister's achievements as a mother meant nothing to Margie since she was convinced they relied almost entirely on Teresa's contribution. This was wrong. She also thought, and had said this to Paddy, that the only reason Steph had had a third child was to move one ahead of her in the family stakes. He told her that was ridiculous. She said, 'Sons don't see these things, especially only sons. They don't sense the mechanism at all. Why should they? They exist as little princes of their own kingdoms. But first I had to fight you, and then I had to fight her.'

'All that aggression, Margie!' he said, laughing.

'It gets channelled. Oldest girls are high achievers usually. But all I managed to do was to appeal to a Canadian.'

'A very picky Canadian though.' She'd met her husband when she was working in the kitchen of a resort in Banff. He was a guest: Brian.

'Oh, he had choices in front of him, I guess. Options.'

'The pancakes or the eggs.'

'I don't know which I am in that line-up.'

'You're the maple syrup surely.'

'The fat?'

'The sweet.'

'Oh, good try, little brother.'

On the phone, Margie had said to Stephanie, 'I don't know what I'm supposed to do. And I can't really understand what you say if you keep crying.' They'd already booked their Christmas holidays but if she had to, she could come over for a week or ten days. She'd have to move things around. She'd email their mother anyway. 'She can operate a computer right?'

'Right,' said Stephanie.

'Oh well, so that would be the end of the world if she couldn't do that.'

'I don't know why you're so horrible about it. She's really in a bad way.'

'Okay. In the meantime, I don't know, give me updates.'

Stephanie told Paddy that he should call Margie at once. 'She doesn't really believe anything I say. She wanted to know if Mummy was having us on.'

'It's what we wanted to know too.'

'"What a weird stunt," she said.'

There was always a touch of conspiracy for his big sister in even the plainest arrangement and everyone believed that it was for exactly this reason that Margie had chosen to live overseas, away from the family, that eternal nest of arrangements. 'Better this way, Old Paddy,' she told him once at the airport when he was asking again whether her sons wouldn't enjoy life Down Under. Brian was an optician, relocatable and totally pleasant, but it would never happen. Margie was their blot, Steph had once said. Not in the way of a blot on the landscape that needed to be removed, she added quickly. But the little darkness always in view. A shadow, and one cast by us all, she said. 'I think about her almost every day. Do you think she knows that?'

'Yes,' said Paddy.

The subject of Margie bothered them all. Which was also the

intentional effect of her absence. She was no longer the girl in the boat stamping her foot up and down, wearing out her petulance in mysterious little acts of mayhem. That aspect of fieriness had dwindled with their father's death. Instead there was the peculiarly barren space between her and Teresa. Negotiations there took the form not of tantrums but a kind of carefulness, an excruciating politeness, which was often even harder to take for everyone. It was bleaker that was for sure. And it had zero entertainment value.

It wasn't dawn in Vancouver but Margie sounded lively. 'You know when I got off the phone from Steph,' she said to him, 'I just laughed and laughed.'

'Fair enough,' he said.

'Come on! It's hilarious.'

'It's got that aspect to it.'

'Over here, we put people like that on TV. We give them their own shows, Paddy!'

'I don't think she's quite there yet. Presumably that would take more than looking scared and whispering things.'

There was a silence on the phone, and then she said, 'Anyway, I'm sitting here with my cup of coffee and everyone else is in bed. Sitting in the dark more or less. Strange. It's usually Brian who's up first, puts the coffee on, empties the dishwasher. It's still incredible to me that I'm with this mild and nice person. My boys are the same, so far. A house of good men and they're all mine.'

'How is Brian?'

'You know, he's great. Kids are great.'

He heard some sounds. Was she moving her cup, drinking? 'Pleased to hear.'

There was another silence. She said, 'But they didn't find anything with the tests, right?'

He explained what Blanchford had done and what he'd said. She listened without interrupting. And then he told her about FAS, the two theories. He heard a sudden noise at her end, her raised voice. 'What happened?'

'One of the damn cats just jumped on my lap. Gave me the fright of my life. Out of the dark, Jesus.'

Immediately he felt weary, irritated. 'Listen, Margie, I've got to go. Get my day started. You know as much as we do now. I'll call.'

'Steph falling apart?'

'I don't think that's happening, no.'

'Okay,' she said. 'Good. So what is this, stay by the phone? It might blow over?'

'Pretty much.'

He waited.

She said, 'Hear that?'

'What?'

'It's the cat, the cat is purring, sounds like an engine. She thinks it's heaven, human voices, company in the dark.'

'Okay, Margie.'

'Okay? So what do I do now, go back to bed or something? Thanks a lot, Paddy.' There was a pause. 'You don't have cats, do you?'

She seemed to want the conversation to continue. 'And you're well?' he said finally. 'Everyone's well?'

There was another silence.

'I can come, you know. Tell me and I'll come.'

'Come if you want.'

'Don't sound so keen, Paddy!'

'No, it's just that it's your decision.'

'So do you think I should come right now?'

'Well, you know as much as we do. She's not, as they say, in immediate danger.'

'Right,' she said. 'Because I'm only flying down there if she's on her deathbed. Ha, ha.'

He thought he heard her drinking again, swallowing.

She said, 'How's Helena?'

'Busy.'

'Don't be angry with me, Paddy.'

'I'm not.'

'Don't be, you know. We've had rain for eighteen days straight.'

'You live in Canada.'

'Am I ever to be forgiven for that? But then this occurred to me. She's done it for me, this French business.'

'How so?'

'Because it's one of our official languages. I could take this as a gesture on her part. She wants to come closer!'

'She does want to come closer.'

'Ouch, so now the cat just dug its claws in. So anyway, I got the maps, Dad's maps. I felt your hand in that.'

'Nothing to do with me.'

'Do I believe that? Okay, I believe it. Top marks for Teresa. The boys took one each for their rooms. They look good. Better here than they did over there en masse. I suppose everything else is gone.'

'A lot of stuff, yes.'

'My fault, I guess.'

'What is?'

'That I wasn't there.'

'Jesus, Margie, you can come any time, you know that.'

'No, that's the thing, Paddy, I can't. She needs a lot of notice for my arrivals and so do I. We both require a period of serious preparation. We need to draw ourselves up for even the simplest hellos. No, thinking about it, I don't think now is the time.'

'Fine,' he said.

A moment passed.

'I heard you had a change of government,' she said.

'Ma was one of the people who voted them out.' She'd told him this when he was lamenting the change.

'Really? Her parents would spin in their graves, and Dad.'

'I can't bear to hear their voices, the new lot.'

'They're all the same, the new lot, the old lot.'

'I happen to think that's not true,' he said.

'Look at the markets,' she said. 'The banks. It happens under anyone's watch.'

189

'And now it's been discredited, that approach. Time for new thinking.'

'Obama?'

'I don't know, maybe.'

'One thing has happened here. On that topic. Two American families from Nathan's school are going home.' Nathan was son number two. 'They came four years ago and now they can face it. They told me they can belong again. They can start to feel good about making a contribution to the grand enterprise of their place of birth. I met the mother the day after the election and she cried in the supermarket.'

'And what about you, Margie? Any stirrings?'

She laughed. 'It doesn't take a world event to make me cry in the supermarket! Besides, go home to a National government? One lunatic in the family is enough.'

'We'll let you know how the lunatic progresses.'

'Call me, Paddy. Any time, day or night. I'm a light sleeper, I don't care.'

2

Without deciding on such a route and without Lant, though wearing his new sunglasses—the same model Lant had—Paddy found himself biking along the Hutt motorway. For his first major solo voyage it was such an obvious bad choice that he wondered what was behind it. Some wish to put himself in danger? The desire to be at the sharpest remove from help? A test of sorts? Perhaps. But it didn't feel that calculated. He'd done the supermarket shopping in the car, delivered the stuff to his mother, who was resting in her bedroom, and then he'd biked down to Thorndon and followed the traffic without really thinking. He was curious, and then he was flying down a ramp heading north, and then he was on the motorway, following the bike as much as riding it.

That was his story.

He went unthinkingly on for perhaps ten minutes before his mind kicked in. Experienced cyclists, perhaps even a pro—he couldn't recall the exact details—had been wiped out on this road. There'd been a campaign a few years back to change the type of marker paint used since one victim had apparently come off when his tyre slid on a freshly applied line. He went under a truck. Paddy wasn't sure what had happened about the paint in the end but he was careful to keep off it. There was certainly no death wish in him. He felt hyper-alert in the traffic, constantly scared, grim and hostile and victimised. Every vehicle that went past seemed malicious. Some moved far out in the lane to give him the maximum space, others crushed the air between them with either fine judgement or vicious disregard. More than a few, he was sure, passed without noticing that there was a man on a bike on the edge of the motorway. They drifted and corrected in jerks. He thought, this last category contains the person who'll kill me, or kill someone else another day.

It was ten kilometres of this, the Hutt Valley at the end of it, that low collection of buildings and houses puddling between the hills. The Hutt, his birthplace, had never seemed such a longed-for thing but he wanted to be there at once.

Of course under normal circumstances he was heading in exactly the wrong direction.

This strip he was on, tossed up by the last big earthquake, consisting of the narrow motorway and the adjacent railway line balanced on the edge of the harbour, had figured, more or less, as a lifeline. Here was the single route of salvation, the means by which he and his friends found a world beyond high-fenced sports grounds, pennanted car yards, shampoo manufacturers, evangelical churches, the flat and wide sleeping streets they'd biked along as kids, speeding up to scare a cat walking lazily across in front of them. The Hutt, you wanted as early as possible to achieve escape velocity.

He cycled hard at first, adrenalised with rage, expecting some wild event to shatter everything. The family SUV with a kid in a car seat, a mother on a mobile phone, clipping him and sending the bike out into the far lane in flesh-tearing circles to land in the path of someone very unlucky; the courier van booming with music, driven by Leo, the name in curly script on the door, swiping Paddy into the gravel on the side of the road and carrying on to his next drop-off; a man in a Mini, looking at the harbour, collecting him from behind. Paddy glanced at his end in many forms.

It was a terrible way to bike.

He was exhausting himself in nervous fury. Most likely it would result in his falling off without anyone else to blame, striking a tree, a pillar, going into a culvert. That was how you broke your arm, your pelvis. A helicopter would come. The

192

irresponsibility of his actions was outrageous. He thought of Helena at the language school, scowled at by Iyob, besieged by Dora, taking the call in business mode. 'I see, I see. Thank you for calling.' He thought of his mother. For years of course she'd been the sole reason to head here.

He slowed down and relaxed his grip on the handlebars and evened out his pedalling. He was still afraid and the air pushed at his teeth, his eyes, but he had a little more control over everything. Normalise, this was Lant's advice. Lift your head and seek the information of your surroundings. There's no panic.

What was the day like?

It was sunny, mild, calm. These weren't the conditions on the motorway while biking in fast traffic but were he to stop that would be the day in front of him. And he had the power to stop at any moment, to get off, to have a sip of water, to regard the whole enterprise from a less threatened perspective, leaning with his bike against the hillside, just out of harm's way. His surroundings? In the harbour there were a few yachts, a motorboat pulling along a water-skier. The unit passed, three carriages, hardly anyone in them, going out to the Hutt. It surprised him how easily and rapidly he was able to take in these things. Where were the dolphins and what were they saying?

He stopped at the petrol station halfway along and had some water and his banana, looking back at the city, which was satisfyingly distant. He was proud then. When he took off his helmet, his hair stuck to it with sweat. He watched the cars pass with what instantly seemed like impossible speed and yet that was the stream that would soon be pulling him along. This was Paddy's new idea about the motorway, that he could make himself part of its patterns and currents. Before reaching the petrol station he'd discovered a channel of air from an intercity bus and had coasted in it for several moments until it weakened, moving ahead of him. He'd seen cyclists in town, often bike couriers, holding onto the back of trucks, getting towed. On the motorway if you were good and had courage, there was the slipstream. He lacked these qualities but even for a novice rider, doggedly in the road's furrows, there were bonuses, surprises.

On his new glasses there was a fine spattering, tiny dots of an oily substance which vanished when he rubbed the lens across his sleeve.

He re-entered the brutal flow. He fully enjoyed none of it and came into Petone sore and dry-mouthed. His water bottle was empty. Lant said always take two bottles. His calves felt tight and his groin and backside ached. But mostly Paddy felt good, vindicated. Wellington glittered over the water, surprisingly tall, a collection of silver filing cabinets. Yes, he thought, catching the image: that is where I keep my problems. And the Hutt? The Hutt was the simple past, wasn't it? It was cats under cars. It was boys sitting in the stands at night watching men play softball under lights. It was John Walker running around a grass track. Arsonists had burned down the stadium and his intermediate school. It was climbing the wall of the Riddiford Baths to take a midnight swim. It was men leaving the RSA holding little overnight bags in which there was a flagon of beer. They looked like burglars. And the walking jolted little burps from the men, as if they were babies.

Tony Gorzo's bowling lanes occupied a bleak gravelly space marked by a chain-link fence between the motorway and the railway line just south of the Petone railway station. There were car parks in front of the bowling building, weeds growing through the broken concrete. A few dilapidated railway sheds sat at one end, their graffitied garage doors secured by large rusting padlocks. At the other end was a group of recycling bins surrounded by several mounds of black plastic rubbish bags that had been torn at by animals. Food scraps spilled onto the ground. A cat was eating there.

He felt very hot suddenly, a flush passing across his back and reaching his ears. This sensation left him. He'd had no trouble with his right ear on the ride.

There were perhaps a dozen cars parked outside the lanes, a flat-roofed single storey building that looked temporary, almost abandoned except for the large new-looking sign fixed above the entrance: The Bowling Place. An old beaten-up painting below this name showed a bowling family—Mum, Dad, two kids— having fun. The son had just bowled a strike and showed a raised fist while his sister was applauding madly and his parents looked at each other in amazement. *Is that our boy?* Beside them were plates of chips, drinks with striped straws. The paint was weathered and the image disrupted by lines that cut across the faces. It might have been a family portrait someone had screwed up in a temper and then tried to smooth out again in remorse. Well, that would have been Margie, except for the remorse.

It was just before eleven in the morning. He locked his bike near the front entrance, chaining it to one of the veranda poles, and went inside. The place was cool and lit oddly so that at first it was hard to make out anything much at all. Pockets of brightness mixed with areas of total dark. Music played from hidden speakers and there was the rumble of bowling balls, then the clatter of pins going down. Cabinets of trophies lined the wall near the entrance. One of these was illuminated and gleaming, while the others were unlit and he could only glimpse their contents. Cups and pennants. A statuette of a figure crouching, his bowling arm thrown up unnaturally behind him as if dislocated. Another of a man holding what Paddy thought might have been a bowling pin high above his head; he was looking up and his neck was visibly straining. These poses, adjusted by shadows and reflections off the glass, suggested briefly people suffering spasms of pain. Similarly, wooden plaques fixed between the cabinets disappeared and appeared as he walked towards the counter, which was the main source of light, a ring of coloured bulbs above the desk, red, blue and green, one or two of which were blown. The first few bowling lanes were in darkness, though the TV screen above each lane showed a single small flashing white light.

195

No one was at the desk. Next to the till was a computer touch-screen with a map of the lanes. A Coke can with a straw coming out of it sat beside the screen and behind the desk were shelves of bowling shoes, cubbyholes with size numbers written in black marker pen onto the wood. There was also a cardboard box on the floor marked in the same pen with the word sox. Paddy looked up and saw a security camera pointing down at him. Was Gorzo in some back room watching him? Paddy slipped off his biking shoes and held them.

At the far end, there were people bowling in the last three lanes. The place smelled of alcohol and carpet cleaner. He heard the sound of glasses being pushed into or out of a dishwasher. More pins went down and someone shouted briefly. A pair of Western-style swing-doors led through into a bar, also mainly in shadow though thin light showed the bulbs of wine glasses hanging upside down above the bronze handles of the beer pumps.

He walked along towards the occupied lanes and then sat in an armchair with broad wooden arms into which a plastic ashtray had been moulded. The wood was marked with white rings from glasses. He was almost completely in shadow. In the nearest lane two men in their sixties bowled in silence. They wore caps and white shirts with some insignia on the back. Between bowls they poured drinks from a jug of beer and watched the cartoon animations that filed across the scoring screen above their lane. A squirrel was being chased by a duck and something else, perhaps an otter.

Further along, a man of about Paddy's age was bowling with two women, one a little older than him, one much younger. The women had to be reminded to bowl. They sat down between bowls and drank from tall glasses with straws, ignoring the man's bowling. The man always stood. He'd set up his drink—a can of beer or something else—on a ledge above a carousel of balls just behind their booth. He moved here whenever the women were bowling, looking down towards the counter and the entrance. Paddy wasn't sure whether the man had seen him or not. He wore a shirt with epaulettes and the women called him Davey.

Between these two groups, a man who looked to be in his early thirties was bowling with his infant son, about four years old. The boy would carry his ball in two hands from the rack and balance it on top of a metal ramp, which his father had positioned for him in the centre of the lane. They would then discuss the best angle to go from, the boy trying to line up his ball on the ramp with the pins by pointing his arm and looking down it, squinting. The father then had to move the ramp a little. Both of them counted off the bowl and the boy would let go. Once it was gone they'd set off after it, walking almost the length of the lane, talking to the bowl, urging it on, flapping their hands to make it stay on course. Curlers did this on ice, sweeping with brooms. Near the end, the father would take his son's hand to stop him banging his head on the board, and they'd watch the ball take out a few pins. The automatic arm swept up those ones and the pair then walked back to bowl again. Between the son's turns, the father bowled mostly strikes. He never missed a spare. His action looked stiff but he kept hitting them. When Paddy lived in the Hutt, they sometimes went bowling but it was an upstairs room near Trentham with holes in the walls where the balls had jumped the gutters. No TV screens, no bar.

When the boy and his father were walking down the lane, the two older men stopped bowling and drank from their glasses of beer, watching impassively. The man with the two women, Davey, stood at the top of his lane with his hands on his hips in obvious disgust. He turned in Paddy's direction and said loudly, 'Put up with this.'

The boy had released his final bowl. Four or five went down. Father and son stood at the end of the lane and before the arm appeared, the boy stepped forward quickly and kicked at the remaining pins. He was snatched away by his father, swung in the air. 'No,' said the father. 'No, no, no!' There didn't appear to be any real anger in the father's voice and his son was squealing and asking to be let down. He was laughing. 'You're a menace and a stranger to me!' 'No,' said the boy. 'No, I'm not!'

Paddy sat forward then, coming into a little light. What was in that voice? Slightly Americanised. The boy was American and possibly Asian, though the father wasn't.

The older men waited. Davey, furious, went to find his drink while the women he was with glanced over at the father and his boy then returned to their conversation.

The father bent down—the same slightly awkward movement as when he'd bowled—and rehearsed a few practise swings as if about to bowl the boy down the lane. 'Stop! Dad! Stop!' Finally he put him down and the boy ran back to their booth to look at the screen that showed their scores. 'I won!' he shouted. 'I won again!'

'Win something from me pretty soon,' said Davey.

Then the boy raced past Paddy and through the swing-doors. Paddy heard other doors open and close behind him.

The father looked at the screen, carrying a ball. He took a few steps and let it go without much effort or care. The ball took out eight pins. He picked up two glasses from the table at their booth, used a paper serviette to wipe the table, and walked in the direction of the counter.

Davey stepped forward and stopped the man from going past. 'Make it hard to concentrate,' he said.

'Pardon me?'

'Rules are keep off the lanes. You and the kid are in my line of sight all the time. Paid for bowling. You want to have playtime, that's a different place.'

'I'm sorry, sir. It's his birthday today. He gets everything he wants.'

'Does he get everything I want too? I wanted to go bowling.'

The two women were calling for Davey to stop talking and come over. Paddy realised they were drunk and had been for some time.

'If you feel we affected your game, I'm going to throw in a free one, sir. How about that?'

The man called Davey looked carefully around himself as if suspecting a trick. 'Free game?'

The father looked in the direction of the screen above Davey's lane, checking the numbers. 'Sir, you feel a little boy made a mess of your game, I'm giving you the free game. He really messed your game, I think that's fair. He's five years old today.'

The women had stood up and were listening now. Their man wasn't so sure of his ground any more. He was hesitating. 'No,' said Davey. 'He didn't mess it up too much. We don't have time for another one anyway.'

'Five years old, sir.'

Davey put his can back on the ledge above the balls.

'Drinks to be kept in the booth, that's a rule, sir.'

Davey picked up his can and moved back to the booth and the women. He said something and one of the women, the younger one, laughed loudly.

Paddy stood up as the father passed him. 'Hello Jimmy,' he said. 'It's Patrick Thompson. You may not remember me.'

'Look at this!' he said. He hadn't seen Paddy on the chair and he stepped back in appraisal. He stared a moment, and then he had it. 'Why don't I remember you, Mr Thompson? I was going to be a retard except for you.'

'And here you are.'

'Here I am, now I get to be polite to retards.' *Raytards*.

Paddy was holding his bike shoes and Jimmy immediately said, reaching for them, 'What size do you take?'

'Tens,' said Paddy.

He went behind the desk where he dumped the glasses. Then he put a pair of black bowling shoes on the counter.

'I'm not here to play,' said Paddy.

Jimmy shrugged. 'You'll be more comfortable walking around.'

Jimmy Gorzo lived in Sacramento, California where he worked in civil engineering, mainly railway-related. Paddy knew this.

199

He skied in the winter. He'd travelled to Japan to study bridges in earthquakes. He heated his swimming pool with solar panels he designed himself. The Christmas cards, then the phone calls, had given Paddy his history, of which his parents were deeply proud and just a little suspicious. Tony wondered about America. He didn't wonder about its politics or its violence. He wondered whether in the end it was a serious country. He'd met many Americans, nice people, but vacant in some way, he thought. Missing something. And those *voices*. He had a sensitivity to American voices, especially the women. 'They grate. I couldn't listen to that for long.' They'd spoken about this one time following a column Paddy had written about regional accent variation across New Zealand. Tony basically thought he was making it all up. We all sound the same here, he told Paddy.

Jimmy now called himself James and on his business card he'd added an initial though he didn't have a middle name. It was 'R' but when they asked him what it stood for, he said he didn't know. What, he didn't know his own name? But it was a made-up name anyway, Jimmy said. It was 'R', the sign of someone filled out and meaning business. It was whatever you wanted it to be. That, for Tony, was a decidedly American touch.

R for real dumb, Tony said.

Paddy sat in the bowling shoes—thin-soled, almost slippers—and listened to Tony's son tell him about his life. He needed little prompting. Of course Paddy was interested in how he sounded. James Gorzo had picked up a few of the politeness markers—the *sirs*, the *pardon mes*—and he pronounced his vowels with greater emphasis. But his birthplace was there in his mouth, and more significantly so was the accident all those years ago when he'd had to learn to talk again. The combined effect wasn't too far off some sort of American. There wasn't a sign of his old trick of waiting for someone else to supply the lost word, but he drawled a little. Paddy remembered that when Jimmy was at university some people still thought he had an intellectual disability. A girl in one class offered to take his lecture notes for him, Tony had told him. Perhaps in California James had the

200

perfect cover for the slight slowness and elongation, the added care. They might consider him a transplant from somewhere south-west on their own continent.

They were sitting in his father's office, a small room behind the bar with a window looking out onto the motorway. There was a kitchen too and he'd glimpsed an elderly woman stacking plates. Paddy had a glass of Sprite and James had a Coke. James had poured these from the nozzles at the bar, shooting the glasses as if he had a gun, which made Adam, his son, laugh and shout, 'Do it again!'

'Want me to do it again?'

'Yeah! Shoot 'em again!'

So he did. The drink overflowed the glasses, frothing through the metal grate. Adam wanted it a third time but his father wiped the glasses down and told him the show was over.

In the office, Adam played a game on the computer and took sips from his father's drink. Paddy hadn't known about Adam but it turned out he was new. James was on his honeymoon. He'd married Sue, a physiotherapist he'd met in January in Sacramento when he was having one of his regular back sessions. He went in, he said, with chronic pain and now he had a wife and a child! They'd arrived in the country two weeks ago, having been married the day before the flight. It was all a surprise—not just the visit but also the marriage, Sue, Adam, the works. 'I hadn't really gotten around to the whole disclosure thing. Then we thought, this will be our gift!'

Paddy considered how well this would have gone down with Dad, and he admired the son's nerve in attempting it. He'd always been brave, tenacious. In the hospital he'd wanted Paddy to stay longer each session, asking to be pushed harder, given tougher exercises. Jimmy turned up the cassette-radio to make it more difficult. He practised shaping his mouth, positioning his tongue, making the sounds until sweat ran down his face, but he wanted more.

'Because we were thinking of what gift to bring.'

'For whom?' said Paddy.

'Okay, sorry. My grandmother. She turns one hundred next week. The big century!'

Paddy remembered the time Tony had kept the grandmother from Jimmy's hospital bed. 'How amazing.' Clearly the reasons for Tony's failure to call him about his last column were multiple.

He thought again of his own mother. Already he'd decided to catch the train back into Wellington.

He asked where Tony was this morning and James explained that his father and mother had gone shopping in town with Sue, supplies for the party, decorations.

'So what about you, Patrick?' he said. 'Still at the hospital teaching some poor crippled guy to talk?'

'Me?' he said. 'No, I left there a long time ago.'

'For real?' James had leaned across to his son, who was having trouble with his computer game. He struck a few keys and watched the screen for a moment. The game appeared frozen. James stood up and moved his son out of the way, placing him on a chair directly opposite Paddy. 'You talk to Mr Thompson for a minute. Tell him how you like his country.'

The boy looked at him, then down at his feet in the bowling shoes.

'Happy birthday, Adam,' said Paddy.

'Oh, it's not his birthday,' said James.

'It's not my birthday,' said Adam.

'Okay,' said Paddy.

James was pressing a button on the hard-drive tower, trying to eject a disk. 'But life's good? You look good.' He glanced at Paddy, making some quick calculation, and then he frowned. 'I need to get a bike and do something.' He was getting annoyed with the computer, shaking his head. Paddy saw Jimmy's body properly now as he leaned forward. Gorzo junior was chunky all over, thickening around the middle. He was a little like Paddy, which may have been the calculation he was doing. Wasn't he supposed to be a lot younger than this figure from the past, and therefore in better shape? His skin was somewhat sallow. His hair was thick and black, packed in tight curls mostly towards the top of his head, exposing a large brow. Where was his mother in all of this? Paddy remembered Ellie's slim neatness. Jimmy had her eyes—light-coloured, almond-shaped—and the same upward curve to the eyebrows. It made them both—mother and son—look slightly quizzical, or as though they were about to deny something, *Who me?* They looked like eyes capable of quick tears. And of course Paddy had seen both these figures crying and crying. Jimmy frustrated, his mother sorrowful.

'In Sacramento,' he said, 'we have lots of tracks. I could go down by the river and follow it along for miles. I see people doing it. I could get one for Sue too and we could bike together. But what about Adam? How would that work?' He regarded his son with seriousness, momentarily stuck. He was used to solving problems more quickly than this.

'Get a seat on the back,' said Paddy. 'A little kid's seat.'

'There you go!' he said, though he sounded unconvinced. He liked to solve his own problems. He returned to the computer. He'd taken a paper clip and was jiggling it in the jammed disk tray.

It struck Paddy then that James R Gorzo had no interest whatsoever in Paddy's life and also, more surprisingly, that he'd received no information about Paddy from his father. The Christmas cards, the phone calls, the columns—none of this had touched Jimmy. Paddy was cast forever in the role he'd had when Jimmy was seventeen years old and his world had changed. Paddy belonged there, not here. If he'd produced from the back pocket of his biking jacket the flash cards illustrating a mouth in the act of delivering a diphthong, Jimmy would not have blinked. He would have mimicked the card and asked for another.

And really who was he to Jimmy? Twenty minutes ago Paddy had risen from the chair by the bowling lanes out of the shadows like some ghost and he'd gained little more substance in the time they'd been talking, or rather in the time Jimmy had been talking. Forgetting for a moment the bigger questions—What had Paddy done since leaving the hospital? How was life for him?—even the smaller questions—Why was he in the cycling gear? Why had he ended up here? What did he want from his father and was there a message?—carried zero appeal for him. Did Paddy have kids?

Here was a curious mix of considerateness—the bowling shoes, the drinks, the time out to spend with him—and disinterest—the cheerful egotism of his stories, the unruffled ignorance about Paddy's existence. And tempting as it was to draw a line under this and call it the habits of his adopted home, that didn't seem accurate. He may have had his mother's eyes but Jimmy appeared to Paddy from this angle not American but quite a bit like his Dad. One could have chosen to be depressed by the thought yet oddly it pleased him. There was something in the continuity of a temperament that was moving to observe. Great and unlikely things had happened to Jimmy after that night he'd fallen out of the quad bike onto the fine sand of a Northland beach and in his life he'd been thrown further than anyone might have imagined—California, Japan, a solar-heated swimming pool, a son who looked different from him. Yet he'd also landed close, it seemed. Here he was. He stood in his father's office in the Hutt, working unhappily with an improvised tool, swearing softly at an old computer, determined, as Paddy heard him mutter, to fix the fucker.

Adam said to Paddy, 'You got hairy legs.'

James walked Paddy to the entrance, with Adam insisting on holding his biking shoes. Paddy changed out of the bowling slippers at the doorway. The daylight was intense after the interior dimness. The three of them stood blinking, looking out on the car park where the two older men who'd been bowling were getting into a car driven by the woman from the kitchen, who looked to be in her eighties. They got into the back seat and she pulled out, tooting her horn. James raised a hand in farewell.

'They're brothers,' he said. 'They come three or four times a week. They live at home and that's their mother. One of them can't really see and the other one can't really hear but I never remember which. Ron and Harry. Ron was once married, I think. Now they all live back together again. If there are lanes free, Dad lets them play and doesn't charge them. They pay for drinks. They help out too. Harry was a mechanic, cars, but he can tweak the insides of a bowling machine no problem. And the mother, that's Annie, does all the club stuff, the tournaments, emailing people, treasurer, whatever. She was here before Dad bought the place. She's Mrs Bowling. Amazing. You come on a morning like this and you think what a dive and you meet this guy in there who wants a fight and you think where am I? Loserville? But on a club night, this is a community venue, Patrick. It can be pretty fun, pretty serious too. You saw the trophies. There's blood in those cabinets. There's history. Here's what Dad says. He says we're not the owners of this place, we're the guardians. That's all. Guardians. Albeit with a rock solid profit motive!' Jimmy smiled. He was reaching into his pocket, taking out his wallet. 'Here I am.' He handed over his business card.

Paddy read it and put it in his back pouch, apologising for not having his own with him.

'Second thoughts,' Jimmy said, 'I need it back.' He reached inside Paddy's pouch and took the card out. Then he produced a very thin pen from a compartment of his wallet and told Adam to turn around. Resting the card on his son's back he wrote something on it and put it in the pouch. 'I put the time of Yaya's birthday. Patrick, we'd be honoured if you could make it but no pressure. It's going to be right here, at the lanes!'

No, he wouldn't be there, Paddy thought. But almost at once he was reconsidering. Why not? Wouldn't it be interesting? Suddenly it seemed important to be there. Paddy said he'd try to make it. 'But maybe check with your father too.'

'Why? You're invited. Consider it done.'

They shook hands and Paddy put on his helmet. Paddy bent down to say goodbye to Adam and he rushed forward, hugging him. Paddy almost toppled.

'Easy chief,' said James.

They watched the boy run back inside the building, frightened at what he'd done, ashamed, uncaring? Impossible to tell.

'Sue says it's the travel and everything being foreign. He's not sure where to put his affection so he tends to give everyone the benefit of the doubt. He ran into the arms of the supermarket checkout girl the other day. I think in your case he showed good judgement. You're going to come to the party, right. You gotta. She's one hundred years old. I said to Dad, can you believe it? He said, a hundred is nothing. Why not a hundred and twenty or thirty. Technically he has a point. We keep on riding bikes, why not?' He touched the handlebars of Paddy's bike. 'Did you have a health scare?'

'No.'

'Okay, you just thought—'

'I turned fifty. I suppose that was involved in it.'

'Fifty? Hell, you're not even halfway, Patrick. Come to the party and see the evidence, the path ahead.'

3

At the barbecue fundraiser they ate coleslaw and rice and chops off paper plates, scooping at the food with plastic forks. The plates bent in their hands. Lant wore his denim jacket, cowboy string tie and his boots, his band costume. He was surprisingly agitated. It was a crowd of a hundred or so parents and their kids, the teachers, a few others such as Paddy and Helena who'd been roped in, grandparents. Already they'd applauded a couple of musical items performed by pupils. Hardly a tough audience, yet Lant had made two trips to the school toilets and he was sweaty around the temples. He kept looking at his watch and walking across to speak to the guys in the band and to fiddle with his amplifier, the height of his microphone. The gear was set up on the veranda of one of the prefabs. 'This is terrible,' he'd told Paddy after making another nervous circuit of the school grounds, drinking perhaps his third or fourth paper cup of water.

'What's the matter?'

'I don't know. But why are you even here?'

'Wanted to come.'

'I'm surprised you came.'

'I'm here, Lant, ready to enjoy it.'

'Jesus Christ.'

The two of them now stood with Paul Shawn, Stephanie's estranged though periodically present husband, talking about Teresa, who was in her apartment, hopefully having an early night, as she said she would. Probably it was a mistake for Paddy to have come. He was considering going back to check on her soon. It was certainly a mistake to have raised the subject of Foreign Accent Syndrome.

Paul said, 'You're telling me bang, I could wake up one day and be Nigerian or something?'

'Possibly.' Paddy had told them both about the cases they'd found on the Internet.

'Big Chief Paul!' he said laughing. Paul was most recently a travel agent, having tried a few things. His only formal training, as far as Paddy knew, was in repairing photocopiers. Paul moved his chop around with his fork. Paddy saw one of the tines was already broken off. 'Freaky stuff. When does she snap out of it?'

'Depends.'

Lant was also looking at Paul's broken fork. 'Lesions?' he said solemnly.

Paddy told him that nothing had showed up on the CT scan.

Lant put down his plate, the chop untouched. He felt again for the lump of rosin he had in his pocket. 'CTs miss tumours, you know that. Get an MRI.'

'I know that. We're getting an MRI.'

'A tumour!' said Paul. 'That's bullshit for you, if it's a tumour.'

'Nothing showed up,' said Paddy.

'She hasn't got a tumour, Jeremy, so why say it?' said Paul.

'I didn't. I was asking.'

'Then don't ask such bad luck questions as does his mother have a tumour.'

'It's not bad luck to ask a question, Paul. Not since the Middle Ages. His mother starts talking French, you ignore it?'

'People always think it's a death sentence. I have a pain in my stomach, it's a death sentence, I'm dying! It's negativity's the real killer.' Somehow Paul managed to spear his chop with the broken fork. He brought the meat in one piece to his mouth, preparing to bite. They both watched Paul twist the fork around, looking for the best angle to attack it. He looked like some animal given cutlery for the first time.

Paddy didn't think it was just he alone imagining the fork piercing Paul's cheek.

Paul was a figure of fun, always had been. Obtuse, transparent, immature. This was what Stephanie had fallen for, somehow perceiving Paul's desperate display as a simple and attractive desire to please. He was puppyish, she'd thought. He was straightforward. In high school she'd gone out for a year with a prick who'd actually bashed her on what she later confessed was a 'semi-regular basis'. Paul Shawn had seemed at least a respite from that. From time to time she saw Paul clearly enough and talked of the fourth child she had, aged forty-two.

Teresa in her undemonstrative way had always loathed Paul Shawn. Characteristically she refused to take anything at all he said seriously, and she achieved this by appearing to listen to him with deep respect. She never contradicted him, since even that would have been a kind of compliment.

He began to chew the chop off the fork.

Lant was about to speak but then they heard him being called over by one of his band-mates. Paddy looked for Helena and finally found her over by the fort, talking on her phone. Her briefcase was on the ground between her legs. She'd put her plate of food and her drink on the bottom of the slide that came down from the fort. They'd had the briefest conversation when she arrived, small talk only as they were in a group of parents and children. The Ministry person was arriving the following day. Paddy wanted to ask about Iyob and Dora but there wasn't an opportunity then. Nor had he told her about biking out to the Hutt and meeting Tony Gorzo's son. A vast web of unfinished business held them—together and apart, since clearly they occupied different parts of the web. They could only wave at each other, which they did now in the school grounds.

Paul and Paddy looked out over the concrete playground where a game of soccer was being played between the staff and the senior students. One of the male teachers tried to dribble around a girl and knocked her over. She landed hard on her backside on the concrete and looked up and laughed, her eyes starting to glisten with tears. The game went on beyond her while she remained sitting. It was Crystal, Lant's twelve-year-old daughter. He was on the sidelines of the game, unmoving, staring at her. He turned to look in the direction of his bandmates and actually walked a few paces in their direction, seemingly oblivious to his daughter. Lant's ex-wife, Melinda, who stood a few yards from them, called to him to attend to Crystal and it was only then that he seemed to remember her.

Paul made a sound with his tongue. He was sucking at the bone of his chop.

'What?'

'Pussy-whipped,' said Paul. 'No offence of Steph.'

'You're an idiot, Paul.'

Paul Shawn dropped the chop in a rubbish bin beside them and ate some more rice. 'Lucky she's got you, Paddy. Teresa's lucky. You'll therapise her then?'

'Pardon?'

'Whatever you do, you'll treat your Mum. She's lucky. Keep it in the family.'

In Paul's mouth this sounded somehow obscene. He must have seen Paddy's look.

'By "keep it in the family" I don't mean hide it or anything,' he said. 'Why hide it?'

'Why hide it? Because it's embarrassing, Paul. Because it's really fucking silly. Like you said, one day you could wake up and sound like a Nigerian, Paul. Which would be absurd. You'd be a laughing-stock. A skinny white guy walking around sounding like that, are you kidding me? You think you could do your job like that? You wouldn't have a friend by the end of the week.'

'Steady on, Paddy.'

'Then there are your kids. You think they'd adjust very quickly to their new Nigerian-sounding Dad? They've got to think you've lost your mind. A nutjob father.'

'In time they'd make adjustments.'

'You reckon? They'd get used to it? Good luck with that.'

'No, Paddy, but all I was meaning was just that you're well-placed to help your Mum, and it's great to be able to use what you know to help family. Because of my job, I got Steph and the kids a good discount on tickets to Christchurch.'

'Why would they want to go to Christchurch?'

'It's a gateway.'

'To where?'

'In two hours you can be in the mountains.'

'To what purpose?'

'Or the lakes.'

'Why?'

'Water-skiing, boating, fishing.'

'Steph has three small children, Paul. She can barely crawl out of bed in the mornings.'

'I'd like them to be safe in the water, to learn the skills.' The statement emerged with the wounded tone he could summon at will. He was charging Stephanie with a dereliction of duty. When the youngest girl, Niamh, was two months old, he walked out on them, claiming he'd never wanted a third child, he'd been tricked into it. It coincided with a development course for real estate agents in Queenstown and he stayed down there for six months. Even during this initial period of abandonment he made sure that the signals and the interpretation of those signals were horribly contradictory in a very Paulish and manipulative way. Either he was completely through with being a family man and had gone forever—good riddance—or he was making an extreme sacrifice for his family's benefit, attending the tough Queenstown course and learning skills in a highly competitive market which would eventually secure them all a better life. Stephanie herself didn't help matters by failing to settle on a single version. This was still the case several years on. She claimed Paul was capable of great kindness. Or that he was a jelly and the question was finding the right mould to pour him into, to set him in the optimum shape. Steph thought he'd never

211

had the right guidance. And perhaps this was Paul Shawn's greatest accomplishment, to persuade people that they could, indeed were obliged to, save him.

Paddy always argued for the clean break. 'But he's their father,' Stephanie told him. Let him be that, he told her, but nothing else, with no other prospects. 'It sounds so simple, Paddy,' she said. It was simple, he said. Time to move on, he said. 'Yes!' Steph always said, grinning. Time to stop forgiving him. 'You're completely right, Paddy!' Okay, he told her, good. Okay then.

Next he'd hear Paul was staying for a month at the house because his flat was being painted or he'd arrived for dinner and stayed the weekend. Proper reconciliation would be threatened but it always evaporated. Paul would leave again or he'd be chucked out. Stephanie would ring her mother in tears. Could she come round with the girls?

Given current circumstances with Teresa, this seemed intolerable. Yet it was exactly the sort of situation that Paddy expected Paul to take advantage of in some way. Even his presence at the fundraiser was tactical surely. Paul Shawn specialised in acts of ingratiation, and he savoured a Steph who was upset since in a low state she became available to him again.

'Take them yourself, Paul,' he said. 'Go water-skiing with them.'

'Paddy, I've made offers, I have. I just keep getting turned down.'

'Maybe something in your past record doesn't inspire confidence.'

'We've all fucked up once, Paddy. Me, you, Lanting. Everyone.'

This was also familiar. Paul thought bad behaviour was a bond between all men. 'Maybe once is okay,' said Paddy. 'It's repeat offending that starts to grate.'

The sound of a snare drum being struck pulled their attention over to the improvised stage where Lant's band was strapping on their instruments. Lant was still with his daughter, though

212

now he was looking across at the band. The soccer game had finished.

Two big boys were riding tiny bikes in tightening circles around the netball poles, trapping a group of girls who'd been shooting goals. A female teacher was walking over there.

'Maybe you should meet Camille anyway,' said Paul.

The name meant nothing to Paddy. He forced himself to look questioningly at Paul.

'She's Thierry's mother, you know. The little French boy in Isabelle's class.' Isabelle was Paul and Stephanie's oldest daughter.

Paddy nodded. It was unbearable for Paul to know such things. 'Where is Camille? Can you see her?' said Paddy. They both looked around, then Paul pointed out a shortish woman with dark curly hair. She was standing next to the bookstall, flicking through a book. 'Oh yes,' said Paddy, moving off in that direction.

'Good luck with everything,' Paul said behind him.

Paddy had no idea what he was going to say to this woman. Did he imagine she could help them? Mostly it was to escape Paul. For a moment he considered turning away, leaving the school without talking to anyone and going back to the apartment. He could text Helena and say he had to go. Lant didn't need him in the audience. He'd already said hello to Steph and her kids. He'd eaten off the paper plates and paid his four dollars. It was a mistake to leave his mother alone in her state.

When Paddy introduced himself, Camille took a step away from him and her head made what seemed like an involuntary movement backwards. She waited a moment, and then they shook hands. Paddy thought she was simply trying to work out what he'd said. He was so full of conflicting thoughts that he'd garbled stuff at her, about Stephanie, Helena, the fundraiser, the food. He slowed down. He told her that his niece attended the school. Again there was hesitation from her. Was 'niece' a common word for non-English speakers to know? Perhaps not, although from what he remembered of his school French, they'd spent a lot of time on relations: frères and soeurs and oncles. Ma tante me donne un baise—there, a phrase! Aunts were always arriving from Londres to kiss you. The train station was a crucial site for affection. He had no idea what 'niece' was. He pointed to Stephanie who was serving behind the food tables. 'My sister,' he said. 'Ma soeur.'

'Yes,' said Camille. 'I know Stephanie. I know Isabelle, she's with Thierry, my son.'

'Yes!' he said, foolishly excited at the breakthrough. 'My niece is Isabelle.'

'Sure,' said Camille flatly. 'You're her uncle.' She spoke excellent English with a slight American accent, otherwise she sounded a lot like his mother. She replaced the book she'd been looking at on the stand. 'Do you know the good ones here?'

Paddy glanced at the display. 'No, sorry. I don't have kids, just nieces and nephews.' He didn't know 'nephew' either. What was the mechanism by which people accumulated some nouns but not others?

She shrugged. The shrug was difficult to interpret. It was close to 'who cares' but it wasn't quite that dismissive. Perhaps it simply meant, 'I understand, now let's move on.' It was, he considered, an especially French gesture. His mother may have had the sounds, now here was the body, or the entire culture vibrating through the body. Paddy started to ask about her son but the band was making more tune-up noises and they both looked over. Lant had his violin ready. He had a red spotted handkerchief or a piece of silk to rest his chin against the instrument. 'My friend,' he said, pointing at Lant. 'Violin.'

'Okay,' said Camille.

'What's it called in French, violin?'

'Violon.'

'Violon. Close to English, eh.'

'Your word is from the French, from viele, Old French, then from Provençal, viola. The Italian violino is . . . how do you say? A smaller type—'

'Diminutive?'

214

'Okay, violino which then becomes violin, the English word.'

'Interesting. But what are you, a musicologist or something? Music specialist?'

'No.'

'You seem to know a lot about it.'

'I teach.'

'Music?'

'Sure.'

The use of this 'sure' was vaguely idiomatically wrong. It gave Camille's manner an offhandedness he wasn't sure she fully intended. Then again, she did appear rather brusque.

'Where do you teach?'

'No, not here, not now.'

Again, what did this mean exactly? Not now because of something that had happened? Or just not at this time?

The band wasn't quite ready. The drummer was out of his seat, rearranging the position of his cymbals. Lant used his spotted silk to wipe his brow. 'Very nervous, my friend,' he said to Camille, who nodded. 'Do you play as well?'

'Of course,' she said.

'What do you play?'

'Many things. Piano, flute, I don't know. Violon.'

'Ah, the same as my friend. La même chose.'

'Yes before any concert I am like him.'

'Really?'

'Sure. I'm sick a few times. Feeling dizzy, all this.'

'That will make my friend feel better.'

'No, because this is normal. This is the pain of the art. From the art? I don't know how to say this thing.'

'The pain of the artist?'

She wasn't convinced. 'Maybe, yes.'

'Let's not call it art before we hear it though.' He smiled at her.

Camille remained earnest. 'Amateur is art, I believe. The arts. I think the arts are very important.'

215

'Me too.'

'It doesn't matter who is doing it.'

'Right.'

She half turned from the band to look at him. 'What do you do in your job?'

Camille's question made him think immediately of Bridget and her advice about fielding this question all those years ago. *Don't tell people what you do.* He'd never forgotten it. How did one forget what was said over a lifetime? He'd tried to write about this in a few 'Speech Marks' columns over the years. What was memorability in speech? Why should we retain some things in great detail that are said to us while forgetting most of it?

There were plenty of theories to do with the mind and memory. But what was this thing called talk and why was it so inefficient? Was it a numbers game? Did we have to listen and listen and listen, or talk and talk and talk, just to produce the material in sufficient bulk to allow our brains to sieve the good stuff? But then clearly we were still in danger of retaining not the good stuff but apparent dross also. It was dross Paddy was drawn to.

He'd asked readers to send in examples from their own lives of things that had been said to them or which they had said, perhaps a number of years ago, which seemed to lack any obvious qualifying features—beauty, wit, poetry, context of speech, valued speaker and so on—but which they nevertheless held firmly in their heads. It was not a line of inquiry that pleased the paper at first. He received over two hundred replies. They were for his research mainly. But kindly, grudgingly, the newspaper printed a few of these.

One woman described how she couldn't remember her son's last words with any precision. He'd died of cancer ten years before and she'd been there with him at the moment. He'd been an academic and was lucid and articulate until very near the end but she'd forgotten what he said. Well, she'd been overcome of course. Hardly in a good state to take notes, to gather her thoughts. But she had an idea he'd been wanting to relay messages for other family members through her and the loss of these was shaming, a matter of regret always. Did he say anything? This was what everyone wanted to know. The answer was yes, but then she drew a blank.

Yet here was the thing. She remembered with utter and pointless accuracy what a neighbour had said to her when she was a child and they were picking lemons together. This neighbour had only lived beside them for a couple of years before moving on and she'd not been close to the woman's family in any way. On this day she'd come over and asked whether one of the children could help with her lemon tree. That was all. The neighbour wasn't full of the poetry of lemon picking. She had nothing earthy or strange or memorable to say. But it had stuck for more than sixty years: not only the sound of her voice but her unremarkable talk. You picked the yellowest ones, you left the rotten ones, you didn't throw them in the bucket, you could make marmalade. The talk now ran in the woman's head as if she were listening to a bad radio play. She could turn it on, or it would turn itself on, and it was there again. Most weeks she had to hear it. Why? The neighbour had a ginger cat, the woman wrote. And while they worked, the cat watched them. The column Paddy had written had made her wonder, for the first time, whether this connection—lemons, marmalade, a ginger cat—was enough to make her remember forever that day. Lots of people called their ginger cats Marmalade.

Paddy didn't have an answer to this. But now he remembered in detail the woman's story. He couldn't forget it.

Once at intermediate school—the one burned down—a boy he didn't really know had said Paddy had a fake face. The boy had been sitting along from Paddy at assembly, presumably studying Paddy's face. His judgement was mysterious but it also chimed with something in Paddy's twelve-year-old self and perhaps still did though he'd never been able to say exactly how. The boy was a person who never figured again in Paddy's life, and that school morning was their only contact. Yet he lived on. A look in the mirror while shaving might readily bring him back. Hello, old fake face.

'I'm a speech therapist,' he said to Camille. 'I work with children who have difficulties.'

She gave one of her French shrugs: *who gives a shit*. He was beginning to like Camille. Her clothes were almost dowdy: a long, shapeless greenish dress, without a belt, sleeves that puffed out girlishly, sandals. Her skin was colourless, as if she spent all day inside. Her hair was pulled back in a harsh knot.

The band started playing. It was the first time Paddy had heard them. Once or twice Lant had invited them to the gigs at the last minute, his way of ensuring they could never make it. Or, as in the case here, he'd become vague about the details: were they even playing? He wasn't so sure.

They sounded all right, pleasantly folky, competent and well-rehearsed. Lant's violin ran under the music sparingly, tastefully. It was hard to know what the fuss was about with his nerves—but Camille had said she would have been the same. The guitarist sang and Lant and the bassist provided very passable harmonies. Paddy had never known Lant could sing. His face changed when he sang, it grew appealingly earnest. The first song got loud applause. Two parents started dancing carefully with each other in a kind of waltz as the second song started. Some of the kids whistled at the dancing couple and then stopped. It was a mild evening, windless and with a dusky light softening the sharp outlines of the school's silvery roofs. A few more couples joined in the dancing. Helena was suddenly beside Paddy. She smiled at him and kissed him on the cheek. She put her bag down and they held hands, watching Lant's band and the dancing parents. He felt a tremendous warmth spread through him. Camille had been pulled away by her son towards the food.

Paddy glanced behind and saw that in the shadow of the school's only tree, one of the boys who'd been circling the netball pole was now making figure eights through the hopscotch markings. He rode the same path each time, waving the bike through its route with the smallest movements of his body weight. There was something dreamy about the scene. He was in his own world. Boys led demented solitary lives. We turned and turned and made our paths on the concrete playground under the tree at dusk while our parents danced and forgot us. Every father, every man who is not a father, would recognise himself in that boy. There's no one else around, no one watching except me. And yet he'd connected himself to the rest of the evening by finding in his movements the rhythm of the music. He was cycling to Lant's band, weaving in and out, making the shape of his eight, moving to the lines of the bass, turning on each special guitar strum, as if they'd worked it all out beforehand, boy and bike and band.

It might have been a film Paddy was watching, complete with soundtrack. Did the thought arrive before or after he saw Dora and Medbh? They were standing by a classroom door, behind the tree. Medbh was pointing a small digital camera while Dora talked into her ear, directing. They were filming the boy on his bike. It annoyed Paddy a little. The boy hadn't given his permission. Paddy thought of Iyob at Helena's language school.

He looked back at the band, intent on regaining that pleasure. Lant was handling a nice little solo. While he played he looked different somehow. The position of the chin, his concentration, his slightly pursed lips, gave his face this serious solitary aspect Paddy had never seen before. It was not that he was simply hoping to get through it without a mistake. He was better than that. The other band members had stepped away to let everyone see Lant and his instrument. He quickened the attack with his bow, playing faster runs with equal smoothness. The drummer and the bass player were grinning at each other. Paddy and Helena and everyone watching understood this moment to have become successful in ways the musicians themselves had perhaps not anticipated. It was a concert in a school playground but it was also something else. Was this what Camille had meant by the arts? The pain of art. Lant played on, utterly absorbed. Here was the reason he'd been so ambivalent and cagey about them attending the band's performances. It wasn't that he was worried about any sloppiness or them not enjoying the thing or the chance of seeing him make a fool of himself, at least not in the way that might be imagined. Music required of Lant absolute commitment. Nothing was held back. There wasn't a trace of irony. There wasn't any space for his usual battery of tricks and deflections. He was afraid of Paddy seeing him like this. He was lost to himself in a moment of devotion as powerful and unthinking as the boy riding figure eights behind them. As he played he couldn't account for himself.

Beside Paddy, Helena squeezed his hand and they exchanged a look of delighted surprise, which meant exactly this: who is that on stage?

When he was thirty-eight, Paddy's father had surgery to remove varicose veins. Shortly after this, he bought a second-hand bicycle from a work colleague. These two facts must have been related though at the time Paddy wasn't interested in putting them together. Paddy was eight or nine years old. The veins were not something he remembered thinking about though he did have an image of his father peeling off a tight sock-like bandage from his leg while sitting on the edge of the bath. The bandage was pale pink, skin-coloured he supposed. Paddy's mother had to wash these special vein socks and they'd be hung on the washing line. This disgusted Margie, who would later develop the same problem in her legs.

Paddy however was interested in the bike, which had originally come from London. The work colleague had been English. The bike looked a little like a Raleigh Twenty, with smallish wheels and an angled frame, except that it had a clip on its central shaft that allowed the bike to be undone and carried in two parts. At the time, no one had seen anything like this. When later Paddy went to England and Europe, he saw these bikes everywhere though he never saw them taken apart.

His father now began riding to the Lower Hutt train station and taking the bike to work. On the platform, he'd unclip the

220

bike and tuck both parts under his arm. Probably there was no need for him to do this since there was a special compartment at the back of the train for bikes. He could have stored his there. When Paddy had caught the train back from Gorzo's bowling lanes, he'd thought about all this. But Brendan stepped into the carriage with his bike under his arm. He did it, according to Paddy's mother, because he was a show-off. Much later, when Paddy considered his father in these years, he didn't disagree with this and yet he also thought there was something else. His father had wanted to meet people, yet he needed a prop. He was basically a shy man. His parents shared this. His mother didn't need people but his father did. Or rather his mother needed his father to meet people for her, she relied on that. Her shyness was the blunt variety, the sort that worked upon over time came to look like self-reliance, or was self-reliance. Whoever visited their house, unless it was family, came as the guest of Brendan first. These were the people she called 'your father's friends'.

He'd always unclip the bike while waiting on the platform at both Lower Hutt and Wellington, for the return journey. He made sure that as many people as possible witnessed the bike becoming two pieces. Without seeing it for oneself it was difficult to grasp the oddness and unnaturalness of this parting, wheel from wheel, front from back. In time there were bikes that folded through a hinge and of course people regularly transported bikes by taking off the front wheel, but his father's bike, with its complete bisection, remained in his mind as a one-off. He'd seen it done many times of course and it still made an impression. No wonder people came up and talked to his father. They asked where he got it and was it available in New Zealand and had it ever come undone while he was riding it. No, the clip was secure.

He worked in the Records Office of the Wellington City Council, about a ten-minute bike ride from the station. At work, apparently he unclipped the bike and stored it in a cupboard. He'd completed a library diploma and was in charge of the housing section dealing with requests from homeowners who wanted to learn about their houses or who needed original plans for renovation work. It was where he'd first met Teresa. She'd brought in her elderly father, who was interested in getting a copy of the original drawings of their old Miramar house. He wanted to frame the best drawing and hang it on the wall of the Naenae house. The story was Teresa had booked, or almost booked—the story wasn't definitive—her passage to Rhodesia, where she planned to live with Pip, her cousin. Brendan prevented her escape.

Paddy didn't imagine his father ever went for recreational rides in his lunch-hour—was this ever done back then? The bike was solely to get from A to B, and of course to provoke the sort of casual contact with strangers his father enjoyed.

At his father's funeral, when they were having cakes and drinks in the church hall, his mother was approached by a man she didn't know. Paddy was standing nearby, behind his mother and with his two sisters in a tight group, a huddle. They were all trying to hide. Their family group of four occupied the smallest space possible. They'd spent almost an hour in the room, though it felt like days, trying to find the best place to be, or not to be. Having tried to disappear into a corner, where it turned out they became highly visible and caged, they'd moved to an awkward space in the narrow gap between the two food tables. They fingered the edges of the white tablecloths and longed to lie under the tables, hidden from view.

The man said he was very sorry to hear about Paddy's father and he hoped she didn't mind that he'd come to the church but he'd got to know Brendan a little over the past few years as a fellow commuter.

Paddy wasn't sure whether his mother really understood what he meant. She wasn't capable of much more than a poor imitation of nodding on that day, or for a long time afterwards. It was ghastly to see it. Her head seemed barely stuck on. It was not an exaggeration to say they thought it might simply fall off. His sisters had the same feeling about this because he talked to them about it years later. 'Like a wooden head at a fair, a clown's head that you toss balls into,' said Margie.

Their mother may have believed she was nodding properly but she lacked the control and her head wavered around on an elastic neck. She gave the man the same unfocused wandering nod and tried to smile and move him on; her hand fluttered briefly as if waving at an insect. The man had never met Teresa before and may have thought this was more or less how she always appeared. He certainly missed her hand gesture. Or he may simply have felt the pressing need to say what he'd come to say regardless of the reception he was getting. He told her that Brendan had been known to everyone on the 8.13 into town and the 5.43 back. These numbers seemed to Paddy incomprehensible. He thought they were connected with money. There had been a lot of talk over the preceding days of money, of mortgages and interest rates. His mother's beloved older brother, Graham, was a lawyer. More or less, he moved into the house at that time, then he died too, delivering what Paddy came to see as an almost fatal blow to her. He thought that for many years Teresa was scarcely alive though for their sakes she did a sometimes-frenetic impersonation of a living being. She went back to work as a typist. She drove them around to their sports games on weekends. She talked to their friends. It wasn't until they'd all left home that Paddy thought she began to recover, if that was the word.

During this period, among the children, the threat was often made that one day, without warning, they'd be off to live in Africa. Margie was especially good at tormenting her sister with this. Pip, the mythical cousin, had come back for the funeral and was seen in private conversation with their mother—conversations that stopped the moment anyone came near. Apart from Graham, Pip seemed to be the only person Teresa could cope with. They overheard a fluency in their mother's voice, laughter even. What could she be laughing about except some crazy scheme to leave all this misery behind? Yes, their futures were being plotted, and more or less, they'd wake up one morning in Africa, every aspect of their lives changed.

Pip had given each of them books connected with Africa as presents, which they refused to open.

Paddy saw his mother blink and try to remain fixed on the man, their father's commuter friend, who continued to talk. Finally the man seemed to have finished. There was a pause and he looked around, searching for some excuse to leave her. He didn't know anyone else of course and he seemed stuck. Teresa was incapable of making any of the usual noises of goodbye. She'd spent all this time hardly saying a word to anyone despite the fact that she'd been approached by almost everyone at the reception. They were two adults, marooned. He turned back and said, 'So what will happen to the bike now?'

'Happen?' said his mother, shocked.

'Where will it go? Who will get it?'

'Who? Him.' She pointed at Paddy with a sort of violence. 'He'll get it.'

Nothing previously had been said about his father's bike. Paddy was certain his mother had been panicked into making this declaration. Perhaps she thought the man himself wanted it, or thought that he was entitled in some way to it as a keepsake of all the good times he'd had with their father on the trains between Lower Hutt and Wellington.

The man looked at Paddy approvingly. 'Good,' he said. Then he shook Paddy's hand with great firmness and moved off through the crowd.

As it turned out, Paddy found the bike very awkward to ride. He wasn't that much shorter than his father yet the distance between the seat and the handlebars was a little too great, forcing him to sit forward on an uncomfortable angle or to pedal while standing and use the seat only when coasting. It also had just three gears and its small wheels made it a tiring bike to ride up even low hills. There was something else. Boys at school liked taking it apart, which was a pain. But they also paid attention to it in a slightly mocking way. They were not like the adult commuters on his father's train. They regarded the bike as freakish and strange and something to be attacked.

It was impossible to lock securely since there was no way of threading a chain through the clip. Often Paddy would discover the front half only of the bike still locked to the bike rack; the other half would be hidden around the school—in a classroom cupboard, in a bush, or once, hanging in a tree down by the stopbank of the Hutt River.

Paddy used the bike for a few months, and then he put it away in their garage. His mother made no fuss at all when she found out. She confessed later that she hated the bike because she'd never trusted the clip to stay in place and had imagined a horrible accident happening to anyone riding it at the time it came apart. When he heard this, Paddy was surprised. Firstly, his mother was mechanically minded and must have known the clip wasn't dangerous; if it had been, she would have done something about it. Secondly, this was exactly what everyone thought, a conventional idea. It was the sort of thing strangers said to his father at the train station. Paddy had previously considered his mother as different in some uplifting fashion, secretly intelligent, utterly penetrating. A typist but also quite brilliant. But she could be this too, he thought, and not entirely unhappily, she could be quite average, nearly normal.

After Lant's band had finished, they went to speak to him. He was in high spirits, waving the red silk cloth he'd used under his chin, comically fanning himself. 'Phew,' he said. 'We survived, I think. No rotten fruit thrown. A few walkouts but what can you do?'

He was back. The old Lant. For a moment this felt disappointing, as if Paddy had hoped it would have been possible for his friend to maintain that other intensity. Yet there was something a little sheepish too about him. Helena shook his upper arm and told him how much she'd enjoyed the music and how wonderfully well he'd played. For perhaps the first time, Paddy thought, she appeared genuinely taken by something in his friend. Lant waved this away, said some things about the sound, that the bass was too loud in his ear. The rest of the band was actually deaf, he told them, which presented problems. But this all seemed a bit half-hearted and obviously throwaway. He was aware something had happened and that they'd seen it, which was pleasing, worrying also. They'd uncovered a part of him and that was moving to him—Paddy saw this; it was also causing Lant a sneaking regret. He'd been outed, it seemed. Where to from here?

Unusually for Lant, he now appeared speechless. He looked back at them, grinning and shaking his head. He held his violin up and pointlessly inspected it. As a kind of tribute to him, and in friendly contest, they too remained silent. Helena and Paddy were both extremely happy to observe this new Lant trying to fend off their appreciation and understanding. Fortunately for him, a couple of his band-mates called him over and he left them, holding his bow up in farewell.

Paddy turned around and found himself in the line of Medbh's camera. Dora was with her.

'Carry on as if we weren't here,' said Dora, coming forward and kissing her mother quickly on the cheek. With Paddy, she shook hands, which was their comic routine. The first time he'd met her, he'd shaken her hand, which she'd apparently found odd. She also liked to call him Thompson. Usually they met in the style of business associates or old boys from an English public school. He often said, 'Pleased to see you again, Price.' It was a failing sort of levity. They always ran out of it fast and lapsed back into mutual incomprehension.

He'd tried hard at the beginning to earn, if not her friendship, then at least some sort of respect. The truth was he couldn't understand how Helena had ended up with this person for a daughter. Paddy credited the father. Dora seemed to be waiting for Paddy to be gone from their lives, much as he was waiting for the exit of Paul Shawn. In asserting her rights as Helena's daughter, she always gave him a clear image of his temporariness. That was how it felt. She was the institution; Paddy was the interloper.

'Where's your permit to film?' he said.

'You don't even have a child at this school,' said Dora.

She'd meant this lightly perhaps but Dora could never quite do lightness. There was always a creeping hostility. The spell of the music had vanished. Lant was packing away his violin in his case and Paddy saw Camille leaving the school grounds, holding her son's hand. She glanced back in his direction just before she disappeared around the corner of the building, as if she realised she was leaving without completing their conversation. The French were big on greetings and farewells so maybe she was only thinking of observing the forms. Whatever, Paddy was annoyed he'd not had the chance to talk to her further. Somehow the presence of a real French person, even one as un-chic and unsympathetic as Camille, created an indefinable hopefulness. Anyway, maybe most French people or at least quite a few were a lot like Camille. He'd never been to France. The closest he'd come, apart from England, was Northern Italy in his early twenties, just after he'd finished university. Indeed, he'd waited five hours for a train at San Remo to go for a day-trip to the Côte d'Azur. First the train was late, then very late, and then no, he wasn't going to France.

He decided he would try to get Camille's phone number, perhaps through the school.

Dora and Helena were talking a few feet away. Next to him, Medbh was reviewing something on the camera. 'The silence project?' he said.

'We're calling it *The Silent Treatment*,' she said.

'Nice. It's a doco then?'

'We're not sure.'

'You don't like labels.'

'Except for funding applications.'

'You got the boy on his bike.'

'Quite good shadows.' She passed him the camera and on the little screen he watched the boy go round and round under the tree, head down, asleep at the wheel. It was black and white. There was no sound but the boy made a rhythm anyway, just as he'd thought when he'd seen him. It made Paddy think at once of the footage they'd taken of him when he was being assessed at the bike shop. Black and white. The gulf between the automatic movements, the sensuality and completeness of the boy, and his own uncoordinated adult striving was immense, laughably so. Yet he'd been the boy. Paddy thought of saying something about this but he stopped himself. Too maudlin, too much about the passage of time. These filmmakers considered Sam Covenay a hero of sorts. Had it been Medbh's project alone, he might have spoken. Dora's involvement was a turn-off. He gave Medbh back the camera. What had also come to mind on this theme was his cartoon portrait—still unreturned. In the confusion of Geoff Harley's entrance with his mother the day before, there wasn't a chance for Angela Covenay to fetch the defaced updated version from her car.

'I heard about your mother,' said Medbh.

'You were the first to hear it,' he said.

'I should have realised something was wrong.'

'You told me and I did nothing.'

'Because I'd never met her before.' Medbh seemed on the point of getting quite upset. He was also aware that Dora had become interested in their conversation though she was still talking to Helena.

He lowered his voice. 'No one blames you, Medbh. I just didn't take it in properly at the time.'

'I was an idiot.'

'I was the idiot, believe me. But in the end, there was nothing anyone could have done. It had happened.'

'Is that true, Patrick?'

'She woke up in French.'

'Will she be all right?'

Helena and Dora had now moved back to join them. 'Is she in the hospital?' said Dora.

He told them that Teresa was back in her apartment, resting.

'By herself?' said Dora accusingly.

'We have our phones,' said Helena. 'One of the doctor's pieces of advice was we should treat things as normal. Keep it as normal as possible.'

'I don't want to cast aspersions on the medical knowledge of our fair city but have they treated this before?' said Dora. 'Do they get a lot of people turning up speaking in different accents? Is there an accent and emergency ward?'

This was another thing that rankled, he thought. She could actually be clever, she had something.

Medbh stifled a laugh. 'Shut up, Dor,' she said.

'But seriously,' said Dora. 'Seriously Medbh, have you heard of this before? No? Have you?' She was looking at Paddy.

'Sure,' he said. He tried to shrug.

'Really?' She turned to her mother. 'I'm really sorry for his mother but treat it as normally as possible? If I started speaking with a full-on French accent, can you please do something for me? Could I just get that established as a basic principle? Dora turns French, do something. Okay?'

'Hey, Dora,' he said, 'we'll put you on the first plane to Mururoa, I promise.'

Helena, moving to mollify, started explaining about the scan and what Murray Blanchford had told them but Paddy raised his hand in Lant's direction as if acknowledging his call and, apologising to Helena, he walked quickly away from them.

He'd expected the musicians in Lant's band to need a drink after their gig but they all had young children and it was mid-week. The men simply packed up their instruments and left in their cars. A couple of them were picked up outside the school by their wives, which made Paddy think of mothers collecting their kids after school. A few times he'd had to get Isabelle, his niece, when Stephanie couldn't make it.

It was dark and only a few helpers remained at the barbecue, clearing up rubbish and putting away chairs and tables. He'd used the toilets and then he'd spoken with one of the teachers

229

he met inside and when he came out, Helena, Dora and Medbh had gone. He had his phone but for some reason he didn't text Helena. She could text him if she wanted to tell him anything. Besides, she was the one who'd left the school, although perhaps she'd looked for him when he was in the toilet and not seeing him, had assumed he'd gone home.

He suggested to Lant that they go to a bar in Courtney Place. Lant said he was keen. Paddy watched him talking to his ex-wife and kissing his daughter, and when they left they walked to the bar. Lant was carrying his violin case. He'd taken off the string tie and put it in his pocket. His boots made crunching sounds when he stepped on gravel. Neither of them said much. Paddy found himself preoccupied with thoughts of Helena and Dora. By now Helena would have been home and found the place empty. Why didn't she text? Perhaps he'd annoyed her by walking away in the middle of the conversation. But surely she understood how offensive her daughter had been. To walk away had been the best option. He asked Lant whether his current girlfriend, whose name he'd forgotten, had seen the band play and Lant claimed not to know for sure whether she had or not. Her name, he admitted when asked, was Alice. She was forty-three.

'A younger woman,' said Paddy.

'Not that young,' said Lant. They walked on in silence after that.

Once they'd sat down with their pints, Paddy wondered whether they'd done the right thing and if either of them really wanted to be there. This was unusual. They met regularly. Maybe Lant was suddenly thinking about his girlfriend and hoping to see her that night, or perhaps it was connected with Melinda, his ex-wife, who'd told him in front of everyone to go and comfort their daughter when she'd fallen in the soccer game. He'd placed his violin case on the table beside their drinks. Paddy had suggested putting the case on the floor to avoid spilling anything on it but Lant had said the table was better because if he put it on the floor, he'd forget it. Paddy told him that seemed unlikely but Lant didn't move the case.

Not being a member of his band, or a musician of any kind, Paddy felt that on this night he was the wrong person for the job. Probably on any other night, by tomorrow even, there wouldn't have been an issue, but Lant's fresh triumph at the school, which was how Paddy saw it, made things awkward. Lant was in a kind of shock from his performance. Words were no good. He needed time. He needed his violin case in view.

Paddy raised his glass. 'To the National government.'

'To prosperity,' said Lant, keeping his glass on the table but tipping it forward a little.

'And equality.'

One of the bar staff, a young woman, carried a plate of fried calamari past their table.

'Hungry?' said Paddy.

Lant shook his head. He kept looking in the direction of the door as if expecting someone. His band-mates? But they were at home with their families. Paddy anyway was insufficient, and he was already thinking about heading back to the apartment. Was it too late to check on his mother? For the first time since his ride to the Hutt, his legs began to ache. He rubbed at his thigh under the table.

Had Dora and Medbh been here with their camera, they would have secured footage. Here was the silence between old friends, but not exactly a companionable one, a new one, of uncertain quality and duration.

The bar wasn't crowded. They sat in an alcove as far away from the big TV screen as possible. Golf was on, and the green drew them in no matter how strongly they resisted it.

The other unsatisfactory thing was that Paddy seemed to have recently lost his taste for alcohol. The beer didn't interest him though he'd looked forward to it. Since he'd begun to bike, alcohol was not what his body required. Even after rehydrating, and several hours after a ride, he found wine and spirits to be strangely unappealing. Water was about all he could take. He had a more or less constant thirst and a single means of addressing it. He'd never been a big water drinker before and it gave him no great pleasure. He was just stuck with it. He mentioned it now to Lant, who grunted and muttered something about rehydration, as if he'd missed that part of Paddy's explanation. Paddy said he wondered whether he should try PowerAde or something like it. The flavours might help him back to his normal likes. Lant said he didn't advise it. Too expensive, unproven results, no. Then he looked up and said, 'Did you ride today?'

For a moment Paddy considered telling the truth. 'No.'

'Why are you sitting like that then?'

'Like what?'

'You look stiff. Where'd you go?'

'I didn't go anywhere.'

He studied Paddy. 'Okay, where didn't you go?'

'Where didn't I go? A quick blatt out to the Hutt. I didn't go there.'

'You didn't go on the motorway.'

'That's right.'

Lant breathed through his nose. He sat back in his chair and moved the violin case a little by pressing his beer glass against it. Paddy didn't know how he would take this. For a moment Lant looked on the point of some outburst. The trip along the motorway was something they said they'd do together. Lant, as a novice last year, had been taken out there by a more experienced rider, and it was his task to pass on the knowledge to Paddy. That was how cycling worked, through a careful series of initiation rites, through the obvious hierarchy of expertise. One rider handing down to another. It was collegial in this way. It was safe and efficient and moral and humble. In other words, profoundly adult. They both believed that. This was how cycling worked. Not through stupid whim, not through overreaching and arrogance. Not through one man against the world. Paddy was guilty of all of this, he knew. Lant saw it. 'Was your heart pounding?' he said.

'It was all right,' said Paddy.

'To the point of nausea?'

'It passed.'

'Did you imagine yourself knocked off, being killed?'

'Not all the time.'

'You would have deserved it.'

The distant sound of cries and applause came from the TV on the far wall.

'I wasn't planning on doing the motorway at all.'

'What happened, you went over the bridge and you couldn't turn back?'

'Pretty much.'

Lant lifted his beer. He was still undecided about Paddy's punishment. 'Card, have you got yourself a pair of magic glasses yet?'

'I have.'

'I think they saved you.'

'Was that it?'

'I think so. Something did.'

For the first time, they both took long decent drinks from their glasses and put them back on the table. The beer still failed to do any of the beery things Paddy had enjoyed in the past but simply the idea of its level going down in his glass was satisfying. Lant moved the violin case off the table, resting it by his feet, and leaning forward towards him. 'What will you do about your mother?'

'What do you think I should do?'

'Murray Blanchford's a good guy,' said Lant. 'For a mountain-biker.'

'He bikes too?'

'He tears up nature. He rips through trees. But he retains, for all that, some skill. I don't know how he gets the dirt out from under his fingernails though.'

'We may not need Blanchford's skill or his fingernails.'

Lant finished his beer in one long gulp. Paddy followed him.

'Aspies do it, you know,' said Lant.

'Who? What?'

'Asperger's people, they adopt foreign accents. They mimic the accents of people they're with. A lot of them do it. They have to work hard not to do it because they think it's insulting to the people they're with, that they'll be accused of making fun of them. It's quite a common issue.'

'My mother's not aspergic.'

'No.'

They both looked over at the golf on the huge TV. The cameras were flying over a hole, zooming in on bunkers, then pulling out again. They were briefly mesmerised. Endless lawn. Endless lawnmowers. Then the screen filled with names and numbers they couldn't read from their table.

'France produces fewer top twenty professional male golfers than any other major nation in the world, and a whole lot of small ones too,' said Lant.

'How do you know that?'

'Name one. Name a French professional golfer.'

'I can't.'

'See.'

'There must be one.'

'Where's their Ballesteros? Where's their Vijay Singh? Where's their Padraig Harrington? Where's their Michael bloody Campbell?'

'It's not their tradition, golf,' said Paddy.

'Interesting, isn't it?'

'They like clay court tennis, pétanque.'

'Where are their track and field athletes?'

'Not a strength. Good at soccer though, football. Handball.'

'Handball? Already that sounds like a mistake, you get penalised for handball. Where are their sailors for God's sake? All that water.'

'Where?'

'Around them.'

'A lot of the place is landlocked, then it's the English Channel and the Mediterranean, I guess. But wait on, I think they do have sailors.'

'Well.' Lant examined the dregs at the bottom of his glass. 'I'll tell you what they do like. Cycling.'

'Right.'

'Bikes.'

'Tour de France, yes.'

'Cycling around their own country, through beautiful mountain villages.'

'Ah.'

'Last year I watched it for hours and hours on the television. I was addicted.' Lant seemed to have forgotten Paddy's hubris on the motorway.

'I can see that happening.'

'Card, it was beautiful. A very human spectacle, very simple and with all its skill somehow invisible. Men on bikes, that's all. In their coloured jerseys. Riding in the country, which just— sparkled. They went past a woman milking a cow!'

'Wow.'

'Supporters suddenly run out of the crowd, on the hill-climbs, and push their favourites, to give them help! Big fat rustic guys puffing away for a few seconds, shoving these sleek athletes, trying to make a difference. Some of them fall flat on their faces afterwards, happy.'

'Is that legal?'

'This is France we're talking about.'

'Right.'

'That lovely sound of a mass of bikes. Teams working together. Heaven.'

They sat for a moment, enjoying the image. Then Lant slapped the table. 'Doped to the eyeballs naturellement!' They both laughed. 'Do you feel like another one of these?' he said.

'No,' said Paddy. 'But I could go a whisky. I need to find the thing that will get me back in love with alcohol.'

After two more whiskies at the first place, they went to another one nearby, up a narrow flight of stairs, less pub-like, no TVs, and drank spirits whose names Paddy forgot as soon as the barman announced them. The drinks tended to be colourful, blue or green, and oily. He felt them on his lips, a coating that needed to be licked off.

235

They'd not been out like this together in years, serious drinking. They sat in half-darkness in a corner booth. Chinese lanterns hung from the ceiling and low dubby music vibrated the air—he could feel it in his elbows when they rested on the table. A few couples spoke together in whispery voices and occasionally Paddy heard the electronic bleep of the cash register, which sounded within the music almost like an added synthesised effect. The barman moved soundlessly between the tables, whispering the names of the drinks, laughing quietly with some of the couples. They were the oldest people there by some margin.

'Okay, let's end the torment,' said Lant. 'What did you think of the band?'

Paddy was genuinely surprised. Hadn't this been covered? 'Like I said at the school, very nice.'

'Nice?' He made a face. 'We can play better than that, you know.'

'Harmonies too.'

'I think we were off a couple of times.'

'Didn't notice.'

'Huh.' Lant bent down and adjusted something on his boot. Maybe they were pinching. '*Nice*? I don't know if I'm happy with *nice*.'

'You were pretty good.'

'Jesus, I'm going to start blushing soon.'

'You can really play.'

'Well.' Lant's head drooped. 'Anyway, I was surprised Helena liked it.'

'Why?'

'I find her hard to please.'

'How strange.'

'Because she's never liked me.'

Paddy weakly denied this. Lant waved a hand: Let's move on, I don't care.

They were tired now, slumped against the deep red cushioned seats. Lant started talking about the other band members,

236

what they did that annoyed him. Paddy didn't interrupt. Each successive drink produced a softening, a luxurious feeling of fatigue that was special in that it didn't seem to promise sleep but a sort of endlessness. It was now very late, easily into the next day, yet they seemed to have hours ahead of them and this was deeply pleasurable. Paddy was aware that at certain moments each of them nodded off. Clearly they were close to that end. But these little breaks in consciousness didn't appear damaging. They woke revived and picked things up again at once. As often happened, they had begun to talk about their hospital days, the same stories.

When they'd worked at the hospital together all those years ago, it was natural for them to hang out with the junior doctors coming off their shifts. Lant and Paddy tended to work regular hours but were pulled into the off-kilter worlds of their colleagues, and this was where they learned to drink. The content of these sessions was fairly standard issue. Someone was usually in tears, someone was having a crisis about being a doctor, someone was angry about something or someone—an injustice had been done—someone else was extremely happy, revenge had been enacted or was being plotted. Paddy saw no violence though from time to time it was threatened.

People got together, declared passions, lusts, moving from the long table in the hostel common room, where they usually drank, to couches, chairs, slipping to the floor in a wrestle, or quietly leaving, perhaps to return later with grins, flushed faces, or pale and shamed or flushed with shame, pale with pleasure. There were various combinations. Some even stayed sober, drinking tea or juice, watching everything closely—these were the strangest among them. A brilliant young Chinese doctor always brought along a textbook and read it, or pretended to. A cheerful teetotal girl off a Southland farm baked cakes for everyone and occasionally handed out bags of frozen meat that her father had sent up. Her cheeks always looked as though someone had just rubbed them. There was an older man, in his thirties, whose surname was Major. He marched in the Salvation Army Band and sometimes he wore his uniform to the drinks and lugged a tuba case. Everyone called him 'Major Major' and saluted him.

Paddy remembered a pair of interns originally from Australia who, once they learned that he was speech therapy, liked to have him on. 'Hey, Thommo, do you like eating *cun cun cun cun country* cooking?' They were both blond and blue-eyed, twins almost, creatures from another planet, Brisbane.

A period would usually arrive, towards the middle of the session, when the table broke into Serious Conversation. Politics, music, ethics. For some this spoiled things; they'd move over to the dartboard or start making hoax calls to the nurses' hostel. Lant and Paddy knew each other a little before this but now they found themselves in a sort of alliance. Many of the junior doctors were, unlike them, conservative, religious. They came from doctoring families, boarding schools. There was an active Catholic wing: bright, well-educated boys who'd gone through school on debating teams and who could knot ties. Two of them knew all the words to 'American Pie' and sang it in harmony when they were drunk. Of course they dismissed psychology as a science, and speech therapy rated somewhere down with reflexology as a medical tool. Lant and Paddy were oddities. For their part, they considered these others to be decent, well-meaning, narrow arseholes.

Lant, who felt the Catholics' kindly contempt more strongly than Paddy, sometimes tried to bait them with hypothetical moral dilemmas. The object was to get the young doctors to make a statement that appeared to cast into doubt major doctrinal matters or simply to upset them enough that they lost for a moment their infuriating calm and superiority and niceness. The treatment of homosexual patients was a favourite, and Paddy recalled one very devout bloke running from the room at some suggestion that in A&E he'd had to remove a rectally inserted object from a Marist Brother.

This was cheap though, and they desired a more forceful and wide-ranging riposte.

Lant had noticed that a surprising number of young Catholic doctors were planning to go into paediatrics. He'd discussed this with Paddy. It wasn't necessarily, he thought, because they were all still kids themselves. His theory was that they believed children's medicine offered innocence, whereas most illness was about sin. The smoker with lung cancer, the sunbather with melanoma, the drinker with sclerosis, the junky with hepatitis, the overeater with diabetes and heart disease. There was just punishment in that. Whereas kids, they were plain unlucky. They got what they didn't deserve: broken legs, dog bites, asthma, a marble lodged somewhere unpleasant. What they forgot, these idealists, these moralists, was the children's oncology ward, Lant said, where the really unlucky hung out. Hardly any of these young doctors stayed around that field for long.

At the drinking sessions this wasn't a topic that could be visited often but Lant and Paddy tried it a few times. Some of the Catholics wore crosses tucked into their shirts although this was forbidden by regulations. At the drinks, with their shirts loosened, sometimes these banned crosses could be spied.

What sort of God allowed a girl of six to suffer terribly for months and months and finally die in agony from leukaemia while her parents watched helplessly?

Years of debating had prepared their opponents for this and it wasn't at all clear whether by the end of the argument much had been won on either side. The Catholics always pretended to be meeting Paddy and Lant halfway, to be acknowledging their feelings. They were clever and the smartest of them seemed capable of drawing on centuries of thinking about these matters. Paddy tended to lose interest.

One time, however, after Paddy had made a version of the now-familiar plea, one of the Catholics said straight off that it wasn't a very subtle question. Lant immediately took the subject off Paddy, launching into an eloquent and stirring speech, lasting for several minutes, about the unfortunate lack of subtlety when it came to the pain a body experienced when facing extinction through disease. He stood up as he spoke. He'd counselled these dying children, he told them, and when he came to do his end-of-month notes, he had to fill in a box that said 'Result'. 'Result? What was the result? Oh, that's right. Death. Which wasn't very subtle either, was it?'

Lant paused and looked around the room.

For a moment it seemed he wasn't going to be able to carry on—his own statement had caught him out, he was choked up—and this had an amazing effect. Previously it had all been about ideas. Everyone stopped and watched him. Then he resumed speaking. He said he'd been trying to think of a less obvious word than death but it hadn't come. Lant said the emotions people felt tended not to be very subtle either. 'Grief-stricken, we say. Grief-struck, like lightning struck. And that's what it feels like, to lose someone. You're struck down. To lose your own child. These people sit across from me most days and it's very hard to know what to say, believe me. I mean, I've read all the textbooks, all the grief literature, I've been trained and trained for this but I'm sorry, I haven't thought of an argument yet, a nice, subtle piece of thinking that helps with this sort of pain. Frankly, in these circumstances, I find subtlety out of place. I think it's offensive. I think it reveals a shallow understanding of what it means to be human.'

By the time he'd finished Lant had tears in his eyes, for which he apologised. He sat down. The tears fell from his face onto the table and Lant wiped at them quickly. The Catholics were silent. They stared at the table. One of them, Paddy noticed, tucked his silver cross back in his shirt and kept his fingers here. Another of them went to speak but trailed off quickly, mumbling a sort of irritated apology. Finally, someone who might have been a member of their group, a newcomer, turned to Lant and said in a conciliatory but firm way, 'I don't believe my faith allows me to escape from any of the questions you raise. My faith was raised out of these very questions.'

'That's circular, what are you saying?' said Lant. He rubbed at his eyes. 'And why do you always say faith? Say religion. You say faith and it sounds as though you own it, you have it, and everyone else is lacking it. I have faith too. I redeem the word for humanism. I have faith minus the other stuff.'

'The other stuff is my way of examining these questions, of suffering and pain. It's a help to me. I find what's human is the desire to understand and one approach is to use these tools.' The speaker was not one of their usual opponents. He was a recent arrival at the hospital and had, up to this point, never said a word. He spoke with his head slightly averted and only looked up when he'd finished, at which point there was a slightly unnerving and unabashed stare. He had a large forehead and a purple birthmark down one side of his neck.

Lant was momentarily knocked off course. 'Tools! Like it's a kitset. Put part A with part B and you shall get, what, the meaning of life, I suppose.'

'No,' said the new arrival, smiling slightly, 'probably you'll still be left with parts C, D and E.'

'Right! Listen, I'm in awe of your composure. Really. I envy you that. But I've done my share of examining these questions too, my friend. End of the day, I have a box to tick. Result, she died. Age, six years. Enter mother and father. At that moment, the abstract contemplation of these questions becomes a little trickier, I think.' He held up his hands as if offering the table something, moving his hands forward as if bearing an object. 'Here is the body of your child.' Several at the table swayed back slightly, to put themselves out of reach. There was something blasphemous in Lant's gesture, priestly. He was compelling. 'We're all too young to know what that means. We're all still children.'

Afterwards as they walked back to their respective flats in the early morning, Paddy asked Lant about the box on his notes. What box? he said. Paddy reminded him of his speech to the Catholics, the result box where he had to fill in the word 'Death'.

'But Card,' he said, 'dear Card, there isn't any box.'

'No box?'

'No, I made it up.' He was grinning at him. 'What kind of form would have a box like that? Come on. It was a rhetorical device. I wasn't going to let those smug bastards off this time.'

They walked a bit further. It was raining lightly. A few cars passed with their headlights on. They'd only get a couple of hours sleep before they needed to be back at work and they'd have to walk back the same way in the rain. Sometimes they could find a place to sleep at the hospital but not that night. They'd had more drinks after the doctors had all gone to bed.

The session had been a strange one, not quite the vindication they'd hoped for and Paddy felt it now in the joyless tramp through the rain. Lant had derailed it with his speech. People had drifted off earlier than usual, leaving only a few at the table and things had continued with an odd sort of willed enthusiasm. Then there'd been the matter of the guy who'd challenged Lant. Forehead, they'd called him. Birthmark. He'd not recoiled when Lant had held up the phantom body of the dead child. In fact he'd folded his arms and looked out the window, in the pose of someone thinking of something important that could not be mentioned just then. What was his story? Not knowing gave him a troubling power. He was a far more serious adversary than the boy-doctor who'd once told them all to keep talking because hell wasn't full yet.

'Lant,' said Paddy, 'do you even counsel dying children?'

'Do you think they'd let me? It's a specialist area, Card. Besides, I couldn't handle it, could you?'

Lant turned off at his street, lifting a hand behind him in farewell. Three trolley buses went past, heading into town, going at great speed. The sound of them gave Paddy a fright. The first one had its cloth blind pulled down: 'Sorry not in service', and the other two were following so closely behind that he couldn't read them. There was only a foot or two between each bus. It was like one long demonic vehicle. The drivers, sharply illuminated in their stations, were laughing—he could see that. They were playing some game, racing each other home. Maniacs.

They left the upstairs bar just after 3am. Paddy had been talking about Jimmy Gorzo and his father, the bowling lanes. Earlier he'd told Lant about Iyob and the whole deal with Dora, then the scene at the school. Lant had listened very carefully and then he'd asked Paddy whether he thought Dora and Medbh had got any film of the band playing, which had then started him on a long riff about plans to go on tour with the band. The problem was the other guys were all fairly housebound types with kids and wives. They'd all done their wild on-the-road stuff years before whereas Lant was just starting out and he had a hunger for it. He thought about it all the time, about playing, about turning up somewhere, no one knows you and an hour later, you've made a connection. Even more than the bike now, he said, he thought about music, playing the violin in this little okayish band. This *nice* band. He knew it wasn't respectable. It was crazy. He was fifty years old. Of course all the punks were fifty years old now, older. Joe Strummer had died of a heart attack, yes, yes, and the Rolling Stones could get into the movies for half-price. But they'd been into it from a young age whereas he, Lant, had been doing music exams and playing in cold halls in front of his parents and a row of hatchet-faced judges accumulating his third places, his runner-up medals. Then he'd thrown it all in because no one was going to keep that up. Now he had a decent adult profession. His daughter hadn't wanted him to play at the school, nor had Melinda, well, that wasn't a surprise. Had Card seen how she'd tried to get at him about the soccer thing with Crystal, which was clearly nothing, the girl got right back up and started playing again. But they had a point. Jesus, he wouldn't have liked to see his father play in a band in front of people. He didn't even like it when his father walked down a street with him. It was against the natural order of things, he understood that. He'd stopped talking then and he looked at Paddy, who asked him what was wrong and he said, 'Your mother, Card. Your poor mother.'

'Yes.'

'Why do you think she's done this to you?'

'Eh?'

The Chinese lantern above them swayed a little. Paddy heard someone nice talking to him. The barman had appeared as if summoned by some inaudible but massively effective bell. Your thought rang it and he came. The human brain was an extraordinary thing. The barman was about twenty-five. He wore a black waistcoat and his sideburns were shaped into a fine point that went just under his cheekbones. He was the polite face of the underworld. He bent down to talk confidentially about their requirements.

'Two for the road,' said Lant.

The devil disappeared.

'What did you say about my mother?' said Paddy.

But Lant said he'd forgotten already. Paddy repeated what he'd heard. Interesting, Lant said. What was interesting, Paddy asked, that he was claiming agency in this case? That his mother was authoring her own affliction? What, she was *putting it on*? She was aiming this at them in some psychic war? If so, she was probably overdoing her own trauma, didn't he think. If so, Lant should take a ticket behind poor paranoid Margie, his sister. No, no, Lant told him. What was interesting was that Paddy had heard him say something he hadn't.

It was an outrageous lie.

'Okay,' said Paddy, 'now the mind games begin.'

Lant shook his head. He had something else he wanted to say, he said. In the ballpark of France. Before he could be stopped, he was into it. 'When Melinda and I went to Paris, before Crystal was born, she was in a clothes store, in the changing rooms, and they had a sign which said, "Please keep your panties with you at all times." And that became our sort of catch-cry the whole trip. It was a very sexed-up sojourn, I remember. Of course now if I said that to her, remember when you saw that sign, "Please keep

244

your panties with you at all times", she'd not find it acceptable at all. It'd be inappropriate, crude. I'm no longer allowed to talk about her panties, the mother of my child.'

'Is there a problem?' said Paddy. 'You're divorced and she hates your guts.'

'Thank you for that. But you're right. Yet I'm thinking, what am I thinking? Intimacy is very fragile. And life is—'

'What?'

'Oh, I don't know. Look at poor old Helen Clark. You define an era and then what? Booted into oblivion.'

The change in topic was highly irritating.

'Poor Helen,' continued Lant. 'Such intelligence and strength of character, rewarded how?'

'The writing was on the wall.'

Lant sighed. 'Truth is, Card, I felt sort of sick of Labour too, you know. I mean it's sad. But finally not so sad perhaps.'

Paddy studied the speaker. 'You voted for National, didn't you?'

'Come on.'

'Jesus. I don't believe it. You voted for National.'

'Well, I'm not proud of myself.'

Lant had sent out invitations for an election night get-together. Paddy and Helena were going. Then a couple of days before, Lant cancelled. Something had come up, he explained, taking him out of town. Here's what had come up. He'd suddenly thought, I'm betraying my ideals and an audience was usually not desirable for apostasy. Paddy said as much now.

'Punish me, Saint Patrick,' said Lant, 'I deserve it.'

'You've voted into power a man with a speech defect.'

'There's no defect. What are you talking about defect? You of all people. As you've said yourself more than once, there's only speech. And anyway, Churchill had a speech defect.'

Yes, they'd had that conversation.

They finished their final drinks in silence.

'I've lost her,' said Paddy. Immediately he despised himself for cracking, for the grandiosity.

Lant was way behind. Perhaps still on the former PM. 'Lost who?'

'What if, I mean. What if I've lost my mother?'

Lant leaned forward. 'She's not doing anything on purpose, you know.'

This made Paddy stand up. He was furious.

Outside it was still mostly night though the sky was lightening close to the hills above Ngaio, where Stephanie and her kids were hopefully asleep. The cool was vaguely beneficial. Paddy felt his body start to work. There wasn't a sign of stiffness or pain from the bike ride or perhaps that was safely masked now by the effects of the alcohol. The streets weren't empty. People with recent histories similar to their own wandered along, trying doors, making sudden movements as if to avoid objects only they could see. Paddy and Lant made way for a group of young women taking up the whole footpath, swaying and tripping. The women called out something in their direction, and then Lant chased after them. He came back with a cigarette.

The men kept a steady and superior course, bumping harmlessly into each other as they walked. Lant's boots made a different sound, a sign that he was moving his feet in some new way. They hit the ground with an odd flappy noise as if the soles had come loose from the uppers. Paddy realised this was drawing attention to them. A few people across the street had stopped to watch. Then Paddy was aware of footsteps coming from behind them and a raised voice. Someone's after us, he thought. This was what the people were watching, some interesting disturbance safely removed from them. 'Who is it?' said Lant. His head was hanging down, the cigarette stuck on his lip. They were both quickening their steps.

'Keep moving,' said Paddy.

The voice was closer now. 'Hey! Hey!'

They were travelling as fast as they could without breaking into a run. But why not run? Because they thought they could escape this without showing that they were even aware of it.

Paddy's mind went back to other pursuits where Lant was involved. They'd run from parties before, jumped fences in Naenae holding LPs they'd tried to put on—*Never Mind the Bollocks* in a very brown disco house where they knew no one—and another time from some cops who'd happened upon them urinating in an alley probably not far from this same spot. The good old days.

'Stop! You guys!'

Lant was breathing heavily beside him. He took the cigarette out and spat something from his mouth.

'Hey!'

'Wait on,' said Paddy.

'Jesus,' said Lant.

'Wait a moment, Lant.' Paddy took his arm and made him stop suddenly. They almost fell together.

'Guys!' The voice was with them.

They turned.

'You forgot this.'

It was the barman. He held out Lant's violin case. Lant reached for it rather blindly, almost doubled over. 'Yes,' he said. 'Very kind of you.'

'All right?'

'We've had a wonderful evening, thanks.'

Three men, breathing heavily.

'Who'd you think I was?'

'No one,' said Lant. 'We just have very guilty consciences.' Somewhere he'd lost his cigarette. He looked for it for a while, muttering to himself, and then gave up.

Another group went past. The girls didn't look older than sixteen. One of them was saying, 'Just the idea of him with someone else makes my skin crawl.'

Lant said to Paddy, 'First you feel flattered to hear something like that because you think they've sort of trusted you with it. Then you realise you only heard it because you were invisible to them. They speak because they don't see you. Girls don't see us any more.'

Paddy said, 'Please tell me that you've not just thought of that now.'

'Knowing it, even for years and years, doesn't prevent it from being a recurring pain.' He took a few more paces. 'I'm struggling with the fact that my normal partner is now a woman of almost my age.'

The almost was good. It was a joke. But Paddy didn't want jokes. He said he didn't feel that way at all about women. And as he spoke, he believed it. Did Lant believe him? Probably not. Fuck Lant.

But Lant stopped for a moment. He looked at Paddy. 'I respect that,' he said. He appeared to be sincere.

They walked on towards the corner of Dixon Street and Cuba Mall, where they were to part company. Lant lived in the top storey of a house he owned in McDonald Crescent, a few minutes away. He rented out the bottom of the house to a physiotherapy clinic and received free sessions in return for letting them use the space in front of his garage for client parking. The physio, he said, was what got him through the first months of cycling. He was speaking about it now. Paddy knew all of this and didn't want to hear it again. He also said the physio was good for post-violin playing since he often got a sore neck, which shouldn't happen but his technique was rusty. He'd have to see them tomorrow if he could. Was Paddy still sore from the ride to Lower Hutt? No, Paddy told him. He said he couldn't believe Paddy had gone out there solo first time. What did it feel like honestly? Good, said Paddy. They were walking more slowly than before and Paddy had the sense that Lant wanted to delay their arrival at the corner. He'd moved into the sentimental phase of the evening and Paddy, longing for his bed and feeling hostile towards his friend, was not with him.

But why hate Lant? For fucking with his mind about his mother? Because of the National Party? The violin incident and the chasing barman was nothing, a laugh. Paddy thought again of the time when Lant had lied to the Catholic junior doctors about his work, fooling everyone with his emotional

248

speech. Could it be that he resented him for that still? But Paddy admired him for it too, sort of. Maybe his disenchantment had a plainer source: the coloured alcohol he'd poured into his system. Paddy wasn't used to it and it had poisoned him. Toxic was a good word for his state.

Lant stopped for a moment, moving the violin case from one hand to the other. 'Whenever I'm feeling lonely or a bit depressed,' he said, 'I go downstairs and sit in their waiting room until an appointment comes free.' They were back on the physio stuff.

'Sounds good.'

'Then you feel the hands on your body, and that helps.'

'Yep.'

'Not sexually. I mean, Bruce is like this short, ex-hockey rep guy.'

'You don't fancy him.'

'No, and Rae, his wife, she's . . .'

'Not your type.'

He stopped again in the street and turned to face Paddy, fully exasperated. 'It isn't about that, Patrick! Can you be serious for a moment? Listen, it's about human contact.'

'I understand. It's about physios in the basement.'

'Oh, you're a cunt.'

'I know I am.'

Lant regarded Paddy with hostile disappointment and Paddy saw that he'd succeeded in giving him a portion of his own temper. Paddy walked on. At the corner, as a precaution against any sudden embrace, Paddy made sure he kept a few feet away from him as they said goodbye. There seemed little danger now, Lant was stewing. Paddy could do nothing about his own mood and he felt sorry about it standing with Lant early in the morning but that made it worse. Anyway, neither of us will remember these details tomorrow, he thought. They nodded at each other and turned away.

'Au revoir!' Lant called out as Paddy walked off. Was it spite or solidarity? Paddy couldn't tell.

The Mall was deserted except for two buskers standing in the doorway of a shop playing acoustic guitars. They looked like students and they were singing, of course, 'American Pie'. They'd opened a guitar case to collect the money. Paddy didn't want to get too close to them so he was unable to see whether there was any money in the case. There was no one else around. Staggeringly pointless. He thought at once of the two Catholic junior doctors years ago. It was a song he'd always hated, the song of bores who saw in the interminable lyrics special meanings, deep symbolism. The buskers sang with the sort of pretentious emotionalism, the whiny pleading that this song always drew from its converts. Maybe they were med students. They threw their heads back as they sang, giving each other little looks of encouragement. They weren't real buskers, they only did this after they'd had a few drinks and on deserted streets, hoping to be seen by one or two people so they could claim it as a great night. They must have been aware of Paddy though they showed no sign of it. He counted as an audience, as part of their 'great night', which made him resent them viciously. What he hated most was the idea that this pair was actually Lant and himself. Hadn't they too entertained the same idea—to sing on the streets at night? He was sure of it, and sure they hadn't done it. Even more strongly now he felt the desire for his bed and to be close to Helena's sleeping body. He wondered again about his mother and a useless alcoholic irritation gripped him. Perhaps it was in his power, in his range, to therapise her, just as the fuckwit Paul Shawn had said.

The city had grown unlikeable or Paddy was unlikeable in the city—one of the two. He was moving quickly, wishing for a sort of invisibility, keeping his head down. He was Sam Covenay, he was.

He thought in a rush of sentences. You need to see life as a story with meaning. But you impose this meaning on the world. Thus spake Susan Neiman in *Moral Clarity*, recently in from Amazon. This need was crucial to human dignity, 'without which we hold our lives to be worthless'. He'd written out the stickie earlier that day. Cf FAS? he wrote. Could his mother hold firm to her dignity? What was her story now? Contingency came a-knocking one morning on her new apartment door, where Paddy had placed her. Teresa opened the door and said, 'How do you do?' He thought in one moment, she'll be all right, and in another, but what will all right look like?

Ahead of him a man stepped out of an entranceway carrying a stack of long cardboard boxes. He was adding these to an existing pile on the footpath. A yeasty blast of air came from inside. It was a bakery. The man was wearing a paper hat and an apron. He was re-entering the place as Paddy passed and he gave Paddy a quick look and then glanced at the boxes on the footpath. He seemed to be sizing up whether or not Paddy presented a threat to the boxes. They must have contained something—bread or pastries—which were to be delivered to cafés for the day's trade. He'd decided Paddy was harmless because he closed the door.

A part of Paddy wanted to repay the man's scrutiny by scooping up one of the boxes. Not that he was hungry at all. Paddy looked in through the window and saw him moving behind a counter into a back room, which was well lit. Just as Paddy was about to move off, another figure appeared near the counter, also wearing a hat and apron. He first thought it was a boy. The figure bent down then moved back into the lit space and he saw that it was a woman. She opened an oven and slid a large tray out before disappearing from view for a moment and when he saw her again, she was carrying another tray that she put in the oven, closing the door. At this point she took off her hat and ran her fingers through her hair, itching her scalp. She looked straight out at the street, past the counter to the window where he was standing. It was Camille, the French mother from school.

Mon Dieu a French baker!

He wasn't sure whether she'd seen him. Maybe the light on inside hid him because she showed no sign of being watched. He moved his head slightly and she peered in his direction, trying to work things out. She stepped a few feet into the bakery, into the shadow, still looking towards him. Could she recognise him from where she was, or would she think he was just some strange man cruising the streets, pressing his face against shop windows, hoping to spook people? She turned her head slightly and said something to the man Paddy had seen with the boxes. From outside he couldn't hear anything. The man appeared by the counter. There was still time to walk off before he was recognised.

He realised what this was like. It was like watching a silent movie. A *French* silent movie.

Paddy raised his hand and smiled. Hello, he mouthed. Finally she came towards the door, still looking. The man was talking to her but she was obviously telling him not to worry, she knew this figure at the window.

Camille opened the door. 'Hello?'

'Paddy Thompson,' he said. 'We met at the school thing today, yesterday.'

'Yes? Hello.'

The man still waited by the counter. He made a gesture, checking with her that everything was all right before moving into the back room again.

'I just looked in and saw you.'

'I work here.'

Paddy looked inside the bakery. The glass cabinets were empty but there were handwritten signs fixed to plates. They were all in French. He must have passed the place before but he'd never been in. It was quite new. 'Is that your husband?'

'Yes.'

'He's French?'

She seemed to agree with this. 'Pierre,' she said.

Pierre! 'It's an early start. Hard work, I imagine.'

'Yes,' she said. She was puzzled and wary.

'Okay.' He started to turn away, suddenly exhausted at having to do the work of talking to this woman.

She scrunched up her cap in her hand. At once she seemed

to have changed her mind about him. 'Yes, when I was at the school and meeting you, I was just woken up. I was not so good. It was very early morning for me. Now I'm better. I'm alive, you know.' She gave a little smile. 'And then I had to go. I was taking Thierry to his friend's. But what are you doing on the street? An emergency, I hope not.'

'No,' he said. 'I was at a bar with a friend. No emergency. You remember the violinist from the band?'

'From this band at the school? Of course. I liked them.'

'I'll tell him. We were celebrating. It went on a bit longer than we were expecting. Sorry for interrupting your work.'

'No because we don't see many people, it's a change.'

'Not many of your friends drop by at three or four in the morning to say hello.'

'You are the first.'

'Maybe we could meet again some time.'

She studied him. 'Sure. If I see you at the school maybe.'

'It may sound strange,' he said, 'but I'd like you to meet my mother.'

'Okay,' she said. She took everything in complete earnestness. See the drunk person's mother, why not.

Pierre came to the door with more boxes and they let him past. Camille then spoke to him very fast in French, explaining about Paddy. He shook Paddy's hand, saying quite sternly, 'Pleased to meet you.' He was only a little taller than Camille, olive-skinned, stocky, with strong forearms. He smelled of sweat. They spoke together again, something about the boxes, Paddy thought, and then Pierre went back inside.

'Attendez, wait. He wants to give you something to eat,' said Camille.

'No, I'm fine.'

'No, but he will bring it. You can't refuse. He's from Bosnia first. Can't refuse. You're lucky he doesn't want to give you something to drink. Do you know rakija?'

'No.'

'Good.' She laughed and then he laughed.

'Okay. Pierre doesn't sound very Bosnian though, the name.'

'When he comes to France, he changed it. When he *came* to France. Change the name to make things easy.'

'When was that?'

'After the war, you know.'

His mind was so bleary he couldn't think for a moment which war Camille meant. The war with Serbia.

'Who is your mother?' she said.

'Who?'

'No, I mean, you want me to meet her?'

'Yes! If you could, that would be great. It's difficult to explain, sorry.'

Pierre was heading back their way, carrying a small square box. 'For you,' he said and gave Paddy the box.

'That's very kind! Merci!'

Pierre shook his head, it's nothing. Paddy looked at the box. It was sealed with a simple fold of cardboard flaps. He wasn't sure whether or not he should open it. The three of them looked at each other.

'You can see,' said Camille. 'It's fine.'

'Yes?' said Paddy. 'Open?'

'Open,' said Pierre.

But Paddy could hardly move his fingers to lift the flaps. He felt shaky and uncertain, as if anything might happen to him outside the bakery of these near strangers. A huge wave moved through his entire body. It was a definite physical feeling starting at the backs of his ankles and passing along his legs, up his spine and ending at his ears—the sudden release that could come from massage. Lant's point after all? But it was also more than that. Here was the emotion too, that he'd denied Lant and which shook him and which hadn't been released even yet but was held, trapped, as if he'd just prevented himself from sneezing. Was this hidden from his companions by the half-dark? He fumbled with the lid. The box opened and there was a single pastry, a thing of obvious delicacy and skill, two different-sized balls, the smallest one on top covered in a coffee-coloured icing. It was architecture, clever and witty, artistic even. He'd never had a sweet tooth. The thing was astonishingly pointless to him, and that was suddenly affecting too. All that effort.

'It's la réligieuse, you know it?' said Camille.

He shook his head.

'Also you can call it the nun. Here is the body and then the head.' She pointed. 'Oh. I'm sorry,' she said. 'You have these—'

'Tears!' he said. 'Yes. Strange person that I am.'

Pierre was staring at him, then at the pastry.

'Sorry for this,' said Paddy. He was holding the box and he couldn't wipe his face. He was powerless to do a thing, his cheeks wet. He was half-blinded and he felt the box being carefully removed from his hands.

'Come inside,' said Camille.

'No, no,' Paddy told her, wiping at his eyes and at his nose. 'I'll be fine. I'm so sorry.'

Pierre spoke in French or Bosnian or something to Camille. 'He says,' she said, 'maybe he could bring you something else, not this one. People are not so often upset with his baking.'

Paddy laughed. He was feeling better, less shaky. The immense rogue wave had crashed on his head and he was still standing upright. He gestured that Pierre could hand him back the box. Paddy was muttering something about work pressures and family issues. He tried to make a joke of it, telling them he wasn't réligieux at all. Camille bent close to hear but he wasn't making much sense. He thanked them again. He shook Pierre's hand and said goodnight. 'Bonne nuit,' he said, not at all sure this was the correct French for the occasion. Maybe this what you said to a child who was going to bed? Sweet dreams. Camille took his offered hand and drew him down towards her. In his confusion he thought she wanted to say something to him and he turned his ear to her mouth. In the confusion she kissed him there, on his right ear. He had an image of Sam Covenay kissing his mother outside their apartment, the careful proffering of cheeks, the lightest touch of faces. Had he practised

255

this? Paddy had seen it and then he'd forgotten about it but it was remarkable. Better than this bungled thing. I need to see the Covenays again, he thought. More unfinished business. They have my picture after all. 'Thanks,' he said. He was walking off, full of blue liquid, carrying his box, his little building, his sculpture of sugar, his edifice of mainly air.

4

It was the morning of the review and still dark outside. Paddy was instantly awake. He lay in bed listening to the far-off rumble of the building. He'd been dreaming about being caught in a volcanic eruption. The noises in his dream were obviously connected with the building's sound. It was all reasonably apocalyptic, with a German theme too, of explosions, wartime panic. Astrid L., the Norwegian head-injury and FAS pioneer, was involved somehow.

At the moment he'd seriously miscalculated his heroic move— to re-enter the threatened house, to find Helena's laptop—the dream ended, or he made the dream end and he woke hot and alert, sweating from his stomach. He put his finger in his belly button. It was damp.

The Ministry was coming to Helena's school. He concentrated on that fact as the volcanic eruption feeling gradually faded. One world slipped behind the other. He could hear Helena in the kitchen, banging the coffee grounds into the rubbish bin under the sink. There was a sharp guilt for Paddy in this sound, if not rebuke. The coffee machine was his domain, his responsibility. Who knew how such things developed within a household? Both of them understood the washing machine was hers. The dishwasher was jointly managed, as was the recycling. Anything involving a ladder—changing light bulbs, looking in high cupboards—was Helena's, he didn't know why. She possessed no cat-like qualities of climbing or balance. If anything she was a bit clumsy in her movements. Nevertheless, she commanded the little stepladder, pulling it into position from wherever she'd stored it previously. There were other divisions. He cleaned the bathroom but she vacuumed. He took things to the post office but she managed their joint bank account, keeping an eye on the automatic payments and all other bills except those connected with their various insurances which were somehow his area despite the fact he'd overlooked a double payment on their car insurance for several months. This had all developed mysteriously, in some cases with a kind of illogic, and lying in bed, stunned by the dream he'd just had, it was nice to gather up a few domestic details.

He thought, though without any kind of criticism, how Helena was a rather casual, almost heedless, washer of clothes, ignoring instruction labels and seldom addressing problem items separately. She threw everything in together, crushing full loads into the small machine and closing the lid by dropping it from its full height. There was something punitive and unacknowledged here. This didn't seem to affect the way she looked at all. She was an exceptionally good ironer of clothes, which may have saved her. Paddy had once tried to get to the machine first and she'd intercepted him, simply taking the washing basket from his hands. That was that. Probably he guarded the toilet cleaning with a similar and similarly strange sense of ownership. She'd told him that there was a good chance he was the only male anywhere on the planet, not remunerated directly for it, who cleaned the toilet. Yes, he said, and he'd also been the only male in his second-year Women's Studies tutorial. Who says the liberal arts aren't worthwhile, she said. To cap it off, he'd entered a profession dominated by women.

Listening to her bash around in the kitchen, Paddy knew he had to intervene but by the time he got there, the coffee pot was on the stove. Helena stood watching it. She was dressed for work. He was still in his pyjamas. He was filled with blue alcohol, though for now this seemed to pose few problems. The hot flush from his suicidal act in the dream of the volcano had gone. He felt all right. Perhaps the barman, notwithstanding volcanoes, really was a kind of magician and not a poisoner.

'You didn't need to get up,' she said.

'Today's the day,' he said. 'How did you sleep?'

'It's out of my hands now. There's nothing more I can do. I had a good sleep, didn't even hear you come in.'

'I'm glad. Lant needed company.'

'They were good, weren't they, his band.' She poured some milk into the pot—his pot—and put it on the stove. The coffee was only just starting to come through. She was getting to the milk earlier than he would have done. It irritated him this tiny detail. It horrified him that he registered such a measly emotion. He had to fight hard not to say anything. Today was the day. Someone was deciding his beloved's future, someone who lacked any insight into her character. He loved Helena ferociously and he thought she was the best thing that had ever happened to him bar nothing. He thought, my sisters are right: she is a sane, grown-up person. He thought, she has a mind greater than your petty apparatus. She'd ruin the milk in front of him. They'd not made love in more than three weeks, going to bed at different times.

'Let me,' he said, trying to manoeuvre closer to the stove.

'No, it's all right,' she said, holding the space she had. 'Come any closer to the flame and we'll all go up in smoke.'

'Is it that bad?' He sniffed his own sleeve. 'We went to a bar, two bars.' He apologised for not texting and she shrugged dissociatively. Her plate was full of bigger fish. But so was his.

'Careful you don't scald the milk,' he said.

'What?'

He gestured towards the pot.

'Scalding is what we're aiming for,' she said. 'Scalding is just heating. You mean scorching, which is burning.' She gave it a glance.

Let's not, he thought.

When she'd poured the coffee, he asked about Teresa, whether Helena had seen her last night after the school barbecue. She said she'd phoned her and spoken briefly, things seemed okay. Teresa said she'd been sleeping and sleeping, as if she'd come back from some mammoth journey involving numerous time zone changes. She'd wake for a few minutes, feeling fine, knowing she had things to do, before being struck down again by the need to collapse into bed.

'I told her that was all normal and good,' said Helena, 'the body's way of telling her it was fighting a battle on her behalf and needed all the energy it could get.'

This general practitioner voice of reason was infuriating somehow. He asked about her accent.

'The same.'

'Perhaps after one of these sleeps she'll wake up talking normally,' he said, with strange flippancy.

'That's what she said to me. Crossing so many time zones, she said she's bound to end up home again. She sounded quite jolly when she said it.'

The coffee tasted different but Paddy didn't say anything. There was Helena's laptop, on the table in front of them. He put his hand on it and it was warm. She'd already been working. The warmth made him remember again the crazy search during the eruption, the heat coming up through the floorboards of the house. In the dream he'd looked for the laptop in concealed or semi-concealed spots whereas maybe it had been out in the open all along. Dreams were engines of regret.

They talked about what would happen at her school. There were a few small matters to be addressed before the Ministry person arrived. Her name was Trish Gibbons and apparently she was new to the role, which could mean bad things, Helena said, if she was the sort looking to make a name for herself by coming down hard. Plus she was a woman. Or good things, he said, if she was the sort looking to prove her fairness and decency. Helena nodded automatically at this, then stood up abruptly.

'What is it?'

'Morning tea,' she said. 'What should I give Trish Gibbons for morning tea?' She walked over to the bench and opened a cupboard. She seemed a bit mad.

'Don't bake her a cake, will you.'

'A small cake, an orange cake.' She looked at her watch. It was just before seven.

'Don't Helena.'

She was looking in the fruit bowl. She picked up two oranges. 'It's a quick cake.'

'No cake. Buy the cake. Go to Moore Wilson's on your way and get a cake.'

She hovered with the oranges. 'Quick cake for Trish Gibbons. Yes or no?'

'When did you last bake a cake?'

'When?'

'When? I've never had a cake that you've baked.' That had the potential to sound whiny.

'You?'

'Never. So that's three years of not baking a cake.'

She dropped the oranges back in the bowl. 'Fuck, you're right. I can't bake, what was I thinking? Should have got Medbh to bake a cake!' She turned to face him. 'But what is the thing in the fridge, Paddy? We have a white box in the fridge.'

'You can't give that to Trish Gibbons. It's my réligieuse.' He told her quickly about meeting Camille at the school, then their later encounter. He didn't say anything about how he'd responded to the gift. Helena was only half listening by this stage anyway as she tidied things up in the kitchen. He told her to stop doing that, he'd do it later.

'What do you think this Camille will do for your mother though?' she said. It was a dispiriting question, not unfair, but posed without her usual tenderness. Helena was firmly in her work sphere.

'I don't know.'

Ten minutes later she was ready to leave. He followed her to the door. 'Probably this is exactly the wrong time and you've got it all sorted out but what about the Iyob and Dora situation? I mean from a Trisha Gibbons perspective.'

'Sorted,' she said.

'Good. But how?'

'Iyob had some leave owing.'

'Okay.'

'So that's all good.'

'So Iyob won't show up.'

'Exactly,' she said. 'He's on leave.'

'By which time things might have cooled off.'

'After which time we review everything.'

Paddy heard his voice adopt a fake note of objectivity, as if he were interviewing her. 'I see. Everything being?'

'Everything related to the employment situation.'

'Vis-à-vis Dora.'

'Everything,' she said, an edge to her voice. 'Our lawyer's on it.'

This was the time to pull back. 'On what?'

'The harassment et cetera, the things he said.'

Of course to provoke her, challenge her at this moment would clearly be a thoughtless act. He had no idea whether it was justice for Iyob he wanted or punishment for Dora. He heard himself begin again on the inquiry, sounding official. 'Harassment? Okay, that's new.'

'Anyway, the things that he said.'

'The things he said being part of a conversation, an exchange, also involving the things Dora said and did. Those being the two that it takes to tango.'

Helena took a short breath. She could have slapped him hard across the back of his head with her bag. 'All that, yes. Paddy, I've got to go. I've got to buy my fucking cake.'

He hated when she swore. She had bursts of it and so did he, related usually in his case, and he guessed something similar in hers, to spending time with people who did so regularly, without hearing themselves. Tony Gorzo. Paddy had once worked as a consultant on a TV documentary. That world ran on a stream of it, with the natural force of dialect. For the first couple of days they actually struggled to understand what he was saying to them. He was visiting a foreign fucking country.

He could tell she was prepared not to kiss him goodbye. This was about as harsh as they got with each other. Up to now. He possessed an astonishing complacency to think they'd reached some immutable comfort zone. Yet he was also deeply attached to, and proud of, that very zone. He thought of it as the principle achievement of his adult life. They were civilised. He leaned forward, determined. It was will-power. The day was a significant one, requiring a show of male maturity, even one as shallow as this. They kissed and he wished her luck and told her he loved her and that she ran the best language school in the country if not the world. She looked at him as if to say, why do you sound so pro forma? He did sound pro forma, yet he meant every word. She knew this too. She was being frosty and fed up. The door closed but then she knocked on it almost immediately. In that moment before he saw her again, he imagined a scene of intense reunion.

She was bent down, fiddling with things in her bag. 'Paddy, call me or text me if anything happens with your mother. I can come, you know. Trisha Gibbons means nothing to me.'

'That's not true but thanks.'

She stood up. They kissed again, she leading. She kissed him as though she meant something. It was emphatic, which slightly spoiled it. He was critiquing *this* now?

'Soon,' she said, 'this will all be over and we can both be more human, sorry, my love.' She slapped her forehead with her fingers as if she were in a movie. 'God, I almost forgot. Your mother's cousin rang last night. Pip.'

'We were supposed to call her.'

'Anyway, I filled her in. She's going to call again today.'

'Right.'

'Then when I was talking to Pip, Tony Gorzo left a message. I saved it.'

'A veritable tsunami of messages,' he said.

They heard the lift doors opening down the corridor. 'The other thing of course is they have a new minister.'

'Who does?'

'Education,' she said. 'So they'll want to please the new minister.' She was scattered to the winds, his normally together partner-for-life. Was there a chance things at the school could go wrong?

'By showing him things aren't all bad in the language school sector, that you don't all drive black Mercedes, that there are still shining lights.'

'Okay,' she said, nodding. 'Where's your bike by the way?'

'In the morgue,' he said.

When he pressed the button to hear the message, Gorzo's voice came on so loudly he had to put the phone away from his ear. Normally he didn't speak at this volume. 'Come all the way to my place and you don't bowl a ball! On a bike! What's happened to you? Car broke down? So anyway, this is a late late call. You know I walked around all week last week knowing I'd forgotten some fucking thing. Like a headache. Turns out it was you, Paddy! And I thought it was something serious. Nah, nah, I'm kidding. But listen, you gotta come to the party. My eternal mother! If I don't die before then from organising a centenary. Like all week I think I've forgotten some huge obvious thing, something I had to do for the party I don't know. Logistics. Logistics are coming out my ears. But it was you, Paddy. And don't tell me about the new column, will you. I'm a bag of nerves just waiting to see what it is. The suspense is killing me. Ciao! And did I miss a fucking column, did I? Shit! Blame my family, blame—' Then his message cut off.

Paddy left a message for Murray Blanchford at the hospital, reminding him that he said he'd call, and then he cleaned up the kitchen. It was still too early to ring anyone else or to go next door to see his mother. He put on his cycling gear and took the lift to the basement.

The floor above where his bike was stored in the lock-up was for residents' car parks and he could hear a car starting up and the automatic gates sliding back to let it out. There was no one else around. He hadn't yet had the chance to explain anything about his mother to Geoff Harley, who'd found her and brought her up to them and so was probably entitled to a few facts. Still Paddy was pleased not to run into him now.

Outside the day was boringly blustery, the sort of conditions that turned even a short easy ride into something more effortful. He went down to the harbour and biked past Te Papa along the waterfront, moving against the thin stream of commuters heading towards Lambton Quay. The harbour was a mess of whitecaps, the water jerking around as though being carried in a bucket. Above him a silent passenger plane that looked too big and heavy and close tipped jerkily on its wing and entered the clouds. There were people on that plane, poor souls, most probably doing nothing more than going to Auckland for a day's work. It was his thought; it was also what his mother was prone to offer whenever she saw a plane. She hated flying. Not a phobia Margie in Vancouver believed in. Paddy cut back towards Mount Victoria, completing a small circuit of hill streets before rewarding himself with a homeward downhill coast.

In forty minutes he was back at the apartment, where he showered and, having forgotten to drink water after the ride, he drank some directly from the showerhead. It was warm and it made him feel sick at once. To act on such an impulse was curious. It wasn't something he'd done since he was a boy and he regretted it. There was now this liquid sitting on top of what he'd drunk the night before. He stood over the toilet bowl and slowly the nausea passed.

He had some cold water from the jug in the fridge and ate half a banana and a piece of cheese while looking at the paper. Then he remembered to check for phone messages.

Pip introduced herself as Philippa from Africa, 'your mother's ancient relative'. She apologised for calling so early. She said she'd talked to Helena last night and she was very grateful to get the news on Teresa, although now she knew she should have been in touch the moment his mother had left her house. She'd spent a lot of time thinking about her during the night. 'I was sworn to secrecy, Paddy. She said she needed a little more time. Clearly that was wrong. I'm very sorry.'

Pip was coming to Wellington that day and she'd like to meet him if it was possible. Did he remember her at all, she wondered? The last time she'd seen him was at his father's funeral.

She spoke in a quiet, even voice that dropped to a whisper at the end of sentences. Paddy imagined her smiling as she said her words, which were clipped precisely in a British way though they spread and opened on certain sounds.

She said she hadn't told Teresa that she was coming down and perhaps it was best if he didn't mention the visit. Despite everything, they'd spent a 'most marvellous' time together, full of 'memories and tears and laughter'—*lawfter*—but there was something that she'd like to talk to him about. She gave her phone numbers.

Pip answered at once when he rang. She was just walking out the door, she said. Paddy invited her to come for lunch at the apartment, or they could meet at a café if she preferred not to risk seeing his mother, if secrecy was utmost. She laughed and apologised for giving the impression that the meeting had to be all hush-hush. There was probably very little need for precautions of any kind. 'I was just hoping to speak to you on your own for a bit, Paddy.' It wouldn't take long. Then she could see Teresa, she was desperate to see dear Teresa, and without making a nuisance of herself, to offer any assistance, if only to sit in a room with her, keep her company, or do the shopping, whatever. 'I'm a free agent now,' she said.

He thanked her and they arranged the lunch. She knew a great place for strawberries on the way down. After further negotiations, they settled on meeting at midday, then they could do the lunch thing with Teresa, and eat strawberries.

'Can I just say, Paddy, how wonderful it will be to meet you after all this time. Of course I've been reading you for a long time, your column online. I often thought of writing you an email, a fan letter. It sounds silly but to be even distantly related to someone so distinguished is enough to feel excitement and pride.' *Prahd*. 'But listen, I'm not fully convinced of the wisdom of speaking to you about the subject I have in mind. So if during the course of driving to Wellington I change my mind, I hope you won't be too annoyed.'

He told her it was very intriguing and that he was looking forward to seeing her again, whatever she had to tell him.

'She's a very strong woman, your mother,' she said. 'Living alone all this time.'

After finishing the call, Paddy went downstairs into his office and sat in his clinic chair, listening hard. At first he thought he heard something through the wall. Then he became aware that it was coming from his own ear. It was the old figure leaving the room. Paddy went upstairs and in the bathroom he turned on Helena's electric toothbrush. The act was more in the spirit of random experimentation than any developed theory and in this way it was a bit like drinking the warm water from the shower. He switched off the toothbrush and walked out of the bathroom. The sound in his ear had gone.

When he rang his mother's number, the phone went unanswered for a while and then it clicked through to her voicemail. Here was Teresa as she'd been, asking him to please leave a message, speaking in her old clear unaccented voice— that is, accented in the familiar way, in the way of their family too. It gave him a shock. He remembered that after the death of a friend, the friend's widow couldn't bear to change the answer phone greeting and so you listened to the voice of your dead friend saying he'd get back to you soon. This wasn't as hopeless. Teresa was alive and she lived next door after all. But it wrenched him briefly. He put down the phone without leaving a message. Where could she be? It wasn't late, almost 10am. She could still be sleeping, or showering. Or she could simply not be answering her phone. Would she have the confidence to pick up the phone and speak to whoever was there?

He decided to go next door and knock on her door. He

also took their key to her apartment. He was prepared to enter now.

There was no response to his first knocking but after a while he sensed someone waiting behind the door and he spoke, letting her know who it was. He knocked lightly again, aware that the noise carried swiftly and clearly along the corridor. Finally, the door opened a little. He couldn't see anyone through the gap.

'Bonjour?' he said.

'Don't,' said his mother, her voice a thin rasp. The protest was desperate.

He asked if he could come in and the door opened wider.

His mother stood against the wall, appearing to use it for support, though the moment she understood he was staring at her, she attempted to stand straight. She even managed a weak smile. 'Paddy,' she said. 'I've just woken up.' She put out a hand to steady herself once more against the wall and knocked a little picture that was there. The picture appeared to confuse her. Who had put that up? It was a still-life oil painting of a bowl of fruit. It had hung in their old house in a similar position, by the front door. On one of the lemons there were a couple of brushstrokes that looked like two eyes and as a girl Margie had drawn a nose in black pen to finish the face. There was nothing experimental here, just plain defacement. It went unnoticed for days until finally at the dinner table their father said, 'I think we have a budding artist in the family.' Margie instantly went red, stood up and ran from the room in tears, saying, 'It wasn't me! It wasn't!'

The next evening their father told her they'd arranged for her to take art classes on Saturday mornings. Impossible to tell whether this was a very subtle piece of punishment—as punishing as their father could be—or a hopeless misreading of Margie's malevolence.

His sister went along perhaps three or four times to the lessons then stopped going. The still life by the front door remained her only work, since despite cleaning, the nose remained in ghostly outline and it became known as 'Margie's painting' after that.

Paddy straightened it.

'Margie's painting,' said Teresa, suddenly finding the information at her command once more. During the move, she'd been adamant about keeping it.

His mother looked ghastly. She looked neglected, and not simply for the ten or twelve hours since he'd last seen her, but neglected for days, weeks, longer. What had Murray Blanchford been thinking to suggest they could keep things normal? What had Paddy been thinking to go out drinking with Lant?

She was in a white nightie that was dotted in places with sweat. The nightie had ridden up one thigh, exposing the mottled skin of her upper leg and the edge of her underwear. He quickly pulled the damp material down. She accepted this with a quick look of annoyance. She knew something was wrong but she didn't know what exactly. Had she lost weight? Her hair was pressed in a wet mass against her forehead. He took her hand and led her into the sitting room where she brought herself down with a thump onto the sofa. She seemed surprised by this fall and opened her eyes wide, as if she'd only that moment woken up properly.

'Hello, Paddy!' she said, perhaps seeing him for the first time. *Ello Padee.*

Had everything at the door been forgotten now? 'How are you, Ma?'

Her gaze wandered uncertainly around the room though gradually she seemed to be gaining focus and alertness. She saw an object and nodded, as if mentally ticking it off. The table with my green vase. Tick. The cabinet with my glasses and bowls. Tick. The cord to pull the blinds up and down. Tick. Through there: my kitchen. The door to my bedroom. The inventory may have been more sophisticated than that or there may have been no such ticking at all. Whatever was happening, the process worked. Something began to reshape her features. When she turned to him again, her face was more animated, intelligent-looking. She's almost herself, he thought. The stare was collected and then it grew faintly ironic. She brushed her hair away from her eyes with one deft movement of her hand. She said to him, 'You look terrible.'

In the context, this was quite witty; she also meant it and she was almost certainly right. The early morning rise, coffee with Helena, the bike ride—this all represented a long false dawn. He had started to feel seedy and rough. African Pip would be there in less than two hours.

He told his mother he'd been out with Jeremy Lanting and had got in late. Then he asked her whether she'd eaten any breakfast. She was unsure about this and Paddy went into the kitchen to see whether there was any evidence of activity. The benches were clear. He looked in the dishwasher and that was also empty. He made tea for them both and some toast with marmalade, which was her favourite, while she went to the bathroom. When she came back she was wearing her dressing gown and her hair was brushed. She said she'd decided to wait until after he left before having a shower, if he could bear to look at her in her current state. 'Oh, Paddy,' she said. 'I—'

'Never mind,' he said.

They sat together in the kitchen without saying much while she ate the toast and drank her tea. Soon the colour returned to her cheeks. He watched her flex her foot which she did tentatively at first as if unsure how far to go with it. The movement and control she had seemed to satisfy her. She also rotated her left shoulder, feeling at the joint. She stood up suddenly and was clearing the cups and plates away before he had a chance to stop her.

'Your sister rang,' she said.

'Margie?'

'At some point in the early morning I was dead to the world and then I found myself with the phone in my hand talking to Margie. I don't think I'd called her.'

He was looking at his mother's mouth. The articulation was clear and very frontal. He'd been reading up on the French accent. Most vowels weren't diphthongised as they were in English. The French speaker of English therefore tended to stress vowels evenly, in effect substituting pure vowels for diphthongs. 'What did she say?'

She sat down again at the table, folding her serviette and smoothing it in front of her. 'She said I should go and live in Montreal.'

The effect on her face was to produce animation, which was new. The absence of diphthongs meant her mouth was moving much more rapidly than in English English, changing position after almost every syllable. There was no relaxation. He stared. 'No she didn't.'

'She did! First she'd asked me to say things, pronounce words. She was testing me, I think. It was a strange experience. Maybe I passed the test? "Very cute, Ma," she kept saying. "Very cute." Oh, she sounded quite— In Montreal, they'd accept me, she said. So I said, but I don't know any French, Margie. How would it help? The whole conversation was surreal and maybe I'm getting it wrong. Anyway, I don't think she's very happy about it.' *Appy*.

'It's Margaret, she's not very appy full stop. Don't worry about her.'

She looked up at him sharply. It was his imitation that had wounded her. 'Paddy, it's not how I sound is it?'

'Sorry, I was exaggerating.'

'No, I'm ridiculous.'

'Why ridiculous, there are sixty million people who sound like you when they speak English.'

'As a second language. This is my first. My only.' There was dread in her gaze now. 'And why are you looking at me all the time?'

He apologised again. 'Most of the English that's spoken in the world today comes with some sort of accent. Well, come on, actually *all* the English that's spoken. All of it! I'm speaking with one right now. What's the big deal?'

'That's just a clever thing to say.' She'd spoken with bitterness.

'It's a true thing to say.'

271

'But Paddy, the people you're talking about are *adding* a language to their existing knowledge.' She slumped back in her seat, the energy of her outrage expended. When she spoke again it was softly. 'It's different with this. What's happened to me? I've suffered a . . . subtraction.'

'But you still speak in a sophisticated way, don't you, as yourself. That hasn't changed or been subtracted. Mentally, you're the same. You can communicate me with me just as you've always done.'

'Can I?'

'And you can understand me. We can talk at our normal level.'

She nodded slowly, stroking the serviette again with both hands.

'Say "reading", "I was reading my book".'

She pronounced the word.

'Hear that? It's uvular.' He opened his own mouth and pointed his finger inside. 'The back of your tongue is touching your uvula. It's where you make that slight trilling sound. You've changed from the English "r" sound, which isn't usually trilled. Say "jew".'

'Shoe.'

'Okay, your tongue, the blade of it, which is here—' he showed her his tongue, '—goes up just behind your teeth, hits the alveolar ridge, while at the same time the front of the tongue is raised towards the hard palate, roof of your mouth. We call that a postalveolar articulation. In French, je. Je suis fatigué. See? Small movements of the tongue and palate. So what's happened to you is really something quite superficial, in the sense that certain aspects of your communicative style, the things going on in your vocal tract, have been altered, while the essential core remains in place. The voice is one of the easiest mechanisms to fool around with, to manipulate. Actors do it all the time. Imagine if you'd been paralysed by a stroke and couldn't move your arm. That would have been a nightmare of rehab and no certainty that any of it would work. All we're talking about is the position of the tongue, the lips, the soft palate and so on. Easy. I can help with that. It's what I do! And if it's not with me, because it might be better with someone else, I can arrange that. I can recommend someone. There are exercises and routines. Software you can use at home. It can all happen in private. Like your game. It would simply be another computer game for you. We can work something out.'

While he'd been speaking, his mother had kept her eyes fixed on the table. She now raised them and regarded him with a look of such gentle pity he was startled. She'd reversed in a flash, completely and mysteriously, the flow of emotion and for a moment he couldn't think what the meaning of this look could be. Surely he should have been pitying *her*. As a kind of reinforcement of this feeling, she reached across and put one hand on top of his, smiling at him reassuringly. She triumphed wordlessly. Without questioning or challenging any of his statements, he understood that she'd gently removed herself from their power. The effect was that his arguments suddenly seemed gestures of hope not for her but for him. Paddy appeared as well-meaning and ineffectual as anyone turning up with a message of cheery revival in the house of someone whose sense of life had shifted profoundly.

He still thought she was wrong. She was stubborn, afraid and wrong. Yet it made no sense to pursue things further then. Besides, he saw one way in which she was right and it stopped him. He'd spoken to her not as if she was his mother but someone else that he knew only vaguely. Someone less intelligent, less knowing, less familiar with the world she'd arrived in. At some level, I must think she's changed.

She had her computer set up in an alcove off the sitting room. Paddy could see the cords running down the wall. 'Have you been online at all?' he said.

'No!' She looked almost insulted at the suggestion.

'Murray Blanchford says you should just return to your normal routine. It might help. Do the things you always do.'

273

'But the things I always do have landed me in this.' Had she heard anything he'd said?

'We don't know that. Maybe there's no cause. The brain is a mystery.'

'Except they insist on poking around in it.'

'Some things they know about.'

'And with all the other things, they pretend they know about them.' She looked over towards the computer, and then glanced at her watch. She was being drawn towards it.

'Go on, Cleopatra,' he said.

'Who? Oh. Very smart, Patrick. Very smart.' She was still considering it, then with a shake of her head, she appeared to free herself again. Her eyes searched the room in a sudden arc— was she getting her bearings once more?—and she found Paddy. 'Has he called? Why hasn't he called, Dr Blanchford? Did he call you and you won't tell me what he said? Paddy, what did they find?'

'He hasn't called, Ma, and there's nothing more to find. We just need to get an appointment for the MRI scan, that's all. Things just take forever in hospitals.'

She watched him carefully as he said this, weighing things. Finally she nodded cautiously.

'I don't have the radio come on in the mornings any more. Its that crazy.'

He told her it wasn't.

'I still watch the six o'clock news,' she said.

Good.

They talked about other matters for a while—Stephanie and her kids, the school barbecue, finally about Murray Blanchford once more and the message Paddy had left at the hospital for him—then, at the door, he told her about the lunch with Pip.

'Pip is coming here? But when?'

He told her.

'But I just saw her.'

'She's coming.'

274

'Oh,' she said. She spoke with such gloomy disappointment, he had to laugh. 'Do you think she'll want to—help?'

'It's shaping as a real possibility that a lot of people will want to do exactly that.'

'That's what I'm afraid of.'

5

It was hard to remember whose idea it was to go on the ride in the first place, Pip said. This was more than fifty years ago and quite a few things were now lost. She couldn't remember where they got the bikes from, for instance, since they weren't theirs. Did they have panniers full of provisions, bedding, water? She had a vague feeling they decided against carrying any water because it would be too heavy—could that be right? Visions of drinking from fresh streams? Bathing under waterfalls? They had a little two-man tent. A billy. He had to understand to a pair of closeted Wellington girls in the early 1950s, the country beyond their birthplace was largely unknown. Her impression anyway was that they were foolishly ill-equipped for such a journey, four hundred miles or so at the height of summer. The bikes were old and heavy but she couldn't tell him what colour they were, for instance. By the same token, she said, a surprising number of things were still there, locked in the memory banks, seemingly unlosable.

They were in the sitting room. Pip sat on a sofa, right on the edge, her hands folded neatly in her lap. Paddy was in an armchair facing her. He'd slept for fifteen minutes before she'd arrived and he felt better. There was anyway something immediately soothing and undemanding about her presence, the sort of guest who'd slip from the dining table and have all the dishes done by the time you noticed her missing. Did this mean there was also something subservient in Pip? He wasn't sure. One imagined a life of service, self-deprecatory and resilient.

Already she'd washed the strawberries she'd bought and put them into a bowl she'd found in one of the cupboards.

She wore a faded floral sundress under a black cardigan. Her shoes were brown and looked heavy. Her white hair was cut severely across her forehead, just a fraction shorter than it should have been, as if someone else with an idea about Pip had gained the upper hand and despite misgivings, Pip had consented. He thought there was something childlike about her—the haircut and clothes contributed—though this may have only been because he'd always put her together with his mother when they'd been girls. Pip had been fair once but now her skin was sunned to the point of wearing a coating—like one large freckle or a stain—and it seemed unlikely this would fade and return with the seasons.

He couldn't think what she'd looked like at his father's funeral. There was only the strong and uneasy sense of Pip with his mother, two heads close together, a cousins' conspiracy.

Now there was also a briefcase, which she put down beside her.

She'd wasted no time in starting her story. Having taken care of the strawberries, she'd moved to the sofa, refusing any refreshments. She'd shown no interest in the apartment itself. She'd shaken his hand, ducking easily away when he tried to kiss her. She was light on her feet and Paddy had the impression of swiftness, of a woman disappearing around corners, an elusive spirit, unused to being the focus of attention. She was close to her cousin, his mother, in all of this. And once she'd found out Teresa was resting next door, she wanted to begin. It seemed that if she failed to start telling him immediately what she'd come to say, it would all be over. Hesitation was the end. Nor was he allowed to interrupt. He'd tried at first, prompted by things she was saying, looking for clarification, but she'd held up her hand, smiling. Paddy was her audience no matter how much that may have pained her.

He'd been right when he'd listened to her voice on the phone. Smiling for Pip meant little; it was simply the way she talked to people and it didn't express anything except that she was speaking. Silent, her face lapsed into a dullness that was at first disconcerting. The talking smile, this rather fixed arrangement of her lips, seemed to hold everything at a certain distance of politeness. Paddy had no doubt she was a kind person too, yet he suspected her sympathy might easily grate. He recalled the odd thing his mother had said over the years about 'Pip the Good' and 'poor old Pip'. She was a loved figure, important in ways beyond their understanding, and these veiled criticisms were similarly impossible to pursue. His mother protected her cousin and kept her to herself. Over the years they'd stayed in touch, but he had no real idea what they said to each other or even how they said it.

Yet here Pip was, telling him something he'd never heard his mother speak about and which he'd never known had happened. It was hard to believe she'd appeared like this, ready to narrate. It was exciting, and partly because she herself seemed excited by such an unusual event. Paddy had no idea what she was going to say from one moment to the next. He also had the impression that when Pip had confirmed for herself that this was the case—that she was novel, that it was all new to her audience—she spoke less with the smile and with greater flexibility and emphasis, if still perhaps with the solitary person's uncertainty as to whether she was wanted in this unfamiliar role.

What had she never forgotten? The weather on the first day of their biking trip, she knew and could recall with absolute faithfulness, the weather. How they'd watched the clouds move out to sea as they biked along the coast, settling over Kapiti Island like a . . . white crown! Pip laughed shyly at her own image. 'We thought they were making way for us,' she said. Sunshine marked the route ahead. The road was still wet from the night's rain, and as the day heated up it steamed up beneath their tyres. 'We joked that we were causing the effect because of our extreme speed. Of course it had probably taken us a few hours to get even that far. We were so badly prepared really, with only the natural fitness of two averagely healthy teenage girls. We were members of the Miramar Tennis Club but that was about it. No one ran or jogged in those days. Oh, there must have been clubs of course, harriers. But normally you didn't do such things. If someone ran in the street, they were up to no good.

'Poorly organised no doubt about it but I do remember I had an utter faith in your mother with the bikes since she was good with machines of all sorts. She had a surprising skill there.

'Anyway, that only went so far. Teresa quickly had blisters from pushing against the pedals in a new pair of tennis shoes she'd bought for the trip. I had very sore thigh muscles after the first hour, plus I'd fallen off when I was looking at something in the distance—a train, I think. Ran straight into a hole. That would be me not the train. I grazed my elbow quite badly. Amazingly, we did have some bandages. We collapsed at regular intervals by the side of the road, inspecting the damage we'd done to ourselves.'

It seemed both incredible and perfectly normal to Paddy that Pip's story should involve bikes. Here was the sort of coincidence that encouraged people to think the world was a quilted thing, each person carrying a patch, the bearer of an illustrated scene or design which made sense once it was joined to its neighbour, creating overall an effect that was pleasing, cohesive. Still he wondered what part Pip had brought him? He'd never even seen his mother on a bike.

'Maybe this won't surprise you, Paddy, but here's the thing,' she said. 'Cars would stop, they'd always stop when they saw us by the side of the road. We must have looked pathetic. But it was a different time too. It was a kinder time, I think. I want to say "innocent" though that may be pushing it, especially given what later happened. Yet people thought nothing of stopping their cars to ask whether they could help. It was just a different idea about manners and community. That's my opinion. Historically, I may be talking rubbish. But as someone looking back fifty plus years, I can say with all honesty, things happened to us that would never happen now and there must be a reason. We must have lost something, I think. I'm out of touch with New Zealand of course but that's still my sense.

'We had many acts of kindness come our way and we were always being offered lifts. Farmers in trucks would want to throw our bikes in the back and drive us wherever. And we didn't have to be stopped anywhere to be asked. We'd be biking along perfectly well and someone would want to help us. They'd pull alongside and wind down the window. On the first day we'd decided it was a rule not to accept these offers. Apart from our minor aches and injuries, we were going along quite well and the weather, as I said, was beautiful. Not too hot, very little wind, the clouds parting for us. So we always said no thank you. I think they thought we were mad. We probably were mad. No one really cycled long distances back then, is my impression. I think we were an oddity. People stopped to find out what it was that we were doing exactly.

'Anyway, day one ended in Levin, which made us proud, I remember. We'd reached Levin! That seemed a long way on the map—not that we carried a map. I think my father had told us the way to go and we were quite happy to have his extremely basic directions to guide us. It was straightforward, right up State Highway One until we hit Auckland. "Don't go to Napier" was one thing he said. No idea why. Once we hit Auckland, he didn't have a clue and we were on our own and good luck to us. That was all right, we'd just ask someone. We were going to stay for a few days with one of my mother's relatives whom I'd never met.

'You've got to understand, the arrangements, the planning was very loose. We weren't silly girls by any stretch of the imagination but we liked to pursue a notion. Your mother was great fun and very determined, up for anything.'

Paddy wasn't sure if Pip had seen something pass across his face, a questioning look, some doubt, for her to say what came next.

'It's sometimes hard for children to accept any image of their parents which is not the one they've developed through that relationship. But this was well before that relationship, Paddy. You were not even thought of beyond the most abstract abstract. We were still children ourselves. We encouraged each other. We were a good team. Always laughed a lot. We had no fear or trepidation about the biking, despite never having been on a bike for more than about forty minutes, never having been further north than New Plymouth in my case and somewhere similar in your mother's, and only having a very faint idea about what Auckland actually was, how big, how easy to get around in, how it looked and felt. None of this made us pause for a moment.

'I got a puncture just before we stopped for the night and your mother had the tyre off and repaired in minutes it seemed. I remember looking at her while she worked and just giggling. She put the plaster on the tube and I think I said, Thank you, nurse.

'Day two was always going to be harder. You wake with all of day one's previously hidden problems now exposed. Where did we sleep though in Levin? I don't know. There were towns where we slept rough. Can't really remember being inside the tent. We wheeled our bikes onto farmland, or down beside rivers, and slept under trees. That was perfectly acceptable too. If we were found, and once or twice a farmer's wife or a worker spotted us, perhaps, we weren't chased off or suspected of something. We were invited into houses and fed and, very gently, questioned. I remember telling our story to a family of wide-eyed listeners on a farm near Bulls. They listened as though we'd decided to circumnavigate the globe. *Auckland*? They inspected our bicycles as though they must have been fitted with rocket technology. Teresa could hardly keep a straight face.

'Am I making this sound dubiously idealised? Was it a nation of generous, simple, good-hearted people on the lookout for those in need? I don't have statistics to back me up but as two teenage girls biking the length of the North Island, we took this sort of treatment as a given. I don't think we thought we were charmed. We biked on with simple confidence, communicating to those we came into contact with the same unselfconscious and unexamined faith they too possessed. If we were unusual, and we were, for taking on such a journey, then this only increased the kindness.

'But that second day was hard. Our bodies weren't ready for it. The sky, I remember, was bare. It was boiling hot. We'd decided we had to get to the coast, to cool off, but we took a wrong turn somewhere and biked for a long time in the afternoon sun down deserted roads that circled back on themselves.

'"We should have stayed on Highway One like my father told us," I said.

'"Shut up," said Teresa.

'And she was right. Shut up.

'At one stage we emerged onto a major road and set off in what turned out to be completely the wrong direction. We were heading back south! We weren't speaking to each other by then, blaming each other. I wanted to stop and bike down a long gravel road which looked like it led to a farmhouse we could see on top of a distant hill. But Teresa had already passed the driveway, her head down, pedalling blindly. It was the only time I wanted to go home, well, one of the few times. I hated her back. I hated her pedalling. There was a pointless aggression in her pedalling, her legs were going round too fast. I could also see that her shirt was soaked in sweat, as mine was also, and I even hated her sweating like this. You understand how it can get, Paddy, do you?

'I followed behind her, furious. She disappeared over a little rise and just as I was fantasising about a big hole swallowing her, I came to the top and we were looking at the sea! She'd stopped her bike and was gazing out. Then she turned to me. "Told you," she said. It was completely the most stupid thing I'd ever heard in my life and we both burst out laughing. We were dehydrated too, I'm sure. Brain-fried. We had to get off our bikes and fall into the grass, still laughing. We let our bikes crash down. We didn't care. We loathed the bikes right then and hoped they'd break and we wouldn't be able to carry on our journey to Auckland. Who cared about Auckland anyway? It was so delicious to lie in the grass, delirious and exhausted.

'Eventually we stood up, picked up our bikes and made our way down to the beach for a swim. And this was where we slept the second night, just up from the beach, on a springy stretch of sandy grass, with a few sheep moving around us. You could hear them munching in the night, a sound like someone tearing their hair out but we didn't mind. What did we eat? Certainly we didn't have dinner—we were going to get that further on at some town. What town? Well, we didn't know names, we just took what came at us. We felt amazed people lived here.

'Anyway, the third morning we got going very early and made great progress. We biked seriously, hardly talking the whole time. There was no bitterness or bad feeling at all. We knew we had to rely on each other. It was as if we'd used up all our emotions the previous day, and we pushed on automatically and very efficiently. And maybe for that reason, I have no memory of where we stayed the next night or what we did there. General tiredness might be the cover-all phrase, and a sense of satisfaction, we were really doing it!

'One of the days, however, we didn't go anywhere. Because I'd stupidly taken off my tennis shoes and put on sandals to ride in the heat. Guess what? I woke up with the tops of my feet badly sunburnt. I remember the tent then, lying in agony by myself. I think your mother had gone off in a huff. She came back later on and she rubbed cooling cream onto my feet, which was lovely.

'I'm sorry, Paddy, if this is all going too slowly. It probably seems to you as if you've been asked to experience our epic journey in real time. I'll try to speed it up. I've never told this story out loud though I've said it to myself many many times over the years and things can go faster in one's head.

'You've heard about Bulls. Let's move on.

'We arrived at Waiouru hopelessly under-dressed. I don't think either of us knew what the Desert Road was. Perhaps we

283

knew about the mountains but even there I'm not sure. In winter, snow sometimes shut the road, we knew that in an abstract way but we would never have asked ourselves why this road and not others? It was just something odd that people mentioned happening somewhere else. Could we have been so lacking in curiosity? I fear yes.

'Actually I was terrified and trying not to show it. At the tearooms there was a strange feeling suddenly. There was a table of young soldiers who kept looking at us, and there were truck drivers. We had no idea what the army was doing here. The presence of the soldiers certainly didn't help our nerves. They were eating raspberry buns that left cream all over their faces and they were drinking milkshakes. Not much older than boys, about our age, but dressed in uniforms. It was all strange. We sensed that we'd come to a kind of portal. That's the only way I can describe it. A place where you *go through*. That was the talk. We overheard things at the other tables, talk of slips, and corners, accidents. I mean, it wasn't intimidating talk, it was just how people thought of that stretch. Is it still the case? Not sure. But we knew we'd come to somewhere important. We felt very girlish in those tearooms, in the middle of a male world so different from our fathers' world—my father was an accountant—and the mountains loomed, it's the only word I can think of.

'There was a chill in the air that took us by surprise. It went straight through our thin summer shirts. Even inside the tearooms we couldn't escape it. It was as if we'd biked into another month altogether when of course all we'd done was ascend to the volcanic plateau. That phrase itself—"volcanic plateau"—would have been meaningless to us before this moment. We put on jerseys but they were lightweight summer ones. I remember Teresa slipping her jersey over her bare knees and hugging herself under the table. I told her she'd stretch her jersey and she said she didn't care, better than freeze. But she stopped doing it and smiled at me. "Let's go then," she said, and she stood up and clapped her hands. I was so grateful to her, so impressed and buoyed up by that clap! It was all an act but it was a good act. People turned to look at us. The soldiers stared, a couple of them were grinning. One gave a clap just like Teresa's but we pretended not to notice or care. We wheeled our bikes out of sight of the tearoom. Didn't want them to see us getting on our bikes. We walked a bit down the road, wheeling them, then took off as if nothing mattered.

'I was biking at first with my breath held, if that's possible. Teresa was out in front and I had no idea how she was feeling but immediately I was getting very tired. I had so little energy, despite having just eaten at the tearooms. It was because I wasn't getting enough oxygen and even though intellectually I knew this, I didn't seem able to adjust. My heart was racing and my breaths were like hiccups.

'I remember a terrific wind had come up and it was buffeting us from the side. I knew that if I tried to shout out to Teresa she wouldn't be able to hear me. She was further ahead of me now, perhaps fifty yards or so. I saw a sign by the side of the road warning about army testing. We had to stick to the road, to leave it would be a "grave risk to civilian safety". I thought of the soldiers back at the tearooms, eating their raspberry cream buns. We didn't even know how long the Desert Road was and how long it would take us to get to the first town on the other side and now we wouldn't be able to get off our bikes and rest because of the army testing.

'As you know, it's the landscape which gives the road its name. It's not a desert as such but it chimes with something in our imaginations connected to the word. Inhospitable would be part of it. A duney place, isn't it, but without any hint of the beach. Pumice, scorched rock, scrubby plants, and running alongside us, telegraph poles. I've travelled a bit and I've never found a counterpart for that geography, have you? If the rest of the country is all done and made, more or less finished, completed, beautiful in many instances, this is the place left over, exhausted from all that making, ground zero if you like. Or the geologists might just say, typically volcanic.'

Paddy thought of his volcano dream.

'With a great conscious effort I slowed down, concentrating not on keeping up with your mother but just getting my breathing right. I couldn't see her now since she'd gone around a bend.

'I don't remember much traffic on the road. This only contributed to my idea of the strangeness of the place. No one much came here, as if they knew its dangers, its graveness. I know this sounds melodramatic, Paddy. It was after all the main highway of the entire country! Still I must be accurate to how it felt then, to a young girl out on her own for the first time. It was like biking on the moon. Perhaps that family in Bulls hadn't been so silly after all.

'Gradually I calmed down and it became easier to maintain my speed, though the wind was getting worse. I still rode anxiously. Had your mother not been out in front, I might have turned back to Waiouru. It was already late in the afternoon. We'd never reach the lake by dinnertime. It was another thing my father had told us, "Stay at the lake. Don't stop at Turangi. Push on to Taupo and stay at the lake." All of his easy-sounding instructions now seemed to me very hateful and cruel. I regarded him as highly irresponsible for letting us go on the trip.

'From nowhere, an army truck went roaring past me. It blew its horn. My bike wobbled in the wake of the truck. I caught the voices of the soldiers shouting something at me. They were sitting in the back of the truck, which had canvas sides, looking at me, shrieking and pointing. Then they were gone. I was close to tears.

'I came around a bend and I saw Teresa waiting for me at the bottom of a slight dip in the road. Her clothes were being plastered against her body and her hair was wild in the wind. She was having trouble standing up, holding the bike. Good, I thought, she's had the same idea as me, we're going to turn back. We could spend the night at Waiouru in a motel. Reconsider our options in the morning. It was an achievement to have reached the mountains. We already had plenty of stories to tell everyone. The bare-chested man who stopped to fix a puncture on Teresa's tyre, when she could do it better than him, with a tattoo of an eagle across his shoulders. Once he'd finished, he ran back to his car lifting his arms up and down in bird-like swoops and making crowing noises. We'd laughed every night about him. We made the same noise whenever we overtook each other on the bikes.

'I pulled alongside her. "My God, Pip," she shouted, "isn't this great!"

'I couldn't understand what she'd said at first. "Are you loving it?" she yelled.

'And she wasn't being ironic, she was dead serious. I could see it in her face. She was alive, on a high. I shook my head. No, no I wasn't loving it. I wasn't. "I want to go back," I shouted.

'"Can't hear, what?"

'I screamed it again and this time she heard.

'"Philippa Macklin," she said, "don't be such a little fool. Pull yourself together." This was something one of our teachers used to say. We were all little fools.

'"We could be in grave danger," I said.

'Teresa stared at me.

'"We could!" I said. "We're civilians."

'She waited again, not speaking but looking right at me. And the pause, the waiting, had an effect. I felt my words crumble. I felt my fear crouch down low and hide. I won't say it was banished but there was no longer any courage left in my fear. It was like a pain I could cope with, say to myself I could cope with. I've always had basically a timid disposition. I think that's why I've ended up in some dangerous places in my life. I went to Africa to spite people, because it was the last thing expected of me, that I would have the gumption to do such a thing. Timidity and pigheadedness in combination, that's probably more common than we think. But I'm wandering now. Sorry.

'On the Desert Road, Teresa motioned with her head for me to start riding, to take the lead, and I did. I pushed off into the sideways wind and began the slow climb up again.

'Did I mention how dark the sky was? Black clouds. Further

287

in, cars had their lights on. It was as though normal time had been suspended and we were travelling through a special zone, somewhere not made for civilians. It seemed very unlikely anyone would stop for us here. A few cars slowed down to get a look at us but that was all. Plus we didn't have lights on our bikes. We had reflectors. It was unsafe.

'I felt spits of rain against my face. To the east, near the horizon, we could see a patch of horizontal lines connecting the sky with the earth. We knew it was a storm. There was no downward direction implied in these smudged lines however. It wasn't obvious that rain was falling. It may just as easily have been something being sucked up into the clouds from the land, as in a tornado though there was no funnel shape.

'Having had the whole trip so far in sunshine, we'd just assumed things would carry on in this way. The rain was an outrage and I know that I took it personally, yet another slap in the face, literally! My face hurt. The rain dripped from my nose. It was coming down more heavily now. Rain from the road was getting sprayed up against my legs then running into my shoes and I could feel my lower back also getting wet from the rear tyre. I could see when I glanced around that one of my panniers was flapping open and the rain was soaking everything inside.

'These details, Paddy! It's hard to imagine I'm a person who has had a gun pointed at her head, isn't it?'

She stopped abruptly, as if she'd felt something touch her. Metal?

'I'm someone who has been blindfolded, tied up and put in a chicken coop with my own birds. But those are other stories, with their own context. I didn't like the blindfold one bit but once I was in there, I knew—I guessed and I was right—that was all the harm that was coming to me from those people. Probably they also thought it was clever and humiliating and horrible to be in the coop but being with my chooks was calming. We knew each other. Those people misjudged that.

'What I'm trying to speak about, not very well at all I know, is this particular feeling, in this particular time. Historically, it ranks very low. On a scale of suffering, it doesn't make the scale. You see a child dying of cholera, well. A man beaten to death. Yet I can still feel the rain on the backs of my bare legs and the way it drained into my shoes. Horrible! It makes me shudder now. And of course my failure to rid myself of what was only minor physical unpleasantness, this must be connected with what happened later. Everything's connected.'

She looked down at her brown shoes and moved their toes together and then apart again. 'May I have some water?'

'Of course,' said Paddy. 'Anything else? A snack?' Pip shook her head. She looked pale and tired suddenly, a bit shaky. He went to the kitchen and brought back a tray with the jug from the fridge together with two glasses. They drank some water and Pip sat for a moment in silence. His mind was racing with questions—about their ride but also about Africa, the gun, the blindfold, the chicken coop. Not the time.

'As you know,' she said, 'the road twists and turns and has lots of hollows, but it also has flat straights, sections which grant you the larger view, across the plain, where you think it wouldn't take much to go over to one of the mountains and tap it with your foot. You feel close suddenly. We were on one of these. To the east, the storm seemed to have moved off somewhere else and there was a bright margin of sky lighting less dense clouds as if it was clearing. It was still raining but lightly now, a steady drizzle. Teresa rode up beside me. She was soaking like me and grinning just as she'd been when I'd thought we should turn back. More than an hour had passed since that bad moment.

'"Good afternoon, Miss Macklin," she called to me.

'"Good afternoon, Miss Fulton," I said.

'"Nice day for a ride."

'"Perfect, Miss Fulton."

'"You look a tad damp, Miss Macklin."

'"Do I? I wasn't aware of it. Though looking closely at you, Miss Fulton, the phrase 'drowned rat' comes to mind."

'"Why, Miss Macklin, I do believe you're right. Kind of you to point it out."

'"What friends are for, Miss Fulton."

'"Is that what friends are for, I'd always wondered what they were for."

'She overtook me, a faint crowing sound coming from her, and we biked on through the rain, past signs which warned of firing ranges and military vehicles crossing the road, though we never saw any of this activity and never saw another soldier. Maybe their canvas truck had been sucked into the air.

'I'm not sure how long it took us to get through. We moved ahead in numbness. I think all our vigilance was exhausted long before we left that road. By evening, there were simply no vehicles going either way. It was less gloomy. A clear night, the air warmer now. We began to dry out. We went on like this for quite a time, owning the entire place, biking automatically.

'At a certain point I became aware of a different kind of shadow and a scent too. I lifted my head and saw that the road had entered a forest. Pine trees lined both sides. There was an apron of ground maybe ten yards wide leading up to the trees and this was covered in brown pine needles. Clumps of these needles had been blown onto the road and swirled into largish neat piles. It looked a bit like someone had raked them into these piles. So we rode over them, through them. We kicked at them with our feet. The setting was suddenly private, as if we were biking along a friend's driveway, ruining someone's hard work. We shouted with all our strength, whooping in the deserted alley of those trees. It was a huge and inspiring freedom after the tense watchfulness and doubt of the Desert Road. We were alongside each other and we took turns to ride out across the other side of the road, shouting at the nonexistent oncoming traffic, daring it to appear and crash into us. There was even a gentle downward slope to the road and we went fast, eating up the distance. The mountains were no longer visible behind us. We knew we'd made it! We'd got through to the other side and now all we had to do was carry on to the lake, or perhaps even risk stopping in nearby Turangi since it was so late. We could ride to the lake in the morning and swim before lunch.

'Then far ahead of us we saw something shiny by the side of the road, on the apron. As we got nearer, we could make out the shape of a car.

'Do you believe in presentiment, Paddy? I mean in some notion of foretelling?'

Automatically he touched his ear.

'I do not,' said Pip, 'unless it's tied to human agency. To the ordinary powers we all have of paying attention, of noticing, of surmise, of guesswork. Do I believe objects tremble with their own futures, signalling their import to us? No.

'The African day the people came to our property with the gun and the blindfold and the rope for tying me up, I thought it a day like any other. Later, I thought of certain things. Afterwards, I considered the signs. A broken bottle by the mailbox that morning. A dog I didn't know walking in the middle of the road. A commotion nearby, raised voices, angry shouting, that was quickly over, too quickly perhaps, as if someone had had second thoughts and then he was silenced, everyone on edge? Were these signs, or even part of the thing itself? At the time I thought I was hearing an argument between the labourers working on the little relay power station at the end of our street. They were patching its crumbling concrete walls. I'd gone past them a few times that week and they were a rowdy, good-humoured bunch. Signs? Dogs walked everywhere. I didn't know them all. Bottles broke. No, these weren't harbingers. But you think on things after the event. It's a helpless act, to want to have seen it coming. Ah, yes, obvious.

'Where we were living, at that moment in history, in Zimbabwe, you could argue we saw it coming, some might say even that we had it coming, and if we didn't know we were just too—blind, stupid, for our epoch. Look I've gone off track again.' Pip reached for her glass of water and as she drank she was looking at Paddy through the bottom of the glass. It gave him the sense that she doubted he'd been listening or thought he would stop listening to her now. She had to keep him engaged, even while she was drinking water. 'Where was I?'

'The car,' said Paddy.

'Your mother and I both saw the car at the same time and we wondered. We looked at each other quickly, just a glance but enough to see the smallest disturbance in each other's eyes, nothing like fear or fright but the upset of our joy, a sobering, and of course we'd left off shouting and kicking the needles. Certainly the car put a stop to that. It was as though we'd come across the owner, the owner of the road, of the forest. The Master. Hushed, we heard our tyres against the surface of the road and the tiny crunching of the needles we passed over.

'We biked close to one another on our side of the road, heading towards the car.

'Concentrating so tightly on the car, trying to make out its purpose, whether there were any occupants, created an odd alternating feeling in me. At one moment it seemed we were reeling in the vehicle, drawing it to us along the avenue of trees, and then the opposite. The car was like some magnet, it sucked us towards it or sucked our ideas about the day out of ourselves. I may be dangerously close to what I've just denied about foretelling, presentiment. Yet I thought of the rain clouds we'd seen far off on the hills by the Desert Road, the dark band connecting sky and earth but without a sense of direction. It was similar. I didn't know what was happening.

'I could see Teresa had a similar intentness on her face. She was peering, trying to work it out at the earliest possible moment. And all the time a million innocent explanations went through my head. The car was abandoned. The car's owner was going for a walk in the bush, or he was a hunter. Someone had stopped for a rest, for a drink from a thermos. The call of nature. A man would appear soon from the trees pulling up his trousers, a bit sheepish, and he would wave at us. The obviousness of its position—parked just off State Highway One—worked in its favour.

'Getting nearer it looked as though the car was empty. There were no signs of movement. I felt the tension ease up through my legs and shoulders. I'd been unaware of this nervous grip. I gave Teresa a smile when she looked at me. She returned it.

'We were almost alongside the car when its driver's door swung open and a man who'd been slumped down in his seat stretched a leg, then got out of the car quickly. He took a few steps towards us, holding up his hand. We braked and stopped. Perhaps that was the moment when we should have accelerated past him, swerved out onto the other side of the road and biked off. I'm sure we both thought of it.

'"Girls," he said. "Girls! Are we pleased to see you!"

'We looked towards the car and saw a young woman, a few years older than us perhaps, who'd also been slumped down in the passenger seat, gradually work her way up. She didn't get out of the car, however, but she was looking at us carefully. I wasn't sure whether she'd been asleep and we'd woken her. It wasn't a friendly look. The man was stretching his arms over his head as if he'd been sleeping. "Our saviours," he said.'

At this point Paddy became aware of the phone ringing and although he told Pip that they could ignore it, she was insistent that he pick it up. She would use the break to go to the bathroom. 'Comfort stop,' she said, moving from the sofa as he answered the phone.

It was Murray Blanchford from the hospital. He'd just spoken to Teresa. They'd set the MRI appointment for the following day. Obviously this would give them a clearer idea of what, if anything, was going on. From his conversation with Teresa, he understood that she was in the same position as when he'd examined her—was this Paddy's feeling too? It was. Excellent. The line seemed to go dead for a moment and then Blanchford came on again, apologising. A moment later, they were saying goodbye.

At once Paddy thought of the things he hadn't asked. He'd wanted to get Blanchford's opinion on her tiredness, the pattern of sleeping and waking. Also he thought he should have said how they'd been expecting him to call earlier and his failure to do so had caused anxiety. Doctors should know this stuff, even very important brain doctors. The conversation had gone so fast. Blanchford had given the impression that Paddy was in a queue, which perhaps he was, and their time was extremely limited.

Pip came back into the room and sat down again. 'Is it all right to go on, Paddy?'

He told her what Blanchford had said.

'I can be there at the hospital, if you want me there, that is.'

'That's very kind.'

'But I'm very worried now. I'm using up all your time.'

He waved this away, continue.

'Okay, if you're sure. I'm not entirely without hope that maybe this long-winded anecdote has some bearing on what's happened to Teresa.'

'What do you mean?'

'Not sure. Sorry. I'm ahead of myself. Anyway, it's information I'm . . . relieved to share finally with someone. You can do with it whatever you like. Where were we?'

'"Our saviours",' he said. 'The man in the car. He called you his saviours. With the woman.'

'Yes! The man. Funny, I have trouble picturing him. He was maybe in his early thirties or a little older. Clean-shaven. Average height, thin. Light complexion. No scars. It was how I went over in my mind the description I'd give to the police when they asked for a description. In truth, I can't remember really what his face looked like to see into. Or I've preferred not to remember for so long that now I can't.'

'The police?' said Paddy.

Pip held up a hand, begging him to hold off. 'Perhaps it was because we'd been in, I don't know—the rhythm of strangers' kindness for the previous days, throughout the trip, and here was an opportunity to repay some of that but Teresa said at once, very brightly, "How can we help?"

'It was painful to hear these words. I felt we were immediately in further than we should have been. This is stupid of course. What were our options? We were on bikes, in the middle of

294

nowhere and it was night though still easy enough to see twenty or thirty yards ahead of us.

'"Hear that, doll?" the man said to the woman in the car. "So nice! *So* nice!"

'The woman's lip curled back slightly and she turned away again. She had messy blond hair. Yes, I'd made a judgement on her already! Caught out here with this man and now involving us in whatever was going on. I was not much more than a schoolgirl and my imagination was as conventional as they come. I couldn't understand a person like her at all.

'Then the man explained they'd run out of petrol, which was his fault entirely though the gauge was temperamental and he thought they had enough and then it had plummeted suddenly and without warning, giving him just enough time to swing the car around and drift to a stop here since they had been going in the opposite direction but figured it was safer to fill up this side of the Desert Road, hence their predicament. He addressed most of his speech to Teresa, I noticed, as if already identifying her as an ally and myself as something else to be decided on later. Divide and rule was a phrase I'd heard without completely understanding it and now I wondered whether this was it in action. He had a rapport at once with her.

'"Oh, that's bad luck!" said Teresa. "How long have you been here?"

'"Not long," said the man. "But there's no one out tonight, not a soul. A logging truck went by but maybe he was on a mission, I don't know." He held up his hands and shrugged, smiling. Small teeth. I remember now he had small teeth. He approached Teresa's bike and put a finger on her handlebars, his index finger. "You girls been biking through?"

'"We've just come through," said Teresa.

'"That's a good effort! Hey, doll, that's a good effort, isn't it, these girls have come through right now." He held out his hand to Teresa. "My name's Duncan. Dunkin' Biscuits is what they called me, I don't mind. You are?"

'We gave him our names. He shook my hand too. My mouth

was so dry that Teresa had to repeat my name so he could understand it. Then he told us the woman's name was Ginny. "Genevieve really but I shorten it, which she doesn't like."

'Teresa told him we were heading for Taupo that night but we'd probably stay in Turangi since it was late. We didn't know anyone there or anywhere since we were from Wellington en route to Auckland where we only knew one person. When we got there, she said, whenever that was, since we didn't have a strict schedule, that person would ring our parents to say we'd made it.

'Duncan listened to her story with a smile and lots of appreciative nodding. At every new piece of information she gave him, my heart lurched.

'Now your mother was no fool, Paddy, and, out of the pair of us, I'd have had no problem in being judged the one who possessed the greater naivety. I was unworldly and guileless on a grand scale, I remember. If I felt our journey suddenly compromised and threatened in some unknown way by this pair by the side of the road, I also wondered whether Teresa, in her apparently mindless chirpiness, was playing the situation in the only way she could. I simply found myself unable to speak. The man saw my terror as obvious as day. It was only Teresa's sweetness and openness that could distract him.

'But distract him from what? We didn't know. He stood again in front of Teresa's bike, gently touching the handlebars. We both still straddled our bikes. I thought then I might just have a chance of biking off before he could catch me. There was still a slight downhill slope on the road and I'd be a few good pulls away before he managed to get out from in front of the other bike. In the time he was chasing me, Teresa could head off as well, either in the same direction, and attempt to dodge him on her way through, or back the way we'd come. She'd eventually come across someone who could help or somewhere she could hide. We'd be separated and I had no idea where I was going or how I'd find her again but we'd be free from the forest. These thoughts were making my pulse race so much

296

I had to run my hands down my sides to wipe the sweat off them.

'Meanwhile Teresa and Duncan were trying to work out the best way of getting petrol for the car. Suddenly I wondered whether the car even needed petrol. The whole thing might be a trap. This meant that if we tried to bike off, he'd just come after us in the car.

'I heard Teresa make an offer that was the first sign she was thinking along similar lines to me. She said that we'd carry on into town and tell the man at the petrol station about Duncan and Ginny stuck out here. They could then send someone out with petrol.

'Duncan shook his head and said that was going to cost a lot of money because they'd have to pay for the car with the man in it as well as the petrol. Then there was the issue that some people, especially those who ran petrol stations, weren't always as nice and understanding as people like us. They'd want to go home for their dinner ahead of driving five miles to help a fellow human being.

'"If I could borrow a bike," he said, "I'd get the petrol and bike back here fast as, then we could all get going again on our little journeys."

'We looked at our bikes with their loaded panniers. "They've got all our stuff on them," I said croakily. "Won't work because it's our gear."

'Duncan looked at me with a slightly open mouth. Then he moved to the back of Teresa's bike and flicked at the buckles on the straps that secured the panniers to the frame. "Take two seconds to get those off, Pip. I'm not going to bike off with your things, if you think that. You've got my car back here! You've got Ginny!"

'At the mention of her name, the woman shifted slightly in her seat, glancing out at us. It was unclear how much of the conversation she'd heard. She appeared completely hostile to the entire scenario as if she might have preferred us never to have stopped and that somehow it was our fault they were there.

Maybe they'd had a fight about running out of petrol and she was sulking.

'"Where," I said, "where are you two going? Eventually."

'Again Duncan shot me the look before speaking. I was very irritating to him but he needed to replace any aggression with his carefully casual tone. That was what I thought. This time he also gave the impression that he was buying time to think of a fact that would be silencing, something to shut me up. He couldn't do it. He didn't know where he was going or he didn't want to tell me. He turned and looked down the road, gesturing with an arm. "Through the way you came, Pip," he said vaguely.

'He rested his hand on Teresa's panniers. "Of course it's an imposition, I know. You girls have had a tough day's biking, my goodness. The last thing you need is the day to get any longer. Right, Pip? Listen, I told Ginny we can walk back. It's about five miles. Or I can walk back, do the round trip. But she doesn't want to be left out here in the dark is what she says. Doesn't like the trees apparently. She's not from round here, you know."

'All three of us looked at the pines above us, the furry branches shifting slightly at their tips, darkening as they thickened closer to the trunk.

'"Why don't you both walk back together," said Teresa, "then get a lift, hitchhike or something back to the car with the petrol?"

'"Hitch?" said Duncan. "But there's no one about."

'"Or just wait till tomorrow morning?" I said. "Both walk back to town, then come back out here tomorrow and start again?"

'"That's a good idea!" said Teresa.

'Duncan looked at us both, still smiling, scratching his head. "These are good ideas, girls, and I'd be a starter for any of them, only Ginny can't really walk anywhere at present."

'"Why?" I said. It wasn't boldness I felt but the recklessness of disbelief. The idea that the woman couldn't walk was so outrageous to us, that he'd offer such a weak excuse, it was incredible.

'"Hurt her foot."

'"Really?" I said, openly dismissive.

'Duncan called to the car that Ginny should show us her foot. At first she didn't respond but Duncan asked again with a sudden harshness in his voice, and with difficulty she raised a foot, which we saw was in plaster. She lowered it again unhappily.

'We all stood in silence for a few moments. A big bird, a wood pigeon, came out of a tree nearby in lumbering flight, sending a trail of debris spinning in the night air down to the road. The sudden sound of the bird made me duck my head. I had a taste in my mouth from those dry dry needles simply by watching them rain. A few fell on the car roof. I had a strong and upsetting image of the vehicle eventually being covered over, buried by the forest litter, sinking into the earth in some undiscoverable patch inside the band of pines.

'He was telling the truth.

'The foot in plaster was a bitter defeat for us. It threw everything into doubt again. By how much had we misjudged this pair? It was an odd sort of shame we felt. We'd met the first real test the world had sent us and having studied it, considered it, here was the result: we'd failed. It *was* a test too. I knew at once this was the reason we'd come on the trip, to face this, the car by the side of the empty road at night with its human questions. And what had happened? Faced with a man's story, we'd put in place of its ordinary reality a schoolgirl fantasy of evil intentions. We'd imagined all sorts of unnameable horror. Things buried.

'Duncan and Ginny had run out of petrol, didn't we get it? Now we did. Teresa had already stepped off her bike and was unlacing her panniers. Duncan was helping her, kneeling at her back wheel.

'"How did she do that?" I said. "Get the cast on her foot?"

'The man didn't look up. "Tripped."

'I looked over to the woman in the car and our eyes met for the first time. In that instant everything changed, or changed back. In place of the cold hostility she'd been showing us, there was now a pleading sort of look, a quick terror of her own, pure alarm. She was begging for help or sending a warning or both. Her eyes widened with it. She showed me this for only a moment, while Duncan had his back to her. When he stood up again, taking the bike from Teresa, the woman slumped down in her seat and resumed staring out the front window of the car.

'I was staring at the ground, unable to meet either Teresa's eye or to look at the man who was now adjusting her seat to his height. He made some joke about his legs being longer than ours but not as pretty, and I heard Teresa's dutiful laugh. She sounded strange, unwell.

'I heard him speak though I was unaware he was asking me a question. He repeated it. "Will you ride with me, Pip?"

'"Me?"

'He explained that I could stay in town once we'd reached it. He would bike back with the petrol, then rope Teresa's bike to the back of the car and drive her into town before setting off on their own trip. The car could only take one bike, he said. The rope was too short and weak for both.

'I found it hard to follow any of this reasoning. Ropes? The word made me feel ill. I only knew that we had to stay together. That was our only hope. Two against one, possibly three against one though the woman was not to be counted on, her fear was so complete she might not be able to do anything when it came time for it. She was trapped in the car, trapped in her terror, but I had no idea about her loyalty.

'"Can't," I said.

'"No!" said Teresa harshly, as if suddenly waking again into her buried fright.

'"Why not?"

'"My father told me not to bike with strange men," I said.

'He laughed loudly and briefly at this, then he was earnest. "If we don't do it this way, it'll be pitch black and very late by the time you girls reach town. You don't even have lights on these bikes. Do you have food? Maybe a dry biscuit or two but not dinner."

'"We had a big lunch at Waiouru," said Teresa.

'"We'll stay here with Ginny and wait for you to get back," I said. "That'll be fine. We can sleep somewhere off the road, we've been doing that, you know. Then in the morning we can take off again."

'He looked from me to Teresa, as if trying to find a crack to slip through, some path to win back the advantage. Finally, he could do nothing except lift his shoulders and drop them, signalling that we were stupid girls who couldn't be helped. Then he got off the bike, letting it fall roughly to the ground, and went over to talk to the woman.

'He spoke through her window in a low voice and we couldn't hear what he was saying. She didn't look at him as he spoke but kept her head still, fixing her gaze on the road back to town.

'He went around to the boot of the car and took out a can and a long length of plastic hosing. He tied this around his waist.

'He came back, picked up the bike, loathing for it written all over his face and got on it. Then he said to us in a voice of sternness, "She needs to rest. Her foot in the cast is sore and she's not feeling great. You girls stay over there and try not to make too much noise." He pointed to a spot in front of the car. "I'll be back soon. Don't go anywhere, don't wander off, and don't bother her. Now I'm offering one last chance. Who wants to ride with me and make the whole fucking mess of this night come to a quicker end?" He waited, looking up at the trees. "No? Want the longer version? Frightened of your own shadows, whoever sent you pair out on this adventure had no idea!" He spoke these words with real venom, almost spitting them. His face was mostly in darkness now but you could see little flecks of silver where the saliva flew. Plus he had more for us. "You don't come with me, you insult me, you think I'm something I'm not but it's you who fit into that camp. You think you're grown-up but you're two kids, scared out of your wits and making everyone else's life harder as a result. I've got one piece of advice. Go fucking home!" He was breathing heavily from this outburst. We didn't dare speak. He tightened the strange belt he'd made of the plastic hosing. "Coming? No? Suit yourselves."

'We could hardly bear to watch him bike off. We both had our heads down. Finally I looked up and he hadn't gone very far at all. He was wobbling, trying to get going, surprised by the bike's weight, as I said he wasn't a big man, his legs were slight, and it might have looked comical in another situation. I don't think he'd been on a bike in years. We heard him cursing. Then he disappeared in the gloom.

'I'm not sure who started first but we both began to cry. We wept as the children he said we were, out of our depth, missing our families, hopeless. We wept as babies.

'But we also wept as young women, humiliated and terrorised and resisting. Yes, that as well, I think. Hadn't we sent him away? It was relief and exhaustion that rushed from us, and a kind of immobilising grief for versions of ourselves he'd shredded and yet also a feeling now that we had a future to decide on, if only we could bring ourselves to stop crying.'

Pip stood up and moved to the window that looked down on the alley between their building and the neighbouring one. Paddy stayed sitting.

'We wept standing in exactly the positions he'd left us in, upright and fixed, as if he watched us still, keeping us in place, as if we knew he could come back at any moment and punish us for even the slightest physical move. It was extraordinary that feeling of stone that was in our feet and legs, that idea of him over us, even though we'd seen him wobbling away on Teresa's bike. We knew he was gone and we believed he was here. We were forbidden by that presence to touch or console each other. I think it the loneliest I have ever been, Paddy.

'In the chicken coop, I had the birds. I keep coming back there when I don't mean to. I think it's because when I was in the coop, facing all that, I thought a lot about your mother. I'd had a letter from her that very day, always a good day when I got a letter from darling Teresa. And I thought especially of our famous bike ride up the North Island, though famous only to us. Anyway, in the coop, the birds came to me with curiosity. They knew I was in the wrong place but they came to me. In the forest, I had no one though with an arm I could have reached out and touched your dear mother, whom I loved and loved.

'These were not silent tears either. We encouraged each other with our misery and we cried loudly, the clear shame of it making us give in more completely to the emotion. It seemed as though nothing could stop us ever. Perhaps when the man came back we would have had enough. He would make us stop. Duncan? I couldn't stand to have his name in my head, that he even had a name seemed absurd. We howled and howled, statues, howling, inconsolable, the sounds carrying far into the ugly forest.

'Next something odd happened. We became aware of another person standing between us. I saw the foot in the cast. The woman he'd called Ginny was there! We swallowed our crying almost immediately and looked at her. She stood unsteadily, balancing her weight on her good foot. Feeling herself topple, she reached out and caught our shoulders and we found ourselves joined, the three of us. It was an amazing thing, yet another amazing thing!

'"We must have a plan," she said. "I am Genevieve."'

Pip moved away from the window and came towards him, her eyes alive. 'Paddy, she was French!'

It was difficult to know what to do with this piece of information. It took Paddy a moment to understand what she'd just said. 'How strange,' he said.

'When your mother came and saw me in Palmerston North, we looked it up on the Internet. People who suddenly take on a foreign accent.'

'Snap,' he said.

'She hadn't thought of doing that. She was in a state, you know. She thought tumour but she didn't have any pain as such, no headaches or dizziness even. She was tired. She was tired I think from oversleeping. Anyway, you'll know it too, that there's a connection between something that's happened in the person's

303

life and the type of accent they suddenly acquire. I mean, why French?'

'And you think Genevieve?'

Pip's story at once seemed both less and more important than he'd thought it was going to be. He didn't doubt her sincerity and he was grateful to learn about this episode in his mother's life. Yet a wave of disappointment went through him. This?

Pip had probably armed herself against this response or she might have seen something of it in his features because she immediately nodded, as if agreeing with his thoughts.

'You're right!' she said. 'Of course you're right, Paddy. She was French, so what. Yes. Too far-fetched, yes.' She sat down again opposite him, deflated.

He waited for her to say more, to advance her theory, to convince him of the connections, yet she'd lapsed into silence, her face a blank. No longer animated by her narration, she looked immediately older.

'Did you talk about this possibility with my mother, this connection with the woman in the forest?'

She shook her head. 'It occurred to me much later, after she'd gone. She'd already told me about hearing the item on the radio. But to me that sounded so minor and inconsequential. Of course what do I know? Maybe that would be enough. And how anyway does this help?'

They were silent for several more moments.

Of course he also wanted desperately to know how it would all end. Because he didn't yet know. And maybe this Genevieve had a bigger part to play. 'But you can't leave it there,' he said.

She seemed surprised by this and looked at him with curiosity. Leave what where? Now that her feeling about the French connection had been revealed and made to look weak, did this mean the tale really lacked a point? Of course Pip knew the ending. To her there was no mystery. She was the story's ending embodied. She sat before him, so obviously they made it out of the forest. What did he want to know?

'How did you get away?' he said.

304

'How did we get away?' She was foggy and tired. 'Oh, that. You'd really like to hear?'

'Pip,' he said, 'I have no idea whether or not this all relates to what my mother has got now. I'm not ruling it out. The brain is an astonishing thing. Yes, she'd also heard the story on the radio about the French truck drivers. It might all be in the mix. But anyway, the French woman, Genevieve, has come to life and she's asking what your plan is. Me too. What's your plan?'

'Okay.' Pip rubbed her ankle thoughtfully. 'Our plan. Didn't have one. Not immediately. Because we were too dumbfounded. We were in shock from this person. The cast on her foot. Her accent! Paddy, all right, I won't make a thing of it. But her French accent!'

'Where had she come from?'

'But we didn't ask her! She was standing with us, talking, being held up by us! It was as much as we could take in, that she wasn't with the man, she was against him! That was all we could digest. I remember looking at Teresa and she just had this happiness in her face, utter surrender to euphoria I suppose. I'm sure I was the same.

'We were all panting, Teresa and I from our outpouring, Genevieve because she found it difficult to get around. Somehow she'd hopped soundlessly from the car. "We must go!" said Genevieve. "Before he comes back, yes?"

'"Yes!" we said.

'She was looking along the road in both directions, listening. The night was completely silent except for rustling from the trees, birds, insects. Teresa slapped her own leg. "I'm being bitten," she said. Genevieve glanced at Teresa, briefly annoyed. Problems on that scale, we understood, were not worth mentioning.

'"We push the car into the trees," said Genevieve. "Hide it. He comes back, he won't know where. The road all looks the same."

'"And we hide in the car?" I said.

'She shook her head. "Too dangerous, he finds us. We hide

305

further away over there." She pointed up the road on the opposite side. "I can't walk far."

Teresa picked up my bike. "On this," she said.

'"Yes, you must ride away, both." She pointed to me. "You ride with her across."

'"Giving her a dub?"

'"She sits on the front, the back wherever. But first can you help me? Look in the car for blankets or something warm. Get anything. Then push the car away. Last, take me across the road. Just a little way. He won't find me."

'Sitting in the car, she'd been thinking it all through.

'We eased her down so she was sitting on a patch of grass and then we went to the car. We found a Swanndri jacket in the back seat, which we took. In the boot there was a large bottle of water that looked too old to drink safely. He probably kept it there to fill the radiator. Teresa tipped this out on the grass and put the bottle back in the car. There was also a short piece of rope. She lifted up an old mat underneath which was the spare tyre. "Come on," she said to me. Together we pulled the tyre out. Teresa then rolled it away, taking it thirty or forty yards off from the car before pushing it into the forest. I heard the tyre moving across leaves and fallen branches and then nothing. Teresa ran back to the car. "Get the handbrake," she said.

'I took the handbrake off and we started to rock the car back and forth, trying to get it moving. I had one hand on the steering wheel.

'"Wait!" said Teresa. She walked around to the passenger side and opened the glove box. She came out with a screwdriver and she told me to open the hood. I couldn't find the release handle at first—it was getting quite dark. Finally I found it and Teresa opened the hood.

'"What are you doing?" I said.

'Her head was lost in the engine and she was grunting with effort. I could hear the screwdriver scraping against metal. Something gave way and Teresa stood up, holding a piece in her hand. "Distributor rotor!" she said. She put this in her pocket.

'Where had she learned about such things? I didn't ask her then. I've never asked her.'

'It's true,' Paddy said to Pip, 'she knows about cars. Her brother Graham taught her, I think. He built a car in their garage and she watched.'

'Ah, poor Graham,' said Pip. 'Yes, that rings a bell now. Anyway, we went back to our positions and this time we got the car rolling. I aimed for a gap in the trees and the car went through easily. It must have struck a small ridge though because it stopped and we couldn't get it moving again. This wasn't far enough. Anyone could see the vehicle from the road, even in this light.

'We lifted Genevieve up and walked her to the car. She leaned her weight against the back of the car and with Teresa and I also pushing—no one steering—we managed to get the car over the ridge. Genevieve fell down with a cry at the same time the car left our hands. There must have been a slope because we heard the car carry on for several moments, bashing down through the undergrowth until it came to a thudding stop. The noise gave me a shock, it was so final. We couldn't go back now. We stood looking after the car, with half an idea it might come back up the slope and offer us a second chance, a chance to reconsider what we'd done.

'Genevieve was already getting to her feet. She was in pain, you could see it, but she didn't say anything. She pointed to the other side of the road.

'"No," said Teresa. "We're not throwing you into the bushes. We'll put you on the bike and we can wheel it along the road until we've gone far enough, then we'll get off the road and wait with you."

'"Yes," I said.

'Genevieve refused this at once. She told us we'd do much better by ourselves and that she'd be fine if we left her. She'd wait until morning and then cars and trucks would start using the road again and she'd get a lift. But we held firm. We weren't going anywhere without her. She threw up her hands in the air. I remember the gesture so clearly! She said something in French, a long string of—exasperation. So strange to hear that, Paddy, in the forest, but nothing could happen which wasn't an inversion of normal life, our normal lives up to this point.

'We worked to conceal the car's location, spreading pine needles over the tracks with our feet and dragging branches to obscure the gap we'd pushed it through. It was difficult in the night to know how successful we'd been. Perhaps we were making things worse, making it look too obviously like the site of a cover-up. The man would notice everything. Yet his car was down the bank, undriveable.

'Finally we got Genevieve on the bike, her bad foot sticking out awkwardly, and we started off slowly down the road, heading in the same direction as the man had gone on Teresa's bike.

'I wheeled the bike while Teresa carried the panniers which the man had stripped off.

'We thought we could travel like this for about half an hour at the most before the risk of meeting him on his way back became too great. The plastic hosing, Teresa explained, was for siphoning the petrol. Most likely the petrol station would be closed. The man would simply take petrol from the first parked vehicle he came across in a suitable location, that is one that allowed him to steal without detection. If he was lucky, and we were not, he might come across a car, perhaps a forestry vehicle, nearby on a side-road or on a farm. Forget the petrol, he could simply break a window, touch a couple of ignition wires and steal the car. He wouldn't have to go the five miles at all. He might be returning our way now and so we needed to keep as far to the left as possible.

'I remember listening to all this coming from Teresa and knowing absolutely that it was extraordinary, that her composure and expertise were startling, but also understanding that it was necessary simply to listen and act on what she was saying. There was no time for marvelling. Danger made everything clear, like ice. Speaking of which, the temperature had dropped a good deal. We were cold and this seemed better than drugged by heat.

The air itself was pure in our lungs, I felt. The handlebars were cold, almost sticky with cold.

'We pushed the French woman on the bicycle down that dark road without any effort it seemed and with no thought now as to our own strangeness. Certainly I wasn't thinking about her story. How did she get here? Who was she to the man? What was the danger he represented? No. All the normal questions were utterly suppressed. It was your mother, Paddy, who showed how it was to be done. And I understand completely now what it is to obey an order. To hear a voice. We were a tiny female army, more army than the boys we'd seen with cream on their faces in the tea rooms.

'No one talked on that journey.

'All our senses were trained on the distance, trying to hear or see him first in the incomplete darkness, to find some reflected glow off the road's surface that would give us that moment's warning which would let us fall into the shadows by the trees before we were spotted. I was conscious of a terrific headache from staring and staring ahead but I couldn't break away.'

His mother's cousin opened her eyes wide and blinked slowly several times as if she'd been back on that road just then. She rubbed her face, covering a yawn with both hands. Paddy asked if she wanted a rest. They could resume later, after lunch. She looked at her watch, apologising again for how long this had taken, but she thought she should finish it now. There wasn't much left.

In the midst of many other thoughts, he was considering what was surely a tangential if not meaningless connection between the story Pip was telling and the films Dora and Medbh made about female hitchhikers in trouble. Of course Teresa had never seen these films; the connection was in his head only. Still he wondered what the two cousins would have made of them.

'After thirty minutes of that, we left the road and pushed the bike carrying Genevieve between the trees, entering the forest for several minutes until we came to a small grassy clearing. We helped her off and she sat down, the Swanndri covering

309

her shoulders. She rested her head against Teresa's panniers and while we spoke about what we'd do, she fell asleep. One moment she was wide-awake and listening closely, next she was sleeping. It gave us both an idea about what she must have been through. It was enough, you know, to tell us something. Of course it was also what we both wanted to do as well and now we couldn't. Suddenly I looked at her with wild resentment. But it never crossed my mind to leave her. She was vital. One good thing, I didn't like listening to her voice, and now she was, thank goodness, quiet. I was still blaming her for everything, I suppose.

'Your mother and I took turns to watch over the road. We were on a slight rise and we could see sections of the road down in a valley beneath us. We lay on our stomachs, really again like soldiers. Sentinels. And we waited for him. We did thirty-minute shifts, any longer and we would have all been asleep. Of course we couldn't be sure we didn't nod off occasionally. Lying on my stomach, I did feel the strong temptation to turn my head and sleep. To avoid this, we agreed to lie with sticks near our faces. If we felt droopy, the sharpness of the sticks would wake us. The cold helped too. Even with this precaution of the sticks, did we miss something? Did he bike past at just that moment? It's possible. But we never saw him and I don't think he came back at all.

'You know, Paddy, when I was in the chicken coop, with my hands tied and the blindfold on, those people didn't come back either. But they want you to think they will. That's the trick of their terror.

'I remember when I was on watch I kept myself alert by going over my police description of the man until that too took on a mantra-like feeling, height, weight, eyes, height, weight, eyes, and I had to stop in case its rhythm sent me off to sleep.

'In the forest we were all awake at dawn and we went out carefully to the road. It was deserted, though not for long. A logging truck went past after a few minutes, too sudden and too huge for us to react. We watched it disappear into the valley.

No one felt like moving so we simply sat down and waited. I'd imagined a kind of triumph but there wasn't any of that feeling, none at all. There was no conversation, no planning. If the man called Duncan had appeared, he would have had us. I suppose sleep-deprived we lost our purpose.

'Ten minutes later we heard another vehicle in the distance and Teresa and I stood up and started waving. It was a farm worker, a Maori guy, a bit older than us. He put the bike on the back with his dogs and said one of us had drawn the short straw because he could only fit two more in the cab. Teresa was the first to move, climbing into the back, and we drove into town. Actually I would have preferred the back too. The idea of talking to the Maori guy, explaining any of it, was hard to take. But he didn't seem to care that my answers were so vague. Once he knew Genevieve was a foreigner, it seemed any explanation carried equal plausibility. We were soon bumping along in silence. I looked back through the cab's little rear window. The dogs were ignoring Teresa and barking from time to time, their heads stuck far out in the wind. They were alive in the morning air, telling everyone about it. They were alive. And I thought, we were those dogs too.

'When we got into the town, it was still early morning and there was hardly anyone about. The wide streets were misty and damp. Genevieve looked out the window and suddenly asked the guy to stop the truck. She pointed across the road to a walkway between houses. She said she lived down there and thanked him for the ride. I hadn't been prepared for this and she had the door open before I could think what to do. I looked quickly at Teresa through the window. She didn't know what was happening of course. I told Genevieve I'd help her across the road but she was now standing on the street, leaning against the door. No, she said, she'd be okay. "Thanks," she said. She closed the door and we drove off.

'I was stunned. Teresa knocked on the window and gave me a frantic questioning look. Behind us I saw the French woman hopping across the road and disappearing down the walkway.

The Maori guy was asking where we wanted to be dropped off. "Here!" I said, pointing to a dairy we were passing which was closed. "Right here?" he said. He pulled over sharply and we heard the dogs sliding on the tray, their claws against the metal. The bike also knocked against the side, catching one of the dogs who yelped. The guy leaned his head out the window and told the dog to be quiet.

'He got out and helped us with the bike. One of the dogs jumped down, did one mad circuit around the truck, and jumped back up again.

'"You girls aren't in trouble, are you?" he said.

'"No," said Teresa. "My aunt lives here."

'"What's her name?"

'"Polly."

'The lie was so swift I almost believed it myself. Maybe she did have an aunt here. Was I also related to her?

'"Polly?" he said.

'"Do you know her? Polly Purvis?"

'"Purvis? There's Purvises from Bucknell's Bay but not any Polly."

'"Different ones must be," said Teresa.

'"Polly Purvis," repeated the Maori guy, moving back to the cab of his truck.

'Once the truck had gone, I biked back as fast as I could to the walkway but there was no sign of the French woman. A few of the houses now had lights on, most had their curtains closed. The lane went on for some time and I biked the length of it but Genevieve wasn't there. I went back to Teresa.

'What had we been imagining would happen once we reached civilisation? We'd imagined telling our story to the police. And for that, we needed Genevieve. Without her, what did we have? A man runs out of petrol and borrows a bike to get some. For that, we vandalise his car and take off with his girlfriend, or whatever she was to him. We required her terror, her evidence, her foot in the cast. Without her, we were the ones in trouble with the police.

'Then we imagined Duncan out on the dark road, having biked ten miles, lugging the petrol, looking for us and for his car, trying to piece it together. If he had gone out there, what would he then do? Bike back most likely, another five miles. The man was somewhere in this town, furious, having lost everything.

'It was hard to believe that the nightmare was continuing, that the nightmare had a place in broad daylight. But of course, yes, it does.

'We had to get out of the place as fast as possible. We decided to risk going to the bus station though we figured there was a chance he'd be waiting there for us. He wasn't. And there was an intercity bus for Rotorua that left within the hour. We didn't know where that was. "Hot pools!" said the man behind the counter and we nodded. We bought tickets and waited in a playground near the station. I remember there was a concrete tunnel for kids to crawl through and we lay down in this, at either end, our heads almost touching, our legs dangling out the ends as the town slowly woke up.

'When we heard the bus start up, we ran across to it and got on. We'd already been able to store the bike and our panniers in the luggage bay after buying the tickets. We pulled the little curtains across our window and slumped down in our seats and I think we were asleep or unconscious before we left Turangi.

'The rest of the trip, well, I can hardly remember it, Paddy. I was keen to abandon the whole biking thing and catch another bus to Auckland but your mother said she thought we should complete what we set out to do. It didn't make sense to give up now. In Rotorua we bought a second-hand bike at a garage sale just down the road from the hostel we were staying at. Teresa rode this.

'I remember we were horribly lost riding into Auckland and finally got another lift with a postal truck to the North Shore, bikes in the back, right to the door of my mother's relative. You know I've forgotten her name. She was very nice, an old woman, rather bemused to have us and not at all sure how to treat us, whether as children or adults. She settled for children, which actually was lovely. We had lemonade in her back garden under a fig tree when we arrived and she put out a bowl of lollies in our room. There were soaps in the shape of animals on our beds.

'It was so lush, tropical almost. Like something kept from us. Hot at night. It was then I think I had the idea of leaving, leaving the country for good. I think so. Not because of what had happened but because of this place we'd come to. I had a sudden strong feeling of what might be possible or impossible. I woke up, I think. I thought suddenly, Wellington was boring. I don't know my motives. Some have them perhaps.

'One day we caught the ferry to Waiheke Island and I saw Teresa leaning her hand over the edge of the boat as we moved out into the middle of the harbour. I could tell she had something in her hand. She caught me watching her and she opened her hand to let me see what it was. As she did so, the object tumbled into the water, sinking from sight at once. It gave me a fright to see it happen. It was the part from the man's car that she'd ripped out in the forest that night.

'In Auckland, we never spoke about what had happened to us or what had not happened to us. We went home after a week of lemonade and lollies. We took the train back to Wellington. I went down to Otago a few weeks after that, by which time your mother had started doing her secretarial training. We never spoke about it again, ever.

'You, Paddy, are the first person I've ever told. I never even told my husband.' She smiled at him and brought her shoes together with a soft click. 'Fini.'

They sat without speaking for some time. Pip looked drained. Paddy told her he was immensely grateful she'd come all this way to tell him the story. It was remarkable. It was also mysterious, he said.

'Yes!' she said.

She looked at him expectantly, as if hoping that he might say more. Might he have an opinion on their behaviour? What had

314

been the proper way to react to their situation? How would he have handled it? He could condemn them even, she seemed to be urging with this look. He understood Pip was fully prepared to be punished somehow. When she saw his hesitation, there was a flash of disappointment in her eyes. His recoil briefly hurt her. She'd set everything out so carefully and he was withdrawing. Did Paddy, the figure she'd thought of writing a fan letter to, really have nothing more than this?

'I didn't know any of it before,' he said.

She smiled at him, nodding. His statement struck his own ear as not-very-interesting on a major scale if interpreted as filial bleat: why'd my mother keep it to herself? The longest story Teresa had ever told had lasted in the telling probably about two or three minutes. She didn't speak a lot, in general. Her favourite reading was thrillers. She despatched them five-a-week. She spoke, a little, in thriller mode. In compressed units that eschewed personal feeling. But he was guessing here. He'd not read much in the genre.

But what could he say now?

Pip said something about being very young at the time.

There was that.

'Bit of a shaggy dog story, sorry,' she said.

'No,' he said. 'The *point* of a shaggy dog story is its shagginess. Too much psychology in yours, too much tension.'

'But not many bodies, dead bodies I suppose I mean.'

'Pleased about that,' he said.

'And now I feel—'

'What?'

'Disloyal. Your mother should have been here, to help, to correct. Lots of things I'm sure I got wrong. Probably you should get her version first before you come to any conclusions. Conclusions about what, I don't know.'

Nor did Paddy. He was held by another something. It was approximately this: he thought the story of their bike trip wasn't over somehow. It went on. It was still in progress. This was its impossibility and its delicacy, moral delicacy. And the ingenious

315

notion that the French woman Genevieve could be connected with the sounds now coming out of Teresa's mouth was another instalment, instalment was the wrong word. Interpretatively depleted, he thought the following: if Pip's effort was proof of something it may have been only this: that the cousins had never stopped telling each other the story of the man they met that night who terrorised them and who went off on one of their bikes and was never seen again.

Anyway, it was all he could think of, and scarcely in language. He was stunned.

Then randomly: by what whisker had Teresa, as a young woman, not ended up in Africa?

There were great-looking strawberries in the bowl.

Pip realised the impasse in front of them. Without Paddy really noticing, she'd left the sofa and was in the kitchen, preparing the lunch things. She'd fallen back into her role of kindness and service and invisibility. It wasn't her role, she was built this way. He went to help her and they chatted about the best roadside places to buy fruit and vegetables outside Levin. She talked about Palmie. She'd lost her letterbox one night to students or someone.

When everything was ready, he went next door to get his mother. There was no reply when he knocked and he'd forgotten his key. He went back to his own place and rang her number. After a while his call went through to her message. Paddy had told her to expect a knock at around 1pm. The session with Pip had taken them past that. He hadn't said anything about seeing Pip before the lunch. As far as his mother knew, the knock on her door meant Pip had arrived. Perhaps she was dozing. He used his key to open her apartment and he called out her name. There was no response and no sign of her inside. The things from their tea earlier that morning were on the kitchen bench unwashed. Paddy had the feeling nothing was different from two hours before when she'd been wearing her dressing gown. Her bed was unmade, clothes were draped over the back of an armchair. He stood in the middle of the sitting room and became aware of an electrical hum. It was coming from the computer. The screen was off but the tower, which sat on the floor, was on, as if either she'd been on the computer and switched the screen off or she'd changed her mind about it and having started it up hadn't gone through with it. Why was he thinking like the police? In thriller mode.

Pip suggested that maybe Teresa had grown tired of waiting and had gone out to get a little treat for the lunch. Paddy noticed her handbag and her car keys on the hall table, though it was possible she'd taken her purse, which he couldn't find. 'Maybe she's just gone for a walk,' said Pip.

They waited another ten minutes. Then he told Pip that he'd have a quick look for her and it would be good if she could stay in his mother's apartment in case she came back. He gave her his mobile number and took the lift down to the street.

6

It was normal for him to let a week, ten days, two weeks even go past, without knowing where his mother was and what she'd been doing. They lived in the same region, under the same weather, and this was enough for Paddy, if not to have certainty, then to be able to imagine her routines, her days and her nights, that is if he chose to. He saw her in their old house. He saw her folding the gardening mat and brushing at her knees. Later, it was at the computer, doing her stuff. It was as thoroughly complacent an adult son's purview as they come.

One time they'd met by chance at a supermarket in town and both felt a shyness, as if they'd secretly arranged to bump into each other. She'd been in Wellington for some reason and had decided to do her grocery shopping. They looked in each other's trolleys and made comments about what was there. His mother reached into his, picked something up and read the back of it. Okay, she said. Interesting. A great current of intimacy went between them through this simple, meaningless act of reaching into his trolley. It was terrific to have come across her like this, to stand in a public place and for no one to know that she was his mother and he was her son. It was as though they existed at the heart of a grand conspiracy. See you by the fish. I never buy the fish in these places, she said. Too pricey? Exactly, and the looks on their faces. Whose faces, the guys selling them? No, on the fish.

Anyway, Stephanie was in contact almost every day and she'd keep Paddy informed.

Invariably, at some point in the period of not seeing her or hearing his mother's voice, he'd experience a sharp feeling of loss. There was often a connection between this feeling and his poor long-dead father. The prompt might be that Paddy had come across something his father would have been interested in, a minor thing. A book for sale, the demolition of a house. And he'd have the urge to call the old place in Lower Hutt. Sometimes it wouldn't concern his father at all. It was her alone he needed and whom he'd tried to summon and couldn't. That was crucial, to be unable to imagine her. It was a strange ache, a kind of despair. Was he being a child to react like this, or a sentient being? The feeling was that he'd forgotten what she was like and what he was like with her. The moment she answered the phone, his mind was at rest. Here she is. Here we are.

Perhaps the three of them—Paddy and his two sisters—despite their differences, were all somewhere along the same scale. Stephanie had once told him that if a day went past without making contact with their mother, she felt terrible and lost. 'Like the day didn't really happen, Paddy.' Margie could last longer than any of them, months, years in fact, but that was exactly what she savoured, the sensation of being outcast on a daily basis. Pocketbook psychology, not Lant's: she took strength from her feeling of exclusion and courted it through a series of imaginary rebuffs. The facts: messages that were left for her she claimed never to have received. Things sent to Vancouver went missing in the post. Margie refused to get Skype, rarely sent photos, then complained her boys were growing up unnoticed by any of them. Two gangly Canadian boys who said they liked to fool around in *boots*, sailing boats. They were extremely tall but was anyone interested?

Outside his building, Paddy looked both ways down the street. To find that he had the task of looking for his mother in the city they'd helped persuade her to shift to, this gave him a sudden moment of fright. Which direction to go in? The lunchtime crowds were still out. Bodies moved along the pavement. What were her habits? She had none. There hadn't been time to establish routines. She'd recently bought a pair of shoes with Helena from a shop around the corner and, for no other reason than to start moving, this was where he headed.

She wasn't a missing person.

Almost immediately he became aware of someone walking alongside him, keeping pace. Paddy started walking faster and the person kept up. He glanced across. He knew him of course. The figure was all in black. Black sneakers, black jeans, oversized black sweatshirt. He walked with his hands in his pockets, head slightly bowed, letting the dark hair fall over his face. He should have been in school. Paddy kept moving, even faster now, and his companion had to take his hands out of his pockets. Glancing down again, Paddy saw the scribbles on the back of one hand as it swung awkwardly. The large feet fell without rhythm on the footpath, as if he might trip up, and the breathing had started to struggle. Paddy slipped quickly between two people and accelerated away. The figure was trying to get past but the gap had been closed by people coming the other way and Paddy heard him grunting, breaking into a jog now to catch up. They'd reached the corner of the Mall, where Paddy stopped suddenly. There was almost a collision. They were outside the shoe shop, standing side by side, looking at the window display of women's summer sandals. His pursuer's chest was heaving and he was swallowing hard.

Paddy looked at him directly as he tried to recover. He was bent over, his fists resting on his knees. Hair hid most of his face, leaving only a jaw-line of acne, and a pale neck of clear glistening skin. His eyes flicked briefly at Paddy then back to the shop window.

Teresa wasn't in the shoe shop.

The noise of the bucket fountain made Paddy look in that direction and he set off again, jogging this time. He was followed. The heavy feet, the helpless grunting as if someone was punching him. Paddy skipped between people. Looking back he saw how his running mate went through them blindly, without apology,

320

scattering the footpath. Paddy heard a few curses. The figure kept his head down and ran.

His mother wasn't among the people by the fountain. A woman of about her age sat on a bench feeding pigeons, while a young mother waited for her toddler to go down the slide. Office workers ate their lunches perched on the edge of the planters. People smoked, leaning against the streetlight poles.

He arrived beside Paddy, panting, just as the water began to crash from bucket to bucket. Spray hit the tiles near the feet of a couple having lunch from paper bags and they looked down at the damp spots and continued eating. The pigeons lifted a few inches off the ground then settled again.

Paddy was suddenly hungry, with a sick feeling too.

At the noise from the buckets the toddler on the slide had looked around, startled, and begun to cry; his mother was reaching for him but he'd retreated inside the little turret and she couldn't get him. She took a few steps up the ladder but he screamed at her to get down.

In the corner of his eye, through the open doors of Farmers, Paddy thought he saw a familiar shape, a woman carrying bags, heading for the escalator. At that moment a group of six or seven shoppers came from the doors and he couldn't get through quickly. When the way cleared, the woman was gone. He took the escalator in large steps, hauling himself up. The black-clothed figure was just getting on it when Paddy was at the top. Lingerie.

He moved among the displays of bras and knickers, searching for the woman who might have been his mother. He had to squeeze past a middle-aged woman with an armful of underwear who gave him a filthy look, as if he'd caught her wearing the things she carried. This was Paddy's sense too. What was the expression on his face except a strange and heated neediness? He was sweating now, having dressed too warmly for the pursuit, the mad search, the hide-and-seek with his Boy-Man companion, who'd also now entered the lingerie section. Paddy could hear him blundering about, knocking into things. A sharp, reprimanding female voice was saying something to his follower but by now Paddy was in Toys, which had aisles and was empty. He completed a circuit and headed for the stairs. There seemed to be no down escalator. From far across the floor, the figure saw him just as Paddy went through the fire doors.

At the bottom of the stairs he paused, looking up and down the aisles, trying to see as far back into the store as he could. Menswear, shoes, and further on, homeware. Behind him, he heard his pursuer thundering down the old springy wooden stairs, the heavy noise as he took the last few steps of each flight in a leap followed by a different, more sinister thud as with the full weight of his body he flew out of control against the wall before bouncing off and starting down the next flight. He moved as helplessly and heavily as the water falling from bucket to bucket in the fountain outside. He was the water, its wasteful flow, but he was also the buckets, tipping gracelessly and righting themselves with a clangy jerk.

Jerk was the word.

Paddy stood clear of the entrance to the stairs and the body tumbled forward as if sent down a chute, sliding on the linoleum, gripping a counter full of lipsticks that appeared in front of him, looking around wildly to see where Paddy had gone.

They were twenty metres from the Mall entrance and the figure raised his head towards the street, making a strange move with his nostrils as if trying to sniff a scent. Then his head turned swiftly in the other direction and his nostrils again widened. Which way?

He hadn't seen Paddy, who was standing still, very close.

The chest rose and fell but the great wildness and heedlessness seemed to be subsiding. He seemed to be considering the street option but was tempted once more by going further back into the store. Paddy hadn't done that bit, he was thinking, and surely he needed to check there. He peered thoughtfully. He waited with Paddy, still unaware that this was what he was doing. Paddy was a shadow.

His hair was pushed back now off his face in damp strands

322

and Paddy had his first real look. In two months he'd never had this sort of view. Paddy had allowed him to hide, to sink as low as he wanted to go into his chair, to cover himself by whatever means he needed. Paddy understood that formerly he'd had an impression only, a sketch, a smudge. Here was the original.

What struck Paddy was that Sam Covenay really was a child. He was young. To study his face was to know that he was a young fourteen. You needed a view of the eyes to see this and the brow, something incomplete in the set-up, a compression that over time would move, widen, open. The top half of his face was scrunched up. There was not much that seemed knowing here, only a sort of challenge and at the edge of that, the normal things: fear, vulnerability, shame. Paddy had known in the abstract that his patient was a work-in-progress but the physical proof was startling. He'd missed it.

The eyes were pale blue; a swimmer's eyes almost, he wanted to say, a sunniness and squint that contradicted everything the boy was aiming for. They suggested a history or at least a deep unburiable preference for illumination, for summer, for water. He was not the bucket fountain. He was the sea. Or he was the beach. Paddy remembered now that the Covenays lived on the coast behind the airport, Breaker Bay. One photo they'd brought along showed him there in his togs. You ran from your lawn across the road and you were in the water. He was that running boy. He was the bright kid who wanted to speak. Of course he might also have been the boy with the car aerial punishing the piece of driftwood the weekend he and Bridget had somehow decided, or decided not to decide, about children.

'Sam,' said Paddy.

He found Paddy next to him and took a sudden step back. What sort of trick was this? He opened his mouth. He stared at Paddy, his mouth hanging. He had so much to say. For a moment Paddy felt the full weight of that temptation, the voice held there, ready to break. He was on the verge, the teetering brink. Then the boy dropped his head.

Paddy said his name again but he didn't respond. It was

323

crushing. Paddy was overwhelmed at having come so close, and now he could sense the boy's shrinking, the practised retreat, the rehearsed deadness. The boy turned a great lever within himself and came to a halt. It was maddening. Finally too it was boring.

'I'm looking for my mother,' said Paddy. At this, Sam's head shifted a tiny bit. It was if Paddy was speaking to a dreaming dog. 'It's very important that I find her. Did you see her? Did you see her come out of our building? If you were waiting outside there, maybe you saw her. You remember my mother, you kissed her cheeks.'

Sam stayed beside Paddy and didn't move or speak. His hair had fallen forward and through it Paddy saw his ear. It was a small ear that might easily have belonged to a young girl.

'I'm asking for your help,' he said. 'I'm asking because I need it. I'm not asking as your speech therapist. Sam, I'm not your therapist any more. That's finished. I'm offering your parents a full refund. It didn't work. It's over. You win. You get to stay this way, Sam. Congratulations. Now I'm just asking whether you saw my mother. We're worried. She's not well and she walked out of her apartment. Maybe you saw which way she went.'

Paddy looked at this delicate little ear for ten or twenty seconds. A few shoppers moved around them but they stayed in their pose. They might have appeared as two store dummies, modelling some very average clothes. This season's father and son, in greys and blacks.

Paddy leaned very close to the ear and said, 'Can't you say something?'

He lifted his thumb and forefinger until they rested alongside the boy's little ear. 'Speak,' he whispered into it. He waited longer, another forty seconds maybe, a minute. It seemed an age to keep his hand in that position. His hand had a slight tremor. When he couldn't hold it any longer, he took the ear in his fingers, gripping the lobe lightly with no more pressure than an earring. It would have taken nothing to bring the kid to the floor, to have him at his feet in pain. Experimentally, Paddy gave the ear a few gentle tugs, again without any force. He waggled the ear and stroked it with his thumb. Good dog. Good boy. In holding the ear, his hand was relaxed and steady. It was very tempting. He let it go.

Throughout all this, Sam hadn't moved. It might have been a plastic ear Paddy had in his fingers, a fake ear. It had been temperature-less.

Paddy walked at a normal pace towards the Mall exit. Sam Covenay waited. Was this particular game over? At the doors, he looked out into the street. And he saw her. Teresa was walking past, very close to where he stood. She carried shopping bags. She walked upright, or rather with the slight forward lean they'd all inherited, a pressing forward. What are you all on the hunt for, Bridget had said. He assessed her. Teresa wasn't dissolute, unkempt, bag lady-ish in any manner. If she was inward-looking, that was normal too. His mother appeared to be walking home for lunch.

He considered joining her at once.

Paddy turned so he was facing the perfume counters where young women in nurse-style white coats moved around offering samples to those entering the store. They pressed strips of card to women's wrists and offered the wrist back to its owner to smell. Sam had come to stand beside him. Paddy kept staring at one of these women until she looked across and saw him. He made her watch them. He acted nervous, shifting from foot to foot, glancing around. She was curious at first. Did he want to try a perfume? But no, this pair was up to something. She'd started to look around for someone to tell. Then Paddy said to Sam, 'Are you ready for this?' The boy didn't look at him. 'Are you ready?' Nothing. 'Right, go!' and Paddy ran from the store.

He heard the perfume girl shouting after them, moving to the doors, and, glancing back, he saw a white-shirted security guy going past her, running and speaking into his walkie-talkie. He was after them.

Of course Paddy had seen these running figures before in Cuba Mall and Manners Mall and Lambton Quay. Young guys mainly, a little older than Sam usually. White guys, Maori guys. Two Asian kids once. No one as old as Paddy. He'd seen it in their eyes as they went past, that mix of panic and fun, it looked like. A few were even smiling as they pumped their arms and raised their knees, spitting sometimes. Only seconds before they'd set all this in motion, they'd crossed the line, done their bad thing, and this was what it came down to: a foot-race. *This?*

To watch it was to share some of that mixture too. It did seem absurd, two people chasing each other through the streets. Often you heard it before you saw it. The amazingly loud noise of two figures running as fast as they could; their sudden size, since in the natural bounce and uprightness of the running, their bodies grew taller. They were the mightiest things on the street these runners and they made everyone who was walking seem small and tired and uninteresting. Because condemnation wasn't automatic. It wasn't a stretch to think of them admiringly.

For the length of the street, before they disappeared around some corner, even while running through crowds, their pace never altered. With always this difference, the runner who was being chased never had problems with getting past people; the chaser usually did. The chaser, for one thing, wasn't dressed for the chase. He wore heavy black shoes. He had a tie on. He had things on his belt to deal with. Often he ran holding some piece of equipment. And he ran apologetically. He had to say sorry to people and excuse me. He had to be careful. The chaser was corporate fundamentally, and was running further and further away from his work, to which he'd have to return soon. The chaser was running home.

Paddy had never seen the runner caught.

Now they were the runners. They headed up Cuba Street as fast as they could, almost shoulder-to-shoulder. They made that noise on the pavement and they spat and pumped their legs. Paddy's heart was hurting—with adrenaline?—and his stomach was sore almost immediately from being knocked up and down. People got out of their way. They crossed Vivian Street without slowing, somehow finding a gap between cars. Horns sounded behind them but they kept going. Sam went ahead of him slightly, his bulky frame lengthening. The boy had abandoned his hunch, his lumbering strides, his tripping heaviness. Had all that been an act? He was truly fourteen years old and now ran with a terrifically erect posture, shoulders back. There was another round of car horns which must have been the security guard crossing Vivian. Paddy had hoped he might have given up by now.

And running was different from biking. Different set of muscles. A new pain.

Sam pushed on, taking a sharp right turn down a side street, vaulting a recycling bin that had been left in the middle of the footpath. When Paddy tried to do the same, his toe clipped the bin and he almost fell on his face. Somehow he managed to stay upright though he'd lost a lot of speed. Up ahead Sam turned round, waving at him to get going. It was the first purposeful gesture Paddy had seen from him and one not prompted by anyone.

The security guard was still coming. Paddy glanced back and saw his tight determined mouth, the fierce flush. But he also saw the wayward movement of his shoulders, as if he were running into a strong headwind. His hands clawed the air. The day was still and the guard was tiring. He was putting everything into it and Paddy understood why. It's me. He'll never catch Sam but it's become a point of pride to lay his hands on some sorry, saggy middle-aged guy who thought he could do a runner under his watch.

He'd abandoned the rules of the chase. That was the problem.

Paddy saw Sam take another turn, this time down a narrow lane between two old houses. Again he slowed a fraction to make sure Paddy had seen where he was going. Further example of thoughtfulness!

The other option was to run through the small park and head off along the more open streets leading either into town or in the direction of Aro Valley and Brooklyn. Did they stand a better chance if they split up? Sam, in reality, was gone, safe. Paddy looked towards the park. But he didn't have the puff to keep it up for much longer. There was a slight curve in the road so that if he could get to the lane before the guard saw him, he might run on. He sprinted as hard as he could and went down the lane. It was a dead-end. Ten metres away, there was a chain-link fence sealing it. He had no choice but to run to it. Was he supposed to jump it? But it was topped by barbed wire. He looked to his left and there was Sam crawling through some broken boards under the veranda of a derelict house that seemed to be full of car tyres. Paddy followed him.

They stayed under the veranda for several minutes, panting like cats, lying on their stomachs in the dry dirt. There wasn't enough room to sit up. Paddy picked up a nail and it crumbled in his fingers. Light came through the gaps in the weatherboards. Earthy air that also smelled rubbery, perhaps from the tyres. They could hear traffic and snatches of people talking, shouting, but no one came down the lane. They listened to their own breathing. The blood was beating in Paddy's right ear. He shut his eyes but his father wasn't there. He opened his eyes. The beating in his ear slowly faded.

The security guard might have realised they were hiding somewhere, that they couldn't have just vanished, and he might search for them. But searching was different from chasing and Paddy's guess was that, in spite of his need to get the old guy, the guard wouldn't want to become involved in a situation where he found them down some deserted lane, cornered. It was two against one and he'd already done his best. You ran until you stopped and then you went back to the store to fill in your report sheet.

His phone rang. It was in his pocket and impossible to get out. It rang until it stopped.

Paddy couldn't bear the discomfort any longer, and anyway the phone had given up their position. He moved his legs out the opening and backed awkwardly into the daylight. His whole body was stiff and sore and he slumped against the side of the veranda, watching Sam emerge from the hole.

Once he was out, he stood up, staring down at Paddy with a look of annoyance, disgust even. There was, for the first time, a directed emotion. He looked capable of lashing out, or running off. His sweatshirt and his trousers were covered in dust. He seemed to hate Paddy.

Good.

'What did you take?' said Paddy.

Sam recoiled. Held his hands up. *Me?*

Say what you liked, the Covenay kid was good. All this and still no speech.

'What did you steal from there?'

He was filled with disbelief. He mimed it with genuine horror, taking a step back, flinging his arms around. Search me, if you want.

'You take a bra or something?' said Paddy. 'Panties?'

He put two fingers to his brain. You must be mad, what are you talking about?

Paddy took out his phone and checked for messages. There was one from Pip saying his mother was home. He looked at the kid again. 'I don't care what it is, just tell me. You a panty thief, Sam Covenay?'

He was shaking his head. I pity you, you're sick.

He *was* sick. Sick of this. Paddy stood up so they were facing each other and pointed a finger against the boy's chest. 'I think you have female items on your person, Covenay.'

Sam looked at the finger and smiled, baring his braced teeth, still shaking his head.

It was Paddy's first real look inside the mouth. He thought, It's me. I was like this too. Age fourteen, I was on this path. I was this. The Year My Father Died. Same age. Same mouth. But wait on. Did I stop speaking? No. Did I draw stuff on my hand? No. Did I get or seek help? Hell no. So they were different too, he thought.

The Covenay kid was not sui generis, nor was he generic. Okay then, that established it: he was human. The search for Sam had narrowed.

The boy's head-shaking went on. You're a lame fucking therapist, man. You think this will work? Then Sam gestured towards his pockets. Paddy could look if he wanted to. He didn't care. He was clean.

'Why'd you run then?' said Paddy, suddenly losing any playfulness, speaking earnestly, accusingly even. Hating him too. Hating his blackness, his cowardice, his foolish confidence in an act that would have been insupportable without the indulgence of the people who loved him. 'Why are you with me? I don't get why. And I'm not sure I need you here right now. I have serious things to think about.'

Sam stared at the ground for a moment and moved his foot around in the dusty grass, considering. He flicked at some of the dirt on his trousers, brushing half-heartedly at the knees. Then he looked up and said right to Paddy's face, 'I didn't see your mother come out of the building. But then I wasn't looking for her. Maybe she did and I missed her. Or there's a back way.'

'There's no back way!'

He flinched at Paddy's harshness then recovered. 'Okay.'

'Wasted a whole lot of time here.' Paddy tapped a knuckle against one of the tyres on the veranda. Through a grimy double sash window he could see a workbench, a chain winch above it coming from the ceiling and the parts of an engine. It triggered easily an image of his mother, when she was hardly much older than Sam Covenay, working in the dark in the forest to prise the part from the car that would disable it. In fear of her life. Those were stakes, true stakes. He wanted to be at the lunch.

'So can I ask something?' Sam said. 'Why'd *you* run?'

'Why'd I run?'

'You didn't steal anything that I saw.'

Paddy looked at the boy who was now talking. It didn't seem strange at all that he had this power back again. His voice showed no obvious signs of its captivity though Paddy wasn't the best judge of that. Sam needed to stand in front of his parents and say things to them for everyone to know whether he sounded different from before. He didn't croak, he wasn't husky or hoarse. Of course he might have been chatting away in private all this time, keeping the voice in shape. He wasn't aphasic.

'Why'd you run?' he said again.

'I don't know. Wanted to see what it was like,' said Paddy.

'Okay,' he said doubtfully.

They walked into the lane, both brushing vigorously at their clothes. Dust rose up and made Sam sneeze loudly. Again the noise was novel. At once Paddy knew he'd been able to suppress even this. Sam gripped his mouth and looked shocked; as if he'd said something he shouldn't have but was pleased it was out.

'But you know what, I really wanted to see the guy give up, the security guard,' said Paddy.

'He did though.'

'To be aware of him pulling up, stopping in the street, waving his hand after me in disgust.'

'That guy would be pretty disgusted with you right now.'

'You think?' The kid was even experimenting with kindness.

They'd come to the end of the lane and Sam went ahead, checking the street was clear before Paddy emerged. 'I just thought,' said Paddy, 'I'll never be able to go to Farmers again. I'm a wanted man.'

'Wanted for not stealing anything,' said Sam. 'By the way, you checked the basement, right? For your mother.'

'What would she be doing in the basement though?' He didn't yet want to tell him the truth, that his mother was found, was never lost. He wanted a pressure maintained. The kid was speaking, a miracle, but that didn't make him likeable. He was likeable but that didn't make Paddy disposed to like him. That didn't make him, despite the braces, the unaccountable sadnesses, the unreachable desires, a frère.

'I don't know. That's where you keep all the junk though.

Stuff you should have thrown out. All of those things of Dora's. Plus it's where you keep your bike.'

Paddy stopped him. 'All this time, you've been listening.'

'Never said it was my hearing that was wrong.'

'Never *said* anything.'

'That's true.' The smile he gave was wry, slightly remorseful. Was he considering what he'd lost over these last months of self-imposed silence? Did some image of his parents' pain come to mind? That was probably stretching it. He was after all a devious vandal, the kid who'd not only changed the face of his folks' lives but the face of Paddy's cartoon. The smile may have been more smug than anything else. He was speaking again but was he better?

7

Paddy stood just inside the door of the apartment and listened. This pair was having lunch, behaving as if nothing had happened—not in the last hour, not in the last week, not ever. Cutlery knocked against plates, there was laughter. For a moment he thought nothing *had* happened and that everything was back to normal. Except that category had been banished. Then he heard the voices: Southern African English and French Kiwi. The huge oddness of it made him happy and just a little nervous, as if it all might collapse at any moment when the oddness was recognised, the terror of it acknowledged, and he waited. They'd not heard him come in.

Terror? Surely nothing as bad. It seemed like they'd taken in foreign boarders, or that Helena was home with some pupils. He heard his mother laughing, or guessed it was Teresa, or Thérèse, since the laugh followed the low, insistent, smiling sound of Pip who, it seemed, was playing host. His mother's laugh was new, higher-pitched than before and it trailed off shyly, almost as if a third person was in the room with them. Yet the flow between the cousins was completely natural, marked by habits formed decades ago obviously, the patterns relaxed, spirited.

'But I think secretly you like it,' he heard his mother say. 'You like how small it is. A real *town* town.'

Then Pip: 'It's true, I can't be in a big city for long now. Lost the habit.'

'You could move to Lower Hutt!'

'Yes! I should have bought your house, then you could visit and sleep in your old room.'

They laughed at this, and his mother said: 'But Lower Hutt isn't small any more.' Lower *Utt*.

Hear that, he thought, she was remaking the place. It sounded exotic and new, somewhere almost worth looking into.

There was a silence and then Pip said: 'I met a Somalian man in the Palmerston North Public Library the other day. I've been surprised at the number of Africans here.'

His mother said in mock horror, 'They're everywhere!'

When he appeared, they both stood up and apologised for starting without him but they'd been starving and had begun to pick, just pick, though it looked more than that now, sorry. Pip pulled a chair out for him, giving him the briefest look as if to say, everything's all right, play along. It's fine.

He saw that the food he'd bought had been added to. The table was set for a jolly picnic: a bowl of green salad, two types of bread, a plate of ham, smoked fish, cheeses, a jug of water with ice and slices of lemon in it, the strawberries, cloth napkins he recognised as his mother's, also her vinaigrette bottle. In the centre of the table, an untouched pear tart. Their own plates were half-finished. 'Look at this,' he said.

'Your naughty mother went out and bought things,' said Pip.

'Yes, I have it down now,' said Teresa. 'I go, I point. I nod and smile. I hand them my bankcard.'

'She says she's not understood by the locals.'

'I'm not!' His mother looked at his clothes. 'But Paddy where have you been?'

He was still dusty, despite his efforts. 'Oh, mucking about,' he said.

After he changed his clothes they sat together eating and talking. He was admitted into their company by Pip with a kind of pretend deference that was still lovely. 'Here he is!' she said. 'The owner of the house. The great columnist!' She helped load his plate with food. Then she was asking his opinion on the best small town in New Zealand, which had been their topic before he arrived and he was no doubt much better placed than either of them to give an informed view. He said he liked Central Otago, anywhere down there. He was a Central bore. He began to speak of driving through the region in late summer. His mother cut him off. Too extreme, she said. Hot and cold, no. 'Pip,' she said, 'can never handle a real winter again, she's too soft.'

'I am! I am! I'm ruined,' said Pip. 'But forget about me.' She asked Paddy what he liked about Central exactly.

When they retired he and Helena had a dream about a house on a hill, north-facing, solar panels, a river below them, orchards nearby, the sun moving in a great arc.

His mother said a word they didn't catch. She repeated it rather sourly. 'Melanoma, from the sun.' Her mood seemed fully collapsible. Was she annoyed he was there?

Pip laughed and struck her cousin lightly on the arm. She said to Paddy, 'Will you grow grapes?'

'We'll eat grapes. And we'll drink the fruits of others' labour.'

'Exactly! Because there's too much work in a vineyard and you'll be there to—'

'Bask in the summer heat,' he said, 'while covered in sunscreen.'

Pip then asked about Helena, whom she'd never met.

His mother said unhappily, 'She works very hard, very hard. Harder than he does.'

'That's fair,' he said. He explained about the language school, the review. How committed she was.

'What a neat lady,' said Pip.

'There's a daughter,' said Teresa. It seemed an ominous pronouncement.

'There is a daughter, yes,' he said, smiling.

Then Pip was asking about his work. What sort of problems was he treating typically?

His mind went straight to Sam Covenay. What followed now in that case? There was a good chance the boy might simply return to his old ways. And Paddy could hardly give the Covenays details of the 'cure'. Or Sam might go home and tell the whole truth, the chase, the hiding. Could be a problem there for Paddy, although first they'd have to believe the devil.

He found himself telling Pip about Caleb, his most recent 'graduate', he said, and he spoke of the boy's mother, Julie, who'd read him the poem.

'What a brilliant tribute. They put you in poems! Wonderful,' said Pip.

'It's my one and only appearance.' He told them about the baking too.

'How astonishing,' said Pip. 'In our day of course,' she said, turning to her cousin, who'd stopped eating, 'we had nothing like it, did we?'

'Ginger gems?' said Teresa unhumorously.

'Speech therapy.'

His mother now looked in danger of dropping out of the meal altogether. She'd been staring at her food in sullen contemplation. She put down her fork and rubbed at her eyes. 'There seem to be more and more of these problems nowadays.'

'But is that true, Paddy?' said Pip. 'Maybe back then if you had a problem you just suffered it.'

'You just got on with it,' said Teresa. She lifted her head sleepily.

'Well,' said Pip, resting her hand on her cousin's arm. 'Was it that simple?'

'I don't see why not. People were stronger.'

Pip laughed. 'Okay.'

Paddy said, 'Are you tired, Ma? You could go and lie down in the spare room.'

She ignored this or failed to take it in. 'If you can invent a name for it, you can charge people money for it. Slapped cheek syndrome.'

'What's that, darling?' said Pip.

'It's Slapcheek,' said Paddy. 'Quite a nasty virus. All Steph's kids—'

336

'Slapped cheek syndrome,' Teresa interrupted. 'All Steph's kids get it. Off they go to the doctor, paying out the money.'

'Doctor's visits are free for under sevens,' said Paddy, irritated, yet hoping to pass this off as pure information for Pip.

'Drugs aren't,' said his mother sharply. She was reviving. 'Now *we* never had slapped cheek syndrome. Slapped backside syndrome, yes.' She stared at Paddy. 'Another subject, that one.'

'Indeed,' said Pip.

Paddy reached for some more bread at the same time as Pip. 'Please, after you,' he said. They'd never been hit as kids. For Brendan, it would have been unthinkable.

'The child is king,' said his mother. *The child ees keeng.* 'You get arrested for touching them.'

'Actually no.' He'd not intended to make a response. He laughed. 'That is not the case.' It was a mistake to pursue the topic any further. His mother was clearly failing and of course Pip understood this. Yet even when well, Teresa had always been perfectly capable of saying such things and usually he was drawn to answer. There was a goading spirit in her. Its presence now didn't necessarily suggest that she was under strain, perhaps only that she was in the mood to reveal his sensitivities. Right then he discovered he disliked her thoroughly.

'The child is boss,' she said. The stupid accent gave these provoking statements an edge.

He spoke to Pip, still smiling. 'Yes, of course it was fairly recently in history that the child was sent into the fields, down the mines, sold into slavery.'

'Slavery!' said his mother with joyful scorn.

Pip sat back suddenly and brought her hands together in an attitude almost of prayer, bowing her head as she spoke. She was hoping that the table would reconvene itself in peace. 'We've come a long way, that's for sure.'

'I agree,' he said. 'But as you of course know, Pip, children still end up in the army in some parts of the world even now, parts that you'd be more familiar with than us, so notions of progress aren't universal.'

Pip sent a look in which her annoyance at him flashed briefly. She had loyalties. 'Paddy, you're right. It's a terrible thing.' She picked up a pie slice and addressed the pear tart. 'Now, can I cut some of this wonderful-looking creation for anyone? I mean, this is something you just can't get in Palmie.'

'And yet,' said his mother, 'they say the army is exactly what some of these young people need. The discipline.' *Dee-cee-pleen*. 'And they've had some good results with that.'

'Patrick,' said Pip, 'I want to give you a big piece.'

'Terrific,' he said, holding out his plate. 'Terrific.'

'You know he bikes now?' said Teresa, her voice slippery with amusement, veering towards a sort of spitefulness. 'He bought a bike and he goes out on it, he goes everywhere. He dresses up.'

'How wonderful,' said Pip.

'He wants eternal youth.'

'Bit late for that now, I think,' said Paddy. 'Besides, I didn't even like my youth. Happier now than I've ever been.' Instantly he wished to retract the first part of that.

'He's desperate,' said his mother.

'For this pear tart, I am.'

'It's very good for the planet anyway, biking,' said Pip.

'Oh, the planet,' sighed his mother. *Pluneet*. 'Sick of that too.'

Pip reached for his mother's plate. 'Thérèse?' She'd said the name in her best French accent.

'Oh, don't patronise me, please! I can't stand that. Both of you, just give it a rest.' His mother stood up from the table, shaking. Then she caught herself, correcting her tone at once. *Who is this mad woman in my body?* 'Sorry, dears. So sorry. Not feeling myself is the problem here. I'm so tired. Would it be too rude to lie down? I think I have to. I could go home but this is all right, isn't it.' Pip and Paddy were standing now and they reached to take an arm but Teresa waved them off. 'No, no, I can manage. Thank you.' She was walking steadily away from them. 'You know the French for "sorry" is "désolée". Learnt that. Je suis désolée. Now watch the elephant in the room as she moves slowly but with purpose to a place of rest. Did you see many elephants in Africa, darling? You probably kept them as pets. Tell me later.'

While his mother rested on the bed in the spare room, he and Pip did the dishes. Shortly after that, Pip had to leave for a meeting with a lawyer, a New Zealander, who'd been recommended by friends. She was trying to sort out a few things regarding her property, which she'd lost in Zimbabwe. She told Paddy that there was no question of compensation but she was trying to arrange for some people she knew to have living rights there. She'd talked on the phone and the lawyer had told her it was going to be very difficult but he would do what he could. Pip's briefcase contained documents that she hoped might help him. She held the briefcase up and tapped it. 'So many forms! So boring!'

She'd told Paddy all of this with her polite smile back in place, as if he couldn't possibly understand what it really meant and she couldn't possibly explain it to him or was unwilling to try. He recognised again how close she'd come in her story about the bike ride to allowing him to see into a sort of entrance. Now with great tact she seemed to be closing that entrance. Well, could she be blamed? What had he done to meet her?

They arranged that she could stay the night either in his apartment or his mother's, depending on Teresa's feelings, and be present at the MRI the following day. Though again, and despite his assurances that she'd be a great help, Pip insisted that this would only happen if his mother wanted it. If not, she could easily drive back to Palmerston North that evening.

She was about to leave and he wanted to engage with her again. He said something about Mugabe. There'd been stories in the paper about police beatings. A photo that was hard to look at of Morgan Tsvangirai's stitched skull.

'I once saw Mugabe on a bicycle,' she said. 'To carry on our biking theme.'

'Tell me more,' he said.

'A dangerous invitation with me, as you know. But yes, it's hard to believe now. It was in 1982, the year after the election. A nearby high school had been completely rebuilt and they'd put in a new sports field. Mugabe was very big on education back then, having been a teacher himself and then he'd studied for all those degrees. You know he's a very educated person, a BSc, several BAs, a law degree, others.'

'He got them in prison, didn't he.'

'He did. Anyway, he was coming to this school for their opening and we went along.

'We sat in the new stand at the sports ground and waited for ages. I remember thinking, okay Mugabe's not coming. He's a busy man with a big job in front of him. It was a small rural area, nothing much. Then finally a line of black cars comes through the school gates and turns into the sports field, parks in the middle of the grass, and out steps the man himself. Robert Mugabe, the great hero of our nation! I mean, he was a hero.

'Of course everyone goes absolutely crazy, weeping and screaming, men and women. There are children sitting on the dirt behind ropes and they started banging the ground with their fists. And he stands beside the cars for a while, smiling at us. Just smiling. You felt really great to be there that day.

'Then someone from the school comes forward and he speaks with the prime minister. There's a little stage set up near the cars, with a microphone for the speeches. But Mugabe doesn't walk there. He goes to the edge of the running track, and then he sees this bike that's lying on the grass, maybe a teacher's bike, I don't know. Did someone leave it there especially? Did one of his aides bring it and place it there? No one knows whose bike it was. Afterwards, many claimed it of course. Anyway, he picks it up, looks at it for a moment, and then he gets on it. Robert Mugabe on a bicycle! When he was young he would have had a bike of course but that was some time ago, you know.'

'I know the feeling,' said Paddy.

'He wobbles quite a bit too, getting going. He can't do it at first and he has to put his foot down. Finally he's riding. But then he does a circuit of the school track, dressed in a suit and tie. One of the most extraordinary things I've ever seen, Paddy.

'Slowly he bikes around in front of us, still smiling. It's a terrible smile, I think. All around the field there's this great hush now, the applause and everything has just died away completely. No one can believe it, what are we seeing? He looked so strange.

'We should have cheered and laughed, but people were afraid. Suddenly you knew everyone was terrified.

'And you know what? Never once did his hands leave the handlebars. He didn't wave, he didn't lift a finger off the grip he had to acknowledge us. How could he? He was concentrating with all his might on not falling off. He went very slowly and at the end of his circuit, his aides surrounded him, and he biked sort of into them, again in slow motion, all of us frightened, and they caught him, he simply crashed into them and they held him, and we never got to see Mugabe get off the bike, thank goodness.'

'What were you afraid of?' said Paddy.

'I don't know. Perhaps only that we'd seen it.'

'Seen something you shouldn't have?'

'Of course.' She shifted her briefcase into the other hand. 'For a second, you see, he had no power. We had the power. We had the power.'

After Pip left, he phoned Helena. 'How's my Janet Frame?' he said. For a moment she didn't get the reference. 'Running from the room? Running into the trees?' No, she said she was still there, hanging in. He asked about morning tea and Helena said that in some serendipitous way, having in her haste bought a gluten-free cake at Moore Wilson's, Trish Gibbons turned out to be wait for it gluten intolerant. 'We put the cake in front of her and she said sadly, "I don't know if I can eat that." Oh, I could have kissed her!'

A thing like that, he told her, could have an incalculable effect.

Trish was also, Helena said, from the South Island, from near Bannockburn, so they'd talked over lunch about their dream of retiring down there, building a place. Soon they were swapping ideas on heating, wood pellets versus log burner, waste water systems, whatever. 'Incredible,' he said, telling her about the lunch conversation he'd had with Pip, the same topic of their retirement coming up. He felt his optimism begin to return. The lunch had been misery. Teresa was a worry. He was unhappy with his own selfishness. But simply by talking to Helena, he felt better. It was a wonder. He had images of them reading in front of large double-glazed panorama-giving windows. The underfloor heating, heating stones. Snow on the ranges. No doubt he was attracted to it right then because of the promise of escape. It was ten or fifteen years away! Helena already knew quite a bit about septic tanks and even this aspect of their grand plan was thoroughly exciting, romantic. In the space of a year, from when the idea first came, the self-sufficiency angle had already moved in his mind from impossible to daunting to invigorating, and this was fully down to Helena's range of skills. She'd do the landscaping. The garden could grow most of their food. She admitted she could use a rifle. She was some sort of über frontier woman. He could be a worker, a worker bee. And they'd be surprisingly sexual. Otherwise, he'd told her, he wasn't interested. Ditto, she said. They wouldn't have neighbours.

On the phone, when she asked about Teresa, he fudged it a little. He was sparing Helena the gory details because why bother her now, on her day of days. Also he was tired of his mother. Then Helena had to go. 'But things are looking okay there?' he said.

'It's a damn good school, Paddy,' she said.

*

He was working in his office, finalising exit notes for a couple of his patients, when he heard a voice from upstairs. His mother had woken up and was testing how she sounded. He walked quietly to the bottom of the stairs and listened but she'd already stopped. He heard her go into the bathroom, the water running, and then he went back into his office.

Teresa appeared at his door a few minutes later, not looking groggy at all, though the edges of her hair were wet from where she'd washed her face. She asked about Pip and he told her about the trip to the lawyer.

'Poor old Pip,' she said. 'She can stay with me. When do we go to the hospital again?' There wasn't a trace of the aggression she'd shown at lunch.

'Tomorrow,' he said.

'I don't want to go.' She'd spoken evenly, a flat declaration.

'I think it would be a good idea to have the scan.'

'I don't feel anything any more. My head feels normal. I think I'm going to be all right. Tomorrow is my day with the girls. I'm booked.'

All her r's were guttural, the uvula giving its series of taps as the larynx vibrated and the back of her tongue rose towards the soft palate. With effort he prevented himself from staring at this hidden miracle. He had to get used to it. 'I'm sure Steph will understand.'

'It's a real nuisance, Paddy.' She smiled at him. 'I bet you're cursing the day you told me the place next door was for sale.'

'With neighbours, it's all luck, isn't it.' He stood up to open the front door for her. 'I think it's very cool having a French mother.'

'Cool? The word seems too young for you, Paddy. Cool.'

He kissed her lightly on the cheek. Her skin was dry, vaguely powdery, impossibly soft, velvety, and for a moment he rested his own cheek against hers. She let him do this. They'd not touched much. It was for Stephanie to kiss and hold their mother, to rub the back of her hand, to feel the lined and pale instep of her bare foot—he'd watched this the previous summer, when Teresa was complaining of the pinch of a new pair of sandals. Somehow Stephanie had always had this job, this right. She'd held a finger down just below their mother's ankle. 'It's your pulse! Look, your life-source,' she said. Then she'd quickly taken her finger off. 'Don't really like to know that.'

He couldn't sleep. Helena shifted slightly beside him as he got out of bed but she didn't wake up. They'd finished a bottle of wine between them, which was more than they usually drank. This was by way of a mini-celebration. As far as anyone could tell, the day with Trish Gibbons had gone off smoothly, amicably, though the word 'successful' was banned. There were no on-the-spot results and Helena had of course not been present when the interviews of students, past and present, were taking place. But unless Trish was especially duplicitous and tricky, and there'd been some left-field report from a previously silent complainer, Helena thought her school would come out okay. Now she was tired in an altogether new way, relief-tired, and she'd fallen asleep on the sofa, more or less in the middle of a conversation. He'd had to wake her to get her to the bedroom. He helped her take off her shoes and her clothes. She slurred at him. Touching her body, he felt something that must have been close to what he'd read described as a twinge of sadness. It occurred in his penis. So that's what they meant!

He went into his office and tried to read a book but his concentration wasn't there. He read Julie's poem again. He thought, I'll put this on the wall instead of the missing cartoon portrait. This is much better. He put a coat over his boxer shorts and teeshirt and left the apartment barefoot. He stopped outside his mother's door, and then, hearing nothing, walked along the corridor in the direction of the lift. It was just after 11pm. He considered going for a bike ride but his gear was in the bedroom and the noise might wake Helena. There was an unreleased energy in him, something spring-loaded. It wasn't wholly connected with his sleeping beauty.

He was just turning at the end of the corridor, to head back to the apartment, when the doors of the lift opened and Geoff Harley stepped out. He was carrying a solid black case, a little like something used for musical instruments, brass perhaps. It was Thursday night. Geoff's mystery outing. He'd moved a step back at first, trying to take in Paddy's form. The corridor was dimly lit. The lift door closed on his case and he pulled it free, the doors opening and shutting again.

'Hello, Geoff. Sorry for creeping around, couldn't sleep.'

'Thought I was going to be mugged for a second there, Paddy. You almost got this swung at your privates.' He held up the case. 'The lift saved you an injury. Are *you* worried about the people in the alley?'

'The drug dealers? Life's rich tapestry I think. Until they mug me. So far so good.' He gestured towards the case. 'Do you play?'

'Play? Yes, I do. Though not quite what you think.'

Paddy had started to move off. 'Okay. Well, good night.'

'Is your mother well? I hope she's better.'

Paddy turned back. He said she was and he thanked him for bringing her to the apartment. 'It all went a bit crazy for a while. But we're sorted now.'

'I'm so glad to hear that. No problem.' Geoff Harley stood in the same spot, waiting for something. This was what he wanted in exchange for helping his mother, curiosity about his own life. In the stories Paddy and Helena had invented to explain these Thursdays, Geoff Harley was a Mason attending lodge meetings, a preacher in some small evangelical church, a card-player off to a back room filled with other architects, the father of an illegitimate child who had secret assignations, which was why his wife couldn't know.

They'd not seen the black case except from a distance—once they'd come out of their apartment as Geoff was disappearing into the lift. He was some sort of doctor in an occult medicine.

'My guess is the trumpet,' said Paddy, motioning towards the case.

'Sorry,' said Geoff, smiling.

'Clarinet? I don't know.'

'Barking up the wrong tree, I'm afraid.'

He wanted this curiosity endlessly deferred, toyed with, extended.

'You carry a gun in there.'

'Ha!'

'A pool cue, with screw-in parts.'

'Used to play at my uncle's place, but no.'

'Some sort of equipment for measuring the light coming off buildings at night.'

'Oh, it's not work in here, believe me. No.'

Paddy smiled. Geoff Harley was Sam Covenay's inverse image, the speaker who wanted it never to end. 'So nothing medical? A stethoscope? Instruments of torture?'

'I love this! Torture?'

'Okay, okay. There's nothing in there at all, Geoff, you walk around for three hours pretending you have something in there so people think you're a mysterious person but really the thing is empty.'

Geoff touched his chin with a finger pensively. 'Mmm, I quite like that notion.'

They stood in the gloom of the corridor, a wave of tiredness finally passing through Paddy. Immediately he felt sluggish, weak, ready for sleep. 'Will you show me?' he said.

Geoff placed the case on the floor and flicked open the silver latches. 'I warn you, this is something that Rebecca, for instance, finds rather objectionable. You might too. Maybe I shouldn't show you.' He looked up at Paddy, seeming to notice for the first time the coat, his bare feet. 'How often do you walk these corridors at night?'

'Never. First time.'

'Okay. I was just wondering whether I was missing out on something.'

'Nope.'

He lifted the lid of the case and shifted it around so that

346

Paddy could see inside. There were four compartments. In one of them was some sort of electrical transformer, with a cord and plug. Another held a console with dials and switches, and the other two contained toy cars, about eight inches long, fitted into cushioned slots, their sides visible.

'I can see Rebecca's point,' said Paddy.

'You understand now?'

'Yes, I do.' Paddy bent down on his haunches. He was side by side with Geoff, looking into the case. 'May I?'

'Let me,' said Geoff. He gently pulled at one of the cars and it came out of its slot. He handed it to Paddy with some care.

It was heavier than he expected, solid, the body metal, the little tyres appeared to be rubber, not plastic. The blue and gold paintwork shiny and thick, enamel. Expensive, no doubt. Crafted. Obsessed over. He was aware that Geoff was studying his face, gauging his reaction. It was the sort of look new parents gave you when they agreed you could handle their baby for the first time.

'Quite heavy, isn't she?' said Geoff.

They might have been discussing birth weights. Paddy said, 'You go to a club of some kind.'

'A club of some kind.' Geoff considered this.

'Maybe you're even the president of this club.'

'Ha, not bad. Treasurer in fact.' He leaned over and touched the roof of the car Paddy held.

The windows of the car were blacked out. 'You're a sick man, Harley.'

'I know, I know. Do you want to see her run?'

'Of course.'

He removed the console from the case and asked Paddy to place the car on the floor. He moved some switches and then, with his thumb, pressed the central toggle button and the car went forward with slight whirring. He was lining it up. Both men stood up, looking at the car. 'This won't be all-out, you understand.'

'Of course not,' said Paddy.

347

'Don't want to wake the neighbours.'

'I am the neighbours.'

'And your mother, remember she lives here now. Is she French?'

'Partly.'

'How wonderful. What a gift for you. Here we are then.' Geoff fiddled again with the console. He moved his thumb again and the car shot off. It was much faster than Paddy had been expecting and he laughed. The car was already nearing the far end of the corridor, difficult to see from where they were. It stopped just short of the wall. Geoff turned it around with a few deft flicks of his thumb. 'Naughty me,' he said. He hit a button and the car's headlights came on. 'I don't know if you want to do this but—' Geoff lay down on his stomach, the console in front of him. He was looking along the floor in the direction of the car.

What was there to do?

Paddy lay down beside him, and they watched at eye-level as the car sped back along the grass matting floor straight at them. The tiny headlights came jerkily through the dimness. Geoff kept his thumb pressed forward on the controls. Paddy stared into the lights. The car wasn't slowing. He felt it was going to smash into his face. But he kept still.

At the final moment, the car stopped dead. It was an inch from Paddy's nose.

Geoff picked up the car and inspected it. He blew on the wheels and rubbed lightly against a spot on the bonnet. They stood up. 'That wasn't all-out.'

'Goodnight,' said Paddy, and he walked back to his apartment.

8

His mother didn't want to be watched and didn't need to be looked after while she was having the MRI. No tremors this time, no sedatives. She would have to wear earplugs because of the noise as the magnets crunched around. Paddy warned her about this in the car on their way to the hospital and she nodded. Fine. She was in a new state of composure and resolve. 'Go and have a coffee,' she told them once they'd delivered her to the right room. She was filling in forms.

Blanchford wasn't there. He'd phoned to say that he'd look at the images as soon as he could. His casual approach helped them all now.

She sent them away, even Pip, and they had to go, no matter what they said.

They went to one of the cafés across the road from the hospital. Pip was asking Stephanie about her children, showing again a genuine delight in any subject connected with her cousin. She heard about ballet and gym and teeth. Steph talked about their mother's involvement in the kids' lives, how important she'd been, really things would have collapsed in a heap without her, she said, and then she started crying. Pip put her hand on Stephanie's arm. 'You've given her that joy,' she said.

Stephanie shivered, as if shaking off this idea. 'I try to look at her life, to work out whether she's had one, a life. I mean something separate from us. Even this morning when I woke up, I remembered I had an appointment and I thought immediately of dropping the two youngest ones with Mummy. And then I remembered the appointment was this!' She looked at her watch. 'And look, soon I need to go again, pick them up. But I feel terrible leaving you here, leaving her.'

Paddy told her it would be okay, and that they'd call her later. She could speak to Teresa, who was obviously stronger today, properly rested and full of determination. He turned to Pip and said, 'Your visit has really helped.'

'Yes!' said Stephanie.

'No, I was never able to influence your mother a single bit.'

This was said without a trace of irritation or regret, which made Paddy think there'd been influence on both sides. The cousins shared an instinct for facts. Pip was more demonstrative, that was clear. But both of them were clear-eyed to the point of starkness.

'She's so hard to know,' he said, almost thoughtlessly. It came out. His starkness was different—it was the stuff of frustrated feeling. He sounded churlish.

'Impossible to know,' said Pip, quite cheerfully.

Stephanie leaned forward. 'You can't know her, but you can know how she affects you.'

A waitress had come to clean the table. She took their cups.

Branch-to-branch style, and perhaps to escape the previous topic, Stephanie started asking Pip about Zimbabwe. Did she miss it? Yes. Would she go back? Maybe one day to visit. Paddy asked about her meeting with the lawyer and whether things were going to be put into action regarding her land.

'It's wait and see, I'm afraid.'

'It's wait and see everywhere, isn't it,' said Stephanie, gesturing in the direction of the hospital, sounding as though she might start crying again. She managed to hold it off, converting her emotion into a short gulped laugh. She stood up suddenly, and tried to unhook her shoulder bag from the back of the seat. Its strap was tangled; she pulled and the chair fell over with a loud clatter. 'Fuck,' she said. 'Excuse me, sorry.' Paddy was straightening the chair and releasing her bag.

Pip was also standing. 'Darling Stephanie, darling Patrick. How proud she is of you. And Margaret. How she loves you and wishes that you go on and achieve all the things you hope for. Yes. You're what she speaks about when she talks to me. You're the great subject. That's a life, Steph. That's a large life. But I think this too. There's always something else. Don't you think? There's always more. Of course there is. That's the mystery of us all.'

The speech stopped them from saying anything more as they left the café and crossed the road back to the hospital. Paddy had found Pip's presence vaguely irritating. It was also unusual for Stephanie to be silent for long. She was walking slightly ahead of them, a stiffness in her body that he recognised as upset of a peculiarly humiliating sort.

Their mother's cousin, he thought, was both a stranger and not one at all. She was hard to place finally, knowing a little too much about them and not knowing anything, at least through direct experience of their lives. All she'd experienced had come through their mother. That was one reason to resist. Something too in the word 'mystery' perhaps, which suggested Philippa from Africa was on the point of claiming spiritual properties for truth. Was she, endlessly mild and kind and strong, meeting all this through some unannounced attachment to a church? Well, did it matter? She'd been through a real hell in Zimbabwe. The murder, the blindfold, the chicken coop. She'd seen Robert Mugabe on a bicycle. And it wasn't only God she was calling on now; she had a lawyer.

They arranged to bring Teresa home in a taxi.

Mystery, the word still bothered him. He thought of Geoff Harley lying on his stomach, watching his toy car race along the corridor. Was that Geoff's 'mystery' uncovered? Or had it just been the aspect of himself he was prepared to show at 11pm, in a moment of shared weakness, to a barefoot man in a coat and pyjamas?

Of course playing on them all was the terrible anxiety of what was happening in the building in front of them, from

351

which they'd been banished. Their mother in a cylinder of noise, her head fastened in place.

Suddenly he missed Margie.

A few weeks after their father's death all those years ago, a man had come to the house with a box for their mother, who wasn't there. Margie had answered the door. She must have been seventeen. The man asked if he could leave the box for Teresa. It was his doctoral thesis, he said, and their mother had agreed to type it up for him. Inside the box was also an envelope, with the first instalment of his payment for the work. Paddy was standing behind his sister.

They both remembered the period before Stephanie was born, when their mother had taken on typing work at home. She would close the door of the little study, put on the headset, and then for an hour, two hours, three, the only sound they heard was the snapping of the typewriter, the bell sounding at the end of each line, followed by the creak of the paper as it was pulled up across the roller, then the resumed clack. They both loathed this noise. It was as though their mother had become a machine, was remaking herself with the hateful little hammers of each letter behind the closed door, composing a message of fury. Yet when she stepped out of the room, she was the same mild person. She was ready to cook them dinner.

Margie looked at the box in the man's hands. He wore glasses, a blue-black suit jacket greasy around the shoulders. Paddy had no idea what a doctoral thesis was—the word 'thesis' sounded close to faeces which he knew was shit. 'It's all in here,' he said, 'my baby. Three years' hard labour.'

Did they both imagine a foetus in the box?

And then Margie said, 'No, sorry, our mother changed her mind. Perhaps you didn't get her message. She's too busy. Can't do it. Very sorry. Goodbye.' And she closed the door. They could see the shape of the man's head behind the frosted glass panel. He waited a moment and then he left.

They'd come in Stephanie's car, which was in the hospital

car park. 'Stupid!' she said. 'We should have brought two cars. Paddy, why didn't we bring your car too?'

'Didn't think,' he said.

'I should have brought mine,' said Pip.

'No,' said Stephanie. 'You've done too much already.' For a moment it sounded as though she was warning Pip off, or venting a portion of the dissatisfaction she'd felt back in the café. Here was the person who'd first tried to steal their mother away before she was even their mother, and then who'd tried to steal them all away. Quickly, as if to smother her animosity, she embraced their mother's cousin.

The days passed in an odd sort of normality. Pip stayed on with Teresa in her apartment and the two cousins went out for trips in Pip's car, up the Kapiti Coast, then to Eastbourne, and to see good old Lower Hutt and visit the Dowse, recently redesigned. 'Too many doors, entranceways,' his mother said. 'Otherwise good.' They admitted driving past the old house, where they saw that the two small kowhai trees, which over the years had slightly encroached on the driveway, were gone. When the trees flowered, a soft yellow light was filtered into the nearest part of the living-room, where Brendan had had his reading chair, known as 'the yellow chair' though its covering was blue. Teresa met this blow unconvincingly. 'Probably they have a wider car. It makes sense.'

Paddy held his clinics as usual, working unimpeded and, he considered, to decent effect. He didn't feel impatient while his kids were in the room. He gave them all his attention. And he had no problems with his right ear.

Stephanie phoned him every morning and again at night. She spoke without tears, reasonably and in a new mood of resilience. Their mother's example was powerful. One of the girls had a bad cold. Instead of bringing the germs round, she Skyped Teresa whenever she could. She told him she'd picked up part-time work that she could do from home. Before the children were born Stephanie had been a market researcher, on the statistical side of things. Her reputation as a scatterbrain concealed a fine intuitive feel for numbers and patterns. Her old boss had given her the contract and in the future she could increase her hours if she wanted to. That could pay for a nanny. Paul Shawn had also come round and she'd not even let him in the house. 'Are you proud of me?' she said.

He was.

Apparently Paul had acted very concerned about Teresa. 'This is the man who, as you might remember, when Mummy was having her seventieth birthday party, chose to paint the bathroom ceiling instead of come with me to the dinner. He told me he was doing it for me, so I'd be out of the house and the fumes wouldn't make me nauseous.'

'He doesn't need a can of paint to make me feel nauseous,' said Paddy.

She'd laughed at that.

When Pip and Teresa came home from their outings, they didn't knock on his door and they didn't ring him. Perhaps they'd missed a call but this didn't matter—he'd tell them. Later they would come across for a glass of wine and they'd talk about the world, financial ruin, Barack Obama, about Helena's life before she met Paddy. Days in the Alps. The gardening job. They desired news that didn't quite touch them. It was perfectly understood by everyone that the moment Murray Blanchford called, everything that they'd built up over these days would be swept away.

Occasionally he caught a look on his mother's face that gave away the strain. He thought how waiting for the scan results allowed them two kinds of time. There was the easy regular flow of hours, in his case divided into sixty-minute clinic sessions, which you noticed because you were inside it, the day carved around you, like a fingernail going through soap. Then some other kind altogether. A thicker substance, reflective, heavy, possibly harmful. It was as though you were waiting not only for the future—Blanchford's call, the consequences of a single sentence—but for the past too. Events from long ago were catching up, coming closer. Was this what disease meant? All time pressed together into a space that couldn't possibly contain it.

After his father died, he didn't sleepwalk again. Because he'd outgrown it. But how did he know he hadn't carried on doing it? His mother might have chosen to keep this from him. In bed at night during this period he used to tell himself, You were the Messenger. You tried to warn him. Your father saw you were the Messenger and he froze. He developed a long tale about Messengers, probably drawn from his reading, maybe Alan Garner.

He and Helena made love every night for six nights. Outside their courtship, a record probably. It was as though they were in training, he thought, the only difference being that this itself, the thing they were doing, was what they were training for. Which qualified it, in his mind, as the world's greatest sport. Utterly self-reflexive.

When he went to bed, he'd sit up with a book on his chest, while she always read under the covers, lying down.

After The Six Nights, when she'd turned off her side-light, he kept reading. She looked at him and said, And on the seventh night he rested.

They both laughed.

She said, 'You remind me of that bit in *Der Zauberberg*.'

'In what?' he said.

'*The Magic Mountain*.'

'Ah.' He was immediately sensitised. Rapid tingling. He loved her Germanness, her Germany he'd once called it.

'Hans Castorp is reading these heavy tomes, I forget why. I do remember his cousin, what's his name? Never mind. His cousin is puzzled that Hans should have bought all these books when he could have borrowed them, and Hans says, no, we read a book differently when we own it.'

'True,' said Paddy.

'But that's not what I was thinking about just now. Mann writes this beautiful description of Hans reading with a book on his stomach, that's what looking at you made me think of. The book it's so heavy he's not breathing properly, and he reads to the bottom of the page, very slowly, until his chin is resting on his chest. His head following the lines down until the bottom. Donk. Then his eyes close. He's asleep. Wonderful.'

Paddy said, 'A book can knock you out, that's for sure.' He was very tempted to go down to the office and find his copy of The Magic Mons, the English translation. He was still reading Emily Bishop's poems, which he kept beside the bed. 'Questions of Travel' was presently under his thumb. Should we have stayed at home, line-break, wherever that may be. Occasionally he read something aloud to Helena. Gradually self-consciousness evaporated. True even of poetry. He read five poems per night. He'd noticed a mania for numbers. At the supermarket he bought packs of things in threes, or three of things they needed. Three toilet rolls! Chorizo sausages came in a three-pack. He saw it when he got home and unpacked. There wasn't a magic number, simply a repeating one.

He read on. Then suddenly Helena sat up. She'd remembered something. In *The Magic Mountain*, Hans had been reading medical books, anatomy, things like that. The origin of life. He wanted to know what life was, what it was made of. 'So,' she said, 'he dropped all his other stuff, engineering, I think, and read, you know, biology.'

When she'd studied the book at university, they'd discussed this passage in their tutorial. Stage Two.

'We had a very proper tutor. He wasn't much older than us. Quite prim and a blusher. Obviously very bright at languages but, you know, straight through his degree and then he's sitting in front of a class. Emotionally a little boy, I think. He had blond hair with a centre parting. And in the class we had a girl, a woman, who was extremely I believe the word is advanced. One of those people who don't belong in their own sexual cohort at all.'

'Affairs with her professors,' he said.

'Probably. I don't know. I always found her very nice. Anyway, good old Hans thinks about sperm. In the course of his research naturally, the origin of life. And the book he's reading says something like, all sperm is the same. The sperm of one animal looks like that of every other.'

'Really?' said Paddy.

Helena thought, then said, 'Really did we have a class about this or really is the fact true?'

'Sperm is the same across all animals.'

'Did you think you were special? But listen, our resident—'

'Sexpot.'

'No, no. You misunderstand. I haven't explained her right. She was an adult. She'd put away childish things. And so we're discussing this passage, what is Hans looking for, symbolism et cetera, the quest for meaning, and she, what was her name, I'm hopeless, she says something like, At the end has he masturbated? And we all look at her and go, Huh? What did you just say? And the tutor is simply not looking at anyone. So very straightforwardly she explains. Hans falls asleep with the book on top of him, it's hard to breathe, he closes his eyes and that was all the stuff I remembered, I liked. Then a female figure comes to him and it's all very poetic. I think I'd skipped it, lost the sense. In German the novel is a monster. In our class, the girl says, I want to link this moment of Hans Castorp reading with the sperm references. And she reads out a bit, he smells her organic aroma or something, which she says, now that sounds like her vagina. Now you could have heard a pin drop. Vaginas weren't part of the class's argot shall we say. But more than that, we see what she means. Suddenly it's all totally convincing, sort of obvious even. It's a measured argument.

'The room is dead quiet. We're transfixed. And she concludes, I think he's being fucked by the book, only that's not physically possible, so he takes matters into, as it were, his own hand. Is this even close?

'And we all turn to the tutor, who's gone this really strange colour. And he's looking down at his copy of *Der Zauberberg*. I remember it was covered in this dense little writing, every page was annotated. God he must have known that book better than Thomas Mann and rivalled him in word count. He stays with his head down for a few seconds. Then he turns a page, looks at it. He picks up the book to take a closer look. Puts it down again. Thinks. I suppose I thought he was about to run from the room in tears. He was so flushed. Or pass out. He didn't seem to be breathing. I think he was religious too, or at least that was a big interest because we spent long hours on spiritual symbolism, Christ figures. But it was extremely tense, waiting. Finally he lifted his head and said to her, Sie haben alles verstanden.'

'What does that mean?' said Paddy. He was excited by it all.

'You have understood everything.'

'No!'

'That's what he said.'

'My.'

'It was highly memorable.'

'Incredible,' he said. 'Incroyable.'

Paddy put the poems down and turned off his light. They were lying in the dark with, he thought, their minds bright. The sensation was he could almost see by the force of their living thoughts, see in the dark. They were lying on their backs, awake, with this visible humming. Whenever he'd seen phosphorescence in a night sea, he always thought, the human brain!

He said, 'I'd love to read that book again. It's been almost thirty years.' He agreed, he thought, he agreed with Thomas Mann. You were ravished by a book. 'Dirty old Mann,' he said. But Helena, exercising her gift, was almost already asleep. Incroyable mais vrai. Thus ended their record stretch.

He did look in his copy the following day. He'd not placed a stickie in that part but finally he found it. The girl in Helena's class wasn't wrong, except Hans isn't fucked by the book but by life. It's the image of life, 'its voluptuous limbs, its flesh-borne beauty', which comes to him, embraces him 'hot and

358

tender' until 'melting with lust and dismay', he's kissed by her.

Earlier, the hero asks, 'What was life, really?' And answers, 'It was warmth, the warmth produced by instability attempting to preserve form', which Paddy had to make another stickie for. He also wrote this phrase in a notebook he kept for such things. On the first page, dated Jan '97, eleven years ago, he saw he'd copied a sentence from Mavis Gallant's story 'The Moslem Wife': 'Being childless but still very loving, they had trouble deciding which of the two would be the child.'

And this from Yuko Tsushima's *Child of Fortune*: 'Far from being able to give the child what she was seeking, she was seeking the same thing herself.' He couldn't remember much of the book at all.

After the split from Bridget, he'd languished, luxuriated, lost himself, learned and learned, in literature. Absented himself too probably. He had been a kind of Hans Castorp. Not consumptive, but consumed. He didn't stay in bed or anything sordid. He was very active. It was a labour as well as the rest of it. He got up quite early, sometimes at 5am or before, and after breakfast, he read until he had to go to work. He was employed by the Ministry of Education as an early intervention therapist in schools. He had a car and, of his own choosing, a light load. Often he drove somewhere and parked so he could read his book. He had his lunch in the car. He was amazed he could read so much. July the same year he wrote this out: 'She wanted to get away from herself, and conversation was the only means of escape she knew.' *House of Mirth*. Then a gap of months before he entered under the heading 'Peer Review!', 'Whitman wrote 2 unsigned reviews of *Leaves of Grass* himself. Tell Lant re self-belief.'

These traces of himself, his preoccupations, were accurate enough in their solipsism. The car at Oriental Bay, fogging up. The man bent into his book. The pie wrapper on the passenger seat. Lone eater. Lone reader. They also told an untruth. Yes he felt alienated. Yes he discovered adolescents didn't have a monopoly on such feelings. But he was not cut off. Teresa and

Stephanie were wonderful to him during this time. He saw more of them, valued them more than he'd ever done in the past. They really cared for him. Meals arrived. What did he have, cancer? They phoned. Dropped in. Oh he resisted, told them not to worry, but he was kept up to date, he was kept in the loop of unwritten life. Which was warmth. He pretended they were being foolish. They helped him remain functional. He was still working, still contributing. He had a microwave, didn't he. His mother baked biscuits for him! She told him his ex-wife was a complete dolt and got done over for saying it but somehow they all pushed on. And he read. He read like a demonic grad student sublimating an enormous libido.

On another night beside Helena he dreamed of cells, but there was confusion, since the dream was always switching between the cell as biological unit and as the room in a prison, that form of cell. When he thought about it in the morning, the connection felt trite. He wasn't even the sick one. Yet in the middle of the dream, there was sweaty fear. He was sitting in a jail cell, then the walls turned liqueous and pressed in until he couldn't move. His hair caught in the ceiling with the sensation of honey, which was also grey-coloured, and when he tried to free it, his fingers stuck too. He was sitting inside his own brain. Beside him, Helena woke with her normal nightly gasp, waking him. She reached for her water. His stomach and his shoulders were so damp he had to get up and change.

Paddy called Lant to arrange a ride in the afternoon. The weather was warmer and there was no wind. It would be like biking somewhere normal, in a benign city. He ached physically to get on with it, stretch out, feel his heart, little bubbles of unlocking thought travelling from the pedal to the brain, all the greased cogs of body and mind working together. He only needed to look at his bike shoes to feel the potential.

But Lant said he couldn't go for a bike ride. Yes, it was his afternoon off and he'd taken the last available space with the best fiddle teacher in the land and it happened to be that day. Two hours' worth, and then they were going to a workshop in Wainuiomata that his teacher was running and that Lant had been allowed to sit in on.

'Fiddle is what you're calling it now?' said Paddy.

'My mother always called me a fiddler. "Jeremy, stop fiddling!" And now it's come true. On that subject, how is *your* mother?'

Paddy explained about the MRI, the terrible waiting. He found himself giving an account of his cell dream. 'I know you're not much of a Freudian but what do you think it means?'

'It means you should go for a bike ride immediately.'

'That was my diagnosis too.'

'There you go. You don't need me for dream interpretation and you don't need me for biking. You went all the way to Lower Hutt on your own.'

'I've already apologised for that.'

There was a moment of silence. And then Paddy said, 'You make me buy this damn bike because you say I need to be in better condition to face the things I'm going to face, and ever since then I've had all these problems.'

'Maybe you should get rid of the bike, Paddy. Maybe the bike is evil.'

'You never said you'd leave me for a fiddle.'

'I'm not leaving you. I'm taking music lessons.'

'In Wainuiomata? You'll never come back from Wainuiomata, Lant.'

'Go for your ride. Hug your mother. Goodbye.'

He put down the phone and it gave a ring to let him know there was a message waiting. It was Murray Blanchford. He'd tried his mother's number and left a message there too. If they could call him today, they'd be able to discuss the results. Ideally, he'd like to speak to Teresa and one or two family members at the same time. Normally he preferred to do this in person but with the weekend coming up, well, a phone call would be fine. That was it. Impossible to tell from Blanchford's tone what was in store for them.

He rang Pip on her mobile. They were at the Botanical Gardens. Then he rang Stephanie. They would all meet at the apartment in an hour and a half, and then they'd call Blanchford.

He biked up Cambridge Terrace, around the Basin, then through Mount Victoria before dropping down to Oriental Parade, where he bought an ice cream and ate it sitting on the sea wall, looking at the boats in the harbour. Then he finished the water in his drink bottle. Further along the beach people were sunbathing, swimming.

As young men, one night he and Lant had swum out to the fountain, each carrying a bottle of wine, which they'd drunk there. They agreed that they should each sit directly over one of the main spouts of the fountain. They had no idea whether or not the fountain was timed to start that night. Perhaps they knew it was unlikely, yet as he recalled they'd seen it in operation on other nights. But nothing happened. They'd left the bottles on the fountain when they swam back. Better than polluting the harbour. It was hard to swim carrying a bottle.

He walked down to the water's edge and, taking off his bike shoes and his socks, he waded in up to his knees. It was cold, wonderful.

When he turned to walk back up to his bike, he saw a man looking down at him. The man lifted one hand in greeting. It was Iyob. Paddy returned the wave.

'Beautiful day,' said Iyob, as Paddy came up the steps.

They shook hands. 'Good to see you again,' said Paddy.

'I am on holiday. Two weeks.'

'Great day to have a holiday.' In ancient Syria, at Antioch, Saint Paul set up the first organised Christian church. The road to Damascus. In modern Syria, the last forty plus years had been Baath Party totalitarian repression. Behind the window-dressing of constitutional freedom of worship, Christians could be arrested, imprisoned, tortured and killed for proselytising.

362

For Muslims who convert, it was the death penalty. Paddy had looked it up.

Iyob pointed at the water. 'You swim?'

'No, paddle.'

'When I come here first, I run into this water. I almost die. I almost died.'

'It's not the warmest.'

'It's not the warmest, is it. Today, soon, I watch my son in sports, running, jumping.'

'School sports day?'

'School sports day. I have to go to Newtown. It's a surprise for him. I didn't tell him.'

'He doesn't know you're coming? Nice surprise. And how will he go? Do you think he'll win something maybe?'

'Maybe, yes. I don't know. I won't show him I'm there.'

'You won't go up to him? Why not?'

'Too much—pressure, I think. I want him to win, I shout out. Too much, you know. I'm a crazy Dad. I'm very happy for success, too happy, my wife says. I go and watch very quietly. Then after, I can be with him and tell him. "I saw you do this and this." It's better. It's better.'

'Sounds like a good plan.' Paddy brushed the sand off his feet and put on his socks and shoes. Iyob waited nearby, turning away when Paddy lined up the numbers on the bike-lock.

'I am very sorry for when I came to your house, your place.'

'No.'

'Yes. It was not good. It was not you I am having these problems with. It was wrong. I have this holiday, it makes me feel . . . I can breathe? Deep breathe?'

'Take a deep breath.'

'Deep breath! This.' He drew up his chest and exhaled. 'Anyway, I am sorry.' He was holding out his hand and Paddy shook it.

'You had a good point though, you *have* a good point,' said Paddy.

'Oh, I am right. I know I am right. I have a holiday but then that is my job. Goodness me. They cannot make me stay away, are you joking.' He checked his watch and moved off a few steps. 'My son is not very fast. Can he win? We shall see but I think he likes too many of these—'

'What?'

'You know,' he patted his stomach, 'Happy Meals.'

They rang from Paddy's office, since the phone had a speaker facility. Murray Blanchford asked who was in the room and they made the introductions. Pip was there too.

'What about Margie?' said Teresa. She was on Paddy's chair, by the desk, and so had put herself slightly apart from the rest of them. Once she'd taken that position, she looked around, unsure whether it was best. Paddy thought maybe she'd hoped to be away from consoling hands, away from Pip but also her children at the moment of truth, to be there in the room but not be there. And yet by taking his seat, she realised she was the object of attention, easily the room's focus.

Teresa was looking at him. He hadn't forgotten about his older sister. It was just too hard, the wrong time of day. You left the country, you paid the price. Rain for eighteen days straight.

'Yes, we can call Margie later,' she said, agreeing with everyone's thoughts. 'No point in bothering her.'

Her cousin was perched in a temporary-looking way on the chair Sam Covenay used, by the door. She could slip out if that was how they wanted it.

The phone was on a side-table next to the small sofa, where Stephanie and Paddy sat. Paddy adjusted the volume as Blanchford started talking. He was thanking them for their patience. There'd been a few problems. Not with the scans themselves but with the process by which he'd finally received them and he needed to apologise. Things had taken longer than they should have. Now what he was about to say was still in the nature of preliminary findings. He had to say that. He was yet to write up his notes. However, in this context, they should understand that preliminary was not the same as half-baked or sketchy or likely to change. Simply it meant he hadn't done the paperwork. Very well. 'Teresa,' he said.

His mother sat up in her chair, alarmed, with an almost guilty look on her face, as if she'd been caught doing something. The voice in the phone did have a sort of all-seeing quality, Paddy thought. The voice of God, or something from *Charlie's Angels*.

'Yes?' she said. 'Yes, I'm here.'

Beside him on the sofa his sister took a short breath. His own head was pounding suddenly.

'I've looked very closely at the scans from the MRI. We got some very good images, very clean and detailed. I was very pleased with the information we got. And my finding is this. There's nothing there. Everything looks normal. The scans are completely clear. You have a completely normal-looking brain.'

Everyone processed this for a moment. This was a doctor and sometimes doctors said one thing and you heard another. They spoke a different language.

'I'm very happy to say,' said Blanchford, 'the scans are clear.'

Still the language didn't penetrate. No one moved. What was he saying? What were their instructions? Something held them in their places. On the sofa, Paddy was unable to shift even his hand. His wrist seemed locked, and his neck.

They couldn't look at one another. It was an absolute pause.

'So that's good,' said the voice.

Then finally a noise came from someone—from Steph, he guessed. A little cry.

He might have shot up from the sofa then and leaped in the air. Thrown a fist above his head and jumped again. 'Yes!' He might have danced in front of the sofa. He might have sung: 'The scans are clear, there's nothing there! The good old scans are clear!' He was capable of the eruption. They'd all been ready to burst. Yet Blanchford's marvellous and hoped-for conclusion, though an immense relief, was also the curious extension of the status quo. It was progress but also not. It was another deferral, and in its knowingness, there remained a core of 'we don't know'. They knew what wasn't there but this still left the question of what was, since Teresa was the same. She wasn't cured.

This was preventing anyone from doing much with the good thing they'd heard.

And, he thought, it was a good thing. Teresa wasn't going to die from this. She was going to carry on. More or less in the same way? Which seemed the crux—here was the new reality. Murray Blanchford, mountain biker and brain man, meant this, did he?

His mother, he saw, was looking at the floor. Stephanie was glancing around, as if trying to get her bearings, or memorise details of the room. Pip had turned an ear to the phone, where Blanchford was continuing to speak.

In the next week or so they'd receive a letter, which would be the official end to the business or that part of it at least. 'Can I just offer my congratulations,' said Blanchford, 'on—having such a fine-looking brain, Teresa. Of course these are my favourite calls and I do want to let you folk get on with your day. Okay.'

His mother cleared her throat. 'Thank you,' she said. She stood up.

'One aspect remains,' said Blanchford. And here it was, and Paddy wished the voice turned off. 'The matter of the acquired accent. Having eliminated sinister cause, there may still be ongoing consultation with regard to that issue. Paddy will have ideas, therapeutic remedies and so on. It's of interest to me, I must say, if that doesn't sound too coolly objective. Fascinating really. But I'm going to leave that for another day. I'll say goodbye to you all.'

Paddy pressed the button on the phone. 'Well,' he said. He stood.

Then Stephanie let out a choking sob and, without meeting her mother's eye, went towards her in a blind sort of stagger, knocking against her chest. Teresa held her sobbing daughter in her arms, stroking her hair. Then Stephanie straightened up and smiled and went over to Paddy's desk where there was a box of tissues.

'I'll need those too,' said Pip, who'd stood up and was coming towards her cousin. Soundlessly, tears were rolling freely down her cheeks. They hugged, and were fiercely locked together for several moments.

Then Paddy hugged his mother hard, hugged her bones, though she wasn't bony.

Finally Teresa was released.

She alone was dry-eyed. She stepped a little away from them, but only to take them in, to see them in a single view. She was smiling, her mouth closed. Had she ever looked so beautiful, so strange.

'How amazing,' she said, though she sounded not especially amazed. It was almost how she used to sound when they were children and they told her urgent and fascinating things and she received them with a calm curiosity that seemed to miss the point of their excitement, or to make another point altogether, something about preparing yourself for whatever might be round the corner, for what would happen next. It used to drive them crazy, this calm. How amazing.

After Pip left for Palmerston North, and Stephanie had gone off to collect Isabelle from school, they walked into town. Teresa was meeting up with Steph and all her girls later at the playground at Frank Kitts Park in the sunshine. The girls hadn't seen their grandmother since before she'd had to cancel their weekend away, hadn't heard her, though they'd been told Teresa had a sore throat which made her voice sound 'funny'. It was agreed an outdoor reunion would be best. The girls could run off and play whenever they felt it was getting too weird.

Paddy asked his mother if this was a good idea. Didn't she want to rest? The trial of Blanchford's call must have had an impact, he thought. Didn't she need to absorb the information? She said, What information?

He felt flat. Oh perhaps she was right. He wanted to get out of the apartment. Was it time to 'trust a little to the energy which is begotten by circumstances, something something', he'd have to look it up. Good old George Eliot! There were circumstances at hand for sure.

Before they left, Teresa had put a bar of chocolate in her bag. It was all she had. 'Bribe,' she told Paddy. 'And so they'll still know it's me.' She also put in a book, in case Stephanie was late. She loved to sit and read outside. She said she had a few favourite places in Lower Hutt.

'I didn't know that,' he said.

'You don't know everything.'

He asked to see the book. *Le Petit Nicolas,* in French. A children's book, an old paperback, with someone's pencil marks throughout. She'd found it in a second-hand bookshop the other day with Pip. 'It was only five dollars. Can't follow it at all but I like the drawings. And someone else has struggled with it too, which I like. I don't have to look up every word in my little dictionary.'

'Okay,' he said, 'so you're going with it, the French thing.'

'Going with it?' she said. 'Even that sounds a bit decisive. Keeping things open, is that a better way of putting it? I don't know, Paddy. I really don't know. Winging it maybe?'

On Cuba Street, Paddy stopped his mother in front of the bakery that Camille and Pierre owned. Suddenly it seemed a long time ago that he'd looked into this same window on the night he went drinking with Lant. He suggested they buy some things for the girls, to augment the chocolate bribe. Could Niamh, the little one, even eat chocolate? Teresa stared at the pastries and cakes. 'Oh, this looks too rich, Paddy.' Only then did she see that the names of everything were written in French. 'What is this place?'

Camille was at the counter. 'Bonjour!' she said.

'Bonjour!' said Paddy.

'Bonjour,' said Teresa.

'Ça va? You are well?'

'Since the last time you saw me, I am very well, thank you,' he said. 'And I'd like you to meet, how do you say that in French?'

'Puis-je vous présenter,' said Camille.

'Camille, puis-je vous présenter mon mère!'

'Ma mère,' said Camille. 'Because your mother is feminine.'

'Ma mère! But she's my mother and I'm masculine, she belongs to me.'

'It is the noun that rules it, not the speaker.' Camille smiled and shook Teresa's hand. 'Enchantée.'

'Je m'appelle Teresa, or if you like, Thérèse.'

'Ah, vous apprennez le Français? You are learning French?'

His mother laughed. 'No, no.'

'But show her your book,' said Paddy.

'No, really.'

'Here,' he said. He'd slipped his hand inside her bag and was bringing it out, the old paperback. 'Regardez!'

Camille looked at it. 'Petit Nicolas! J'adore! At home, we have these books.'

'I just look at the pictures,' said Teresa. 'Les illustrations?'

'Oui, oui, les illustrations, sont plus belles, ah?'

'I'm sorry, I don't understand you.'

'Beautiful. And drôle, funny.'

'They are, yes.'

'Très simple. Very simple, a few lines.'

'Oh yes, but—'

'Yes?' said Camille.

'Sad?' said his mother.

'Voilà! C'est vrai. A bit sad. Triste.'

'Yes, or something melancholy about them. Melancholy in French?'

'Mélancolie.'

'That's easy,' said Paddy.

'Yes, same word. We make it easy for you English speakers sometimes! La mélancolie.'

'Feminine,' said Teresa.

'Bien sur! Of course!'

They turned to look at the sweet things. They bought up large.

Walking along afterwards, his mother asked about therapeutic remedies, which had been Blanchford's phrase. Paddy told her she would have to make an appointment. But she wouldn't be interested in going to him, she said—he was children. Then he would refer her to someone else who dealt with the elderly. And infirm, she added. Using this comically as a prompt, he linked his arm through hers. Come on then, old dear, he said. Let's help you along.

He felt a gush of privilege. How to put this? He experienced the most sublime sense of being close to a great work, walking with her. He felt astonished.

He said goodbye to his mother in Civic Square. She was crossing at the overbridge to the park. He watched her walking quickly up the steps, under a cloudless blue sky, carrying her bag of French goodies. The sea smelt fresh, almost salt-less. The smell, the sky, the whole set-up, was auspicious, he felt in a silly way, carrying the notion forward from Blanchford's phone call, the meeting with Camille. He recalled something Bridget had once said when they were walking by the harbour, that she'd prefer it if the sea didn't contain fish. She'd not meant it as a joke at all or whimsy. She didn't joke. It was simply an aspect of the world she found wrong. Another thing she said, more helpful this time: always sleep with a pillow between your knees—it was good for your back. And this was what he did most nights. Marry someone, the wrong person, live together for years, stomp around on each other's hopes and dreams, and take this one piece of wisdom from all that.

In the morning the pillow would be at the bottom of the bed, or on Helena's side. They called this pillow Bridget. Where's Bridget? they said. The spirit was affectionate, or Helena wouldn't have gone along with it. In a perfectly low-key way, he was curious about Bridget's life now, where was she? There was no chance he'd seek the facts. Last time, a few years ago, he'd heard Shanghai. Amazing.

He needed a new back light for his bike. The original one had dropped off and cracked when he'd been putting his bike away in the basement. It was now his recreation to visit the bike shops and browse. He found these places intoxicating, sort of blinding. He frequently spent more than seventy dollars on something.

In front of the City Gallery people lay on the grass. Some were office workers with their shoes off, their shirts undone, giving themselves up to the late spring heat. Neil Dawson's shining metal globe hung above them, suspended on wires, a delicate fern cut-out of the planet but strong enough to handle the worst winds. Two tourists were taking a photo of it, craning their necks, pointing the camera up through the earth.

There were also students on the grass, talking in groups, drinking from water bottles. They had their books open in front of them.

Half in the shade, by the library, one figure sat by herself, her knees drawn up, looking blankly out at the square. He recognised her at once, even without fully seeing the face. There was something in the body's sullen pose, in its coiled aggression, that gave him her identity at once. The knees had to be hugged to stop them flying out, to prevent this person from exacting vengeance on the foolish sunbathers, the studious students, the shining filigreed suspended world. And here at a glance was the wide white forehead, the flattened nose. She was covering it with her hands but it was easy to imagine, yes, the surly mouth.

Somebody loves us all.

Did he hope she might not see him? Was she hoping for the same? But they were something to each other, weren't they.

371

Helena had joined their lives together. He waved at her and walked over.

'Hey, Thompson, what are you looking so happy about?' she said.

'Oh, Price, it's possible you know.'

'What is?'

'Happiness.'

'Did you make some poor kid speak properly again? Me talk purty.'

'My mother doesn't have a brain tumour.' He'd not meant to say it.

'Okay,' she said, not pausing before answering.

'That's pretty much how we feel too.'

She looked up at him. 'Right.'

'On your break?'

'Not working,' she said. 'Got the sack, got the boot.'

'From?'

'My mother. Mothers, huh? They put you through the ringer.'

'Sacked from the school?'

'You didn't know? The morning of the review, she calls me in first thing. She says, "Price, we're going to have to let you go." I thought she was kidding at first. Then she said contract is finished, which was true, sort of. Thanked me for the job I'd done. And that was that. I'm out of there. Stressing about whether I'd ruin the review. Okay, I took the hint.'

'I had no idea.' Somehow he was proud of them both, mother and daughter.

'No? Well, it was a crap job anyway.'

'Data entry.'

'Aren't they two of the worst words in the English language?'

'A lot of the people sitting in this square are probably doing data entry for a living.'

'Poor fuckers.'

'What next then?'

372

'Always got the film-making, Thompson.'

'Indeed,' he said.

'You don't take that seriously, I know.'

'I do.' The denial was so weak they were both grinning.

'Of course you do,' she said.

'Medbh was telling me about it.'

'Medbh.' She uttered the name with disgust almost.

Disgust that he'd used it?

They looked around the square. 'Listen, Dora. I've been meaning to say. Well, I'm with your mother—'

'Know that, Thompson.'

'Yes! All right. We live together and I want that to last—forever. I can't imagine that stopping, changing. And you're part of that. I don't have kids, don't know the first thing about that really. But we're together. The three of us, I mean. You're included. So, I don't know. But, okay, listen. I'd like you to call me Paddy.'

'What?'

'Call me Paddy.'

'What are you saying?'

'Go on, call me Paddy.'

'I can't.'

'Why not though?'

'I don't see you as a Paddy.'

'But I am a Paddy. Then call me Patrick if you prefer.'

She shook her head. 'Sorry, Thompson.'

The tourists had moved to the top of the steps that led to the bridge where his mother had walked. They were lining up the harbour with their camera, in the distance the hills around Lower Hutt. It would go in the album, or on the hard drive. They would show people when they got home. Look where we went. Yes, he thought, he lived in a glorious place, fully deserving of any act of preservation. Look. Very gently he bent down to her and feeling a warmth towards this person he'd never felt before, he said as tenderly as he could, 'Then fuck you Price.' He began to walk away.

'Hey,' she called out. 'Great news about your mother. And see you around, Thompson.'

He turned and saw that Dora had a camera to her eye, filming him.

9

The next day was Saturday and Gorzo called. It was 10am. Helena answered the phone at the same time Paddy picked up the one in his office.

Paddy held off announcing himself. They didn't know he was there.

She said at once that she'd put Paddy on for their talk but Gorzo had already started to speak about his mother's birthday, which was that day. He hoped they hadn't forgotten. It was important to the family that Paddy and Helena come to the party. Also Paddy's mother. The two mothers, the two matriarchs. Two great old ladies. Well, she told him, that was very kind.

They shared a connection, he and Paddy, he said, that no doubt she knew about. Yes, she said, Tony's son, of course. Paddy spoke about it often, how wonderfully Jimmy had worked at his rehab and what a success he'd become.

'Okay, sure, Jimmy got us into it,' Gorzo told her. 'But what I was meaning was our fathers.'

'I see,' said Helena.

'Both our fathers dead at the same age. Me and Paddy were the same age, I mean.'

'I didn't know that.'

'Doesn't make us the same. Look at our lives. He's an educated thinking type, and I'm a stupid Greek. But, you know.'

'It's a bond.'

'It's a bond, I think. You know, all the time I'm thinking about my Dad, oh boo hoo I lost my Dad, what a miserable kid I am. But that's all wrong. Why? Because of my mother. Because of what she does. What happened, it made our mothers very important and that's what we honour today. Is your mother still alive, Helena?'

'No.'

'Too bad. Your father?'

'Afraid not.'

'Mmm. You must be an interesting person. Hey, Helena, we'll see you tonight. Now is he there? Is Einstein there?'

Gorzo had read the paper, the new 'Speech Marks' column. Read it fast at first because today was the day, as Paddy well knew, since he was coming to the party, his mother's hundredth and there was a shitload of things to do, and Helena was coming too, with Paddy's mother, all of them. Read it so that this poor guy doesn't have to get on his bicycle and come out to the Hutt, looking for him. Then he had to slow down because he was reading this rubbish about it being the farewell column, what was that about?

'It's my last column, Tony,' said Paddy.

'That's the bullshit I was talking about.'

'Time to say goodbye.'

'Time to say bullshit.'

'No, it's gone on long enough. I've run out of things to say. Time to let the other guy have his moment in the sun.'

'What other guy? You got shafted? Some young hotshot?'

'No, no. Just—time, you know.' There was no one else lined up. In fact he'd had no communication at all from the paper since sending in the column.

'I think you were at a low ebb,' said Gorzo. 'You wrote it in a low state of mind.'

'Well,' he said, 'I have had a lot on my plate.'

'I think you wrote it because for one week I miss making the call and that's the straw on the camel's back. No one loves me, no one cares.'

'Not quite.'

'See, Paddy, you and me. We've been through thick and thin, haven't we?'

'We've been through thick at least.'

'Ha! But this is why I know you. I know you're not a quitter.'

'This is resigning though, bowing out. This is not quitting. I'm not quitting.'

'So what am I reading this bullshit "Thanks to my readers over the years" column for?'

'Tony, here's the funny thing. I quit and no one notices. Really no one does care. No one at the paper even reads the thing!' Probably the deputy editor and the editor were reading it right now for the first time, or not reading it. They'd see it was there perhaps, the stupid out-of-date cartoon, and turn the page. In Paddy's experience journalists read papers, especially their own, in purely spatial terms, in blocks. How many columns of type here and over here. The advertising. They looked at shape, the distribution of picture and headline, and then lastly, a quick run over the squiggly bits filling each column, the words. Yes, a good-looking paper. He thought of Murray Blanchford complimenting his mother on her nice brain. Once he'd accidentally received an email between two sub-editors. The message read, Here's Skid Marks. 'They just see the copy and go, oh fine, another "Speech Marks".'

For a moment this information seemed to have stopped Gorzo. The idea of Patrick Thompson's marginality, his faded power, his irrelevance, disturbed the flow. Had he, Tony Gorzo, been following the wrong man all these years? 'So I'm— . . . I'm going to write a letter.' He sounded half-hearted.

Paddy was on the point of telling Gorzo about the skid marks line. 'You?'

'Letter to the editor, I'm doing it.'

'You never wrote a thing in your life.'

'And I'm starting now! Tell me the fucking address.'

'It's the address of the fucking paper, Gorzo, you idiot.'

Paddy had begun to laugh.

'Tell me. Dear Sir, Madam, what? Dear Arsehole?'

'God.'

'Dear God. Okay. "Dear God, It has come to my attention."'

He expected his mother to turn the invitation down flat. She didn't know Tony Gorzo except by name, through Paddy's reports. And after all she'd been through, which indeed Gorzo knew nothing about. Her temperament even before this had been to decline and decline. In social gatherings outside the family, outside Paddy and Stephanie, she acted awkwardly. Her conversation was forced. She grilled people for a few moments then went quiet, or she appeared to be playing with them in some obscure ironical way, making little comments that might have been malicious had she not appeared so mild. Her voice trailed off. People were frankly puzzled by his mother. In truth, he'd never liked watching her talk to anyone outside the family and over the years had probably contributed to her isolation by failing to extend opportunities to her in which she could practise a wider repertoire. Did that sound too clinical? Yes. Anyway, the old picture he'd created of a mother shutting things down for her children had to be corrected. He wanted her shut down too? Or maybe she just preferred to be left alone. Then the Internet had been invented. She was back playing that too, though not as often, she said. She'd become a little bored with Cushion, her diplomacy pool game. It seemed she was the cleverest player in the universe and he believed it.

When he told her about Mrs Gorzo's party, she said yes at once. 'What shall I wear?'

'You don't have to come.'

'Am I invited?'

'Of course.'

'Then I'll come. I'll say yes. It's a chance to go back to the Hutt.'

'It's Petone,' he said.
'Close enough.'

The car park outside the bowling lanes was almost full. They got one of the last spaces, guided to it by a teenage boy with the squat Gorzo build, wearing a reflector vest over his suit. He opened their car doors for them.

Fairy lights hung from the veranda, transforming the setting quite magically. Had things been painted? Cleaned certainly. There was a grotto effect, all sparkles and tinsel, and hanging on the outside wall, in a ring of small light bulbs, a framed black-and-white photograph of Mrs Gorzo as a young woman. The gaze was solemn: an instructed sort of look, with slightly staring eyes as if she'd had to hold them open for a long time, but her mouth suggested another spirit, playful and self-delighting. They stood in front of the image for a few moments. 'She looks like trouble,' said Helena.

Near the entrance, they signed a giant birthday card. It was covered in messages for Tony's mother, often addressed on the card as 'Mrs G' or 'Yaya'. Inside, the place was packed. There were children of all ages; mothers holding babies; old men talking in groups; women who looked as old as Mrs Gorzo, all in black. Trestle tables lined the bowling lanes and people were finding their seats. The roof was hung with more fairy lights. In the far corner, a string quartet played—they were dark-haired high school-age girls. At the counter with the cash register, women were taking people's street shoes and handing out bowling shoes.

'What size, darling?' said one of the women to Helena. She'd worn boots, a skirt. Helena was laughing as she sat down and pulled the boots off. Beside her, Teresa was being fitted experimentally—a woman in her sixties was down on her knees, testing sizes against his mother's foot, as in a shoe shop.

He put on his 10s. He knew the drill. Then he heard his name being called. Tony, wearing a brown suit and a blue tie, approached and gave him a hug. 'Yassou file mou! My friend! You came!'

'Was there ever any doubt?'

'And this must be Helena. A Greek name of course.' He kissed her on both cheeks. 'Welcome! And this, I know this person. Kalispera, good evening. Madam, I am honoured. I am Tony.' He bowed and took Teresa's hand, pressing it to his lips.

'Efharisto,' she said.

'You know Greek?'

'No, I Googled. Thelo ena poto.'

Tony turned to Paddy and Helena. 'Look at this, she says she wants a drink. I like this woman! From Google!'

'Me lene Teresa.'

'It's very impressive. All these years, your son never learns a word of Greek.'

'You've never said a word of Greek to me,' said Paddy.

'I wrote the phrases on my wrist,' she said.

'No, you didn't,' said Tony.

'Look.' Teresa rolled up her sleeve and showed them the tiny writing that extended almost to the crook of her elbow.

Tony took her wrist and read the phrases. 'Pos se lene? What is your name? Apo pou eisai? Where are you from? Okay, this is good stuff. I love it, you know. Should do it myself.'

Teresa pulled her sleeve down. 'Something that's not there, is "I feel funny in these shoes."'

Tony looked at her feet. 'Are they the wrong size?' His own bowling slippers were brown, to match his suit. The ensemble, marvellously, worked. Many of the other men looked bad, their trousers sagging unsupported at the cuffs. It occurred to Paddy that Gorzo might have engineered this advantage.

His mother moved up and down in them, reconsidering. 'You know, Tony, they're actually extremely comfortable.'

'I know! At home, this is what we wear. Exactly this. Ela. Come, you must meet someone.' He started to lead Teresa off through the crowd. He hadn't seemed to notice Teresa's French accent at all. Well, there'd been such a swirl of languages. But he'd had no issues with it. Surprisingly, he had a good ear. Gorzo lived in exactly this flow. Turning back, he said to Paddy and Helena. 'I tried, I tried very hard. But you are on Table Two. Okay? It's the problem with this effing family. All the aunts, cousins roll in, you can't move. I got you shifted up from Table Four, in Siberia. So it's not a bad outcome. But the good thing. Your mother, Table One.'

'She's Table One?' said Paddy.

'Sitting beside my mother. Even before I knew about the writing on her arm. I made it happen. Okay.' He winked at them and moved off.

'He's the man to know,' said Helena.

'Did you know about that stuff written on her arm?'

'I saw her in the back of the car, looking down. She must have been memorising it.'

They found their places, exchanged connections with the people around them: a retired couple from Kilbirnie, also Greek, who'd owned a sports shop; the London-based middle-aged daughter of a cousin on Table One, travelling with her father to make sure he arrived in one piece; and a couple whose five-year-old son sat between them. The father of the boy had been Jimmy Gorzo's best friend through school. No, he hadn't been there on the night of the accident on the beach, though he had visited Jimmy in hospital. He'd brought him comics. What did Paddy think of Jimmy's accent now? 'I have a tough time talking to him,' said the father. 'I want to say, cut the crap, speak normally, you're back in New Zealand. It's a put-on, right?'

The retired sports shop owner said to them, 'Gorzo, originally, where do you think that name comes from?'

Paddy said he didn't know much about Greece. The man opened the question out to the whole table. Where was the name Gorzo from? No one knew. 'You don't know?' There was a shaking of heads. 'Hungary,' said the man with strange, bitter emphasis. Then he sat back, content to have outed the hosts.

A bell was rung, bringing the room to silence. At Table One, Tony rose to his feet. 'Okay, okay. Before we get started, I got

381

some announcements to make. It's nine dollars fifty an hour and if anyone throws ten strikes, I give them a free game!' There was laughter and people called out things. 'That's a good deal, I think. Anyway, shut up everyone and behave, don't you know my mother's here.' There was more laughter and some whistling. 'Behave! So, I gotta say thanks to you all for coming, for some it's been a long journey. There are some from Ngaio. No, no. I understand some of you have lost your luggage, or at least that's your excuse for wearing those terrible clothes you got on. Just kidding. Seriously, it means a lot to me and my family and especially to the person we're honouring and celebrating tonight that you made the effort. Tonight is only the first event and we'll be seeing a lot of you over the next few days. Hope we don't get sick of each other, eh. But before we eat, let's put something in our glasses, you've all got something on the tables, and if you haven't we're firing those useless boys from Dino's. Hi, Dino! You out there somewhere?'

'Table Four, Tony,' a voice called out.

'Table a Hundred!' yelled someone else.

'Lucky's you gotta seat at all,' said Tony. 'There's people from Patras sobbing in the car park.' A cheer went up. Someone started singing and was quickly shushed.

Tony's wife, Ellie, who was sitting beside him, poked him in the leg with her knife. 'Hey! All right, all right, getting stabbed up here. Right. And maybe you gotta stand for this, don't they darling?' He bowed in Ellie's direction. She nodded. Her ears carried great golden loops that moved and shimmered. 'I think so. Everyone stand, except not you, mana. You deserve a break. Sit back and enjoy it. As many of you will know, it's very hard for my mother to ever sit back and enjoy anything. Tonight she said she wanted to help in the kitchen. Actually she's tied to that chair with rope. Nobody try to take her dancing. So.' Tony held up his glass as everyone stood. 'You know. Chronia pola, mana!'

The room rumbled. 'Chronia pola!'

*

382

Throughout the meal, Paddy's view of Mrs Gorzo and of his own mother was obstructed. He got only occasional glimpses. Mrs Gorzo bending her head slowly towards her plate; Teresa, beside her, smiling at something that was being said to her, wiping her mouth with her serviette. From time to time, people would approach Tony's mother to say a few words and to touch her shoulder or her head, sometimes pressing the back of their hands to her cheek, as if testing her temperature. Mrs Gorzo displayed little reaction to this. She appeared almost immobile. Invariably these visitors to the top table would then be shown the writing on Teresa's arm by Tony. Paddy caught sight of his mother's wrist lifted above the table and he could hear the laughter that followed. Men touched Teresa's back lightly, gracefully, bending to hear what she was saying.

On Table Four, in the lane closest to the front entrance, he recognised the two men who'd been bowling on the day he'd biked here. Their mother sat next to them, occasionally putting food into one of her son's mouths.

Where would we be, he thought, without our manas.

There had been platters of food on the tables when they sat down and these kept being replenished and added to throughout: cheese eggplant rolls, grilled bread with feta and tomatoes, dolmades, filo pies filled with spinach or various spicy meats; a myriad of sauces and dips: hummus, taramasalata, he knew, but there were others. These finger foods were gradually augmented by more substantial dishes: moussaka, chicken, kebabs in tomato sauce, roast lamb with sun-dried tomatoes. It all came through the swing-doors that led to the bar and the offices, carried by waiters wearing monogrammed white shirts, D for Dino's.

Helena was involved in a long conversation with the cousin's daughter, who wanted to start her own clothes label in Australia, where she had contacts. Meanwhile the five-year-old's mother was worried about the boy's speech. They'd found out Paddy's profession. Her son seemed well behind the other kids of his age, she told Paddy. 'Say something,' she said to him. 'Say, "Please may I go to the toilet?"' The boy looked at her and shook his head. 'Because he doesn't want to go to the toilet,' said the boy's father.

As dessert was being served, people were moving freely around the tables, making the pilgrimage to see the birthday girl or going outside to smoke. He spied Tony leaving with a group of men, already peeling the wrapping from a cigar. Plates of unattended baklava, figs in honey, chocolate-filled filo parcels and other sweets were everywhere. He had sticky fingers. The older children were gathered in groups by the entrance, looking at one another's mobile phones, while the younger ones had taken over the free lane at the far end where they were rolling themselves over and over in the direction of the pins. Some of these kids were lying in the gutters, pretending to be stuck, their feet waving in the air. He recognised Jimmy's son, flat on his back, staring at the ceiling.

Paddy walked over to Table One, where a space was free opposite Jimmy and his wife Sue, the physiotherapist. She told him it was a pleasure to meet the famous Patrick Thompson, without whom she wouldn't have a husband.

'Or any of this!' said Jimmy. 'Had I not come through, Yaya would have died years ago. I was her darling, don't you know.'

Paddy said that while he didn't doubt Jimmy's special status, he hadn't saved his life.

Sue had a lovely open face, long dark lashes. 'But,' she said, 'you taught him to talk again and I don't think I'd marry a man who could only grunt and groan.'

'Most people do, honey,' said Jimmy.

She laughed and hit him hard on the shoulder.

'Ouch,' he said. 'Now I need some physio on that, darling. Gimme a rub.'

'I'm sorry for us, Paddy,' she said. 'The bubbles went right to our heads. We haven't even had the ouzi yet.'

'Ouzi, listen to her. *Ouzo*, it's ouzo, dummy brain.'

She made a face. 'Anyways, don't let me near it.'

'Honey,' he bumped her on the nose with a finger, 'you

wouldn't be able even to sniff it. No way you could actually drink it.'

'Oh yeah?'

'Oh yeah.'

'That right?'

'Thass right, baby.'

She looked around. 'Where's Adam, sweetie?'

Paddy said, 'He's in the gutter.'

'Okay,' she said. She turned her face to Jimmy's, an inch from him. 'Are we fine with that? Our son is in the gutter.'

'Looking at the stars,' said Jimmy. They kissed. Then he put a fig in her mouth.

I'm in the middle of a romantic comedy, Paddy thought. And not just this pair. He looked around. Greeks were a fairly short race. Shortish and homely. He meant it kindly. They'd discovered the mind. He always thought well of them because of their ancient achievements, even Gorzo. The men were a bit beetly. Hirsute. He thought again of Elizabeth Bishop's begonia.

He caught his mother's eye at the head of the table and they raised glasses to each other. She hadn't moved from her position. She looked content. Beside her Mrs Gorzo may have been asleep. But then the old woman roused herself again and appeared to be speaking to Teresa, who leaned close to listen, nodding and smiling, looking into the centenarian's face. Of course maybe nothing had been said; the pair had simply mimed it all. Paddy didn't think Mrs G looked any older than the last time he'd seen her, when she was in her eighties.

He excused himself and moved along a few seats, to sit next to Ellie. Over the years he'd met her only a few times and always by chance, in shops, once coming out of a cinema with a group of women friends. They'd talked only briefly, always about Jimmy. At once, she stood to greet him, putting out her hand. He took it in both of his and thanked her for the invitation. It was a wonderful party, a privilege. No, she said, the privilege was theirs, to be able to share their mother with so many kind and brilliant people. They sat again and looking down the table in Jimmy's direction, Ellie said, 'So happy. She's a lovely person. And Adam, have you met the boy?'

'Really liked the whole family.'

'Bit of a shock, but now—'

'If it works.'

'Sure, it's what I said to Tony. Only now we've got to call him James. Sorry, no.' She laughed. She looked tired. Most likely she'd shouldered a good deal of the organisational burden of the birthday celebrations, despite what her husband had said about all his work. 'For me, I told him. It's too late. If you're going to change your name, do it earlier please. I'm too old to start having to remember a new name. A funny thing is Tony doesn't mind now. He says he can call him anything Jimmy wants. The most important thing is to keep calling, keep calling. We know who he is. If he decides to be Ringo or Tonto or something, we know who this boy is. It's Jimmy Gorzo. Anyway. He's got his life now, the full package, as Tony says.' She drank some wine and, noticing he wasn't drinking, poured him some in a fresh glass. 'Cheers!' she said. 'Yiamas!' They knocked their glasses together.

'Ah, Patrick,' she sighed. Her eyes were prickling with tears.

'I know, I know,' he said.

The children who'd been playing in the free lane were being rounded up. The lane was needed for something. Beefy young men, still beetly, began carrying sound equipment forward, arranging the boxes, readying an assault.

Ellie shifted back in her chair and looked towards the top of the table. 'Here's something.' She gestured towards Tony's mother.

'What an incredible achievement,' he said.

'Oh, a hundred years of course. Yes but also the two of them together. Look at this. It's incredible, Patrick. Yaya has lived in New Zealand for, I don't know, almost sixty years, and never speaks English. Never. A lot of people say, oh but she understands everything. Mmm. I know her very well, I think.' She took another sip from her glass.

'And what's your feeling?'

'A lot of what's going on, she doesn't understand at all and has no interest in knowing! See, always in her mind, there was this idea she'd go back home, to Greece. She was here temporarily. But she never did go home. And she never learned English. She speaks the Greek of her village, in the thickest accent. She comes from a tiny place outside Patras, in the west. A lot of these young people here have no idea what she's saying, and she really doesn't understand them either. With Tony and me, with Jimmy, we've built up communication, and a few others who've known her a long time, but it's a small group. Yet here is your mother.'

'The Greek phrases written on her arm.'

'Can you believe that? I was so touched. I mean, no one knows Greek but the Greeks, and a few old Classics professors in the university. We're only a step up from Portuguese, also at one time a great nation. But I've got to say, your mother's gesture, that meant nothing to Yaya. I mean, she doesn't see very well but even when we explained, it didn't go in. No, it's strange. Nothing to do with talking, a language, I mean. It's just a—connection, I don't know. You're the expert, Patrick. You tell me. Anyway, Yaya won't let her leave!'

They looked along the table again. Everyone else had left now. The two women weren't saying anything to each other but they sat close, absorbed in each other, if that could be guessed at, and they seemed always on the point of confiding, readied in intimacy.

'You can't see it,' said Ellie, 'but Yaya has her walking stick hooked over your mother's leg. Twenty minutes ago, I went and asked your mother if she wanted to move around, to leave the table, she could do this, no trouble, and I'd sit with Yaya. But she said she didn't. She wanted to stay there, if it was okay. She likes this, I don't know. Do you think she's okay? She's happy?'

'She would say if she wasn't. I think this suits her very well.'

It occurred to him then why Teresa was like this. It was the closest she'd allow herself to be celebrated, fêted, paid attention to. That it was happening without it happening was perfect. It wasn't her party. Yet she was at top table. She was a prisoner there. She was stuck, couldn't move even if she wanted to. Ah, and to be fair Patrick Thompson, she didn't want to.

The trestle tables were being dismantled, and behind a pile of speakers the DJ, clearly one of the diners, about twenty years old, in his white shirt, tie, black trousers, now put on a baseball cap and addressed the dials on his console. Paddy and Helena had retreated into a small alcove along the wall from the trophy cabinets, though at Table One, his mother still sat with Mrs Gorzo.

He leaned into Helena, pressing his knee against her leg, feeling tremendously horny, possessive, zingy from the sweets. Her bowling shoes may have been bedroom slippers. He rested his chin on her shoulder for a moment.

'Hello you,' she said.

'Helena of Troy,' he said.

'I don't really know that story.'

'A woman drives everyone crazy.'

'The wooden horse.'

'Forty men inside a wooden horse.'

'You're always trying to find a way of describing me. I'm a bee, I'm this or that.'

'It's true. How shall I compare thee.'

'Did you have the figs?'

'Of course, I love figs.'

'Very sticky, weren't they.'

'Exceedingly.'

She laughed and bit him on the nose quickly. He straightened and they looked out at the room. A dance was being organised. People were being drawn up out of their seats, some unwillingly, and they were forming a long line, everyone holding hands. A few boys ducked under the line and ran out into the night, laughing.

'Do you think we can sneak out too?' he said.

'No.'

'Smoke a cigar. Celebrate.'

'Celebrate, I like.'

'You never told me you fired Dora.'

'Fired? Her contract had finished, that's all,' said Helena. She looked at him. 'She was terrible at it. Data entry.'

'I'd rather be locked inside a wooden horse.'

A young woman was in front of them, smiling, holding out her hand to Helena. She was part of the line, now trying to shape itself into a big circle, though the division between each bowling lane made this awkward. 'Kalamatiano!' she said. Music had started and the girl was tugged. She shrieked and grabbed Helena's hand.

Helena turned to Paddy. 'Kalamatiano!'

'Speak to me in English,' he said.

Helena grabbed his hand. 'Kalamatiano!'

He stood firm. 'No really, I think I ate some of that already.' Then they were both yanked forward.

There was a step, a twelve-step in fact, though he never got it, at least not in the timing that was required. Beside him Helena was rapidly expert. On his other side an older man grinned encouragingly and tried to show Paddy, but it was useless. It was wonderfully useless. 'Sorry!' he kept saying to the man. 'Sorry!' But the man didn't seem to mind. 'I'm a cretin,' Paddy shouted at him.

'Which town?' shouted the man.

Paddy tried to put him right.

'It was a joke,' the man called out before he was whisked off.

Helena was laughing hard, calling out instructions he couldn't hear. The circle turned with the music and Paddy tried to keep up, skipping and stepping. There were figs in the gutters of the lane, they stomped in their soft slippers on flakes of pastry.

People shouted and clapped. Across from where he was, he saw Tony dancing. He'd not talked to him since they'd first come in. He should go over, he thought. But how? Tony was caught up. The patriarch danced with determination. On either side of him, his son and his daughter-in-law were lifted and dropped by Tony's exertions. They were almost having their arms yanked off. He was treating them both like weights, they went up and they went down on the movements of his arms. Up and down they went. Up and down.

And in a booth at the far end of the room, half watching, in utter stillness, very close together, sat Tony's mother and his mother.

Paddy tried to wave but he didn't have a free hand, the circle claimed him, threw him this way and that. He submitted. It had a mind of its own.

10

A few days later he had a call from Alan Covenay asking for a meeting. Angela would be there too, but not Sam. They could come at any time that was convenient for Paddy. Immediately Paddy felt guilty. There should have been some kind of exit interview and a new feeling gripped him that nothing really had been sorted with Sam Covenay. For a start, none of the paperwork was done. There was the refund. He'd get on to that. He supposed he'd been hoping that the Covenays would fade away. But of course here they were again. Were they going to confront him with the whole chase episode? He apologised and told the father that he should have called them. 'No,' said Alan, 'there was no need for that.'

The following afternoon they arrived at the apartment.

He found himself being kissed in greeting by Angela. It was the first time this had happened and he wondered whether it was connected again with the kissing that had taken place the day his mother had been brought to the apartment by Geoff Harley. Or a celebratory kiss perhaps? Except they both looked tired and drawn. The kiss was only to revive herself, he thought, to generate the feeling that was missing. He shook hands with Alan, and saw he was carrying a package wrapped in brown paper: his picture. There was a slight move on Alan's part to give Paddy the package then but he moved it away again, a little behind his back, on some quick glance Angela gave him. Not yet.

Rather than using the office, Paddy took them upstairs to the living-room and made tea. He hoped here to set a new note, with the business removed as far as possible from the bad old days of Sam slumped in the chair by the door.

Angela was looking out the window. She told him the view was surprising; they were higher than she'd imagined. Could they see the sea? Only a tiny corner of harbour, he said, from the top room. She could go up if she liked. He gestured towards the stairs and for a moment she seemed to consider it but then she turned back to the window, as if the stairs, all six of them, were finally a little too much. No, it's fine, she said. Alan went over and stood beside her and pointed out the roof of his workshop. 'Needs a paint job actually,' he said. He'd rested the package behind the sofa. They moved there as Paddy brought the tray over.

'How is your mother?' said Angela.

'My mother is wonderful, thank you.' It was the truth. Teresa had made up her mind not to seek further help—from him or anyone else. He'd supplied her with the contact details of the speech therapist to whom he'd send a referral letter. He'd drafted the letter and shown it to her. She thanked him, read it, said it was an excellent letter, and then she told him she didn't want to go ahead with any treatment. She'd not seen Murray Blanchford either. She felt fine, she said. She was sleeping properly, eating normally. She was okay. Do I look okay? she asked him. Yes. Then that's that. And Pip wanted to get her overseas for a holiday. It looked like happening finally.

Her speech was the same.

He noticed she'd photocopied some drawings from the *Petit Nicolas* books and stuck them to her fridge. Those, she said, were for Steph's kids.

At the end of the Gorzo centenary celebration, Mrs Gorzo had wept when Teresa was saying goodbye, but Teresa hadn't cried.

Angela told him she was so pleased about his mother.

'Great stuff,' said Alan.

Paddy dreaded asking it. 'What I want to know is how is Sam?'

They looked at each other, figuring out who would answer, who was up to it. 'He's talking!' said Angela finally, breaking into a broad smile. 'He's speaking again!'

'That's great!' said Paddy. 'How fantastic.'

'Yes,' said Alan, nodding earnestly.

Angela put her hand on her husband's knee briefly. 'I mean, we don't always like what he says—'

'No,' said Alan.

'But, it's . . . speech. It's his voice. And he's a teenager, you know. Anyway, it's a breakthrough. Totally.'

Paddy repeated that it was wonderful news.

Angela looked at her feet. Work shoes. Had she got the job? It looked likely. 'So we feel—'

'Stupid,' said Alan.

'A bit stupid, embarrassed,' said Angela.

'Why though?'

'For wasting your time. You were right, Paddy. We should have been patient, we should have waited. He was always going to come right, wasn't he? Like you said. He went into his cave for a while and now he's come out.'

'Covered in— . . . something from the cave,' said Alan.

'In the profession we call that cave goo. Cave gunk,' said Paddy.

Angela ignored this. 'And that's developmental,' she said.

'Of course,' said Paddy, serious again. 'The brain, at that age, it's still completing its circuits, making the connections. You acted in Sam's best interests.' He told them he was arranging for the refund.

'Don't start that again, please,' said Angela.

'Really, I don't know how you put up with him,' said Alan.

Did they or didn't they know about the Farmers run, hiding under the veranda from the guard?

Paddy said, 'Sam was a great challenge.'

For the first time, Alan laughed. He thumped the side of the sofa in a way that made Angela sit up and give him a disapproving look. He shook his head and gazed off in the direction of the window. Then he felt around the edge of the sofa and drew out the package. 'You know about this already,' he said, handing it over to Paddy. He continued to shake his head. 'A great challenge,' he muttered, amused, bitter, as if caught in some recent memory connected with his son.

Angela leaned forward to pat the package. 'Paddy, if you tell us the amount, well, you're not going to tell us the amount, but please we'd like to make some kind of contribution—'

'Yes, absolutely,' said Alan.

'No, no,' said Paddy. 'That won't be happening.' He held the package in front of him. 'Besides, I have it back. I'm not out of pocket or out of anything.'

Angela suddenly stood up from the sofa. 'Our idea, Paddy, was that we wouldn't have to be present when you opened it. Unless you wanted us to be present. But our preference is not to be present.'

'We've seen it,' said Alan.

'I made myself look at it a lot,' said Angela. 'I had to know what my son was capable of. I had to see what he could do. Because really I had no idea he had this kind of behaviour in him. But of course he does, of course he did. But now I think of this as, it's the old Sam.'

Alan leaned forward and knocked the table with his knuckle. 'Touch wood.'

'It's who he was. He's someone else now. We think.'

'I'm running out of wood to touch.'

'He's a new person.'

'Oh no, here we are, safe.' Alan Covenay was grinning, tapping his knuckle against his own head.

When they'd left, Paddy opened the package to look at himself updated.

The details were as Angela had warned him. But how had it been done? He looked closely. With some Twink-like substance, the hair had been deleted. Then the artist had applied shading to cover the patch before the new, more accurate, more spartan hair was put in. On examination the entire head had been treated this way, the old drawing eaten alive, though maybe the nose was original, and the ears. The mouth was still open but something was different there too. In place of Bill Golson's dental injunction—Open wide—there was an effect created that said, Man speaking. That was it, here's a person in the middle of saying something. The picture achieved live action. The kid had talent, the little vandal.

Of course if it had been a photo, you would have thrown it out. No one liked such photos.

Part Three

Stephanie arrived at the apartment with her three girls just after 8am. She needed to get Isabelle to school by nine but she was desperate for them all to see their long-lost grandmother, gone two weeks. He had coffee ready for her, which she took and drank at once, moving through the apartment. She asked to borrow his hair-dryer and went into the bathroom. 'Still assembling myself,' she said.

Helena was already at work. She'd just been appointed to a government taskforce charged with reforming their industry. Step one: ban all black Mercedes.

The girls were in their coats and hats and mittens, bundled against the cold, and he helped them take a few layers off. He rubbed his hands over the cheeks of each of the girls in turn and they laughed as he did it. In friendship, the middle one, Sophie, showed him a small plastic creature that he recognised as the sort of thing teenage girls hung off their mobile phones. 'Where'd you get that from?' he said.

'Daddy gave it to me,' she said. It was the first he'd heard of Paul Shawn in months. 'If I give it to Niamh, she'll choke and die.' There was nothing dire in the prediction, only a kind of curiosity.

A few minutes later, the Skype call came in on Paddy's computer and he sat Isabelle and Sophie on chairs in front of the screen, while Paddy stood behind, holding Niamh, the toddler. A moment of black and then Teresa appeared, and beside her,

Pip. They were sitting in their hotel room, a bed could be seen behind them. They waved and called out to the children and Stephanie ran into the room, still brushing her hair, laughing and waving back.

'Bonjour! Hello! Hello you people!' said Teresa. Her mouth moved slightly ahead of the sounds.

'Say hello to Nana,' said Stephanie.

The girls sat and stared, mute, unmoving. They didn't have access to Mummy's computer at home. They were watching two things: Pip and Teresa but also themselves in the small box at the bottom of the screen.

'Ça va?' said Paddy.

'Oui, oui,' said Pip.

His mother said, 'Look at you all! Hello Izzy, hello Soph. Where's your sister?'

Isabelle turned slowly from the screen, all the time keeping an eye on her grandmother and on herself, as if the images might disappear, and slowly pointed at the child in Paddy's arms. He bent down to show Niamh to the camera. She too had stopped wriggling in his arms and was focused on the heads inside the computer.

'They're in shock, Ma,' he said.

'The first time they've been quiet in days!' said Stephanie. 'Come on you lot, that's your Nana there and Pip, you know Pip. Who can tell me where they are? Sophie, do you know where Nana and Pip have gone?' The girl moved her head slightly. 'I think you do. Isabelle?' But Isabelle had leaned closer to the screen, lifting one finger. She wanted to touch it.

'Are you going to school today, Izzy?' said Teresa.

'Answer then!' said Stephanie.

With great reluctance, the girl slowly nodded her head and glanced at her sister, who sat back suddenly, afraid something might be addressed to her, fascinated too by the picture of her sister's head moving up and down in the little box.

'What are you doing with your hair, Steph?' said Teresa.

'Running a bit late this morning, Mummy. Sorry.'

'Going okay?' said Teresa.

'Going great,' said Stephanie. 'We've hardly noticed that you've been gone. You know.'

'How's Paris?' said Paddy. 'How was Bastille Day?'

'Marvellous!' said Pip. 'A million people on the move.'

'But they don't call it that,' said Teresa. 'They call it Quatorze Juillet. July the Fourteenth. We stood on the Pont du Carrousel, which is a bridge, not a carousel, though it felt like we were at a fair, and we watched the fireworks standing on the bridge, with a million other people, looking along the Seine, the river. The most incredible fireworks, girls!'

'And we had a great view of the Eiffel Tower, all lit up,' said Pip. 'Fireworks would go off on the other side of the river and then they'd shoot out of the Eiffel Tower itself. Beautiful. Do you know the Eiffel Tower, Isabelle? Maybe Sophie knows it too. The big tower in Paris with the pointy top.'

'They don't know anything, Pip,' said Stephanie. 'They've been turned to stone.'

Teresa said, 'We caught the Métro from near our hotel, thought we were very clever, leaving early and only travelling on the one line, no changing trains.'

'We *were* clever,' said Pip.

'And so were about ten thousand other people who had the same idea. We got on the train and it was full. I mean, we had to squeeze in. I was bent over, to fit the shape of the curved roof, pressed right against the door. So was Pip.'

'So was I.' Pip mimed the position, hunching her shoulders.

'Then the train got to the next station, doors open, and some more people get on. Not sure how they managed that but they got on and we were squeezed further into the compartment. Next stop, more people. Everyone going to see the fireworks. Okay, so now we are completely jammed in.'

'Really tight.'

'Tight? It was more than tight. Not just shoulder to shoulder. This was chest to chest, hip to hip, all body parts in contact.'

'The woman beside me more or less had her nose in my ear.'

'Yes!' The two women were laughing now. The children remained silent witnesses. They studied the faces, the voices, reaching no conclusions, glancing at their own filmed heads. What was this strange performance? They didn't even have TV. One day Stephanie had put it in the attic to save space, and to prevent Paul Shawn from turning it on when he visited.

'Sounds awful!' said Stephanie.

'By the end Steph, the last few stops, and the train kept filling and filling, the people waiting on the platform would simply back in. Reverse in! They'd turn around and using their backs and their bottoms, insert themselves on board. A very effective technique actually.'

One of the girls sniggered: bottoms.

'It saved them having to look anyone in the eye,' said Pip. 'So they didn't see the "You have got to be kidding" look from the people already on the train.'

'But that was the thing, no one said a word!'

'No one said a word.'

'No one could breathe,' said Pip.

'No, it was just—accepted,' said Teresa. 'It was Quatorze Juillet. It was the big day. Let everyone come! Everyone had to get on the train, all humanity. Young and old, tourists, locals. Everyone. To honour the Revolution.' She'd read books throughout the summer. In English, she'd read Zola and Balzac. Then Victor Hugo. She still munched through her thrillers. She'd also borrowed primers from the Alliance Française, but she wouldn't take lessons, that would be too much, she said. She'd met Camille regularly for coffee. 'It was very important that no one got left behind. I think that was the spirit. People were laughing.'

'Groaning.'

'Laughing and groaning. Some Americans were near us, crushed but safe, it was safe too, somehow. An old couple, like us.'

'Like us, exactly!'

'And he said to her, "Was that our stop back there?"'

'As if he could do anything about it!'

'As if he was going anywhere. Everyone was going to the same place!'

'Quite marvellous really,' said Pip. She wiped her eyes from the laughter.

'Anyway,' said Teresa. 'What's your news?'

'Oh, nothing much,' said Stephanie. 'No fireworks, no revolutions. But Isabelle lost a tooth.'

'Oh, Isabelle! Lost a tooth! Can I see? Let me see, please. Open your mouth and show me or else I won't believe it.'

The girl put her finger in her mouth and then she turned around and showed Paddy the gap before sitting back down and resuming her vigil by the screen. She could demonstrate to humans but not to those others.

In Paris, Pip and Teresa laughed.

Niamh slipped from Paddy's hold and walked out of the room. Sophie saw this and got off her chair to follow. There were things in Uncle Paddy's house that looked promising. He'd never shown them his office cupboard stash—that needed to stay there—but on the weekend, Helena had brought up a box of some of Dora's old toys from the basement: dolls, plastic things, board games. Why not use them, she said. They were for Stephanie's girls, only no one should tell Dora. They'd spent over an hour sorting the safe stuff from the hazardous. Isabelle waited a moment, and then she too was gone.

Stephanie and Paddy took the children's places. 'Got rid of the deadwood,' he said.

Stephanie asked when they were leaving Paris and they went over their itinerary again. Capetown in two weeks. Originally they'd been looking at Canada, to take in Margie, but that had proved too difficult with the schedule, which was another slight for everyone in Vancouver. After Paris they were heading south, where apparently the accent was more musical, sing-songy, said Teresa.

'Bonjour!' Pip sang.

'We've had wine with dinner,' explained Teresa.

'I was going to say, Ma,' said Stephanie, 'your accent. Is it just this line or is it weaker? It sounds weaker.'

'Really?' said Teresa.

'I don't think it does,' said Paddy. He found he was annoyed with his sister for saying this. He felt she'd made the statement because she wanted it to be true. Also because she thought that Teresa wanted it to be true too. But hadn't he thought the same thing, that their mother's accent was a little less extreme? It had been eight months since it had first happened. She'd Skyped when they arrived in London and he sensed it for a moment then though he'd not said anything to Stephanie. Now he believed the accent was as strong as ever. They were getting used to her, that was all. Pip was saying something about a linguistic embarrassment they'd suffered, and Teresa joined in. He had to modify. Listening to the two voices together, he thought the cousins, despite their divergent histories, shared more and more. With her mother, Pip was sounding less, what? African. Teresa still sounded totally unlike her old self. But being together encouraged the softening of difference. They were meeting each other halfway or something. It wasn't hard to imagine them on their bikes riding together up the North Island, speaking in this fashion to each other, flying across the volcanic plateau. He'd never spoken about the trip with Teresa. And he wasn't sure Pip would have told her about telling him.

They were talking about learning French. 'She has this head start,' said Pip, 'which is frankly unfair. Learn it, I say.'

'Too old,' said his mother.

'Old-smold,' said Pip.

'Yes,' said Stephanie. 'But learn it back here, Mummy, won't you. Come back and then transform your life.'

'Oh no, I'm happy with my life as it is, thank you. Anyway, we hired bikes today. Paddy, this is the city for you. We biked all around. And we were approaching a pedestrian crossing.'

'Yes!' said Pip.

'And we saw an old woman on the crossing with her little dog, he was coming along behind her on a leash. Then the woman looks up, sees us, then sees there's a car that doesn't look like it's going to stop, so she pulls hard on the leash and the dog is flipped onto its back and the old woman pulls him over the crossing on his back the whole way! The dog's little legs waggling in the air. They get across and the woman flips him right side up with her shoe. Off they go again, no harm done.'

'I don't think I like that story,' said Stephanie.

Paddy was again thinking about the two cousins back on bikes together.

'What does it feel like Mummy, to be finally there?' said Stephanie.

'Amazing,' said Teresa.

'But do you feel anything, I don't know, special? Given all the bother and everything you've been through?'

Teresa had started to speak over the top of her daughter, as if she'd missed it. The fractional delay on the line made this half-convincing but the stronger sense was that she wanted the subject closed. 'But listen, have you seen what Pip is wearing? Can you see it? Show them, go on. Show it to the camera. She bought it yesterday. The most beautiful necklace.'

'I don't wear jewellery,' said Pip.

'But you should.'

'I don't know. Your mother persuaded me. It was a huge amount of money.'

'No, it wasn't.'

'I like this anyway.'

'Show them.'

Pip stood up and leaned forward, bringing an object close to the camera. It blurred and filled the screen, sparkling briefly in focus and then scrambling, obscuring the women completely, which was probably, he thought, his mother's precise purpose. She had respite for a moment. She was invisible. Or she was the background. She was present and absent.

'Beautiful,' said Stephanie.

*

That morning while he was working with Robert, his nine-year-old with Down's syndrome, a small earthquake shook the room, and as he always did when this happened, Paddy stood up at once, waited a few seconds then sat down again. He considered the doorway. There was nowhere to run. Robert had been building a tower and it had fallen. But the city still stood. Everyone within the earthquake's sphere was fine. He thought of Helena, his sister and her girls, he thought of Lant, all the others. The Gorzos, immune in Lower Hutt.

Why had they ever left the Hutt? But the fault-line went there too, didn't it. No one was safe.

In the apartment, under the stairs they had water that needed to be changed, a torch that didn't work, and no food. They were ready for anything.

Robert looked at him and laughed, and then he stood up and sat down too. Paddy laughed and the boy repeated the action. He did it a third time and Paddy said, 'Okay, Robert.'

'Okay,' said the boy. 'Okay, Robert.'

'Very funny,' said Paddy.

'Very funny, Robert,' said Robert.

After lunch he went for a bike ride out past the airport and it was impossible to resist certain apocalyptic thoughts along the lines of, This is all reclaimed land, loose sediment basically. Later in the afternoon he met Helena at a café. She hadn't felt the earthquake at all, though apparently a few students from more stable places had become quite upset. She found them gathered around the desk where Iyob worked. He was calming them down.

'What was he saying?' said Paddy.

'That our building was wooden and even in the strongest quake, it would move and bend and not collapse. That it was also on bedrock and this was the safest place to be. That there were thousands of earthquakes every year in Wellington but that no one had been killed or injured in over a hundred and fifty years. He spoke very slowly, with great authority. I was convinced myself.'

'Good old Iyob.'

'Then he saw me and he said the *other* language school, which is nearer the harbour, was not built on bedrock, and if a big earthquake happened, the ground would be liquefied and the students of that school would all find themselves in the middle of the sea.'

'I think that should be on your website.'

They had coffee and cake and he told her about the Skype conversation with Teresa and Pip, the frozen girls, the excitement in the travellers' voices. And then, prompted by nothing in particular except her presence and the truth, he told her he loved her.

'I like to hear that,' she said. 'All of it.' Their knees were touching under the table. 'But love does not flourish everywhere. Some bad news. Dora and Medbh have broken up.'

'Oh, I'm sorry to hear that.'

'Dora's a mess.'

'I can imagine.' He thought of the box of her toys, spread over the apartment floor. He'd have to hide all that. She'd be round that evening.

'We'll see her tonight. She's coming over.'

'Of course,' he said. 'Yes. Awful.'

Helena looked at him and laughed. 'God, Paddy, you're a terrible liar.'

'No, I—'

'I mean it's not a bad trait, to be unable to pull off a deception.'

'I must admit, mostly it's you I feel for. The stress for you.'

She shrugged. 'I'm her mother.'

He took her hand. 'You know, I am sorry.'

'Actually more than you know,' she said. 'It means we've lost Medbh too. She rang me at work, such a sweet person, and said in light of present circumstances blah blah.'

He sat back in his chair. 'But—'

'Who will feed us?'

'Yes.'

'Who will look after us?'

'Exactly.'

They looked out the café window. It was a sunny winter's day, with enough heat in the air to confuse people into leaving their coats at home. In an hour or two the temperature would plummet. His mother meanwhile was across the world, in summer. She slept, she said, without blankets or sheets in a tiny room in Paris with an electric toilet. Her bed pulled down from the wall and in the morning she could turn on the jug without sitting up. She'd be sleeping now.

He walked to Manners Mall to buy new batteries for the torch they kept under the stairs. Crossing Cuba Street, he heard loud footsteps and turned to see two figures: the chaser and the chased. There was the security guard, white-shirted, heavy-shoed, holding his walkie-talkie, chest pushed forward, weaving in and out of the pedestrians, struggling; and here was the other guy, arms pumping, sneakers slapping the paving, going straight. People stopped and watched, just as he was doing. The runner came close to him. Paddy stepped aside, making way. He heard the breathing and saw the face. Recognising him, in a reflex, Paddy almost called out his name.

He'd managed to stop himself. The dark figure flashed by. It was terrible of course, what had he done? What had he set in motion? It occurred to him that he was thinking, and not without pride: I taught that boy everything he knows. Then the thought passed and he went into the shop to buy his batteries.

The following morning he hadn't scheduled a clinic. He was going to use the time to write his newspaper column. They'd called him a few weeks after his farewell column, asked him to unretire. There'd been letters. How many? he asked. A number. Yes, but what was the number? Well, he had to understand that for every person who actually put pen to paper, there were fifty, sixty, seventy, more, who shared the same feeling. These were the silent readers. Chaucer, he recalled immediately, was known as The One Who Reads Without Moving His Lips, that was a mark of his genius. Okay then, he'd carry on for his silent readers. And he did have new ideas—that was the real surprise, the marker not of his genius but of his ongoingness. Besides, he had the new image of himself quite literally in the form of Sam Covenay's revised portrait. The paper could use it. He was ready to start. Yet on this morning, he began instead an account of his mother's experience, starting from the moment she'd woken to hear about the French truck drivers making the snail on the motorways, when she knew it was vendredi, a windy day last Novembre. It was the morning she'd tried without success to buy goat's cheese, and had been told how well she spoke English. It was just before he'd wheeled the bicycle into the apartment. For a few months now he'd been talking to Helena and Lant and even to Tony Gorzo about doing it, but it seemed he had to wait until his mother was safely out of the country. How lost he suddenly felt without her! He wished she were back. And was pleased she wasn't. For the obvious reason she was loving it. And for another reason. This. He couldn't imagine writing such a thing with her just through the wall, listening to him.

She'd booked online. The hotel was on rue de la Montagne, handy, and ranked number three in popularity on TripAdvisor for Montreal. His mother, as always, had done her research. She knew not to reserve a room on the side overlooking the street students used as a cut-through to the nearby university. The breakfast she understood to be so-so and overpriced. The staff, unless they'd also been reading TripAdvisor and either wanted to improve their image or go over to the dark side, would be polite but not super-friendly, an observation some people might have justifiably made of her, Paddy thought.

This was two years on from the time he was writing about. It hadn't happened yet.

Teresa was in Montreal for three nights, having flown from Vancouver that day, where she'd visited Margie, an occasion that had been judged a success, even by Margie. Had there been a TripAdvisor on Margie, it was unlikely she'd have rated super-friendly, maybe not even polite. Anyway, everyone had behaved. And Teresa had unbelievably been on a float plane above Vancouver Island with Margie and one of Margie's two sons, Nathan, the little one he was called, though he was over six feet, bigger-looking in the small plane and thin, so thin, folded like origami almost. She'd emailed Paddy. Amazing sights. All is good. Tx. This from a woman with bona fide aviophobia. Perhaps his sister had wanted to terrify their mother by taking her up in the air. Whatever, Teresa had said yes. She'd said, do what you like with me, I'm ready for anything. And she also emailed that she had given Margie the piece salvaged from their father's printing set: the mould of the sun. She'd wrapped it in cloth. What's this, what's this, Margie had said, rolling it open on her palm. Then she saw the thing. Well, I waited. She looked. I waited. And it did not come flying back at me. No. Not at all. The memento was received with a great gulp. Thank you was even said. Of course she soon wanted to know what I'd done with this and that. Of course she did. She wanted to know what you others had got. Dear Margie.

The next evening, the other of Margie's sons, Will, an engineering student, was waiting in the lobby of the hotel to meet his grandmother for dinner. Eventually he went up to the desk. They phoned Teresa's room but no one answered. He sat back down again to think. He texted his girlfriend who told him what to do. Maybe Teresa was asleep. Go up and try again. Break down the door, ha ha.

As a girl Teresa had contracted rheumatic fever, which would now come into play as a contributing factor in her heart failure. Aged eleven or twelve, they knew, she'd had weeks in bed, which sounded great. She told Paddy about this when he was a teenager refusing to get up. You think you'd like to stay there forever but you couldn't do it.

It was about 6pm Montreal time. Their spring. Our autumn.

Teresa was alone and that was hard to take, it would always be hard to take, but it was important to remember she was not a lonely person. Alone but not lonely. Her children would repeat this to each other. Important to remember all of that, the float plane, the success with Margie, the willed trajectory, the firm idea that she was, up to those last moments, doing more or less what she wanted to do, even when—especially when—she was doing what others wanted her to do. They told each other this when the urge to plant one's face in a cushion for a few hours or bike all day in a southerly or find some other way of—fill in the blanks to approximate negation and despair—got strong. Both your parents are gone now, he found himself repeating to himself, at first on an hourly basis. He'd never felt more like a child, like her child.

Helena bought him an anthology of poetry about death. For one foolish instant he was staggered. Why not a card which said Cheer Up. Then he began reading the poems. He felt dumb. She was asking for his intelligence to come back. He was aware that he was reading with an unhelpful aggression, directed against the poems themselves. Okay, then, console me, he said to the poems. He began talking to Helena about this.

First thing Stephanie had done when she heard about Teresa was look for cigarettes. She was a non-smoker, always. But suddenly, she said, it was as if she were addicted. Finally she found a cigar. A cigar in her house, the home of three young girls! It was in an office drawer, left by Paul Shawn who smoked birth cigars in semi-ironic fashion, she remembered. She went into the bathroom, sat on the toilet, and lit the thing. There was no irony. One did not shake ironically, that came from the shaken core. She really wanted to make herself sick, to suck the smoke from a visible fire into her body, expelling what she could. Or she just needed to have something to do with her hands and with her mouth. She didn't have a clue what would happen to her if she inhaled.

Hello, her daughter was knocking on the bathroom door. Isabelle was busting. Of course! The child was what you put in your hands, your mouth. Opening the door, the mother kissed her daughter, pressing her lips long and hard against the girl's cheek.

Isabelle necessary, Paddy said to his sister when she told him what had happened. She didn't get it. It was very lame. She smiled anyway. Good old Paddy.

His mother's last text went to Stephanie. But it got held up in some trans-global phone queue, so that in an echo of a supernatural TV show she thought she'd once seen, Steph got the message in New Zealand the day after Teresa had died. Steph had already thrown the cigar into the bowl where it floated. It looked faecal.

Her phone beeped and the name came up: Ma.

With some difficulty she got herself and the two girls who were with her into the car and round to Paddy's where she handed him the phone. She wasn't going to open any message like that. He had to. He was her big brother. They put the TV on for the girls and sat with the phone on the table in front of them. Wait, he told his little sister, let me get my reading glasses. Here they are. The professor is ready. For the first six months or a year, he thought, the wearer always says something to preface the glasses. No one seemed able to bypass this phase. With kids in his clinic he was still doing it. After that you simply put them on. Ta-da, he said. She looked at him in glasses and for a brief moment the urgency of the phone couldn't be felt. Distinguished, she said. Then Paddy pressed the button.

Teresa was replying to Steph's Are you there yet?

And what did it say? They peered together at once. They were head to head, looking, his ear against her hair. They stared at the small screen.

It read Je suis ici.